CONVICTIONS

CONVICTIONS

Journey Beyond Innocence

Donna Gannon

Sumas Mountain Press

Convictions is work of fiction. While loosely based on certain actual events, all names, characters, locations and events portrayed in this novel are either products of the author's imagination or are used fictitiously.

Library and Archives Canada Cataloguing in Publication

Gannon, Donna Marlene, 1949-, author
        Convictions : journey beyond innocence / Donna Gannon.

ISBN 978-0-9959101-0-2 (softcover)

        I. Title.

PS8613.A5C66 2017   C813'.6   C2017-901371-8

Book layout and design by Ward Edwards (www.BookSmith.ca)
Cover design by Gayll Morrison (www.gayllery.biz)

Sumas Mountain Press
www.sumasmountainpress.com

For Aaron

Who survived mistakes and misbegotten choices of grown-ups involved in raising him, becoming an upstanding person and devoted family man.

PROLOGUE

In the summer of sixty-nine, men landed on the moon, the female sex splintered over liberation and I defied my mother, spending the night in a cabin with a man. We didn't do what my mother thought. An orange glow from the hearth flames licked shadows from the cabin wall, and a brown-eyed hippie who looked like Jesus, lit a torch in my mind and showed me what was there.

What do you most want in life?

Until he asked, my future was without form, and void—like Earth, before God got to work on Monday morning.

I want to feel what it's like to stand on top of a mountain, I want to experience exquisite exhilaration. I want joy. Mount Joy.

Do you dream of love? he asked, a man?

A man? I'd like a man, yes. But I can live my life without him—if I have to. I'm going up on that mountain... with him or without him.

I knew what it would take to get there. Work hard. Do what's right. I didn't know how complicated that is.

I was nineteen.

- from the journal of Shelley Gallagher

CHAPTER ONE

April 1988

From inside my warm cocoon, I heard Ben leave for work, the back door close. Heard his car drone past the bedroom window, fade and evaporate in the cool, spring morning. Hungry for another twenty minutes' sleep before it was my turn to get up, I burrowed deeper into the blankets drifting toward oblivion once more. Almost there, something dragged at me. Something...sounds. I resisted them but they probed, prodded. A car's engine again, the back door, voices. Voices? Footsteps in the hall, in the bedroom.

"Shelley, you have to wake up." Ben's voice was ragged, shaky. "Police are here." I struggled to open my eyes. "They have a search warrant." Like silk collapsing over a lifeless parachutist, a deadly stillness settled over me.

"There's a female officer here," he nodded toward the bedroom door. "She says she has to remain with you." Then he was gone and a stout woman in uniform stared down at me.

Heavy boots sounded down the hall on the parquet floor. Self-consciously, I got out of bed and reached for my robe. Wrapping it around me, I squeezed past her and padded down the hall. She followed me.

The house swarmed with towering men in plain clothes. One or two glanced at me mutely. Another snapped photographs here, there and everywhere in our house... OUR house.

One, smaller than the rest, dressed in a trench coat approached me and thrust a badge under my nose. "I'm Corporal Parker of the R.C.M.P." He repeated what Ben had said, that they had a search warrant.

Parker's words, spoken softly and sounding polite, carried a funereal sobriety. He was barely taller than me, with a baby face; I couldn't help notice his gorgeous long eye lashes. But his eyes were steely blue and I imagined his stare could pin a living butterfly to an exhibit mat. He said I was not required to stay but I had no intention of leaving. I called Agnes at the office and concocted an excuse for being delayed.

Men clumped up and down the basement stairs, lugging boxes and pawing through them. In the den, one scrambled up onto the file cabinet in the closet and disappeared through the opening into the rafters. I thought irrelevantly, *I've never even been up there.* Only the female officer stood idle. But wherever I went, she dogged my heels like a shadow. Rankled, I retreated to the bedroom to put on clothes but she followed me there too and coldly watched me dress.

When I returned to the dining room, Parker had claimed Ben's customary place at the table, while Ben sat on the edge of a chair at the table's corner. Parker addressed him. "It is my duty to inform you that you have a right to retain and instruct counsel without delay. You need not say anything. Anything you do say may be used as evidence."

Ben looked up and locked eyes with me. Parker finished his speech and went back to directing the search, ignoring us.

Ben whispered to me, "Come outside."

August 1983

The teenager sashayed her hips with an impudent, if sensuous tilt, from atop the stout mahogany dinner table. In spite of the pandemonium inside Cottage Three, I couldn't help chuckling at her sass when she stuck out her tongue at me. I leaned back against the wall, one foot up, arms folded. Two adolescent boys in pyjamas streaked through the dining room, the shift supervisor in hot pursuit.

"You g'down from there!" he barked at the girl. He paused leaning on a chair, his paunch heaving, face flushed. "Shelley, can't you get her down from there?" he whined.

"She's not going to stay up there forever, Phil. Be patient."

He scowled. My attitude obviously rankled him. "Well, when she *does* get down, grab her and sit on her."

"Nah, not gonna do that."

Phil's head snapped around. "You *do* know how to do a restraint, don't you?" His upper lip curled as he spoke but I rolled my shoulder affably.

"Even if I did, I wouldn't use it." I knew Phil wanted me to manage the girl so he could wrestle the young male kingpin into submission. I knew too, he would have no compunction about manhandling this fragile fourteen-year-old on the table. That thought made me sick.

It was nearing the end of a twelve-hour shift I'd begun at noon at Calloway Christian Homes. Since the day shift went off at eight, Phil and I had been alone with the six teen-aged residents. They didn't like Phil. The girl on the table had been agitated all day. Since I was just a relief worker, recently hired, the kid wasn't about to tell me what was on her mind. At bedtime, she was still restless. She made several trips to the bathroom and stopped at the doors of the other residents to gab.

It was obvious she needed to talk. But instead of listening, Phil got into a power struggle, trying to get her to stay in bed. She turned defiant. That was all the invitation needed by the two strapping boys now running amok. The three were soon into a full-fledged revolt, howling, taunting and playing "chase me" with Phil. The other three teens joined in the caper briefly, but Phil's bellowed ultimatums had the desired affect and they skulked back to their rooms. It was now two hours past bedtime.

The front door flew open. Grace sailed in with the doomsday air of the Titanic. "Tiffany, what are you doing on the table?" It was not meant as a question. The Director of Calloway Christian Homes was not a woman to be trifled with. Caught off guard by Grace's sudden entrance and authority, Tiffany slumped off the table.

Bone weary, I climbed into my dilapidated Toyota Corolla. The starter whined twice, three times before the engine caught. Gravel crunched under the wheels then a hush followed as rubber met macadam. I blew out the tension in a pursed-lip sigh and left Cottage Three in my wake. At this hour the highway was deserted.

Exhaustion seeped through my body, making me feel older than my thirty-two years. *God, you wouldn't believe what happened tonight…* I found myself slipping into an imaginary conversation with Ben. Well, not a conversation exactly, ours being a correspondence relationship. Letters to and from him had become a kind of lifeline this past year—the year from hell. *No one at Calloway seems to understand a damn thing about sexual abuse. This kid that acted up tonight, she's got all the signs. And this Phil character, he wanted me to* restrain *her! I can just imagine what that would have done. She didn't need restraining. What a jerk.*

I could hear Ben answering, see his handwriting actually, "Sounds like you're working in the wrong place."

I am, I am. But I need the money.

The "vibes" at Calloway had put me off right away, but I'd been desperate for money. The Unemployment Insurance cheques kept food on the table and paid the rent. The mortgage on my acreage though, ripped voraciously into my meagre savings. But I dreaded missing a payment. I'd never wanted anything as badly as I wanted to build the home of my dreams on my small parcel of Lotusland. So I took the on-call work at the group home to supplement UI.

When the recession hit, I'd been eleven months in a position that had been a promotion in Child Protection Services. I loved that job but it was gone now. The day the dreaded pink slip arrived, a dry-mouthed devastation struck and lasted a week. It was no comfort that hundreds of others shared my fate. That was nearly a year ago.

I rolled the car window down and let the late summer wind whip through my hair. The night air smelled sweet with clover. Around me the

Fraser River valley of British Columbia formed a great cradle; the sides were the moonlight-crested mountains, the shadows of the valley, a fuzzy blanket.

I turned off the highway and followed a country road. A few minutes later my headlights washed across the front of a small clapboard house as my Toyota nosed into the drive. Curtains in the front window parted slightly, spilling soft light. *Shannon must have heard me coming.*

Not wanting to wake my boarder, I turned the key softly. But as soon as the door opened, a song issued forth from the outstretched throat of a big red dog. It's not her normal resounding bark but a unique, haunting vocalization I've never heard in any other dog, a joyous, rolling, "Wo-wo-wo-wo". She utters it on rare occasions and only for me. It's love and it melts me every time. "Shannon," I crooned, "Sh-sh, silly puppy. "

I sank into an overstuffed chair and encircled her coppery neck in my arms, burying my nose in the sleek coat. It smelled clean and lightly scented of doggie shampoo. The colour and texture were identical to my own hair. "Of course," I'd quip when people remarked on the likeness. "We share the same ancestry. We're both Irish."

A door opened and a sleepy looking young man in blue striped pyjamas padded by, heading for the bathroom. I was still scratching Puppy's ears when the toilet flushed and he reappeared.

"Sorry, Greg. Did Shannon wake you?"

"Mm," he grunted. He frowned as though trying to collect his thoughts. "There's a letter for you on the table...from Ontario. I think it's from that guy."

"His name is Ben."

He yawned. "How was work?"

"It was a zoo, actually, but I'll tell you about it tomorrow."

"'Kay. G'night. Oh yeah, I left you a note, but it'll keep till morning too." He crooked his fingers in a sleepy wave.

Sweet kid. He'd answered my ad ten months ago when I decided to sublet the second bedroom to help with expenses. A quiet, gentle young fellow barely twenty, he'd been on his own since fifteen. To escape his father's beatings, he'd run away and apart from a few short stints in foster care, survived street life by his wits. He turned out to be good company, like a kid brother. In fact, he reminded me a lot of Jamie, my baby brother.

According to Greg, seeing my ad had been a bit of serendipity for him too. Living with me, he claimed, he felt at home for the first time in his life. I took that to mean that it was peaceful and pleasant to share accommodations with Shannon and me.

He hadn't completed high school so when he showed an interest in taking a trades course, I encouraged him to go for it. He'd finished now, but like me, had found himself competing with dozens of other applicants for the few jobs that come up.

Shannon plopped a huge paw on my lap, rousing me. "Lemme check the mail, Puppy," I said, pushing myself up out of the chair.

Greg's note leaned against the sugar bowl.

> *"Shel, I'm so bored I think I'm losing my mind. I hate having no money to do anything. I'm not complaining. I know it's just as rough for you. I just wondered if you'd like to go swimming tomorrow night at Centennial Pool. It's something we could do that doesn't cost much. If you could spring for it, I'll pay you back when my cheque comes."*

I already knew I didn't have the six bucks for admission to the pool. I felt sorry for him though. He needed an outing more than I did. In the back porch I counted empty pop bottles. *If we cash those in and add the change in my wallet, we could make it.*

A letter addressed to Shelley Gallagher lay flat on the table. I slit the flap with my pinkie and withdrew a single folded sheet.

> *Dear Shelley,*
>
> *You said that if I ever wanted to see the part of Canada you rave about that you'd put me up. If you were bluffing, I'm calling you on it. I can steal away for a long weekend at the end of September. Be my tour guide and take me to Banff. I'll pay.*
>
> *Ben*

Had I been bluffing? Why did this man always make me feel he knew a part of me better than I did? And what was this giddiness in my stomach. Excitement? Or dread?

Greg looked up from his book when I staggered into the kitchen in my bathrobe the next morning and poured coffee into my favourite mug. I eased into a chair, a groan escaping me unbidden.

"Rough night at work?" he arched his eyebrows. This morning, he was the bright-eyed one.

"You were smart taking to the street when you ran away from home, Greg. This Calloway group home gives me the creeps. I don't think the staff even *like* teenagers." I gave him a run-down on the circus the night before.

"I had my belly full of lousy shrinks and counsellors," he said, laying aside his book. "You're the first one that ever passed my litmus test."

I gave a wry smile. "Too bad my talent isn't paying off in a decent job. God, I'm sick of living with the brakes on," I groused.

"Tell me about it," he muttered leaning his cheek on his fist.

I cursed myself for tactlessness and snatched his note still lying on the table. "Swimming! This evening. Sounds splendid."

"Great," he said, brightening. The animation in our voices stirred Shannon from her repose on the floor and she moseyed over to see what was up. I scratched behind her ear. Greg flicked the empty envelope from Ontario with his fingernail. "So, ah, how's what's-his-name, the letter-writing dude?"

"Ben. His name is Ben," I told Greg for the umpteenth time. "He's coming to visit for a weekend."

"Cool." He peered over the lip of his raised mug, a gleam in his eyes. "So...you gonna sleep with him?"

"None of your business!"

"What's the deal? You haven't gone on a real date in all the time I've known you."

"I'm not in the market for a man just now," I sniffed.

He ducked low to capture my gaze, which I sought to dodge by checking the dregs in my cup. "Are you ah...?" His question hung in the air between us.

"What?"

"Well, a virgin."

"No!" I retorted, heat flaming my cheeks. "I ought to say that too is none of your business."

He gave a rueful shrug. "It just seems, well, you know, you're always on a soapbox about sexual abuse of kids and such and you don't seem interested in dating. I thought maybe you had a negative thing about sex."

"I have a 'thing' about exploitation," I qualified, collecting myself, "Not about sex."

He looked dubious.

"Okay, I admit, I was painfully shy and inhibited around boys at one time. With a mother like mine, it's little wonder. Queen Victoria has nothing on Florence Gallagher. She's so sexually repressed that in our home sex had no name. Before puberty I'd never so much as heard the word, and after, it existed only as a dirty secret. She was cold and distant too so I wasn't comfortable even with physical displays of affection."

Shannon propped her chin on my lap. I smoothed the dome of her skull. Animals had been my preferred companions throughout childhood. When other girls were necking with boys, I was still playing horses and filling my need for closeness with a menagerie of pets.

"I think half the reason I went to university was to escape my *uptight upbringing*. Of course, the irony is that I landed smack in the middle of the sexual revolution. Beaded flower children chanted 'Make love not war', a mantra that resonated with my Pollyanna view of how the world ought to be. It dispensed a guilt-free doctrine on sex along with the tiny pills in pretty compacts girls could get from their doctor." I gave Greg a sardonic grin. "I supplemented my academic classes with extra curricular studies in human sexuality; Sex Ed 106, you might call it."

"Now you sound downright promiscuous," he chided, a ghost of a grin curling the side of his mouth.

I shrugged. "I needed to learn."

"Learn what?"

"About... me. About how to be a woman." *Ouch. Even now, that still felt raw.* "Maybe about what I wanted in a man."

"Was there ever anybody special?" Greg asked, heaping sugar into his second cup of coffee.

"Hmm, there was one guy..." A flash of indigo caught my eye as a Steller's Jay landed on a fir bough outside the window. The lilt of laughter on a summer night's breeze came to me with a sudden rush of sensual memory.

In that flurry of sexual exploration, I tumbled headlong into love. Paul hadn't been the first, or second or third. We'd sat on opposites sides on debating teams in a political science class. He and I parried over a charged current of mutual attraction. Then after one such evening class, he asked me along to a dance at the student centre, an informal affair. We flung ourselves into the tribal expression of the times to the ear-splitting acid rock of 1971. When he suggested we leave, I was more than ready to follow. Under a campus lamppost, he kissed me. I revelled in the confidence he exuded and surrendered willingly when he took me to his room.

A crow landed outside the window on the fir bough the jay had vacated. His caw sounded harsh and out of key. With Greg, I glossed over that episode, saying only, "He went into the military. I was such a priggish anti-war freak that I said good riddance."

He nodded pensively, then broke into a sly grin. "So...when you were, ah, studying Sex Ed, was any of the guys, Ben?"

I stared at the crow bobbing obnoxiously outside the window. It was a moment before I answered. "Yeah. He was the first."

————————————

From the back seat, Shannon pushed her snout out the window over my shoulder to catch woodsy scents as the battered Toyota chugged along a gravel road. The handling of last night's insurrection by the teen residents still troubled me. At times like this, when I needed to sort out my feelings, I sought tranquility on my land, a five acre parcel nestled at the base of a mountain. This was my Shangri-La.

When I turned the key off, the engine sputtered on like a beheaded chicken. I opened the door and Shannon leapt out, disappearing into the forest. The hinge groaned as I shut the door.

Silence, glorious silence. No, not quite. The wind soughed through fir boughs high above me. I tramped through the woods from survey post to survey post along the perimeter. It was my ritual. "Come on, Shannon", I shouted. "Do me a favour and don't get lost." There was a burst of copper fur, then the Setter was gone again.

Next, I visited the site I'd chosen for the house. In fantasy, a log dwelling rose before me, a low-slung wide veranda. I mounted its steps and crossed the threshold. In the phantom great room, a cathedral ceiling arched overhead. An ebony baby grand occupied an airy corner. In the heart of the house, a fieldstone fireplace rose the full two storeys. I caught myself straining to hear voices—conversational, familiar, intimate. An ache stole up from some cavernous place inside me. Before it could swamp me, I scolded aloud, "Forget it, Shelley." My voice dashed the illusion into shards of leafy green.

I sauntered to a small clearing and stretched out on the grass. Shannon came by a few times but my thoughts were elsewhere and she went exploring again. When at last I sat up, the sun was past its zenith. My canine companion lay nearby, head on her paws.

"Well Puppy," I mused, "what to do about Calloway?" Shannon cocked her ears adding only her own query. I grunted a sardonic laugh. "Thanks for your input."

Back in the car, the Toyota whined, protesting. I released the parking brake, thankful that I'd remembered to point the hood downhill. The wreck rolled, coughed, chugged and finally roared to life. At the corner, I took the right fork to go round the long route back to the highway. A dirt road wound up a hill narrowing suddenly at the top to a single lane traversing a dam. On the near side, I pulled off the road. Leaving my inquisitive, but reckless companion in the car, I strolled to the centre of the dam. To the north-east, Hayward Lake lay long, blue and serene, surrounded by forest.

Facing south-west, a thick wall reached my lowest rib. I peered over. Water trickled down the algae-discoloured face of the dam to a marsh. Was it a hundred feet below? Three hundred? I had no idea. Anything to do with numerical calculations wasn't my strong suit. It was enough though to give me a touch of vertigo. To quiet the queasy feeling, I gazed toward the horizon. Sunlight glinted off cars on the distant highway, beyond which meandered the wide ribbon of the Fraser River.

Maybe I'll bring Ben out here to show him my future home. Ben. Now that was another problem. I thought about Greg's question. *You gonna sleep with him?*

It had been more than ten years since I'd seen Ben. I'd been a kid when I first met him, a shy university undergrad just beginning to get comfortable talking to guys. We met at the cafeteria for the men's and women's residences. He had tagged along with a friend of my friend for dinner, making it three women and him.

A lean, tall man, with classic Russian Jewish features, he dominated the conversation with his stream-of-consciousness verbosity. His expansive gestures, powerful voice and flashing eyes were impossible to ignore. He didn't converse with us so much as he performed. We women were mere foils for his wit. Impervious to rules and social etiquette, he jumped cafeteria lines, took three helpings of food expressly restricted to one and openly admired the bosoms of female students around the room. I don't remember the topic of conversation now. I remember though, that he teased his female friend with lurid, sexual remarks that made me ill-at-ease. The girl had laughed, but awkwardly as if she too were embarrassed.

He began to call on me and soon we became frequent dinner companions, with or without the others. Without his audience, I found him a fascinating conversationalist. A grad student seven years older than me, he was well-read, intelligent and inquisitive. We discussed religion, philosophy, politics, war, racism; he always had an original perspective. I loved sharpening my mind with this captivating man.

His insight into my personality startled me, disturbed me even. He reflected that I possessed a perspicacious mind, (I'd had to look *that* up in the dictionary). I put things together cautiously, he said, but was wise and comprehensive when I did. He said my mild exterior cloaked a spirited passion and that people were likely to underestimate my strength. If he had not described me so precisely as I saw myself, I'd have thought he was trying to con me. I secretly delighted in his outrageous social behaviour too, envying him the freedom to shock people and do as he pleased.

Before long, though, I began having to fight off his crude advances. I didn't get too perturbed when he blocked me with both of his arms against the wall of the residence's darkened hall one evening on the way back from dinner. I made a joke and ducked under his arm. Another time when he came to meet me, he clutched me to him suddenly and pressed his mouth against mine. I made a sound of protest and pushed him away. I stayed mad for a while but went to dinner with him anyway. Stupid!

Once we were having a lively discussion in my room about the Russian Revolution. As he talked, he moved casually from the chair to sit on the bed where I lay propped on my elbow. He picked up my hand and began playing with my fingers, still talking. After he stroked my arm for a bit, I began to tingle. Fool that I was, I thought it impolite to interrupt him while he was talking to ask if he was making a pass at me. I didn't protest when he switched to rubbing my back, either. It felt good. By the time he slid his hand over my rear, I was becoming definitely aroused.

"Stop it, Ben."

"Why?"

"'Cause I said to stop!"

He squeezed my buttock. I lunged up off the bed and stood behind my desk. "Dammit don't be a jerk!"

He shrugged. "You'll come to me eventually."

Arrogant son-of-a-bitch!

The scree of a hawk above the dam disturbed the afternoon stillness. Now that the vertigo was under control, my stomach complained of other concerns. I was hungry. I climbed in the Toyota, shoving Shannon onto the passenger seat. At the highway, I headed into Mission to an ancient diner that served great chiliburgers.

While waiting for my order, I drank coffee from a heavy china cup and let my mind be sucked back to earlier years.

Throughout my youth, I'd watched my parent's marriage deteriorate into a bitter charade. I blamed it on the sexual repression of their era. This theory propelled me to fulfill Ben's boasted prophecy. I needed to overcome my ignorance and shyness, I reasoned, before I fell in love. That way, when—or if—love came along, I wouldn't screw it up. As I saw it, the practical thing was to seek experience with men I wasn't in danger of falling for. Ben served as a perfect choice to take me across the virginal threshold since his lewd and indiscriminate skirt-chasing left me emotionally cold.

Clearly, he wasn't hung up on me either. I knew I was just quarry to him—one of any number of women whose pants he tried to get into. That suited my purposes. I approached him one afternoon in the men's dorm. With exasperating contrariness, he acted blasé, as if it didn't matter whether we did or did not have sex. I didn't mind; since love and commitment were not at stake, I could relax. The sex was okay too. Pretty good really. He was funny, entertaining. After that though, he assumed he could come back for more, but I drew the line at once. We could be friends, I told him, nothing more. And there were other men. It was a good time in my life. I was, I thought, becoming quite liberated.

The following year I fell for Paul. I'd lacked the courage to tell Greg the real story about how it ended. I was on the pill but I'd missed a couple. Then my period was late. I was petrified. I kept trying to call him but he never returned my calls. Irrationally, I thought he must have intuited my predicament and was avoiding me. One afternoon I was moping on a bench outside the library when I spotted his distinctive green and yellow Datsun station wagon heading my way. He passed by without even a glance. Beside him, I mean right beside him, sat a stunning blond.

It was all over but the shouting. I discovered through the grapevine, he'd been seeing her for weeks. A couple of days later, my period came on and I cried as if I was losing a baby. My pain lasted long afterward. It was through a friend that I heard he'd joined the army. I retreated from men after that. After graduation, I left Ontario. I burrowed into my beloved mountains and devoted myself to my work and to the dizzy Irish Setter puppy I bought. Men, I decided, were too hot to handle for this not-quite-disguised Miss Goodie Two Shoes.

When I was preparing to move out west, Ben asked if he could write to me. I figured correspondence was safe, especially with the barrier of two thousand miles. He gave me his postal box number and we continued our intellectual exchanges in letters. The trouble came when I returned for a visit to my family. He picked me up at my parents' house in his red Corvette. He lorded that car over everything on the road; loved all that hot engine out in front. *A phallus on wheels*, he called it. He took me to one of Toronto's best restaurants. I told him plainly, "I won't sleep with you, Ben." He shrugged.

Throughout the evening, his meteoric, high-strung energy swept over me like a tidal wave. It was *his* car, *his* money—*his* evening. After dinner, he put me back in the 'vette and drove.

"Where are we going?" I asked.

"Don't worry about it. Just enjoy yourself."

I let myself be led. He pulled under the awning of a posh hotel, gave his keys to the liveried doorman to have it parked. He led me down elegant halls, finally opening a door with a key into a suite. I told him again, "No sex, Ben. I mean it."

"Yeah I know. I just thought we could have some privacy to talk."

He asked if he could take my picture. Why not, I thought. Everything just got away from me after that. Bit by bit he stripped me—of my clothes, my strength, my dignity. The camera snapped again and again. How could I let it happen? My protests had been too feeble. He promised he wouldn't have intercourse with me. He promised he would stop. But he didn't.

Only when I was back in the safety of my mountains could I face what had happened and then not for long. I had fooled myself into thinking I was ready to handle myself around men but I had been so easily dominated. Beyond humiliation, I retreated to my little girl identity and four-footed friends. Still, I allowed myself a self-righteous parting shot, a brutal letter in which I forbade him to contact me, and he didn't—for ten years.

The waitress set the chiliburger on the table with a clatter. "More coffee?"

"Hmm?" I blinked. "Oh. Yeah, sure."

Fifteen months ago, that first letter arrived. The return address sent a shock of hurt and rage through me. I snatched the nearest pen to scrawl across the envelope 'Return to Sender'. But something made me hesitate, creeping maturity maybe, and I tossed the letter unopened onto my coffee table. It took three days for my pique to subside and to hear a different voice inside myself. *If you don't believe a person can change, you've no business being a social worker.*

I searched the single page inside the envelope for a clue to his intentions, but he said nothing of his life circumstances, of the intervening years, or even how he obtained my address after I'd moved several times. He only asked that I write. *Don't be a chump*, I berated myself. *Why resurrect all that*? But the simple request laid a burden on my heart I couldn't shake. What if he were in trouble, needed a friend? Still, I didn't let him off easy when I replied. Why was he writing to me now? I had forbidden him to contact me. Did he remember why? I spelled it out in my most acrimonious righteousness.

"Dear Shelley," he replied, "I'm typing this standing up. I have to. You kicked my butt pretty good in your letter. It was many years late and I deserve it."

That's how it started. Now, he was coming for a long weekend and I didn't know what I wanted.

———————————

I ran my fingers through my hair, still damp and smelling of chlorine from swimming. Numbers on the gas pump whirred past my eyes, while Greg scrubbed the windshield. I flipped the lever to 'Off' and stepped inside the glass booth. "Ten dollars," the attendant mumbled.

I'd used all but my last four pennies along with the money from the pop bottles we'd redeemed to pay for the swimming. I reached into my wallet for my credit card and stared, disbelieving at the slot where it should have been. "Oh no," I groaned, and combed the other compartments. Nothing. I rooted through my purse. "I'm sorry," I babbled, "I can't find my credit card." I searched my mind for the last time I'd used it, then froze, my hand still deep in my purse.

"Oh, no!" I repeated, more urgently. An image of paying for the chiliburger materialized. "Oh my God. I'm so sorry. I left my credit card at a restaurant."

The attendant didn't reach for the phone to call the manager—or the police. He looked bored, actually. "Just come back later with the money," he said. "We're open till midnight."

I had no way to get cash until my Unemployment Insurance cheque came next week. "I can't get my credit card till lunch time tomorrow, but I'll leave you my watch for collateral. It's a good gold watch," I offered.

"Sure, lady, that's cool. Come back tomorrow." I pulled from my wrist the vintage watch my grandmother had left me and handed it over.

The next morning, I chose a less direct route to Mission on the south side of the river. White painted fences lined the road, hugging farms and country estates.

I braked at a stop sign, then nudged the Toyota into the intersection. Halfway across, the car made a horrendous "ka-thunk", bucked and stopped dead. Phobic about loud noises, Shannon convulsed and cast about for an escape.

I had a pretty good idea that whatever had made that awful noise now lay on the pavement under the car. It was a suspicion I was reluctant to confirm. I took my time getting out and kneeling down to peek underneath.

Sure enough, my faithful limo was disemboweled; a metallic tube, broken in the middle, lay on the road. I thought back to my 'Ladies Know Your Car' course. "Hmm, is that the transmission?" I muttered aloud, as if the instructor were peering over my shoulder.

To signal that the car was disabled, I propped up the hood. I ordered Shannon to heel and trekked to the nearest house to call for a tow. When I met him back at my Toyota, the operator confirmed that her malady was terminal. He dragged the wreck away.

As I listened to his engine drifting back in diminishing waves, I contemplated my slipping grasp on control of my life; my credit card in one town, my watch in another, my wheels headed for the auto graveyard and me stranded in the countryside with a large dog and no money. One last perverse act of self destruction remained.

A car approached. Clutching Shannon's collar, I stuck out my opposite thumb and peered hopefully at the driver.

Grace's unyielding stare made me squirm. When she spoke, her voice was porcelain, brittle and proper. "I presume this has something to do with the ruckus the night before last. You leave me in quite a bind, Shelley, quitting like this without notice."

I concentrated on my breathing. Despite my precarious financial situation, I felt compelled to follow through on my decision. "It isn't the kids, Grace. It's Calloway..."

———————————

Greg had taken the hint and gone out for the evening. Ben would not arrive from the airport for another hour. Since dinner, I'd changed clothes three times.

First, it had been one of the few skirts and the only high-heels I owned. When I observed the effect in the mirror, I was reminded of Ben's back-handed compliment years ago; that what attracted him to me was my full mane, my smile—and my D cup. I scowled at myself in the mirror, then stripped and retreated to the comfort of jeans and a cotton shirt. But a caustic voice in my head chided, "Oh don't be ridiculous." I took off the jeans and slipped into slacks and a jade silk blouse. Still at war with myself, I rubbed off the lipstick but kept the eye make-up.

Why was I letting him matter? He lived in a different world and I had no intention of ever moving back there. To me, southern Ontario's urban sprawl, the concrete desecration of everything wild and natural, signified materialism, avarice and corruption. Ben Volski belonged there.

To distract myself from the clock, I dragged a shoe-box stuffed with letters from my closet. Sitting on my bed, I dumped the letters and probed through the stash. All bore Ben's return address.

His earliest ones hinted at anguish. "I would like to share certain things with you, but I can't yet. It's too fresh." In others, his familiar arrogance surfaced. I'd denounced a sexist remark he'd written. He responded, "So you think I'm a male chauvinist pig? Maybe so, but I'm not just your run-of-the-mill MCP. I'll have you know I was recently elected vice president of the Southern Ontario Chapter." There was no forgetting the mercurial personality. And there was an outlaw quality in him still. He described how he had exacted revenge on a man he felt had wronged him. Through a dastardly brilliant scheme, he destroyed the man's marriage and professional reputation. The story chilled me.

Yet each time I decided he must be a depraved psychopath, I'd dis-cover another side of him. "My two favourite people spent this evening with me and because of them I'm feeling good enough about myself to tell you the truth. In the early '70's, I got married. Yeah, I was a bad boy when I took you out that time." The first time I'd read *that*, I'd gone icy all over—then hot. *Never* would I have knowingly slept with a married man!

"My wife and I separated recently. I'm feeling rather lost and disori-ented. I was lucky enough to bring two children into the world (my wife helped a little, too). My son, Ari, will soon be six; Sara turned eight this month. I have them tonight." I learned how he adored them, how much he wanted to be a good father, how much he wanted them to feel good about themselves, confident and happy. It surprised me somehow. It didn't fit the arrogant, self-centred bastard image.

Gradually I began venting my worries over my unemployment in letters to him. And he responded thoughtfully, empathetically. I recalled how he used to tune in to me in those earlier years at university with such acuity. I remembered how it used to unnerve me. Now I found it comforting.

In turn, he used me as a sounding board while he fought for equilibrium in the aftermath of his separation. I learned of his worries over his sickly, asthmatic daughter and followed his struggles as he tended his father, who lost a leg and later that year his life, to cancer. He disarmed me with his disclosures. "Do you know how you affect me? When you talk to me, you are a mirror in which I see myself with less distortion. That's one of the reasons you are such a treasure to me. You have the ability to get under my skin and do it in the nicest way."

Shannon woofed. Through the open bedroom door, I saw lights wash across the living room. "My God, he's here." I stuffed the letters back in the box and jammed it in the closet.

He stood on the doorsill, with a devil-may-care grin and an unholy penetrating look. "Hi, kid," he said in a soft baritone. His appearance had changed enough for it to take a moment to see past the differences and recognize the familiar. His six foot one frame had filled out; gone was the hungry weasel look of his twenties. An unfamiliar beard accentuated his dark Russian features.

I clasped his wrist and drew him inside. I arched up on my toes to put my arms round his neck. The rush of emotion I felt caught me unprepared. I buried my face against his shoulder where his musky scent filled my head.

"It's been a long time," he said.

"Yes," I answered. "I expect we've both done some growing up." I exhaled loudly then, breaking the mood. "Well, come in. Sit. You must be weary from the trip."

Ben set his empty teacup on the coffee table. His long legs stretched out comfortably from the end of the sofa. In an overstuffed arm chair kitty-corner from him, I sat with my feet curled under me. A cone of soft light from a floor lamp enfolded us in its tent. My fear that we would be awkward and not know what to say, never materialized.

The clink of his cup on the table tapped me back to the present. I checked my watch—I'd retrieved it along with my credit card the day the Toyota died. "Considering the hour, Ben, we should wrap it up for tonight. A trip to Banff and back in five days is ambitious even with us sharing the driving."

"I s'pose you're right," he yawned.

I hesitated, nervous suddenly over what I was about to say. "Um, there's one more thing. It could wait till tomorrow but..." I faltered under his gaze. I searched for a way to ground myself to suppress the trembling that threatened to unleash itself from the pit of my stomach. Untangling myself from the chair, I moved over beside him.

"In one of my early letters to you, I set out terms, if we were to be friends." He stiffened almost imperceptibly, then with meticulous casualness leaned back, crossing his legs at the ankle and lacing his fingers behind his head. I pushed on, afraid I'd choke up if I paused. "One of those terms was no sex. Ever." His eyes held mine. He unwound his arm from behind his neck and picked up a wisp of my hair and swept it slowly behind my ear.

"Shelley, you know I was attracted to you way back. But it was never just physical. It's you, your smile, your joie de vivre, your innocence. I need that from you." I should have questioned what he meant, but I was absorbed in my own agenda.

He gave a sly grin, "I admit I still want your body. You'll never stamp out the MCP." Then he sobered. "But I didn't come here for that. I screwed up with you once. I hope I'm smart enough not to make that mistake twice."

I felt short of breath. "Are you still attracted to me?" I asked. He lowered his chin and gave a hard, meaningful stare. I felt my cheeks warm. "What if... what if I said I wasn't so sure anymore?" I felt dizzy, like I was standing atop a windswept cliff.

The hand at the nape of my neck slid down and described a circle in the small of my back. I made no move to resist. "I didn't come out here expecting you to put out, Shelley. I took you at your word. I'm flattered you're even thinking about me that way."

Terror battered inside my ribcage like a frantic butterfly. "I need you to know something else," I mumbled, staring at my toes. I fell silent. The wall clock's ticking sounded loud.

"I haven't been with a man for ten years."

To my horror he threw back his head, laughter erupting from him. "Ten years!" he exploded.

I drew up ramrod straight, thoroughly miffed at his reaction. "Yeah! So? Lots of perfectly normal people don't have an active sex life, you know. Besides," I shot back petulantly, "I haven't forgotten how."

"I'm sorry," he sputtered failing to stifle his amusement, "I guess that was a tad rude. But," he shook his head in disbelief. "Ten years? I thought *I'd* had it rough going without for, hmm, eleven months, ten days and uh…" He counted softly on his fingers. I jabbed my elbow into his ribs and he laughed again.

The implication dawned on me. "There've been others recently, then?"

"I won't lie to you. I know only the truth will get by you. Yeah, I've been with other women in the past while. No one special, but hell you know me. I'm an alley cat. That was a tough eleven months."

His utter lack of contrition made *me* laugh then. "You're incorrigible."

———————————

Fields of rich black earth, dairy herds and barns reeled past the window of the compact rental. With Ben behind the wheel, I sank back to survey the Fraser Valley's pastoral countryside. Ahead, the valley narrowed; mountains rose sharply each side of the river. I squinted against the sunrise to glimpse the highway wrapping itself around their giant shapes.

"I'm sorry about the car, Ben."

"Cut it out, Shelley. We've been through all that. You didn't shoot your car; it died of natural causes."

"Yeah, I know. But it was supposed to be my contribution to this trip. Now you're paying for everything."

"Hey, if it'll make you feel better, I'll let you do all the driving."

"Okay, okay," I capitulated.

"You are fond of your independence, aren't you," he said, a statement more than a question. I shot him a quizzical look, yet his very presence distracted me. Here he was, not two thousand miles but two feet away, touching distance. "I'm enough of a chauvinist to want to take care of certain things," he went on "Things I'm good at. Face it, Shelley, you're no good with money. But I'm not just good at getting my hands on it, I'm great!"

"Modest too," I remarked. "It's true though, I'm an abysmal disaster with money. I bounced so many cheques that I got rid of my chequebook. Now I count out the cash for each of my bills and put it in envelopes under my rug till I can pay them."

He snorted, crinkling his forehead in amusement. "You don't really, do you?"

"Oh yes I do. Anyway, I may not have money sense, but it's important to me to meet my obligations and rely on myself."

"Is that why you never married?" There was a slight sting in his question.

"No." I stared out the side window volunteering nothing more.

Undaunted, he asked. "Why *are* you so proud and independent?"

"It's nothing to do with men." I lied, waving my hand in a motion of dismissal.

At the town of Hope, the Fraser River bends at right angles, flowing from the north through a spectacular narrow canyon. Following the river, we began threading a series of rock cut tunnels. Train tracks hung precariously on the opposite canyon wall above the boiling water.

"Did you ever read *The Last Spike* by Pierre Berton," I asked.

"A long time ago."

"You can see what a feat it was to build the railroad through here and why the greatest loss of life was through this section." As if to punctuate my remarks, just then a southbound train appeared. I pointed to it and he nodded, his gaze shifting back and forth between the train and the twisting highway in front of us.

As we came up over a rise, I directed him to pull off into a parking lot that appeared. "This is a tourist trap but worth seeing." We scooted across the highway and entered a gaudy orange structure built out over the edge of a cliff above the river. Ben paid for two tickets and we entered a tram with several other sightseers. Slowly it swung out on its cable, stretched between craggy yellow cliffs. Someone on board gasped as we drifted over the narrow gap through which the river surged.

The operator recited statistics of Hell's Gate, the short distance between the opposing canyon walls, the depth of the river below, how many tons of water passed by each minute at this, its narrowest point. The tram disgorged its passengers on the far side. We stepped out with the rest onto the observation deck and stood by the railing. I don't know why the question, submerged in my subconscious for sixteen months, suddenly bobbed to the surface at that moment.

"Ben, how did you find me? I've moved half a dozen times. How did you get my address?"

"I'm an auditor. It's my business to know how to sniff things out."

"That's not an answer. I want to know how?"

"I pulled up your file."

A firebrand touched dry tinder inside me. "What! My income tax file." Heat built up inside my head and air whistled steam-like through my nostrils. "In *my* work, I am not allowed to snoop in someone's file without a legitimate reason."

"I had a reason. I wanted to find you."

"You violated my privacy!" I turned from him, staring down at the turgid, angry river below. A log spun, caught in the brown whirlpool. "Tell me the truth," I demanded. "Is it against the rules to do that?"

"Yeah," he shrugged.

"Are rules meant for everyone but you?"

"I've broken rules lots worse than that."

He sounded so cavalier. "What else did you learn from my file? That I'm still single, right? Damn you Ben, you're so predatory!"

He didn't answer and I said no more. After a few minutes, he turned his back to me and ambled toward the tram. I followed, not trying to catch up. As we crossed back over the river, my anger cooled and I began to feel ashamed of my sudden attack. At the car, I got behind the wheel.

We made our next stop at Lytton, a sleepy little town that lay between the highway and the river. I drove down a couple of blocks of clapboard houses that looked like they hadn't seen fresh paint in twenty years. A few children, mostly Native, were the only inhabitants we saw.

"Why are we stopping here?" he asked.

"There's something I want to show you." At a deserted high-level bridge, I pulled onto the shoulder and parked. "Come on. Bring your camera."

We strolled onto the bridge deck. Far below, a green river flowed from the northeast. A hundred yards to the southwest, it met the familiar muddy waters of the Fraser which still flowed from the north. "Wow!" Ben exclaimed. It was a sight. For as far as we could see, the waters of the two rivers, the green and the brown, flowed side by side.

"This is the confluence of the Thompson and the Fraser," I informed him in my best travelogue voice. "From now on, we'll be following the Thompson." As we leaned against the railing, I became aware that Ben was looking at me instead of the scenery. Vaguely unnerved, I spoke to distract him. "Imagine the first white men who came down these rivers." I watched the inexorable flow of water below. "It could be a metaphor." He gave me a questioning look and I answered his unspoken question. "Life's a journey down an uncharted river. You never know what to expect. Sometimes it's smooth, sometimes so wild it challenges your very soul. If you capsize, you better be wearing your life preserver."

Warily, he took the bait. "So...what's the life preserver?"

I turned and faced him. "Ethics, Ben. When life is most cruel, that's when you most need them. If you're too arrogant to wear them, you may find yourself smashed to pieces at the bottom of the river's next cataract."

He held my gaze a moment longer then slapped both hands on the railing and said, "How 'bout a picture?"

He pointed the camera to catch the line where the brown and green effluence flowed side by side, with me in the foreground. I smiled for the picture. "Turn this way," he pointed. I did. He looked through the lens. "Put your heel up on the first bar of the railing," he instructed from behind the camera. I obeyed. He stopped again, walked over and positioned my chin.

I remembered another time. "For heaven sake, Ben, just take the picture." When I heard the click, I turned for a last look at the two rivers that were not yet ready to mix their separate waters.

Back in the car, we wound our way up the Thompson River valley. Contradictory images of Ben's character wrestled for supremacy in my mind; at times he seemed warm and genuine but I wondered if he was just a charming, modern-day Rasputin. I'd known for years that he had Russian blood but I knew little about his background except that both his parents were dead. "What was it like for you growing up?" I asked.

He took so long to respond that I'd begun to think he wasn't going to. He wedged one elbow out the side window, the fingers of his opposite hand hooked over the top of the wheel. "I was born and raised in Toronto," he said at last, "but when you crossed the threshold of our house, you stepped into 'little Russia'. My father grew up in the old country, the youngest of nine. When I turned twenty, he took me there to visit relatives—what was left of them after the war. They still lived near the city of Volsk." He glanced at me, brightening. "That's the origin of our family name."

I nodded and he sank back into a pensive mode. "They were so dirt poor that when we left, my father made me leave behind every last scrap in my suitcase except my toothbrush. That grinding poverty," he said through gritted teeth. "It made me realize what he escaped."

"What about persecution?"

"Pogroms? I know little of what he experienced. My brother and I got our parent's history through a straw; a few stories but a lot left to our imagination."

"How did he get out? Weren't Jews prohibited from leaving?"

"Yeah. Refusniks, they came to be called. He got conscripted into the Russian Army and sent to the frontier." He chortled. "Imagine putting a Jew on nighttime border patrol! One morning the commanding officer woke up to find the border left unguarded. Dad sold their rifle on the other side and used the money to get to England. From there he emigrated to Canada."

I laughed. "Sounds like you come by your defiance of authority honestly." He grinned and continued. "Dad went into business manufacturing furniture. In Russia, being a Jew, he hadn't been allowed to attend regular school. Since he couldn't read or write much, my brother and I had to help out with any writing for the business. He called us his secretaries. It's no accident my brother, Martin, became a business lawyer and I became an accountant."

"What about your mother?"

"She grew up in Poland. I learned from a relative that she fell in love with the wrong man—I can only guess what that means—and was sent to Canada to separate them. She worked in a sweatshop. She and Dad met at a dance."

"Did you ask her about her life in Poland?"

"Couldn't." A shadow darkened his face. I waited, hoping he would continue unprompted. After a moment, he did.

"When I was eleven, she had a mental breakdown and never recovered. Dad refused to put her in an institution. So she stayed home, but she lived in her own world. She would talk to invisible people, dance about in the kitchen or worse, outside where the neighbours would see. I was afraid of being humiliated by her strange behaviour so I never brought friends around.

"I felt as if my real mother had died, only there was no funeral." After another long moment, in which I searched for something appropriate to say, he glanced over. The strength in his voice signified his return to the present. "So there you have it. My father distrusted non-Jews and educated people. My mother suffered from paranoia. Between the two of them—and an early diet of Holocaust stories filtering back from Europe—I learned to regard everyone, except maybe Jews, with a large dose of suspicion."

The surrounding landscape was changing. Sagebrush perfumed the dry air, replacing the verdant green of the coast. Outcroppings of rock in hues of red and yellow jutted from dusty hillsides. "I didn't know British Columbia had desert," Ben said, "I thought it was all forests and snow-capped mountains."

"I used to think so too," I admitted. "When I first saw it, I thought the desert was an austere, dead place. But in time I began to appreciate it for its own character. In the late afternoon sun, it glows in such glorious colours, pink and mauve, magenta, blue and gold."

We descended the long hill into Cache Creek, the engine of a transport behind us growling down its tenor scale. We stopped to fill up the tank. Inside the gas bar, I took a cold pop from the cooler and joined Ben at the counter where he tossed his snacks and credit card. "Add in the lady's coke," he said to the woman at the till.

"No! I can pay for my own."

He took the bottle from me and set it on the counter. "Include it," he instructed her. I made a face and huffed at him. When the woman handed him the credit card chit and a pen, he turned to me and whispered audibly, "How many p's in 'stick-up?' " I felt myself flush as I checked the woman's reaction. She shot a nervous look at Ben, then at me. I rolled my eyes and shrugged in an effort to reassure her and to distance myself from his game.

Outside, I scolded. "You enjoy throwing people off balance, don't you."

"Yep."

"Why?"

"Keeps 'em guessing. I like to make a clean getaway."

Ben dozed while I drove through the tranquil upper Thompson River valley, passing places with quaint names like Salmon Arm and Sicamous. I was glad for the solitude to analyze my turbulent feelings. Last night when Ben had caressed my shoulder and back, I'd felt a part of myself awaken that had long been dormant. Over the past year, I'd grown fond of him. I was beginning to trust him. I didn't want to be wrong about him, but he seemed to have so many sides, like a mirrored orb twirling above a ballroom floor. Its reflected points of light—madly whirling fireflies—both dazzle and disorient. He had that effect on me. It wasn't sexual seduction I feared now; it was emotional seduction.

It was just dusk when I pulled into a wayside stop. He woke up. "Need me to take over the driving?"

"After. I want you to see this." A stone cairn stood in the half light near to railroad tracks. A small clapboard building beside it bore the name of the whistle stop—Craigellachie. I led the way to the cairn where in silence, we read the inscription. He whistled. "So this is where they drove in the Last Spike. It's the middle of nowhere."

"Yes," I murmured. "In this nowhere place, east met west and it changed things forever."

We settled on Revelstoke as the town in which to spend the night. Ben took the wheel for this last stretch. By the time we reached the outskirts, it was full dark. Reaching across the space between us, he took my hand giving it a slight squeeze. "Listen kid, tell me now, before I pull into a motel. Should I ask for one bed or two?"

The warmth of his hand fired synapses in my head. It had been such a long time since my flesh had been warmed by another's. "I think... one," I murmured."

Dropping our bags on the floor, he reached for me, drawing me into his arms. Ambivalence buffeted me. He must have felt it because he said, "We don't have to."

I leaned into him. "No," I whispered. "I want to."

"Well then," he said holding me at arm's length, "you may have the first turn in the washroom. But, may I make a small request?"

"What's that?"

"Do you have a robe with you?"

"Yes."

"Just wear that, okay?"

I shrugged. "Okay; if you say so."

I took my time showering, fixing my hair, applying make-up. Now that I had cast the die, I was determined to enjoy this. "Your turn," I said, stepping back into the room.

He reached for me again, then stopped. "No," he caught himself, "if I touch you now, it'll be a race to the finish line and that won't be fair to you." He moved toward the washroom. "There's a package for you on the bed," he said over his shoulder. "I'm sure you'll figure out what to do with it." He closed the door.

The package lay wrapped in white tissue paper secured with a gold foil seal. It was feather-light. I pulled off the ribbon, slipped my thumbnail under the seal and let the paper fall to the floor. A filmy, black garment unfolded from my hands. I held it against me, peering at my image in the mirror. My eyes lit up. I had never worn anything so exquisitely feminine. Dropping my robe, I slipped into the jumpsuit. I loved how it made me look. The tiny ribbons over my shoulders accentuated the alabaster matte of my skin. The gathering below my breasts showed off my fullness. Soft leggings billowed like those of a dancer in the Arabian Nights and gathered trimly at my ankles. My hips began to sway to some inaudible exotic music, my bare feet padding lightly in pirouettes across the carpet. The costume was perfect, sensual but not obscene. *A good choice, Ben.*

With a sudden gasp, I froze. *You rat!*

CHAPTER TWO

Ben emerged from the washroom in his robe. He took in my appearance in an up and down sweep of his eyes. I stood stock still as he approached and slipped his arms around me. "Mm Baby, you look good," he crooned, kissing my neck. A thrill rippled through me in spite of myself but I put my hands on his arms and pushed him away.

I meant to be rational, cool, but in the act of pushing him back, hurt erupted. "You lied to me!"

He jerked back and stammered. "What the...?"

"You meant to seduce me. This outfit, it proves it. I fell for your crap that you didn't come here for that, that you needed me for my smile, my 'joie de vivre'. You haven't changed a bit. You lie! Everything is sex for you, a damn conquest! No wonder you're drawn to my... *innocence*!" I spat out the word. Then the trembling started. "I just...wanted you to like me...for me." I choked then, getting too close to the source of the pain.

"I *do* like you for you," he insisted, reaching for me again. But I thrust up my palm to stop him. He blew out his breath and dropped onto the bed, head in his hands.

Neither of us moved nor spoke. My breath came in ragged shudders. At last, Ben lifted his head. "I'm sorry," he said miserably. "I never meant to hurt you. I meant what I said last night. I didn't come here to fuck you, literally or figuratively. If you hadn't made the offer..."

"But the outfit," I cried.

"Listen, Shelley, I really didn't expect that you would want to sleep with me. I was prepared for that. I'm not so stupid that I can't get the message when it's written in black and white. But I'm the kind of guy who always has a back-up plan, who always thinks *What if?* I bought the outfit on the outside chance that you might have a change of heart. If it'd been clear you weren't interested, that little number would have gone back to Ontario with me unwrapped." He looked almost beseeching. "I want you to believe me."

"How *can* I believe you? First you tell me you're attracted to my innocence then I see you've come prepared to bed me."

He took my wrist and tugged but I balked. "Come here," he coaxed. I searched his face. Reluctantly, I let myself be pulled down onto his lap. "I want more than anything for you to trust me," he pleaded. "If not making love to you is what it takes, then I'll gladly forego that pleasure."

I wanted to believe him. I wanted this not to be happening. "It would kill me if you betrayed my trust again."

"Hey, a guy can fantasize can't he?" he said sheepishly but when I glared at him, he sighed, his level gaze holding no hint of deceit. "I mean it, Shelley. We don't have to. I want your friendship more than I want your body."

I exhaled in a shiver. "You don't understand," I pleaded.

"What?"

I didn't know how to answer. I didn't know what to think. I felt so torn. I bowed my head and shook it in my ambivalence. He took my head in both his hands, threading his fingers in my hair. He kissed my eyelids, moist with unspilt tears, then the points of heat on each of my cheeks. His mouth found mine and held it as he lay me back on the bed. His hand moved over the silky costume, warming me where it made contact. His palm traced my shape. The sounds of battle waging in my head dimmed as my skin began to electrify. He slipped a strap down over my shoulder kissing me in the hollow below it. He kissed a path step-wise behind the retreating fabric as he slowly peeled it away. When his lips brushed my flesh at the lowest curve on my belly, a hard spasm seized me there and my eyes fluttered open in surprise. He smiled then and shrugged out of his robe. I gripped his shoulders, whether to hold him to me or push him away, I know not. He lowered himself upon me and I wound my fingers in his hair, still slick from his shower. The trembling inside me that had begun with the quarrelling, felt shot with quicksilver and then a sweet sensation swept through me, like the quenching of a terrible thirst.

By a stone monument, over-arched with graceful wooden beams, I pivoted a slow three hundred and sixty degrees. Eons ago, in violent upheaval, Earth had turned her craggy soul to the sky. Now, peak after peak crowning Rogers Pass shimmered in the morning sun.

"Isn't it awesome," I breathed. Ben nodded, his expression registering appreciation. "They seem alive," I murmured, "as if they know everything that ever happened since time began." A quiver emanated from deep inside. But this morning, I wasn't sure what triggered it, the mountains or the lovemaking at daybreak. My skin, in a multitude of places, felt kissed into wakefulness, my throat, my belly, my fingertips. I felt at once both drained and full. Back in the car, I chattered about everything and nothing, liberated from an unseen constraint. For once, Ben seemed content to listen.

Farther along, we turned off the main highway and made the obligatory tourist's pilgrimage up a series of switchbacks to the fabled Rocky Mountain jewel. The opaque aquamarine water of Lake Louise lay serene and solid looking, reflecting a magnificent alpine vista.

We strolled along a pine-scented path that skirted the lake. A hawk screamed overhead. Watching it tilt and circle in a thermal, I felt a surge that seemed to meld my consciousness with the raptor. Currents buoyed me. I imagined the tufted carpet of deep green forest gliding beneath me, heard the wind whisper. Ben's warm breath feathered my ear, coaxing me back to earth.

When we turned at the head of the lake, Chateau Lake Louise, the stately Canadian Pacific Hotel, stood sentinel over its treasure. Inside, we roved cavernous marble and mahogany halls. Haunting music drew us down a corridor. In the tearoom, a woman with flowing golden hair, looking every inch a siren, embraced a harp enticing a spell from its strings. Ben whispered, "Maybe someday my daughter will play like that."

"She plays the harp?"

"Mm-hmm. She took it up last year."

"An apprentice angel."

He rolled his eyes, suggesting that there was as much imp as cherub in Sara.

We pushed on. In a motel on Main Street in Banff, we deposited our luggage and went out to see the sights; the Cave and Basin, the hot springs and Vermilion Lakes. We strolled along the parapet by Bow Falls. Above us, the Banff Springs Hotel rose like a baronial castle out of primordial forest.

We explored the park curator's taxidermy museum, viewing specimens of every imaginable creature inhabiting the park. I stared up into the teeth of a rearing grizzly. A sudden ferocious growl made my heart miss a beat. Ben staggered out from behind the case, hands curled into claws above his head and I laughed to overcome my fright.

We combed the shops along Main Street. In one, a large shaggy teddy bear, a grizzly in fact, captivated me. It possessed a comic combination of realism and hug-ability. Unable to resist this second characteristic, I squeezed it in my arms. Ben sidled up and bent his ear to its snout. He nodded and eased the bear from my grasp. Carrying it to the counter, he handed the cashier some bills, then turned and extended it toward me. "He says his name is Beasley. He wants to go home with you." I gave Ben a squeeze then too. Tucking Beasley under one arm, I slipped the other through Ben's elbow for the walk back to the motel.

After that, Ben would settle for no other restaurant but The Grizzly House. Inside, it possessed a rustic-elegant ambience. I donned a soft pink sweater to warm me against the nip in the mountain air. Candlelight cast intriguing shadows on Ben's sculpted face. He ordered for us... a bottle of red wine and the house specialty, a fondue of venison, beef and bison.

While we waited to be served, he reached across the table. "Give me your hand." I obliged. "Do you think maybe you trust me a little more now?"

I didn't want to answer him and looked off in the direction the waiter had gone. But he waited till I turned back. "Maybe a little," I hedged. "But there are things about you that scare me."

He held fast to my hand. "Tell me what."

"I'm afraid of becoming your victim. Your attraction to my so-called innocence makes me feel like the next meal caught in a spider's web."

Coal-black eyes pierced mine. Then his mouth twitched. "And such a delicious morsel you are, my sweet."

"I'm serious, Ben. You have cruelty in you. The way you took revenge on that man you said had wronged you for instance, ruining his marriage and reputation. Yours is an 'eye-for-an-eye' code. If you're capable of that, what else could you do? You frighten me." I drew my hand away, finding the contact uncomfortable now.

He looked at me a long time before answering. "Sometimes I do seek revenge." His voice was deep and sober. "But not for fun and not randomly. If I'm at fault or provoke a person, then I take my lumps. It's when I've done nothing wrong, when I've been treated unjustly that I make someone pay. That man lied and profited at my expense. I'm not sorry." He bristled and I glared.

"You know what's wrong with you?" I remonstrated, "You don't get angry. You stifle your feelings."

"You're quite right. I don't get mad." He smiled a taut, silky smile I didn't like. "I get even."

I could feel my temples throbbing. Such a gulf existed between us, different lives, different landscapes. Thankfully the waiter appeared with the meal. We withdrew from battle, focusing on the delectables he crowded onto the table. By the time the waiter brought desert, Ben's banter had resurrected my carefree mood and made me laugh.

He poured his tea, then shifted again to a more serious tone. "Shelley, I want to be clear that you have nothing to fear from me. You don't have the guile to hurt me vindictively. Whenever I have felt hurt by you, it was because you spoke a painful truth. You aren't the kind of person who would ever become the target of my revenge."

I caught the tang of lemon as he squeezed a wedge into his tea. "I suppose I follow your reasoning, Ben, but I still don't *like* what you believe in."

He gave a kind of sad smile. "That's what I mean. You say what you think." He leaned forward stressing his words. "And I want you to go on speaking your truth to me. I need that from you. You don't know how much I need that." I wondered what he meant but it didn't occur to me to ask.

After dinner, we strolled hand in hand down to the Bow River. Granite and snowy peaks towered above the town, visible against the night sky. Globes shedding ivory light clustered on lampposts on a stone bridge built in grander times. Midway across we stopped to watch the hypnotic flow coursing toward us. It disappeared beneath us, down toward the falls whose distant thunder we could hear. Ben pointed to the near bank.

In the pale light of the moon, I saw a magnificent buck elk. It lowered its bulk into the river. The current caught it, sweeping the huge rack toward us. It propelled toward the left bank but barely reached midstream when the river whisked it beneath us. Traffic on the bridge prevented us from crossing to the other side to see how it progressed.

Ben's vision lingered on the last place we had seen the animal. "Do you think that fellow has any scruples?" I shot him a quizzical look. Mock innocence raised his eyebrows. "He wasn't wearing a life preserver. Maybe he'll be pancaked at the bottom of Bow Falls."

I rolled my eyes. "Brat," I chided, tugging his sleeve to head back to the motel.

After the chill in the night air, the warmth of the room was a cozy welcome. A Spartan kitchenette adjoined the bedroom. Ben produced a package of popping corn he'd bought in the afternoon and clattered through the cupboards. He paused, looking momentarily perplexed, then swept me into his arms.

"Hey Baby," he whispered conspiratorially. "Want to try something wild and exciting?"

"Um, I don't know. What did you have in mind?"

"Want to make popcorn in an open frying pan?"

Shannon bounced around the yard, returning every few moments for me to stroke her head. It was obvious that she had missed me. Lounging on the front steps, Ben and I were dispassionately discussing the subject of marriage.

"Tried it once," he said with a shrug. "Don't think I'll get married again. Next time, I'll just live with the woman."

"What if the woman wants to be married?"

"I'll have to find someone who doesn't."

I laughed. "That may not be so easy."

"*You* don't seem to be too eager to be married." He turned and studied my face. "Or is it men you don't like?"

I laughed again but softly this time. "The idea of marriage doesn't appeal to me. My parents' example turned me off. But," I nudged him, "contrary to your estimation of me as a man-hater, you're quite mistaken. I rather like men."

"But you also like your independence."

"I told you, that has nothing to do with men."

He looked at me levelly. "What then?"

I sighed and tossed a stick Shannon brought me. "It's because I grew up kind of motherless. Your mother checked out mentally; mine simply abdicated."

Ben closed his eyes and leaned back casually resting his elbows on the top step and tipping his face to the sun. "You gonna to tell me about it?"

I studied his exaggerated indifference, knowing full well it was to encourage me to elaborate. I was grateful he wasn't gawking at me.

"Neglect saturated every corner of my childhood," I volunteered. "I was a sickly child. My mother made my sister look after me all the time. Poor Gayle resented me because of it, so I felt doubly rejected. If Gayle was in school, Mom just left me by myself. Maybe she needed to pick up groceries or medicine. Or maybe she just got restless.

"I was seven when my brother came along. Before he was a year old, I was having to take care of *him* on my own, sometimes even late at night. You could say I was *his* mother. I adored him though." Shannon settled beside me, leaning into me as I hugged her close.

Ben opened his eyes and observed Shannon disinterestedly. "Looks like you've someone else to mother nowadays." I nodded, scratching Puppy's ears. She broke into a 'smile' with her jaw parted and her pink tongue spilling forward. "But I still don't get why you're so fiercely independent about money, especially when you're so lousy at amassing it."

"Money was a huge source of conflict between my parents. Mom complained that there was never enough, accusing Dad of being tight-fisted and a poor provider. *He* claimed he gave her his paycheque from the factory and that she failed to pay the bills she was supposed to. I learned not to mention money for fear it would trigger one of their horrible fights. I avoided asking for things I needed. I wore shoes with the soles flapping back to the heels. I got frostbite because I had no mittens or scarf. My Mom didn't seem to notice these things.

"In grade seven, girls were required to wear slacks on days we had physical education. I only had one pair and it had a hole in the bum. I had to wear those pants for months because my mother neither mended them nor bought me another pair. The teasing from other kids was unbearable. I was bullied. I don't think she ever twigged to it. She certainly didn't do anything about it.

"One day after I'd had a particularly bad time of it, I came home and she'd bought herself a brand new winter coat with a fur collar. She was strutting in front of the mirror and bragging about how good it looked on her. I hated her that day. I still don't know whose version about my parents' finances was the truth, Mom's or Dad's. But what I did learn is that I couldn't expect even my most basic needs to be met by the people who are supposed to care. I learned that I'm on my own. If I don't depend on someone else, I can't be let down." I fell silent.

After a time, he placed a hand on my knee. "Thank you for telling me that. I understand a few things better now."

"Hey, it's not all bad," I brightened. "From my father I learned to dream and I learned to go after what you want by watching my mother do it."

An odd look stole across his face. "Maybe you can teach me."

I scoffed. "You? You have no trouble taking *whatever* you want." He turned his face away, making no reply. Maybe he meant my father's ability, not my mother's, I thought belatedly. I cursed myself for the snap judgment and for letting my righteousness spoil the moment.

"Shelley."

"What?"

"It's time."

I felt a slice like a paper cut in the vicinity of my heart. "I'm going to miss you. I had a wonderful time."

"Me too." He stood and drew me up into his arms. "I'm already thinking about how and when I can see you again." He leaned his forehead into mine. "Maybe we'll have one of those 'same time next year' kind of relationships." He kissed me and was gone.

I watched the place where his car disappeared from sight down the road. A yawning emptiness opened up inside, a bottomless pain I had not thought possible. For three days I had felt like a princess, like Cinderella. The power of his personality filled the universe and now he was gone. I sighed heavily, knowing I was in deep trouble. *Shelley Gallagher, for the second time in your life, you're in love with the wrong man.*

CHAPTER THREE

I pulled my snarling, snapping dog back from the door. Ferociousness was uncharacteristic of her with this one exception; Shannon hated mail carriers.

Four envelopes slipped through the slot in the door and plopped at my feet. When she stopped straining against her collar, I released my grip. Indignant, she huffed off to her wicker bed in the corner.

We were alone today; Greg had gone to work. Work! He had been exultant last week about the job. The Municipality of Surrey hired him to start mid-October in the Works Yard, maintaining equipment. We toasted his coup with a glass of wine—a rare extravagance.

I flipped through the mail. BC Hydro's blue and green logo meant a bill. Ugh. The grey envelope was from Unemployment Insurance. The return address on the third bore my brother's address. The last one made my heart sink. I'd applied for a directorship of a new shelter for battered women. The interview had gone well, but successful candidates were not notified by mail. I found little comfort in reading that I'd come a close second. I'd really wanted that one.

Maybe my baby brother would pick me up. I opened his letter.

> *Dear Sis,*
>
> *How ya doin? Good I hope. Any luck finding work yet? Me, I just started a new job driving truck.*

It's your fourth this year, Jamie. You can get 'em but you can't seem to hang on to 'em. He went on about the job, the weather and other trivia. Get to the point, Jamie. You only write to me when you've got really good news or really bad news.

> "I've got some bad news, Shel. Carol and I broke up. I don't know what's wrong with me in the relationship department. Sometimes I wish you didn't live so far away. I know if you were here, you'd straighten me out. You always did. You know just how to help me.

"I did something stupid after Carol dumped me. I went out and got blasted. I was too drunk to drive and fell asleep in my car. The cops woke me. They busted me for having open beer in the car. Spent the night in the can. I could have called Mom and Dad to bail me out, but no way! I'll take the slammer over our dear mother's wrath. Please don't tell her. And please don't be mad, I feel awful enough."

More trivia followed, ending with an affectionate closing. I felt guilty. Maybe I could have steered him away from trouble if I'd been there. I sighed heavily. At least I had my UI cheque to cheer me up. I opened the envelope and withdrew it. The customary reporting cards were missing. In their place a slip of paper announced, 'Notice of change in status'. I skimmed it; my heart skipped a beat. "...voluntarily terminated employment...disqualified from receiving further benefits..." I reeled. Disqualified? *I'm cut off?! Oh God.*

Rent, food, hydro, bank loan; without work, in three months they would devour my paltry reserves. I wouldn't qualify for welfare, even if I could've brought myself to apply, because of owning property. I'd be required to sell it. I'd work at anything, waiting tables even, if it would save Shangri-La. But waiting on tables wasn't going to cut it.

"Come on, Shannon. Let's get some air." I pulled my bicycle from the porch and rode sluggishly with Shannon loping alongside. At the country store, I bought some milk and the morning's issue of the Globe and Mail.

I lifted the receiver as if it weighed thirty pounds and punched out eleven digits. Retired, my father generally hung around home but only answered the phone if mother was out. Since she's a major gadabout, it was a fifty-fifty chance he would answer. I hoped it would be him. On hearing the cheery geriatric male voice say, "Hell-o," I felt a wave of relief.

"Hi Dad. It's Shelley."

"Oh hi, dear. How are you?"

"Well, I'll get to that. Are you home alone, Dad?"

"Yes. Your mother's gone to a church bazaar. I was just getting myself some dinner."

"I won't keep you long. I have a huge favour to ask." I sucked in my breath, then spoke in a torrent. "I haven't been able to find work and things are looking pretty bad. I'm thinking of returning to Ontario. I figure with the larger population, I'll be able to find something." I swallowed. "Can I stay with you and Mom till I get on my feet?" Before he could answer, I rushed to add, "My UI is being cut off and I have almost no money left."

"Don't you worry about that, Dear. You just come on home."
I could have kissed him through the miles of cable. "Thanks Dad. I love you. I'll have to give a month's notice to my landlord."
"That's wonderful, dear. You'll be home for Christmas."
"Yeah, Dad, I'll be home for Christmas."
When I hung up, a mantle of gloom settled over me.

———————————

Greg sat on the edge of the couch leaning on his knees and staring at his bare feet. On the floor, I sat cross-legged, stroking Shannon whose head rested on my thigh.
"So you've made up your mind," he sighed.
"I don't see what choice I have. If I don't find work, I'll lose my land. The economy will pick up here eventually. I'll come back. I feel awful about putting you in this position though."
"Don't worry about me. It'll be good for me to move into town closer to work. From here I wouldn't have been able to cycle to work when it snows and I wouldn't want to rely on that wheezy old bus that does a milk run out here three times a day." He peeked up at me, a smirk lurking about the corners of his mouth. "You sure this has nothing to do with what's-his-name?"
I groaned and curled up beside Shannon, draping an arm over her. She stretched and spread her toes in response. "That's the worst of it," I confessed. "So soon after Ben's visit, I can just imagine what he'll think. I made such a case for being utterly mad about BC that he's apt to believe I'm pursuing him. He knows I'm penniless. God! What if he thinks I'm gold-digging! I'd be mortified."
Greg cracked up. "If he thinks that, then he doesn't know the first thing about you."
I smiled sheepishly. "I s'pose you're right. Anyway, I won't tell him till I'm there. It'll be easier to explain face-to-face."
The jangle of the phone gave me a jolt. Greg picked it up. The polite exchange told me it was not for him. He held his hand over the receiver and said in an exaggerated whisper, "Hey, Gold-digger, it's for you." I felt my face flush. As I reached for the receiver, he added, grinning, "Let's see how you handle this one."
My heart flip-flopped to hear that deep, melodious voice. I hated talking on a phone. But Ben was in his element, like a stand-up comic with his outrageous monologue. Greg yawned at my laughter and monosyllabic responses and retreated to his room.
"There *is* a purpose to my calling besides wanting to hear your voice," Ben said, seeming unconscious of the irony of his comment. "Your birthday's in November, isn't it?

"Yes."

"I want to give you a present. Actually, it's more of a present for me. I want you to come to Toronto for a weekend. I'll send you the air fare."

I opened my mouth but nothing came out.

"Are you still there, Shelley?"

"Yes, I...I'm here. I don't know what to say. It's such a generous offer."

"Say yes. I want to see you."

"I'd like to see you too, Ben. But, um..." I had to tell him something. After all, I'd be there in a few weeks. The truth, as always, proved the simplest approach. He sympathized. He knew how hard it must have been for me to decide to leave my beloved mountains, he said. Then he made a date with me for December.

Tomorrow I turn thirty-three. The plane ticket on my dresser was dated December 2, two weeks hence. It was the first available flight I could get to Toronto in December with a heated cargo bay, necessary for Shannon. I'd scheduled the movers to come for my furniture at the end of the month. It would have to stay in storage for now. How long would I be away? An aching grief swelled inside.

"Come and get it," Greg sang out from the kitchen.

I helped myself to salad, savouring the lasagna with my nose. "I hope your cousin appreciates what a swell live-in chef he's getting." I observed.

Greg tore off a hunk of garlic bread and stuffed it in his mouth. "Maybe that's why he gave me the room so cheap. You were going to tell me about the ad in the Globe and Mail."

"Yeah. It's a supervisor's position in a counselling agency for abused women. Closing date's tomorrow so I phoned. Talked to the Director. She sounded interested in me. Wanted a number where she could reach me in Ontario."

"Sounds promising."

"Well, there's a hitch. The pay is awful."

He looked balefully at me. "When were you ever motivated by money?"

"Okay, I know. But I have to live. Besides, I have a dependent to support, don't I, Shannon." The Setter cocked her ears but continued wolfing down kibble from her bowl.

Greg helped himself to a plateful of lasagna. "So how far is it from this place to where what's-his-name lives?"

I jabbed my finger at him. "Don't start on me, mister. Just don't start!"

The sun dipped westward behind the tail of the aircraft while every sinew in my body strained to resist the eastward flight. It droned on heedlessly, bearing me over southern Ontario's worn winter quilt of dingy brown and dirty white. Lake Ontario crept into view, the point of its almond shape familiar. A trail of lights in the dusk marked the Skyway Bridge crossing from Hamilton to Burlington. I craned for a better look, wondering where in the sprawl Ben lived. Minutes later, a whine and thump of lowered wheels announced my imminent arrival at Pearson International.

Deplaning passengers bolted past me. The crowd compressed through double doors, spilling into the arrivals compound. I wavered, fazed by the wall of waiting faces. Then, without wanting to, I spotted my mother's set jaw and slightly behind her, my father's waving arm. It wasn't till I heard my name that I saw the figure dashing toward me. My shouted greeting came out explosively with the breath I'd been holding and I laughed with relief. Jamie's irrepressible grin shone like a beacon. He caught me in an exuberant squeeze.

"C'mon, c'mon," he said hauling on my arm and cutting short my parents' greeting. "Let's getcher bags. Where's Shannon?" He dragged me bodily back into the arrivals corral, ignoring the 'Passengers Only' sign. We horsed around at the luggage carousel shouldering each other aside like wrestling puppies. "You got a job interview tomorrow," he announced. I gaped at him. "In St. Catharines. Dad said he'd lend you his car to get there." I pointed out my backpack, sliding down the ramp, followed by my battered suitcase. He hoisted them off and parked them by a pillar.

"Watch them for me while I fetch Shannon," I said. "I gave her a tranquilizer in Vancouver. She might still be sedated." At special cargo a baggage handler dragged a kennel through the doors. I knelt and peered inside. A sloppy, doggie grin greeted me. I released the latch and snapped a leash on her collar. She staggered out like a happy drunk careening from the door of a favourite pub. Tail wagging in lop-sided circles and tongue lolling, she lurched along erratically with her claws slipping on the terrazzo floor and her shoulder bumping against my leg. Above the din in the terminal, I heard a loud guffaw. Jamie, clutching his stomach and leaning against the pillar was slipping by degrees to the floor. Shannon shambled up to him with unabashed familiarity, her ears spilling abundantly into his lap. She grinned as he scratched them. "Sedated my ass," he wheezed. "She's stoned out of her gourd!"

———————————

I stepped down from the train into the steamy underworld of Toronto's Union Station. I was to meet Ben by the fountain at Yorkdale Mall. It had seemed a reasonable request since Yorkdale marked the halfway point between my folk's home and his place, but I'd landed in Ontario with a hundred dollars left in the world and it was reckless to spend twenty of them just to see him.

I found the subway and dashed aboard. Every seat was taken so I clutched a grimy pole. I'd got the job in St. Catharines but my initial delirium had enjoyed a brief life. What would rents be like? Could I find a place that would allow dogs? I'd need to be on a bus route since I couldn't afford a car. How would I manage without my furniture?

At Yorkdale station, a solid mass of humanity exited onto the platform, carrying me with it. The mob poured down a flight of stairs and into the mall, like effluent from a drainage pipe. I drifted away from the crowd, a piece of flotsam. I longed for Ben's arms to steady me. I looked for and found the fountain. But he was not there. I was early.

The noise and crowds overwhelmed me. I drifted away from the fountain, wandering in and out of shops in a fugue state. Anxiety welled up inside me. From the dark interior of my mind a voice lashed at me. *Fool! Why are you thinking about this man this way? He doesn't love you back. He probably won't even show.*

Something brushed my shoulder and I whirled round to see only racks of clothing clawing at me. I bumped into a mannequin. It lurched back at me with a sinister leer. I bolted out into the concourse and broke into a run, dodging shoppers, panic rising in my throat. He *had* to be there. I saw the fountain and cast about wildly. Maddening, indecipherable din assailed my ears – scuffling feet, babbling voices, crying children, jangling bells.

Then a fur chupka floated above the throng crowning a Russian Jewish profile. Dressed in a greatcoat open over a three-piece suit, he scanned the myriad faces. Then he saw me. His face creased in a wide smile. I rushed to him and he caught me in a bear hug. "I missed you," he said, with feeling.

I clung, a catch in my throat preventing speech. He pulled me in closer still, kissing me full on my mouth and the fountain's patter washed away my dread.

Steaming dishes of Chinese food crowded the small table in the Chinatown restaurant. "If the salary's so poor," Ben asked, "why didn't you hold out for a better job?"

"I don't have that luxury. I have *no* money until my first paycheque. As it is, I'll have to borrow from my parents to get set up. Besides," I waved my fork, "the position intrigues me. It's exactly the kind of experience I'm looking for. Someday I want to design and develop my own treatment program."

"I see. You'll need a car to get around," he said practically.

I scowled. "I can't afford it just now. I have to find a place to live where I can walk to work or ride a bus."

"What kind of vehicle do you like to drive?"

I looked at him quizzically. "A truck. Why?"

"Shelley," he leaned forward, "come live with me."

My wide-eyed stare must have unsettled him for he added in a rush, "I've lots of room. I live on acreage. I know how you like to live in the country. I...I'd like to have you, help you...out," he finished lamely.

My mind spun. *Wait. Slow down. One Cinderella weekend.* "I...I don't know what to say."

"Say you'll come."

"I haven't even met your children," I said, scrambling for excuses. "What about them?"

"They'll like you. What's not to like? Look, you can't even afford to rent a place. How will you manage?"

"I don't know but, even if I were to accept your offer, I'd need a car to commute from Burlington and truly, Ben, I can't afford it."

"Don't worry about it."

"Don't worry about it!" I echoed. "What do you mean don't worry about it?"

"I'll take care of it." I gaped at him trying to absorb his meaning. "I'll see that you have something to get to work in."

I searched his face for clues to his intentions while emotions boiled inside me. Common sense told me to run as fast as I could in the opposite direction. "There's a problem," I said, stalling.

"What?"

"Shannon."

His shoulders slumped. "Yes, that is a problem. I know you love her, but...I love my daughter. With Sara's allergies, I just can't have a dog in the house. We could build her a doghouse? She'd have lots of room to run outside."

I shook my head. "It's December. Maybe in the warm season she could make that transition, but not now. Coming from the West Coast climate, she doesn't even have a winter coat."

This talk was making me uneasy. It was as if I were really considering his preposterous invitation. And Shannon after all, was my anchor; all that was familiar now. I was grateful for the distraction of the little, balding Chinese waiter who came to clear away the plates. Ben ordered tea for both of us. I excused myself and left the table. By the time I returned, the tea Ben had poured me was cold and a lone fortune cookie remained on a plate that had not been there when I'd left. Ben was solicitous.

"You okay?"

"Sure, fine."

"Have I upset you?"

"You haven't upset me." I cracked the cookie and read my fortune. *Happiness follows a crooked path.* Great, I thought. That could mean anything. "I'm sorry I was away so long. I went to the phone to call my parents. They agreed to keep Shannon for the winter."

He lit up. "Then its 'Yes'!"

I grinned. "I probably need my head examined, but yes. It's 'Yes'."

He leapt from his seat like a schoolboy, kissing my cheek and causing me to giggle. Several patrons turned to gape. Then he sat back down brushing his vest with his hands as if to smooth himself into composure once again. He finished by flashing me a foolish grin that made me laugh out loud.

Mother left earlier for one of her meetings. "I'm going now Dad," I hollered. If I could just get through the goodbye formalities. Dad clawed up out of his chair and shuffled into the front hall where I stood by my bags. He was so much more frail than he'd been last time I'd been home; the salt-and-pepper in his hair had by now turned snowy white.

Shannon sat at rigid attention, watching me with questing eyes. Guilt twisted my gut. She *knew.* "Call when you get settled, dear," Dad said amiably, oblivious to both my anguish and Shannon's. I knelt and took the great red head between my palms. Her ears covered my knuckles.

"How do I tell you it's not forever, Puppy?" Tears clouded my vision. I wrapped my arms around her shoulders. She trembled. Swallowing a lump, I stood and hefted my backpack into place and grabbed the suitcase. Not trusting my voice, I gave Dad a quick hug and hurried out the door.

At the bus station, I boarded a Greyhound. Three hours later, I stepped off in downtown St. Catharines. I asked the ticket master where I could find economy lodgings within walking distance. He directed me to a cheap four-story walk-up. Exploring, I found that it was two blocks from my new job. Back in the room, I sat on the bed and leaned my elbows on the windowsill, looking out into the dark. Searching through the space between buildings my eyes strained to discern the friendly shapes of mountains. But there was only the unending night sky.

Two days later, after orienting myself to my new responsibilities, getting acquainted with my staff and seeing a few clients, I climbed back on the Greyhound. When it wheeled into the Burlington terminal, I spotted Ben leaning against a light standard, waiting, just as he'd promised.

He whisked me off to a car dealership. What colour did I like? he asked, sweeping his arm along the row of shiny new trucks on the lot. Red of course, I told him—for a redhead. He wrote a cheque for the full amount. Just like that.

He dropped the key ceremoniously into my palm. "Follow me," he said and took off in his car. The lights of Burlington fell behind and in a few minutes, he turned onto a gravel lane. Way down the darkened drive, a house huddled in a farmer's field. A floodlight exposed it, all angles and boxes. I tailed his car around the end of it. Two garage doors yawned and Ben signalled me to park beside him.

Inside he toured me from room to room. A barren and lifeless interior confronted me; a bed in the master bedroom and in each child's room, a desk in the den, four chairs around a table too large for the dining room, and in the living room, an ancient yellow sofa. No lamps, drapery, carpeting or pictures. Not a television or radio. No colour or wallpaper softened the stark walls. Our voices and footsteps echoed on hardwood throughout the house. I hugged myself for warmth.

In the morning's bleak wintry light, the outside appeared even more desolate. The house squatted in a flat field devoid of shelter from trees or softening of shrubs. Behind it, a crater filled with water, wounded the earth. Clay from the excavated pond mounded around its perimeter. It was a water source in case of fire, Ben informed me. A woodlot backed the property but could not be seen from any window.

"When my wife and I split up," he told me, "we put our house up for sale. She got the proceeds and contents and moved to another house. I kept this property I'd meant to flip. When my father died last year, the inheritance allowed me to build." I gathered from this explanation that Ben hadn't had enough money to properly furnish the place. Yet he'd paid in full for a new truck. *Is he a wealthy, eccentric tightwad,* I wondered, *or a pauper with champagne taste?* I didn't ask. People could be funny about revealing their financial situation as I knew too well from my parents.

I held the speed down; the new truck needed breaking in. I'd survived the fourth day on the job and tonight faced another first, meeting the children. Ben picked them up every Thursday after work. On Friday morning, he took them to their school bus pick-up point. He had them alternate weekends as well.

Children! The prospect of having them in my life enchanted me. Sara, I knew, was nine. Ari had turned seven two months earlier. Their mother had all the family albums so I had no vision yet of what they looked like. Preoccupied with thoughts of them, I almost missed my exit from the highway and had to cut sharply across a lane to make it. Someone leaned on their horn. I drove up the country road and a few minutes later turned into the lane. In the kitchen, Ben took a moment from cooking to hug me.

"Sara, Ari," he hollered. "Come here."

A lithe boy with baby-fat cheeks traipsed into the kitchen. Intelligent brown eyes looked out from under a shock of brown hair. He wore a white turtleneck, grey corduroy pants, black oxfords and green cardigan with two white stripes encircling an upper arm

"Ari, this is Shelley."

He flashed a disarming smile. "Hello."

A wan pixie, almost the same height as Ari, slipped around the corner behind him. I smiled. "I guess you're Sara."

The girl eyed me with cool reserve, not speaking. She didn't look old enough to be nine. Her limbs resembled matchsticks and her complexion was pallid. Fine blond bangs clung to her rounded forehead; the rest fell chin-length around a white hair band. Her hunter green tunic, white blouse and knee socks were in tune with Ari's attire.

"School uniforms, huh," I remarked. "Where do you go to school, Ari?"

Sara tugged the back of his sweater, distracting him long enough for her to answer in his place. "Hillfield-Strathallan College. It's a *private* school." Her tone and the upward tilt of her chin seemed intended to put me in my place.

"Ari, how about playing something on your violin for Shelley," Ben suggested.

"Come on." He waved me to follow and headed down the hall. Sara shot a look at her father, her eyes smouldering behind narrowed lids. Then she scurried after her brother, clutching his sleeve and whispering in his ear.

While Ari removed a miniature violin from its battered case, Sara sulked on the far edge of his bed. Seated on the floor, I studied them while the boy scratched out a melody. Was my arrival a surprise? Had they met other women their father had dated? I couldn't very well ask them.

When he finished, I tried safer topics—school, music, hobbies. Once warmed up, the boy was quite talkative. "Do you know how to ski?" he asked.

"No, I never learned."

"*We* do," Sara boasted. "*We* ski at *Snowbird*."

"What's Snowbird?"

"It's our *resort*, in the *mountains*." Her cadence worked its way under my skin. "We're *going* there with Mommy and Daddy in *March*."

Sticking his head in the doorway, Ben heard this last and must have caught my bewildered look. "Uh, I was going to tell you about that. I'll explain later. Dinner's ready," he said. "You kids wash up. Let's eat."

Quietly, Ben closed the door to the hallway. He had tried to draw me into the bedtime ritual of quiet conversation and tucking in, but I figured it was too soon for that. Afterward he joined me on the sofa and we caught up on each other's day. Then he asked me what I thought of the children. "They're sweet," I said, deciding to keep my observations about Sara to myself for the time being.

"I meant to give you time to settle in before explaining about Snowbird. I didn't count on the kids bringing that up. You see, Margaret and I own a time-share at a ski lodge in Utah. It's the one thing neither of us could bear to part with when we split. We agreed to each use it alternate years. Last year was my turn. Since we hadn't been apart long, I thought it would be nice for the kids to have both their parents on vacation. So I invited Margaret to come along and she did. This year, she invited me."

I felt something flutter in my chest. "You and she sound very...cordial."

"It's not... We aren't..." he sputtered. "The condo has two floors. We each have our own space."

Something acrid seeped down the lining of my stomach. My face must have betrayed my dismay. "I can't really back out now," he insisted. "These arrangements were made months ago. The airline and lift tickets have already been paid for." I nodded but remained silent. What was there to say?

I stretched out full length on the rug in front of the fireplace and stared into the flames. Shannon pressed against me as if hugging my warmth despite the heat of the fire. The tang of Scotch pine prickled my nostrils. Dad grappled his way out of his recliner to throw another log on the fire. The chair bore a permanent imprint of his body.

I resisted the nagging voice in my head, with its litany, *Go help your mother.* Instead, I hugged Shannon. She'd been like Velcro since I arrived last night, Christmas Eve. I ran my splayed fingers through the sleek red coat, liking the way her hair tickled the webbing between my fingers. Perhaps the three week's separation made me more aware, but Shannon seemed to have more white in her face.

I heard the front door open and the doorbell ring redundantly. Through French doors, I saw two young children in snowsuits spill into the front hall. Behind them a large woman bearing a casserole dish bustled in, followed by a man with parcels to his eyebrows, Gayle and

Tom Preston, my sister and brother-in-law. My young niece and nephew were virtual strangers, having been born after I'd moved out west.

I jumped up to greet them. Mother came from the kitchen, wiping her hands on her apron. We converged in the hall, everyone talking at once. Mother took the casserole and trundled off to the kitchen. Gayle embraced me. "So the traveler finally decided to come home. Did you bring this man we've heard about, for us to meet?"

"No." I brushed Gayle's cheek with my lips. "I didn't think it would be fair to him."

"Fair! What's unfair?"

"Come on Gayle. If you've heard about him, then you know he's Jewish. Meeting all the family at once on Christmas Day might be a tad uncomfortable for him."

"Well he's got to accept who *you* are." I hadn't seen Gayle in three years and it had taken less than a minute for me to feel defensive. I turned to the children.

"Hi Robbie, Jennie. Remember me? I'm your Auntie Shelley." Kneeling down eye to eye with my nephew, I whispered, "Want some help with your snowsuit?" He nodded, sticking out his chest to offer me the zipper.

"I'm going to kindy-garden now," his older sister stepped forward.

"Cool!"

Gayle bustled over to our father bending to kiss him. "Merry Christmas, Dad." She spoke loudly to him as if he were hard of hearing, which he wasn't. "Tom, put the parcels under the tree." As she waddled off to the kitchen, I watched her retreating back. Gayle was everything I wasn't, domestic, conventional and...well...a bit bossy, at least with her husband.

Robbie and Jennie raced off to play with new toys they'd brought from home. I remained in the hall, contemplating the Christmas glitz. Mom always went overboard. The place was decorated to the ceiling with tacky garlands and cutesy angels and Santas. Like make-up trying to hide an ugly face, I thought. Scolding and strident parental quarrelling still echoed in my head.

Behind me the front door burst open without the accompanying bell this time. Jamie's elfin grin greeted me. "Hello Baby Brother," I beamed and grabbed him in a fierce hug.

Steaming platters, bowls, jellies, pickles, place settings, napkins, candles and Christmas crackers covered every square inch of tabletop. Florence Gallagher presided at the end nearest the kitchen. She nodded to Dad, opposite her. "Calvin, would you say the blessing."

I bowed my head with the others but rebelliously kept open my eyes. To my right, I saw Jamie put his palms together. With his blond hair and boyish face he resembled a Sunday school painting. He rolled his eyes toward me, ensuring that I was looking. Then he arched his brows and puckered his mouth in exaggerated piety. I elbowed him. He loosed a stifled snicker, almost causing me to laugh aloud.

With our father's "Amen", the others opened their eyes and reached for the food. For the next few minutes, a general hubbub ensued while bowl after bowl was diminished and passed on. Then silence reigned.

Silence at the Gallagher table held old terrors for me. The vacuum allowed for ugly possibilities from Mother's end of the table. I cast about wildly for something... anything... to say to send conversation in innocuous directions, but as usual I came up blank. Gayle admonished Robbie for his manners, then asked Mother about a neighbour's health. I cringed, cursing Gayle.

"Tom, how's your job?" I blurted, sounding shrill. Still, I heard Mother's serrated voice above my own.

"...had to cut eighteen inches out of the poor soul's bowel." I felt my own gut clench. I didn't hear Tom's reply. "...said for three whole days she was spitting up this thick yellow stuff."

Dad turned a bland, oblivious face to me. "Sure nice to have you home, Honey." I smiled weakly.

Jamie addressed his plate in a low voice. " 'Oh there's no place like home for the holidays'."

"What a god-awful charade," I muttered.

"What was that, Shelley?" Mother's voice arrested me. I felt caught in her crosshairs.

"She said we should play charades later," Jamie said, reaching across her for a slice of bread. Then he sniggered, setting me off. We infected the children and Jamie threw fuel on the fire pulling monster faces. Robbie and Jenny shrieked with laughter. With a wounded look, Mother hitched her shoulder and turned back to Gayle, moving on to the pregnancy of an unwed cousin.

By the time the hysteria passed, Gayle was recounting the itinerary for an upcoming get-away with Tom. "We land in Miami but we've been advised not to stay in the area. I'm told the people are snooty and obnoxious to tourists."

"Oh, yes!" Mom snorted, her mouth twisting in distaste. "It's full of Jews, you know."

My fork clattered onto my plate. I stared at her open-mouthed. She looked blankly at me, then gasped holding her fingertips to her mouth. But she offered no apology. I said nothing. It was no use. She would only act wounded and indignant. *Thank God I didn't bring Ben!*

———————

Six days past winter solstice, the sun fell pale on the walls of my second floor office. In an armchair opposite me, an attractive well-dressed woman wept in a controlled sort of way. I nudged a box of tissues across the coffee table. She took one and dabbed her eyes. Her speech revealed intelligence and breeding, yet she'd told me a sordid tale of perverse sexual oppression.

"What do you want for yourself now?" I asked.

She fingered the tissue. "I don't know. Peace. To get away from him. But it's not easy. He has money, connections, family. The children adore him. No one would believe he's doing these things."

She described how her husband's power and financial resources blocked her escape and as she did so, last night's interchange with Ben intruded on my thoughts. I pushed them away long enough to finish the session and move on to the next. In this one, a thirty-year old woman told me how she'd given up a successful career to stay home with her three children. After her second child, she succumbed to her husband's pressure to move from her hometown. In time he wore her down, relentlessly criticizing her money management. She let him take control. "That was the second biggest mistake of my life," she said. He reduced her to begging for change to buy diapers, cough medicine and sanitary napkins. She knew she would leave him. "It's just going to take time—and money."

Again my concentration broke. Last night I'd taken home my first paycheque and asked Ben how much he wanted for my expenses. "Why don't you sign your cheques over to me?" he'd said. "I'll manage your money for you. You can just ask for whatever you need."

I know I'm lousy with money, I'd thought, *but I'll be damned if I'm going to ask for an allowance.* I stood my ground and negotiated a more comfortable arrangement. Listening to these women, I reminded myself that I knew very little about Ben. These were intelligent, capable women. How easily their men had entrapped them.

I unwound the curling iron from the last strand of hair and let the ringlet fall warm against my neck. Tinny music drifted up from the bedroom. Ben had found a station on the clock radio broadcasting big band tunes. It was New Year's Eve.

I frowned at the reflection in the mirror. A stranger looked back. The heavy make-up, another lingerie outfit, this one more risqué yet, belonged to a seductress I didn't know. Was I merely stuck in the identity of a girl from a house where sex was not supposed to exist? Miss Goody Two Shoes.

I snapped out the light and wobbled toward the music in a new pair of spiked heels. They clacked on the parquet hall floor, echoing in the barren house. The bed in the master bedroom looked lost, like an island in the ocean. Pellets of snow pinged the window. Ben lay back on the pillows in black satin pyjama bottoms, arms behind his head. Seeing the exposed tufts of hair under his arms, I felt a rush of modesty, as if that were more frankly intimate than had he been utterly naked. He took stock of me admiringly. "Baby, you look like a sailor's dream." He got up and reached for me.

I felt wooden. "I can't do this."

"Sure you can, Honey. You look luscious. Here, wait," he backed away, turned up the radio and lay back on the pillow again. "Dance for me. I want to watch you."

I tried to feel the music, tried to oblige him but my blood thickened in my veins. I stopped, paralyzed. I felt humiliated, like a reluctant stripper. *What's the matter with me? This is my partner. There's nothing wrong with what he's asking. He likes how I look.* But pressure built in my chest, pain from some unremembered lesion.

Ben's mouth parted and he ran his tongue across his lips. Unbidden, a picture sprang to my mind of the woman in my office who wept for her own accommodation to an abuser's obscene demands. The pressure screamed inside my head like a steam kettle, then burst in hot tears. I hid my face in my hands and crumpled on the foot of the bed.

He was beside me in a flash. "Baby, don't cry. I didn't mean to hurt you. You don't have to. Forget about it. Please don't cry." I barely understood my own reaction but his arms around me felt reassuring. "Talk to me, Shelley, What's wrong?"

"I just can't do this; it's not me. My whole life has changed, where I live, where I work, who I see. I have none of my belongings around me. I miss my home. I miss Shannon. I miss...I miss my mountains!" I wailed. "I'm living with a man from a different religion, and there's the sex. I've lost all sense of my *self*."

He gathered me onto his lap and rocked me. "I'm sorry," he murmured. "I'm not such a boor as to want you to bend to my will. I care about you; I really do. I guess I'm just too thick to have seen things from your point of view." I looked down into his face. I wanted to trust him. He seemed tender and understanding now. I brushed the tears from my cheeks and moved to sit beside him, feeling foolish.

"There's one thing we could do that might help a bit," he said.

"What's that?"

"Let's send for your belongings in storage in BC. I can arrange it tomorrow."

"I don't have the money," I said testily.

"You're with me, remember. I want you to be happy. Okay?" He tipped my chin up to make me look at him. "Okay?" he repeated.

I smiled faintly. "Okay."

We lay in bed, my head on his shoulder. "Ben, there's something I need to talk about."

"Hm hmn."

"It's what happened all those years ago. The pictures."

He groaned. "I thought we'd settled that."

"It's not settled for me. I wrote you how angry and humiliated I was and you apologized. But I don't understand why you did it. I need to know. I need you to explain yourself."

"Because I enjoyed looking at them."

"It's not just the pictures. I'd told you, no sex."

"I was a seasoned lecher, Shelley. I've learned a great deal from you about what it is to be a woman in a man's world. Back then I didn't have a clue. I got my education about women from Playboy and guys in the locker room. Men conned and women pretended to resist. I thought that was the way the game was played. It was stupid. *I* was stupid."

"Worse than stupid, Ben. You shattered me. You acted as if you had my consent. But consent is meaningless when one is tricked and coaxed into submission. You kept making greater and greater demands, always promising there would be no more. Before I knew it, I'd lost all control over what happened." He didn't respond.

"You made me distrust myself around men," I persisted. "You dominated me so completely. You robbed me of my voice. And now again, with everything so foreign, I can't *hear* my own voice. That's why I cried just now. All I can hear is *your* voice, what *you* want."

He was silent a long time. "You've got a big job in store to re-program me," he said at last. He rolled up on his elbow, his eyes sparkling "I *do* like the way you look you know."

I countered this change of tack. "What did you do with those pictures?"

"I destroyed them when you wrote me last year about how upset you were by that episode."

"You kept them all that time!? Even throughout your marriage?"

He arched an eyebrow. "If I told you I hadn't looked at them in years, would it be a compliment or an insult?"

That caught me off guard and I laughed, unable to stay angry. I pinched him and he grabbed my wrists, pinning them over my head. I struggled but he straddled me and bent to kiss me. I turned my head aside laughing, resisting, but his tongue wet my ear and I moaned. I pulled my arms, seeking release from his grip but he laughed a hard laugh and tightened it. Instead of resenting my captivity, I was the more aroused. He stretched out along my length, a swelling between us telling me he was ready. I parted my knees, inviting him in but he just poised...stalling.

"Come on!" I cried, frustrated now.

"Pardon," he smirked. "I can't hear you."

"Damn you!"

"That's not very pretty talk. What is it you want?"

I squirmed. Again he pressed against me and again he withdrew.

"Fuck you!" I hissed.

"No, my dear," he retorted, grinning. "Fuck *you*," and he did.

Later, I lay with my arm across his stomach, drowsiness pulling me down into velvet depths. Our body heat had cooled and his breathing had slowed. I felt him gently lift my arm and push me away an inch or two.

"What's the matter?" I teased. "Can't you fall asleep in my arms?"

"No. No one touches me while I'm sleeping."

"No one?"

"No."

"Not even your children?"

"*No* one."

I finished clearing away the supper things. Ben's voice, sounding playful, drifted up from the den where he'd gone to take a call. He said goodbye and a minute later he was stretched out on the sofa. I sat on the edge by him and we exchanged anecdotes from our workday. I relished this daily exchange, the ordinary domesticity of it. I asked him about his caller and he told me it was a woman he'd known for a decade. He had a propensity for keeping friends a long time, I was beginning to learn, and I admired this about him. "I can tell when you're talking to a female though," I said. He gave me an enigmatic smile, so I added. "You always sound like you're hustling them."

"Who says I'm not?"

That caught me like a dash of cold water. "What are we talking about here, Ben?" For several long seconds, we stared each other down.

"What had you imagined?" he challenged. My throat felt thick and I couldn't respond. "Is it a problem if I take out other women?"

"Don't answer my question with more questions," I shot back.

"Come on, you're the woman that's living with me."

"Don't make that sound like a privilege!"

"I'm not saying it's a privilege. I like you."

"Like!" I spat out the word "You 'like' me? What does 'like' mean?"

"I enjoy you."

"Oh. So I'm a toy."

"Aw, Shelley, don't get your garters in a tangle. It doesn't mean anything if I have sex with another woman."

"To whom, Ben? It may not mean anything to you, but it sure as *hell* means something to me!" I was blazing now. He opened his mouth to speak but I raised my palm to check him. I sat stiff, eyes closed, my insides on fire. He waited.

"Forgive me if I don't grasp the male mind," I snapped. He reached up to put his arms around me but instead, touched off an explosion. I balled my fists and pummelled his chest. "How can you be so callous? You insufferable brute!"

"Ow! Hey, don't hit. Shelley, stop hitting me."

I froze, my fists in mid-air. How ironic; the counsellor for abused women beating on her lover. I fought for self-control, took huge gulps of air and willed myself calm. "I'm sorry. It's wrong of me to hit you." He started to say something but my hand went up again like a stop sign. "I don't want to talk anymore right now."

The technique was working perfectly. I leaned back in my chair watching my co-leader, Daphne Piccolo, bring home the point. A hoola-hoop occupied the centre of the floor. Each woman in the group had taken a turn claiming the space within it. The others, coached by me, had attempted to "invade" while the claimant "defended" her boundary. Each woman so far, had practiced verbally and physically evicting intruders. But the women were stymied by one claimant's lack of resistance.

"I don't mind," she said sweetly. "I like all of you."

"I'm coming over for coffee," an intruder announced, stepping into the circle.

"Okay."

"Can I borrow a cup of sugar, Phyllis?" another petitioned.

"Sure."

"Can I borrow your pearl necklace? I'm going to the theatre with my friends. It would look stunning with my new dress."

"Okay," Phyllis smiled weakly.

Winking at me, Daphne bounded from her chair. "Come on everybody, party at Phyllis's." With a grin and twinkling eyes, she stepped boldly into the circle, tipping Phyllis off balance. "Come on in, people. Phyllis doesn't mind." Amid much laughter, more women crowded into the tiny space. Phyllis's eyes grew round and the smile slipped from her face. The "partiers" became more raucous and demanding, led by the intrepid group counsellor. A small smothered voice whimpered, "I don't think I like this after all."

"Okay, Phyllis," Daphne grinned. "Do something about it." Phyllis cleared the floor.

The women were still laughing and whooping their congratulations to Phyllis as they filed out of the room. Daphne collapsed in a chair giggling. "Your idea worked like a charm, Shelley."

"Thanks to you."

"Did you see Phyllis's face when she got everybody out?"

"Yeah, she looked like a goalie for the Chicago Black Hawks."

"Her ex better beware. I think he's in for a big surprise next time he tries to order her around."

"Yeah," I chuckled. "I've kept you overtime, Daphne. Your kids'll be clamouring for dinner."

"Actually, I'm a free woman tonight. There's no school tomorrow and my parents took the kids. How 'bout you? In a hurry, or do you have time for a beer?"

Perfect timing, I thought. "I'd love it."

"Jake's?"

"Great. I'll meet you there."

I liked Daphne the instant I met her. Seeming to regard life as a constant source of amusement, she possessed a lively energy, tempered by empathy. I supervised her and admired her intuition as a counsellor. I knew from her personnel file that after getting her sociology degree, she had worked in Italy for a company that did research.

From casual conversation, I'd learned that she had married a native from that country and brought him home. A few times, I'd overheard her speaking to him on the telephone in Italian. Occasionally she'd sounded fired up, almost as if they were quarrelling, but I wrote it off to the excitable Italian style of speaking because afterward she always seemed happy and upbeat.

As my eyes adjusted to the dim light inside Jake's, I caught sight of her waving from a booth against the wall. "This is a treat," I sighed after the waitress plunked down two mugs of beer. "Since I got off the plane last month, I haven't had a chance to catch my breath. The only place that I'm getting to know is the highway between St. Catharines and Burlington."

"The tale of two cities," she grinned. "T-a-i-l, that is." I chuckled. It felt good to laugh.

"I'm glad you're here," she said. "I'm learning volumes from you."

"Really? Like what?"

"You're so knowledgeable about abuse."

I grimaced "Great. What our clients really need is to know what's normal."

"So what's that?" she grinned.

"I was hoping you'd know."

She sputtered, choking on a mouthful of beer. "You think *I* have a handle on functional relationships? Don't follow *my* lead."

"Really? I thought you had it all together. What's your excuse?"

"My parents are religious fruit cakes," she offered. "Their zeal had different, but equally disastrous effects on my brother and me. They were utterly rigid. I coped by being utterly obstinate. They expected us to marry someone from our religious community so for spite I chose an Italian Catholic hippie and political anarchist."

She laughed with merry eyes. Her easy manner of divulging family skeletons made me relax. "I thought he was free thinking," she continued. "Now I realize he's pretty much what my parents said about him—a spoiled, irresponsible university drop-out. I revelled in their discomfort till it dawned on me that *I'm* the one who is stuck with him."

"You put on a good show," I said. "You struck me as a person with no worries and a lot of common sense."

"Gronk," she said, laughing still. "What I am is an eternal optimist and a stubborn ass."

"Useful qualities," I grinned back. "What about your brother?"

"Richard? Ha!" She snorted in obvious contempt. "He learned to play the piety game. He chose the perfect line of work for someone with no sincerity whatsoever. Politics. He's the MLA for Hamilton riding. Let's not talk about him. He gives me heartburn. Or maybe it's the beer. What's your relationship with Ben like?"

Coming at me on the rebound, her question caught me off guard. I shrugged. "I think I'm a relationship hypochondriac," I mused. "Instead of diseases, when I hear abused women describe their partners I wonder, 'Is Ben like that? Is he doing that?' I don't know, Daph. Maybe I'm just unsure because the relationship is new."

"What's he do that you're not sure about?"

I felt myself waver. It felt good to have someone ask, to have the chance to voice my bewilderment out loud. But what if I looked like a naive little fool for trusting him. I told her about him asking me to let him manage my money. "But when I resisted, he didn't push it."

She nodded, looking thoughtful, neutral.

"He and his wife seem to have such a civil relationship too," I plunged on. "Is that normal? I mean, if they're so nice to each other, how come they split? It's pretty unsettling to me that he's going on vacation in March with her and the children."

"Whoa, Shelley! Run that one past me again."

I felt a thickening in my throat. I hated feeling so naked. I explained it the way Ben had explained it to me.

"I see," she mused. "And you're worried that they'll rekindle the old flame while they're away together?"

"Wouldn't you be?"

"How long have they been separated?"

"A year and a half."

She shrugged. "If they were going to get back together, they probably would have done it by now."

"Yeah, that's what I thought too."

I teetered on the edge of telling her about Ben's desire to date other women, but pulled back. That wound from last night was fresh and the friendship with Daphne, new.

I felt like a burglar. The agency where I worked leased the second floor of a graceful brick house converted into tastefully decorated offices. But now at eight p.m. the building stood dark and silent. Letting myself in with my key, I hastily tiptoed up the stairs with my bundles. Once in the familiarity of my own office, I relaxed.

If I hadn't been so pinched for money, I'd have taken a motel room. Instead, I unrolled my sleeping bag on the carpet between the two armchairs. I brushed my teeth in the washroom down the hall, slipped into pyjamas, set my alarm for seven a.m. and crawled into the bedroll. By now Ben would have discovered the note I'd left on his pillow telling him I wouldn't be home tonight, needed time to think.

From my purse I pulled out a pen and my journal and began to write.

Perhaps I expected too much. He made no false promises; never spoke of a future with me in it. He offered me a place to live and financial help; that was all. Maybe my demand for commitment is unfair... dishonest even, for Shangri-La is ever on my mind. I love her and want to return someday. Yet I love Ben too. I think.

My head drooped onto my arm, too heavy to hold up. *Why did I let myself get in so deep? I'm so naive.*

We faced each other across the living room. Ben had not reacted to my renewed apology for hitting him. The longer he went without speaking the more tense I felt. I wanted a chance. A chance to make something happen between us. Despite the warning signs, I wanted the relationship that seemed tantalizingly just beyond my grasp. But at this moment I felt shut out. "Would you prefer I moved out?" I asked.

"Do you want to move out?" he said dully.

I looked away and smiled without humour. "There you go again, answering my question with another question. Tell me what you *feel*." He shrugged but didn't answer. Instead, he stared at his hands, folded in his lap, looking dejected. "Ben... ?"

"I don't know what you want me to say," he muttered. Something flickered across his face. He had the look of a twelve-year-old.

"I don't know if I'm welcome here anymore," I said.

"Of course you are."

"You don't want me to leave?"

"No," he said.

"You know I want more." I waited for a response, but none came. "You don't, do you."

"I uh," he shrugged, noncommittally, "I like you."

My breath escaped through my nostrils. "At least you're honest."

"I know not to lie to you."

There it was again, the twelve-year-old look. "Are you afraid of me?" I asked.

"After the other night? Are you kidding?"

"Come on, you could pin me down with one hand tied behind your back."

His shook his head. "It's not that. It's how fast you changed. My mother used to switch like that. One minute she'd be normal and the next minute there was this... stranger." It was as if a light snapped on in a dark room. What was it he had once said? *My mother had a mental breakdown and never recovered. I was eleven.*

"I see," I said softly. "Look Ben, I behaved badly the other night. But I'm *not* crazy. I'm not *her*," I whispered. "It's just emotions; it's okay to *have* them." I looked for a clue to his reactions but he remained frozen. "I'll make a deal with you," I said, feeling like I needed my head examined despite my claim to sanity. "I'd like to stay... to see how it goes between us." He stole a glance at me. "I promise to work on containing my histrionics when I'm upset. You could work on communicating about feelings—yours *and* mine."

Still there was no reaction. I changed my tack. "I have no right to tell you that you can't date other women. Anyway if I tried, I'd probably be setting myself up for you to do it behind my back. But if we're to have a relationship, I need it to be based on honesty and openness." I paused but he seemed to be struggling to absorb what I was saying. Perhaps it was a fool's bargain, but I had to try. "Here's what I could live with," I said. "If you start dating other women, I expect you to tell me. And if you do date others, you can't keep sleeping with me. I couldn't cope with that. You willing to agree to this?"

He nodded slowly without looking up, like a child who'd been chastised.

He told me he'd be late; said he had something to do after work. I wondered if he had his own surprise. Hurrying home from the office, I got busy setting out candles and preparing pasta and medallions of veal. I changed into a clingy white jumpsuit with a rhinestone bolero jacket and put on a fresh face.

With exquisite timing, headlights bobbed in the lane.

I toyed with meeting him at the door then opted to wait till he shed his coat. He seemed to dawdle. When he came into the dining room, I watched his eyes take in everything. . . the linen, the candles, me. I smiled and embraced him. "It's been one month, hasn't it," he murmured. I nodded, pleased that he'd remembered the anniversary of my moving in. But something was wrong.

"Give me time to change my clothes," he said retreating down the hall.

Through dinner, he talked no less and no differently than usual. Yet my unease continued. "You look tired, Ben."

"Sort of."

"Is something wrong?"

"I have to do some work after dinner. I'm sorry. I'll explain later."

All evening he busied himself in the den. The house was unbearably quiet. With nothing to do but wait, I went over and over the signs, his bearing, the eyes that would not meet mine. The verve, the energy that was quintessentially Ben was missing.

I lay propped up on the pillows when he came in. He didn't look at me, just sat on the end of the bed, his back to me. I wished I could see his face.

"I'm sorry I couldn't spend time with you tonight. I realize you planned a romantic evening. It was a nice thought but I...had some business I had to attend to." He stopped and I waited. When he continued, I thought I could detect a tremor in his voice.

"After what happened to my Dad, I thought maybe I was being paranoid. I didn't tell you, but I went to the doctor last week for some tests. You see, I found this lump on my leg. I got the results today.

"I have cancer."

CHAPTER FOUR

The night was cold. It robbed me of feeling in my fingers and toes. My back ached from craning around to keep an eye on the tractor's blade. Snow arced like surf, spilling to the side of the lane. I hoped it was to the side. In these whiteout conditions, I couldn't be sure if I was on or off the gravel drive.

The blizzard had closed in around seven. I'd been at the hospital. A bed had come available for Ben and I'd rushed him in.

In the four days since the news, he holed up in his den. He did not explain what he was doing. He did, however, take time out once in a while to find me and hold onto me. I had tried to draw out of him what he was thinking, feeling. But he seemed incapable. A few times he gave instructions. He reviewed how to operate the tractor; showed me how to put the charger on in case it wouldn't start in frigid temperatures. Tonight I'd needed that knowledge. He asked me to pick up the children on Thursday. I was surprised at that but he said his wife would expect it.

There'd been one instruction I tried not to think about. But it haunted me. He pointed out two cardboard boxes in the basement. "If anything happens to me," he said, "if I don't come through this alright, I want you to take these boxes out onto the pond. Burn them. Make sure there's nothing left or they go through the ice. Promise me you'll do that. And promise me you won't open them."

I'd been spooked, as much from his oblique reference to death, as from his request. Still, I hated secrets. My childhood had been rife with them. I had learned not to question, not to even wonder about certain things. I didn't question Ben either. "I promise," I whispered.

Through the swirling snow, my little red truck was now visible in the headlights of the tractor. Snow came up to its axles where it had come to a halt, ten yards or so into the lane when I had turned off the road. I cleared snow from in front of the truck as best I could with the blade. Then I grabbed the shovel I'd brought along. The effort of digging snow out from under the truck soon had me heated up and puffing. I had to lie in the snow to hook the chain to the frame underneath.

I climbed back up on the tractor and put it in low gear. The truck inched forward. It took twenty-five minutes to tow it the length of the driveway, move the tractor, drive the truck into the garage and put away the tractor.

It was thirteen minutes to midnight when I got into the warmth of the house and shed my heavy clothing. Exhausted, I fell into bed. With one fleeting thought of the operation Ben would undergo in the morning, I dropped like a stone into the black depths of sleep.

———————

On the threshold of the hospital room I'd been directed to, I hesitated, then entered quietly. Ben's lidded eyes looked dark and sunken. Strong, brawny men weren't supposed to look so vulnerable. I crept to his side and softly stroked his arm. His eyes fluttered open. He focused and smiled weakly in recognition.

"Hello, kid." His voice was more husky than usual, suggesting a raw throat.

"Hi. How ya doin'?"

"I hurt," he admitted.

At his request, I adjusted the bed and helped to prop him up a little. After a couple of minutes, he seemed more alert. "Has the surgeon seen you since you woke up?" I asked.

"Yeah."

"And?" I held my breath.

He placed his hand on top of mine. "He thinks he got it all." My lids closed of their own accord and a balloon collapsed inside, pushing out an audible sigh. "Yeah, me too," he murmured. "I'll have to go to a cancer clinic for check-ups for a few years to make sure I'm clear. And I'll always have a reminder, a big bite out of my flesh at the ankle, but, it looks good for me."

His voice strengthened as he shook off the anesthetic. "I'll be on crutches for a few weeks. My left ankle will always be weaker, the doc says. The muscle and sinew won't fully replace itself. I'll have to take it easy when I go skiing in March."

"Skiing!" my voice screeched. "You're not still going?"

"Sure. Why not?"

"You're crazy! You won't be able to ski."

"I'm going." He set his mouth. It was futile to protest. I pressed my lips together, exasperated and sank down onto the chair beside his bed. I felt drained from weeks on an emotional roller coaster. He must have noticed for he announced energetically, "I made a decision today. It involves you." I stared at him mutely. "This morning as they wheeled me into the OR, I was thinking about my life, what I've done and especially what I haven't. Just before they put me under, I thought, 'What would I really regret having missed out on, if I don't come through this?'"

I nodded but he hesitated, a look of anticipation lighting his expression. "What?" I prompted.

"Disneyland!"

For a long moment, I sat bug-eyed. Then I burst out laughing.

"What's wrong?" he said in wide-eyed innocence. "What'd I do?"

"Disneyland?" I sputtered.

He thrust out his chin. "Well, if you're going to be like that, you don't have to come along with me and Sara and Ari, so there!" He finished by sticking out his tongue.

I rose and sat gingerly on the edge of his bed and leaned my forehead to his, smiling. "Okay, Buster. Disneyland it is."

The house where the children lived with their mother nestled at the end of a quiet residential street. The driveway was empty when I pulled in. I rang the bell. A moment later, Sara opened the door.

"Hi Sara. I'm here to pick you up."

"Oh," was all she said. She turned and disappeared down the hall. I stepped inside and closed the door. She did not return. The sound of cartoons drifted toward me. I stepped to the archway into the livingroom. Ari sat cross-legged on the floor, three feet from a TV screen. He looked catatonic.

"Hello Ari."

No response.

"Ari, hello-o."

He looked up. "How did you get here?"

"If you mean how did I get in the house, your sister let me in. Is your Mommy home?"

"No. She's still at work."

"I see. Well I'm here to pick you two up."

"Oh." He turned back to the cartoons.

"Ari, can you get ready to come with me?"

"Can I watch the rest of my program?"

I checked my watch. "Well...I guess." I chose the chair nearest the hall and sat down. Ben had said Margaret would expect me to pick up the children. Now I wondered. Exactly how did the Volski family communicate with one another? Or did they?

When the show was over, I was relieved to see Ari turn off the television without prompting. "Ari, will you see if Sara is getting ready?" Without answering, he left the room. After several minutes, neither child had returned.

I'd met Margaret only once, briefly and had never been in her house before. I didn't relish being caught searching through it if she came home but there seemed no alternative now. I found Sara in the kitchen reading a book.

"Come on, Sara. Get your things together. We have to go."

The girl moved in slow motion. I watched her, puzzling over what to do. Clearly the children were reluctant to come with me. But I couldn't very well leave them either. What if their mother, expecting to have the night off, didn't come home?

It was another twenty minutes before I succeeded in herding them out the door. Sara locked it with a key that hung on a string around her neck.

"Did you guys know I'd be picking you up?" I asked as I drove away.

"No," they chorused.

"Hmm. Did you expect your Dad?"

No answer. I glanced at them. Ari, sitting in the middle, turned to his sister. She stared straight ahead.

"Do you know where your Dad is?"

Ari shook his head, looking up like a solemn puppy. Sara did not answer. Perhaps I shouldn't have been surprised. After all, I knew how a family could manage to avoid certain topics. It was just that disease, hospitals and death were not on the Gallagher taboo list. Maybe they were on the Volski list. I pulled over to the curb and turned to them.

"Listen, you guys, I'm really sorry you don't seem to know what's going on. Your Daddy couldn't come to get you today because he had to go to the hospital." I explained that he'd had an operation but was okay and should be home in a few days. "He asked me to come for you. I thought he told your Mommy to expect me but maybe he forgot, or maybe she forgot to tell you."

I studied their faces. Ari frowned but whether from worry, confusion or some other feeling, I couldn't tell. Sara's mouth worked as if words were fighting to come out. But none did.

"Would you two like to see your Dad?"

Ari brightened. "Yes," he said, nodding. This time Sara turned to look at me, some obscure emotion burning in her eyes. She too, nodded.

At the hospital, the reunion between them and their father was cheerful enough. At Ben's invitation, Ari scrabbled up on the bed beside him. Normally all elbows and knees, he made an extra effort to avoid his father's vulnerable ankle.

The kids seemed to take the circumstances in their stride. Yet on the way home, I could elicit only monosyllabic responses from either one. Ari, especially, looked pale and sober. I glanced his way while driving and thought I detected moisture on his cheek but when I asked him if he was crying, he said no.

—————————————

Closing my book, I extinguished the lamp over the armchair. The children had gone to bed quite agreeably. All was quiet as I crept down the darkened hall. Sara's door stood wide open. Moonlight streamed through the curtain-less window. She was not there.

I tiptoed to Ari's door which was slightly ajar. I eased it wide. A silver band of moonlight fell across the rumpled comforter that cloaked two mounds. Ari lay on his stomach, face turned to the wall. Sara's slender arm entwined itself around him.

Had she stolen into his bed to offer comfort or to seek it? I had a hunch it was more likely the former. Rascal though she could be, Sara *was* the elder sibling. Perhaps she'd heard muffled sobs that did not reach my ears at the other end of the house.

—————————————

Ben sat on the end of our bed and handed me his crutches. I set them aside. His dressing would need changing twice a day. I knelt to remove the tensor stocking that covered his leg from instep to knee. Little by little I worked at it, inching it down his leg. He sucked in his breath in short little hisses of pain. A wave of nausea rolled through me. Though I minister to the emotional wounds of abuse survivors, unflinching at their horrific disclosures, I cringe before the pain of another's physical wounds.

I fought to keep the bandage from bunching and squeezing the wound. He winced and another wave of nausea hit my stomach. I tugged and fretted at it till it began to ease past the wound and slip over his foot. I lifted the corner of a gauze pad. It had yellow muck on it and some blood. I wasn't sure what the muck was but finally decided it was ointment.

Gently I peeled back the pad, exposing a patch of flesh the size of a man's palm, just above his ankle. The tissue was translucent over the bone and bore the fabric imprint of the gauze. I forced myself to examine it. Not *so* bad. Clean at least. I glanced up. Ben's eyes were closed. He looked so vulnerable.

I put the required ointment on the wound and covered it with a fresh pad and worked the stocking back onto his leg. "Maybe I should sleep in one of the kid's rooms tonight, Ben. I'm scared I'll bump your leg by accident."

But he said, no, he wanted me near. When I crawled in beside him, he pulled me down onto his shoulder. In the dark, emotions felt palpable.

After many minutes, he started to say something but his voice cracked and he had to clear his throat and begin again.

"If you hadn't been here, I don't know how I would have managed. I've never had to lean on anyone before. I'm not used to having someone take care of me. It's not enough to say I appreciate... ." He cursed softly. "I don't know the words to say what I feel," he admitted.

"It's okay. You don't need to say anything."

"Yes, I do." But for a long minute, he remained silent as if scanning the pages of his mind for words he couldn't find. He squeezed me in his arm intermittently, communicating it seemed, in Morse code. With his free hand he reached over and took my opposite hand. "When I looked down at you dressing my wound just now, something reached inside me and clutched me...here." He pressed my hand on his chest where his pyjama top lay open. I feathered his fur between my fingers. "Thank you," he whispered.

It was such a simple statement but it sparked moisture in my lashes. He said no more and I continued to stroke his chest, unable to think of any words that could improve on the language of touch.

Parallel ice-blue troughs lay between me and Jamie's retreating back. The tips of my cross-country skis alternated leads with a rhythmic swoosh, swoosh. A path, wide enough for a railroad right of way led deep into the Ganaraska forest, a stretch of rolling evergreen-shrouded hills an hour by car north-east of Toronto. A fresh dump of mid-March snow and blue sky served up a perfect day.

The snow was causing ice balls to form between Shannon's toes. She flopped down, as she had been doing every few minutes, to yank them out with her teeth. A chittering squirrel caught her attention and the Setter shot down one of the lanes, a red streak between arrow-straight rows of fir trees.

I heard Jamie utter something, but since his back was to me I couldn't make it out. I looked where he was pointing with a pole and spied a hawk circling just above the treetops. Then I lost it against the sun that momentarily blinded me. I failed to see Shannon emerge from the woods and drop down to worry at her pads again. My ski tip collided with her ribs. She leapt away, but not before I lost my balance. With an indignant yelp, I whumped into the snow.

My protest reached Jamie's ears for he looked back. He must have gathered from my cursing and muttering that I was unhurt, for he laughed at me struggling to untangle my skis.

"Damn, Irish Setters are dense," I grumbled.

"Maybe you should get Shannon her own skis," he suggested, offering a hand. "It might not keep her out of our way, but it'd slow her down some."

"I *ought* to get her a brain transplant."

"Hey, Shannon," he said, slapping his leg to call the dog to him, "Do you know your mistress is insulting you?"

"Duh," I parodied Shannon's idiotic tongue-lolling grin as she accepted his scratch behind an ear. "She reminds me of that river."

"The Shannon in Ireland?"

"No, the one in West Virginia. The Shenan...duh."

Jamie chuckled. "You come live with me, Shannon old girl. I'll treat you right."

"No way," I backtracked. "I can't wait till she's with me again. Ben and I've been building her a deluxe doghouse. As soon as the weather breaks, I'm bringing her home. It should only be a few more weeks."

"Oh well, Shannon. Too bad."

"I'm starved, Jamie. Let's find a spot we can sit down and eat."

"Sure. You lead. Stop any place suitable."

I broke trail for the next few minutes till I came upon a granite boulder, large enough for us to rest on. We removed our skis and rammed them upright in the snow. Slipping off my backpack, I produced sandwiches while Jamie pulled a thermal jug and two cups from his.

"So Sis, how's your love life?" he asked, pouring us each a steaming cup of coffee. Of the mix of emotions and thoughts tumbling around inside, I couldn't select one to express.

"Earth to Shelley. Are you there?"

I shrugged. I could feel his eyes on me but couldn't meet them. "You hurtin'?" he asked, his voice liquid.

"No. Not really. Fact is I'm not sure what to feel—or think. I'm still trying to figure Ben out. Sometimes I think the man is a scoundrel, but so far he seems to have been quite honest with me. He's never promised me anything. I just don't know where this relationship is going yet."

"Does it upset you that he's gone off for two weeks skiing with his wife and kids?"

"I'd be lying if I didn't admit it makes me nervous, but I don't resent it. I have no reason to." I took a bite and chewed thoughtfully. "It must confuse Ari and Sara, though. What kid doesn't yearn to have their family intact?"

"Me," he retorted. "I'd have thought I'd died and gone to Heaven if Dad had packed you and me up years ago and gotten away from the Witch."

"I suppose. She was always hardest on you. Maybe she was emotionally bankrupt by the time you came along or maybe she transferred her contempt for Dad's weakness on you, being the only other male in the family."

He kicked at the snow with his boot. "She thinks I'm a bum."

"Who cares what she thinks?" I muttered.

"My own mother?"

"You've got to quit giving her so much power. You keep chasing the carrot of her approval, trying to be good enough for her. But she's the one at fault, subjecting her kids to an endless barrage of negative criticism. She'll never change. As long as you think you need to prove yourself to her, you'll keep getting involved with women who can never make you happy. Look what you choose. They're either dizzy airheads posing no threat to your manhood, or they're domineering bulldozers like Mom. You get bored with the former and pulverized by the latter."

He looked chastened and I regretted coming on so strong.

"You deserve better," I said, touching his blond curls. "There's really a lot in you to love."

"You're just saying that 'cause you're my sister. But women don't want to stay with me when they figure out what a fuck-up I am. They leave—at least the smart ones do."

"You mean, like Carol?"

"Yeah."

"She was one of the bulldozers, James."

He swept a swatch of snow off the boulder with his mitten. "I know."

"Were you in love with her?"

He shrugged. "To tell the truth, it's sort of a relief it didn't work out." He laughed. "She was too much woman for me."

I laughed too, gently. "You mean the way Mom is too much woman for Dad?"

"Somethin' like that. Anyway, how'd you do that? We were talking about *your* love life and you manipulated the conversation around to talking about mine."

"That's what social workers do. They manipulate conversations."

To head off any more questions, I scooped a handful of snow and tossed it at him. "Oh yeah?" he challenged and reached to the ground. I shrieked and leapt off the rock at a run. A snowball pelted dead centre in my back. He chased me, hurling several more. We both ignored Shannon's barking till she grabbed Jamie's pant leg in her teeth, pitching him into the snow. I bent over double, laughing.

"Way t' go, Shannon."

The winter sun threw long shadows across the yard when we pulled into Jamie's driveway behind my truck. His house slouched like a vagabond beneath a once magnificent oak tree. Everything about the place was decrepit. The paint peeled; the eaves troughs collapsed; bricks were missing from the chimney. A "fixer-upper" Jamie had proudly termed it, when he showed me his acquisition. "It'll give me a project to throw myself into," he explained.

It will eat you alive, I thought.

We took the skis off the roof of his rust-bucket Pinto and dumped them in the porch. He carried my overnight bag to his bedroom. "You can have my bed for the night. I'll sleep on the couch."

He insisted that I sit at the kitchen table over the coffee he brewed while he prepared dinner. While he chattered about the renovations he was planning for this old farmhouse on a severed lot, I absorbed my surroundings. For once I agreed with Mother's pessimistic view. This place would swallow every penny he put into it and never return his investment.

He had stripped the walls of the kitchen to the studs. Looking through the spaces between, I could see through to the blackened fireplace in the living room. The hardwood floor heaved. Stained wallpaper hung in strips. Still, I couldn't help but admire the oak cabinets he'd installed in the kitchen and did so out loud. His tooled scrollwork in the doors was exquisite. "I don't understand why you don't go back to school and get your papers for carpentry. You should be doing *this* for a living, not driving a truck."

"Yeah."

He sounded like he was brushing me off. "I mean it, Jamie. You're putting all your talent in this old house and it will eat your money, not increase it."

"Sure it will," he argued. "I'll fix it up and sell it. Then I'll buy another to fix up and sell that too. It's something I can do on the side."

Just like Dad, I despaired. *No lack of ambition, just judgment and follow through.* "Well, there's nothing wrong with having a trade," I said lamely. "Right now what you have is a hobby." He handed me the dishes to set the table and ignored my remark.

After dinner, he made a fire in the fireplace with the scraps of wood from his demolition. When the dust and disarray in his house and life became too much for me, I pleaded exhaustion from the day's skiing and retired to bed.

As I crawled under the covers of the single cot, I thought it odd that already I considered Ben's house my home and wished I were there, even though Ben himself was in Utah.

I felt over-dressed as I observed the airport crowd. I wanted Ben to like what he saw when he came off the plane. I chose a white pleated skirt and jacket in keeping with the spring weather that had at last arrived only two days ago. For colour, I wore a satin tangerine blouse.

I spotted Sara. She darted through the entrance to the carousel area, dodging through the crowd. Her face had an obstinate set to it. Margaret came next craning to keep Sara in her sights. Ari tagged behind Margaret, wool gathering. Ben stared stolidly ahead, not scanning the throng for me as I thought he would.

I approached him. When he finally noticed me, he barely reacted. I stood on my toes to kiss him but he turned his face away. "Don't," he said.

Stung, I stepped back. Fighting for composure, I asked, "How was your trip?"

"I'll tell you later." I tried to hug him but he anticipated my intention and put his hand harshly on my arm. "Don't hug me."

Tears sprang to my eyes and a lump lodged in my throat. *You got back together, didn't you*, my mind cried out.

Sara and Margaret hauled luggage from the carousel and loaded it onto a pushcart. I led the way to the car on the parking ramp. Taking the keys from me, Ben got in behind the wheel with Margaret beside him in the passenger seat. I sat stiffly in the back between the children.

It took forty minutes to get home. Talk was sparse and limited to practical matters. We pulled up to the garage beside Margaret's car that had sat there the two weeks they were away. I left them separating the luggage and went straight into the house. From the bedroom, I heard her car leave. The back door opened and closed. Ben's footsteps sounded in the hall as he approached. He took one look at me. "Oh boy," he said, looking stern. "What's wrong?"

I sat at my vanity table, a box of tissues on my lap and tears streaming down my face. "You got back with your wife, didn't you?"

"Oi gevalt." He took my wrist and led me over to the bed, motioning to sit beside him. I leaned toward him to lay my head on his chest but he pulled back. "Don't lean on me."

I sobbed louder. "Are you mad at me?" I wailed, a hiccup erupting.

"No," he said. "But I will be if you don't give me a chance to explain."

I sniffed and swallowed, wiping my cheeks with the tissue. A degree of control achieved, I nodded, indicating a readiness to listen.

"Believe me, Margaret and I are *not* getting back together. Two weeks with her is quite enough to remind me why we're separated."

"Then why did you pull away from me when I tried to hug you?"

"I'm getting to that. Will you just listen?"

I sniffed loudly, then nodded.

"I had hoped this vacation would help the kids see they will always have both of us, even though we aren't together. But it was far from smooth sailing. Sara was a real pain in the ass. She acted up every day, demanding, bitchy, picking on Ari.

"Yesterday was our last day on the slopes. The kids wanted to ski an area they'd explored with an instructor earlier in the week. Sara led the way on a trail through the forest. She got ahead of me and out of sight. I came to a branch low enough for the kids to ski under, but I had to duck. Right at that moment, she called to me. I looked up in time to catch her grinning. I didn't see the drop-off and I fell—hard. I cracked my ribs."

I stared wide-eyed and contrite. "No wonder you wouldn't let me hug you or lean on you." He tried to take a deep breath but winced instead. "I'm so sorry. Are you in a lot of pain?"

"Yeah, I hurt. I'm royally pissed off too. Sara did it on purpose, setting me up for that fall. She thought it was a big joke to see Daddy go down. I was so mad at her. After all the trouble she'd caused all week, that little trick really finished me off.

"Her shenanigans caused a lot of friction between me and Margaret. She says Sara is trying to show me that she's unhappy. Her answer is to just give Sara more affection. Maybe Sara *is* unhappy, Shelley, but it's not for lack of attention. Margaret never wants to put limits on the kid. Whenever I'm mad at Sara, she can just run for cover under her mother's wing. I end up looking like the bad guy. It makes me furious."

An angry frown creased his face. "This morning was the last straw. I left about twelve bucks in change on my dresser and within minutes it disappeared. Sara and Ari were the only ones who had the opportunity to take it. I asked them and both denied seeing it. I hate to say it, but I'm sure it was Sara; she couldn't look me in the eye.

"We were in a hurry so I couldn't do anything about it right then but on the plane I told Margaret I wanted to go through Sara's things when we got to Toronto. Margaret wouldn't go along with me. We argued about it. By the time we landed, we were all angry and tense. You just happened to be an innocent bystander."

"I guess I didn't improve your day with my hysterics."

He gave me a rueful look.

"I'm sorry," I said again. "But, I still don't understand one thing. Why wouldn't you let me kiss you?"

"Because the sun bit me too. We had a lot of bright, sunny days. My face, my mouth got pretty burned. It's nothing personal, Shelley. I just hurt all over."

"You might have said so at the airport. You would have spared me a lot of anguish."

He brushed back a lock of my hair that tears had pasted to my cheek. "When I look at things from your point of view, I can see why you freaked out. I am glad to be home and I'm glad to see you even if I can't hug and kiss you."

I sat a moment, taking in his explanation, considering things from his side. Then I met his eyes, smiled and blew him a kiss.

———————————

Sara manipulated the origami pyramid she called the Fortune Teller on her thumbs and forefingers in a crisscross pattern.

"Show me again how you make it," I asked.

"S'easy," she said, tearing another sheet from her notebook.

As she turned the paper in a deft, circular motion, folding and creasing, my vision fixed on her dainty hands. "Kids made these when I was young too," I observed, "but I never got the hang of it."

"Done," she announced. "Now you write questions on it, whatever secrets you want to find out about somebody." Her cheeks dimpled and her sparkling eyes insinuated impish thoughts. I chuckled and raised my eyebrows at her.

The phone on the dining room wall pierced the moment of cama-raderie. She bolted for it, jarring the table. Coffee slopped over the lip of my mug. "Oh hi." Her voice shivered, like a tiny silver bell I thought, as I got up to retrieve a rag from the kitchen to mop the spill. Must be Caitlyn returning Sara's call. There was a long pause, bracketed by another "Oh," from Sara, this one muted, leaden. She turned away from my glance, head bowed, seeking refuge in the forward hunch of slender shoulders. I stepped away, giving her privacy. With my back to her, I gazed out the patio door, across the fields.

Spring had come at last, turning the field that Ben had ploughed in the fall into a sea of reddish brown oozy mud. It also had heralded a joyous reunion between me and my dog. I watched Shannon now. Ari, delighted with the entrance of a dog in his life had begged to walk her. Though there was no necessity for her to be on a leash he had tied a rope to her collar. Now though, I noticed my Setter snaking about the field sniffing out quarry with the rope dragging loose behind her. Her beautiful red feathers hung in strings, caked with red clay.

Ari stood rooted to the spot, seemingly unmindful of the dog. The boy never seemed to have his wits about him. Not that he was simple; he possessed a perceptive mind and a wry sense of humour, leaving one with the impression of a wise old man going on eight. He focused so intently on his own thoughts that he'd lose track of what was going on around him. He was always forgetting things, losing things, much to the exasperation of his sister.

Sara, on the other hand, never missed a beat. It was impossible to hide things from her, like cookies, small change, or the inhalers she used to control her asthma. She tended to use them to excess and Ben would try to hide spares in case she ran out and really needed one. But Sara could ferret out anything she wanted. She had perfected her sleight of hand with those pretty slender fingers. One time I'd come around the corner into the kitchen to catch her sitting on the counter, her hand quite literally in the cookie jar. She'd flashed an angelic smile and quipped, "Nice day, isn't it?" Her wisecrack caught me unawares and I'd laughed outright.

Behind me, I heard the phone quietly being hung up. Wordlessly, Sara returned to her schoolbooks at the table. "Hmm," I mused aloud, keeping my eyes on the outdoors. "I wonder what Ari's up to? He's been standing out there a long time just staring at the ground."

A chair scraped and she appeared at my elbow. I unlatched the patio door. The brisk outside temperature raised goosebumps on my arms. "Ari!" I sang out. My voice evaporated into the distance. His back to us, Ari did not appear to have heard. The hood of his jacket covered his ears. I called again. He twisted around awkwardly, without moving his feet. The hood didn't turn with his body and it covered half his face. He shouted something but the hood swallowed his words.

I exchanged puzzled glances with Sara. Leaning out over the doorsill, I hollered louder. "WHAT-DID-YOU-SAY?"

A plaintiff cry drifted back on the wind. "I'm stuck!"

Now I saw that he was more than ankle deep in the red-brown mud. I covered my mouth, stifling the urge to laugh; he sounded so panicky. But the wholesale giggling at my elbow undid me and I dissolved. We two laughed till Sara's wheezing and coughing overwhelmed her and she had to use her inhaler.

Ari's boots stayed behind when I hoisted him. With an anxious whimper, he locked his stockinged feet around my middle. I bent, precariously overbalanced by his weight and tugged at a half-buried boot. It resisted, then with a sucking sound yielded suddenly, nearly causing me to sit down. Ari yelped.

I handed the boot to Sara who held it at arm's length with an expression better suited to holding a dirty diaper. I retrieved the other one and gave it to her as well.

"Come on, you two. Let's go wash off in the creek."

By the time we reached the woods behind the house, my arms ached from carrying the sturdy boy. I deposited him on a fallen log and took the mud-caked boots from Sara, stooping to wash them in the creek. Shannon waded, lapping from the surface, then disappeared in the thicket.

Ari tugged on each boot as I handed them to him. Sara perched beside him on the log. For once, their faces looked open and relaxed.

The Thursday evenings and alternate weekends of the last four and a half months had brought me no closer to understanding what thoughts and feelings went on behind those faces. All too often Sara's expression was pinched and resentful though not particularly directed at me. Ari was an agreeable and placid boy. He chatted amiably about his hamster and goldfish, and of course the dog he wished for. He'd talk about school, playmates and music. Yet I wondered what thoughts and feelings were masked behind that amiable countenance.

"What happened with Caitlyn, Sara?"

"Nothing." A tiny current seemed to sizzle through the girl's body. Her expression turned touchy and suspicious.

"She can't come?"

"No."

"How come?"

After a moment's hesitation and a shrug, she replied, "She's going to a birthday party." She wouldn't look my way.

"I guess you're disappointed."

Ari began kicking a branch that adjoined the log on which they sat. Sara shoved his foot with her own. "Stop Ari, you're bugging me." Her voice contained a bite but he continued as if unaware of her.

"Sara, it's okay to have feelings like that. It's normal."

She shrugged again and raised her chin too high. "I don't care."

"We'll have Caitlyn over another time," I persevered.

"Shelley," Ari broke in, "how long are you going to stay here with Daddy?"

Sara's sharp jab in Ari's ribs produced a protest this time. "Ow! That hurt."

"I told you to quit kicking!"

I studied the two of them, waiting for this artificial fight to subside. They withdrew momentarily, facing off like ear-flattened kittens.

I crouched down to their level and broke off a length of twig from a sapling. "Listen, you guys," I began stripping the twig of its spring growth.

"Remember when your Mommy and Daddy told you that they were separating?"

Two blank pairs of eyes stared back at me.

"You *do* remember when your parents first separated." Nods, almost imperceptible from both of them. "They must have talked to you at some time, explaining what was going to happen."

Ari squirmed. Sara's complexion paled and she blinked. For an instant, I thought of a rabbit run to ground, frightened and immobilized. Why was it so hard for these children to talk about anything that really mattered?

"How *did* you find out that your parents weren't going to stay to-gether?"

Ari turned his downcast face toward Sara. They exchanged furtive glances. I wondered if they felt disloyal to their parents for having this talk, though so far it was a pretty one-sided conversation. I waited in the confidence that someone would fill the silence. Finally, Sara did. "The For Sale sign."

"For Sale sign?"

"We went on a vacation with Mommy to visit Gran in England. When we got home there was a For Sale sign on the front lawn."

"That was how you found out?" Both children nodded, their faces solemn. I blew out my breath in a long, deep sigh. After a pause, I said, "Then what?"

Sara answered. "Mommy said we were moving to a new house and Daddy wasn't coming with us."

"How did you feel?"

Silence again

"Were you sad?"

No response.

"Ari?"

For a moment he looked close to tears, then pulled his mouth in a kind of grimace. "I don't know." But it was an 'I don't know' of denial.

"What about you, Sara? Do you remember how you felt?"

"Yeah, I was really sad about our house. I didn't want to move."

"Mm. You'd lived all your life there, hadn't you."

"Yes. And my best friend lived next door."

"Caitlyn."

Her eyes shone with moisture, but then she blinked them back. I sighed again. "It must be hard for you to understand what the grown ups in your life are planning if they don't explain things to you. Sometimes grown ups don't really know what to say. I know your Mommy and Daddy both love you two very much though. Your parents have been apart now for nearly two years. Do you ever wonder if they might get back together?"

"No," Ari spoke for the first time. "They have their own houses now." *The little old sage.*

"You asked me, Ari, how long I'm going to stay with your Daddy. That's a very fair question. And I'm glad you asked. I wish I could give you a definite answer. But I don't know the answer. Your Daddy and I are still getting to know each other and find out how much we like the other. It could be that I might stay forever, but I just don't know."

Ari's direct gaze seemed to hold no more questions for now and Sara's body seemed to have lost a little of its tension.

I slapped my thighs with both hands. "What do you say we have a boat race on this here creek?"

Ari reverted to a seven-year-old. "How?"

"How? What do you mean, how? Haven't you guys ever raced boats on a creek?"

"No," they chorused.

"Poor little city kids," I teased. "You've got this fantastic outdoor play-land and don't know how to use it. Well, you each have to find a stick or piece of wood that looks like it'll float, like this." I held up the twig I'd been stripping. "Then I'll show you how it's done." They slid off the log and scurried like squirrels through the underbrush to find a suitable 'boat'.

August 1985

I watched the corrugated terrain glide beneath the jet's belly with a tug at my heart. Ben slept beside me. He proposed this trip back in April. It was my second spring with him and for weeks, beginning in March, he'd retreated to his den consumed so it seemed, with the preparation of his tax return. I felt like an accountant's widow. Gone were our routine evening talks. Gone too, was Ben's usual good humour. Like the proverbial bear in spring, he was grouchy and unpredictable whenever he emerged from his den. The vacation, I suspected, was a guilt offering.

I turned from the port hole to find him awake. "See anything?" he asked.

"See anything? Wow! How can you sleep through this scenery?" He leaned over me and peered downward. Then he lowered his chin to look down the front of my blouse.

"Yeah. Nice scenery."

I pushed him back in his seat. "Neanderthal."

"Yup." He grinned, arching his eyebrows. "This vacation, it's just you and me, Babe. Not like last year in Disneyland. It's Margaret's turn with the little rug rats this summer."

Though I wouldn't have said so, I shared his relief. Sara's tantrums, complaints, sulks and defiance through last year's vacation had strained us both. I turned back to the window and watched mountain ranges pass beneath the plane's wing. I felt Ben's hand stroke my back but I couldn't tear my eyes away from the panorama.

"Sorry you left all this?" he asked.

I didn't answer. How could I tell him that part of me had never left? After a moment, I leaned back. "You know I like you."

"Like?" he laughed. "Now that's the pot calling the kettle lukewarm."

"I like things you do for me," I said, evasively.

"Such as?"

"Mm, well, such as how you make sure we talk regularly. I like how affectionate you are, how you don't mind showing it even in public."

The side of his mouth turned up in a grin. I half expected him to do something to embarrass me right then but he didn't.

A 'bing' announced communication from the captain's cabin. "Good afternoon ladies and gentlemen. We should be arriving at Vancouver International Airport on schedule in twenty-five minutes. The time in Vancouver is three fourteen and the weather is a balmy twenty-seven degrees."

———————————

For a moment when I awoke, I couldn't remember where I was. The high ceiling, the room were unfamiliar. But there was Ben sleeping soundly beside me. *Oh yes, our hotel room.* I reached for my watch on the nightstand. Six fifty a.m. I crept out of bed, quietly pulled on jeans and sweatshirt and tiptoed out of the room.

Emerging from the darkened hotel foyer, I stepped into a fresh morning. An ivy-covered vestige of a more elegant era, the Sylvia Hotel overlooked English Bay. On one side were Vancouver's downtown high-rise apartments, close by on the other, the preserved natural estate of Stanley Park. The street had been cleansed in pre-dawn showers, the pavements and lawns still damp. An organic musk from giant rain-drenched evergreens mingled with salt air.

Across the street, the boulevard dipped down to Second Beach strewn with driftwood. To the left, the bay curved round to where Point Grey's forested peninsula pointed westward toward Vancouver Island. The rugged skyline of the Coastal Mountains winged the northwest, the city of West Vancouver stealing up the slopes. Out in the bay, a half dozen tankers lay at anchor.

I crossed the street and spongy lawn to the beach. The retreating tide had left behind broken bits of shell, seaweed and kelp. Hungry gulls swooped, screeched and squabbled over the spoils, their beaks yawning and necks bobbing at each other threateningly. The sand seemed a living thing gurgling through the craters dug by burrowing razor clams.

A light breeze feathered my hair as I tramped the deserted beach just out of reach of the breakers that washed up the sand. I perched on one of the giant logs abandoned by the tide. Pressure had been building up behind my eyes. Being here induced an exquisite pain, as if I'd had rushed into the arms of a secret lover and had but one precious hour. The salt air tingled in my nostrils; I tasted salt as tears reached the corners of my mouth. Uncomplicated but compelling was this love. It was dangerous for Ben to bring me here. Craning around on my log, I could pick out the window of our hotel room. I pictured him wrapped in the sheets, asleep and oblivious to the battle across the avenue, raging inside me. Wrenching, shuddering sobs worked their way out and tears washed my face until finally there were no more. I felt bleached inside, like the driftwood on the sand. Joggers and dog-walkers began to invade the beach. I drew a sleeve across my eyes and reluctantly ambled back.

My key scraped in the lock and the door squeaked when I pushed it to peek inside. Ben stirred, then rolled up on his elbow facing me. "Hi," he said, patting the bed in front of him. I slipped off shoes, jeans and sweatshirt and slid under the sheet beside him. He pulled me close. His naked body felt warm after the coolness of the morning outside.

"You look like you've been crying," he said, matter-of-factly.

"Mm-hmm."

"You okay now?"

I nuzzled in closer—my only answer.

I felt guilty deceiving him; he'd been honest with me. He wanted to try his luck at finding an old flame who'd long since moved to Vancouver. Would I have something to do for a couple of hours if he located her? Sure, I said; I'll visit Greg, my former housemate. He dialled a number from several possibilities in the book. Someone apparently gave the right answer because he gave me the thumbs up and I crept out of the room.

From the phone in the hotel lobby, I arranged to have dinner at Greg's apartment. I hung up and called a real estate agent. I explained that I wanted to know the current market value of my land. It wouldn't hurt to know, though selling wasn't on my agenda. He agreed to pick me up from the Silvia, take a look at my acreage and afterward drop me at Greg's apartment in New Westminster.

I sketched a map for Ben to find Greg's place, letting him infer that Greg would be picking me up. If one of us was guilty of stealing away to a lover's tryst, it was me. To go to my property without him was a hunger I didn't want to explain.

A few minutes after we stepped out of the realtor's big Chrysler and into the trees, I gave him the slip. Survey posts, I told him, were down by the stream we could hear gurgling at the bottom of the slope. I let him get ahead, then stole off in the opposite direction. When I could no longer hear his feet tramping the forest floor, I leaned back against the trunk of one of the firs shooting arrow-like into the sky. Behind me, my hands pressed against the sticky, scrubby bark. My heartbeat slowed finally to match the rhythm of this, my perfect universe, my Shangri-La.

From the twelfth story balcony, I shaded my eyes against the late afternoon sun reflecting off the Fraser River. Flat delta islands, hives of commercial activity, lay between the north and more distant south arm of the river.

I turned to the apartment interior and caught Greg bending to give his fiancé a peck on the cheek. They were working side by side in the closet-sized kitchen, preparing a meal for the three of us. I stepped in through the open patio door.

"I could swear you've grown taller, since I saw you last."

"He only looks tall beside me," Cathy said reaching into the fridge. "I'm such a pygmy."

It was true. Even at five foot eight, Greg towered over her. What she lacked in height, though, she easily made up in personality. I'd liked her immediately and enjoyed the easy intimacy between the young couple. Watching him, I was reminded again of my brother, the likeness between these two. If only Jamie could pull his life together as Greg had done.

"You've done well for yourself," I said. "You should be proud."

He flushed and changed the subject. "You said on the phone you'd explain where what's-his-name is tonight."

"Ben. His name is Ben." The words slipped out before I realized he'd caught me in his old trap. I wagged a finger at him and he chuckled. "He's seeing an old girlfriend," I said.

"You're not jealous?"

"No."

He tipped his head to the side, eyes narrowing skeptically at me.

"What?" I laughed defensively.

"You've mellowed. You used to have this feminist scrutiny of men's behaviour. Made me cautious around you."

"Really?"

He paused, knife aloft. "Have I offended you?"

"No. Perhaps I have mellowed." But the day's emotional roller coaster left me feeling anything but mellow just now.

Ben was cordial but quiet when he arrived to pick me up. I sensed that his day had been as emotional as mine. We rode the elevator in silence. As this was home territory for me, I took the wheel. A heavy rain began. I drove along a commercial artery, the lights from shops and other cars dissolving in a watery smear between passes of the wipers. Ben slouched in the seat beside me staring unblinking into the night as the blades thumped out their lonely beat. Apprehensive about the meaning of his mood after his mysterious rendezvous, I waited anxiously to see if he would elucidate.

"Thanks for letting me do that," he murmured at last.

"I thought this trip was to please me. I didn't know you had your own agenda in coming here."

I glanced across. He offered an expression of contrition. "It was dumb luck that she moved here."

"So who is she?"

He heaved a sigh, leaned his head back on the headrest and closed his eyes. Blocks slipped by and I began to think that he was pointedly ignoring my question. When at last he spoke, it was low and slow, as if in deep hypnosis.

"In *American Graffiti* there was a character named Toad. He was the geek in the gang, the one no self-respecting girl wants to be seen with, chasing girls like a dog chases cars, salivating over them but not knowing the first thing about how to catch one. In my circle, I was Toad. The other guys always managed to snag the women with stunning looks and social graces. I'd see a couple strolling in the park holding hands and I'd feel so alone. I was dying to have a girl hanging on my arm but none ever wanted anything to do with a rowdy buffoon spiked on hormones." He sighed deeply.

"I was equally inept as a scholar, or so I thought. I'd clowned my way through high school and my marks reflected it. So when all the guys were heading off to university I didn't believe I had the brains to cut it. Instead I bought a variety store and went into business. While my buddies were running around wild and having the time of their lives, I was working my butt off twelve hours a day, seven days a week. I made money, though. Fistfuls of it. Then I met Marianne.

"I fell hard for her, like falling off a cliff, madly, totally, helplessly in love. She was everything I ever dreamed of, warm, beautiful, kind. She was gracious and genteel—even when she broke up with me. 'I don't think it will work out between us, Benjamin,'" he mimicked. "She was probably right. A classy Roman Catholic woman like her with a bumbling Jewish shopkeeper like me." His voice cracked with bitterness.

"My father drummed it into me to work hard and save. Save for tomorrow. Save for a rainy day. Save for your old age. But when Marianne dumped me, I realized how useless that was. I'd mortgaged my youth and lost the only woman I ever loved."

"The only woman, Ben? Surely you loved your wife once."

"Yeah," he sighed, "but not the same, not without holding something back."

His eyes remained closed. The sadness in his face was heartbreaking.

"When I lost Marianne, I realized all I had left was money. I went on a mad spending spree. Maybe I thought I could buy happiness or maybe I was just rebelling against my father's advice, but I spent like there was no tomorrow. If I wanted something, I bought it. I traveled Europe, took up skiing in Switzerland, bought expensive clothes, a flashy car, took flying lessons. But the pain never let up."

The light changed and I drove on.

"One day I was flying a Cessna. I began to push it through aerobatics I knew might be beyond its capability. But I didn't care; I *wanted* to die. I finally succeeded in getting into a maneuver I couldn't get out of. The plane was plummeting toward the ground. I'd been taught what to do in that situation; pull the power off and let go of the stick. If you've enough altitude, the aircraft will eventually right itself and fly level. At the last possible moment, I shut down and let go. I'd like to say I chose life, but the truth is I chickened out."

He fell silent again. I reached over and slipped my hand in his. We rode several blocks like that, then he opened his eyes and gave my hand a slight squeeze. "You're a smart woman, Shelley. You don't make a lot of demands on me, don't try to own me. If you'd been any other way, I don't know if I could have become so comfortable with you." A traffic light turned red. I was grateful because mist in my eyes blurred my vision.

"Seeing Marianne today," he continued, "I remembered all the things about her that I once loved. She's still got class. She's good looking. She's sweet and kind. But I realized...I'm not in love with her anymore."

The light changed to green and I pulled away. "Did you cry over her, back then?"

"I wish I could have, but by that time in my life I'd already forgotten how."

"How does one forget how to cry?"

"You tell me. You're the psychological expert."

"You blow me away. I cry so damned easily."

"I know. I envy you."

"People need to cry sometimes."

"I know."

My sister, Gayle had become pregnant again and was due just about the time Ben and I flew to Vancouver. Sure enough, when we got home a message on our answering machine announced the arrival of a baby girl. Gayle was already home and invited the four of us, Sara, Ari, Ben and me, to a family picnic and pool party in their backyard. We hoped this would be one of Sara's good days; they were becoming fewer and farther between. But the conditions were right. Sara enjoyed swimming and she *loved* babies.

I was excited about the baby. Robbie and Jennie were born while I lived out west. I'd missed their infancy. I looked forward to seeing Jamie too. He'd taken a job with a trucking firm out of Sudbury last fall supplying lumber to retailers around northern Ontario and I hadn't seen him since Christmas. He abandoned his "fixer-upper" project and as I predicted, lost money on the sale.

It was a fine August day when we pulled up in front of Gayle's house. I led the way through the side yard to the back. I pushed open the gate in a six-foot board fence and found myself gaping down the throat of a wide camera lens at point-blank range. "Shelley, what are your comments on becoming an aunt?" Tom asked inanely. I tried to step around him out of the camera's unblinking stare, but he tracked me at close range.

"It's not a new experience for me, Tom," I answered with a vinegary smile. "It's the baby that's new." I dodged him and put out my arms to receive the bundle in Gayle's arms. "How 'bout you Gayle," I asked. "How are you doing?"

"Oh I'm fine, Honey. Just fine." I felt a rare moment of kinship with her as our eyes met. Tenderly she laid my six-day-old niece, Chantal, in my arms. She was gorgeous. With a rounded forehead, snub nose and moist puckered lips, she slept with the carelessness of newborns, her miniature fists curled by her cheeks.

I eased into one of the unoccupied deck chairs in the circle where sat my parents, Tom's mother and Jamie. Ari and Sara hovered over me. "Oooh, she's so-o adorable!" Sara crooned, slipping her finger into the baby's curled palm.

"Would you like to hold her?"

"Could I?" she answered breathily. I gave her my chair. Sara emitted mewing sounds in her throat as I lay the baby in her lap.

Tom, by now, had turned his electronic eye on Ben, who stretched out on a chaise lounge. Ari sat squarely on his stomach. "Ben," Tom boomed, "how about a few words for this auspicious occasion."

Tom was one of those flukes of nature that defies Darwinian theory. One hundred million sperm and the one that spawned him managed to cross the finish line first. Ben had as much trouble taking him seriously as I did.

"Have you picked a nickname for the baby yet?" he asked Tom. "It's very important, you know; helps build character. Take my two here." He planted an index finger on Ari's nose. "This is Spot. When he was a baby, every time you held him on your lap, he'd leave a spot." Tom guffawed and Ari wiggled his bottom on his dad's stomach in retribution, making Ben groan.

"He seems to have gotten over that. Fang, now..." Sara's face turned red and taut. She handed the baby to Gayle and stiffly walked away. Ben's gaze followed her to the far end of the yard where she leaned against a tree, shoulders hunched.

Behind his camera, Tom hadn't seen her reaction. He sniggered and urged Ben to continue. Ben shrugged and grinned back toward the camera. "Fang got her name when she could stand up by holding onto furniture. She was really sweet at that age. One Sunday morning I was relaxing over the newspaper in my pyjamas, feet up on the coffee table. Sara made her halting way around the table. She patted my bare feet and smiled benignly at me. I smiled back and returned to my paper. She gurgled and babbled and patted me and then with no warning, sank her single tooth into my big toe." Tom howled. Everyone laughed. By the tree, Sara hunched her shoulders a notch higher.

Mother bustled over the picnic table, shuffling bowls around to add more platters to the already over-burdened surface. Sara hovered around the food like a humming bird.

"Come and get it," Gayle hollered. We swarmed the table, loading paper plates. Ben dropped his hand on Sara's shoulder just as she reached for a pitcher of clear red liquid.

"Sara, I don't want you to have that. We'll get you something else to drink."

"Awww. Why?" she whined.

"It has red dye." She wrenched her shoulder out from under his clasp.

"It's just Freshie," Mother sniffed. "A little bit can't hurt."

"She's allergic, Mrs. Gallagher," he replied. Sara left the line and took her plate off to a corner of the yard by herself.

After the meal, the children put in the obligatory hour's wait to go swimming. Ari and Jennie raced ahead and leapt in the deep end joined by Jamie, wading and sucking his stomach concave as the cool water reached his waist. Robbie hung back in the shallow end. I looked for Sara and spotted her at the picnic table, a tall glass of red drink tipped to her lips.

"Sa-ra!" I chided.

The eyes of all adults riveted on the pixie in the pink bathing suit. She took the glass away from her mouth, leaving a reddish tinge on her upper lip. "Nice day, isn't it," she quipped with a smug grin. This brought a peal of laughter from the circle of adults. But Ben shook his head straight-mouthed and looked away.

"What happens when Sara has something she's allergic to?" Gayle asked him after Sara splashed down in the pool.

"It aggravates her breathing. And her mood."

For a few minutes, the older three took turns stepping into Jamie's crossed hands and getting tossed backward in the water. I noticed though, that my brother took care to keep Robbie in his sight. After a few minutes of horseplay, he waded over to him, speaking in a low voice. I'd never observed this protective side of him before. To me, he'd always seemed impulsive and childlike himself. Something nagged at the edges of my memory that I couldn't quite place.

The shrieks and competition of jumps and dives from the springboard engrossed me for some minutes. When I looked back to the shallow end, Robbie was paddling valiantly toward his uncle, grunting with the effort, while Jamie quietly cheered him on.

It was then that the memory assailed me of another five-year-old boy, pale and still, in a coffin. Davy. He and Jamie had been best friends. They accompanied their mothers on a berry-picking excursion in the country. While the women gathered berries for canning, the boys wandered off exploring. Minutes after Davy's mother went to check on them, my mother heard her unearthly wail and tumbled headlong through brambles toward it. She broke out on the bank of a creek where it curved around a bend. The current had carved a deep hole there. Davy's mother was sodden, as was the dead child she rocked in her arms. Jamie stood transfixed on the shore, dry and silent. I knew all this from hearing the details told over and over again at the funeral home. Watching Jamie now with Robbie, I felt a new appreciation for him.

I didn't see Sara leave the pool. It wasn't till I heard Ben speak that I realized a scene was taking place by the picnic table. "You know the rules, Sara. No more swimming for now," He stood over her where she held a plate with a huge piece of chocolate cheesecake.

"You're always yelling at me," she wailed, half angry, half tearful. Ben's voice was low and I couldn't catch his reply but there was no mistaking hers, as she stalked into the house.

"It's not FAIR!"

In time, she re-appeared fully dressed and sat sulking under a tree, looking daggers at her father. She got up presently and moped around the pool deck watching the others with green-eyed envy. On the diving board, Jennie shouted at Ari to look her way and cannonballed two feet from him. He shrieked, then pulled himself out at the side of the pool. He walked purposefully toward the board past Sara. It happened so fast, my shout came too late. Ari screamed in pain. His shoulder blades protruded backward. Four livid red lines ran down the length of his back where Sara had raked her nails.

Ben flew up and leapt the fence in a bound. He scooped the boy up and sat on the bench, rocking and soothing him. Ari's back ran blood. Sara shrank away and skulked out of the yard.

"Maybe I should go after her," I murmured to Ben.

"Let her go. Don't give her attention for this." His fury and my own pumping adrenaline advised me not to pursue her.

———————

I wakened with a start. The red numbers on the clock beside the bed showed 2:42. Then I heard Sara cough again and realized what had roused me. A light went on down the hall. I heard the bathroom door close and she coughed again, the sound more muffled. I considered getting up, not that there was anything I could do. Most nights the children spent with us were like this. It was rare for Sara to sleep through the night.

Sometimes when her coughing was bad, Ben would go to her to try to ease her distress. Being a lighter sleeper than him however, I awakened more often and consequently the nighttime visits became part of my routine. I felt helpless though and ached for the wheezing child. I would rub her fevered back as she gasped for breath.

At night, Sara kept her puffer on her headboard. Ben and I knew she was overly dependent on it, using it more often than recommended. Talking to her did no good. We'd tried all sorts of strategies to manage her abuse of the drug. She always outwitted us, hiding and hoarding them.

The light went out down the hall and I heard her go back to her bedroom. I listened to hear if the coughing continued. It was sporadic, but not serious. Eventually the house grew quiet except for Ben's sonorous breathing.

I'd almost dropped off when I felt the blanket slowly lift on my side of the bed. A small body eased in beside me, still gasping slightly. My heart tugged for this feisty, sick little girl and I spooned around her slender form, stroking the damp hair back off her hot temple. *Why do you always have to swim upstream, Sara?* I thought, kissing her shoulder and hugging her close.

A pair of doves burst up with protesting chitters from the stubble of the mown field, startled by the streak of burnished copper. Shannon trotted in my general direction, her fringed banner waving behind her, jowls open in a smile. I wondered what she would have been like as a properly trained bird dog. This would have been working season.

It was not often that she looked this happy anymore. For twelve years we'd been together. Since getting her back from my folks a year ago last spring, we had both struggled to adjust to her fate as an 'outdoor' dog. I'd hoped she would revel in the freedom of fifteen acres of field and stream. But she kept to the porch. In cold weather, she retreated to her doghouse. Shannon was lonely.

I tipped my head back to gaze at the October sky. Soon enough the north wind would howl down the expanse of field along the escarpment. Several nights last January, the mercury dipped to thirty below with the wind screaming around the house. I wanted to bring Shannon in. Ben refused. We quarrelled. He was implacable; Sara had to breathe, he said. I wept while Shannon shivered in her thin coat.

The approach of another winter sickened me. These two years I'd been vacillating. Never sure I belonged with Ben, I incubated my dreams of Shangri-La and my mountains. If I went back, Shannon would go with me and be restored to her place by my side. But the right time to leave never came and Shannon just grew older.

"Here, girl." The setter lifted her head from the stubble, where she'd been zigzagging, following mouse trails no doubt. She bounded up to me. Kneeling, I took her head in my hands. One could drown in those limpid golden eyes. The face had grown grizzled. Silky ears fell over the backs of my hands. As a puppy, she'd have squirmed, eager to run and play. Now, she received my embrace with patience and dignity.

I stood and turned back to the house. At the garage I opened the door to the truck. "Get in, girl." She leapt handily into the passenger seat. Fifteen minutes later, I pulled into a parking lot and snapped a leash on her collar. Together we entered a low building. A young woman behind the counter looked up from her books. "Miss Gallagher?"

"Yes."

"Come right in." Shannon's claws clicked on the tile floor. "He'll just be a minute," the woman said, closing the door. A stainless steel table occupied the centre of the room.

"Sit, girl," I whispered. She obliged. A moment later a man with salt and pepper hair entered by a different door. He smiled kindly at me. I recognized him from previous appointments.

"Can you lift her onto the table?" he asked. I clasped Shannon's body around the chest and rump and hefted her sixty pounds onto the table. I expected her to struggle and try to jump down but she stayed put, shivering slightly.

"Let's get her lying down shall we," he said.

"Lie down, girl." This time I had to press lightly on her rump to get her to comply. I eased her front paws forward.

The doctor turned away to the counter. When he turned back, he held a syringe. A worm in my stomach writhed. I massaged the sides of Shannon's head while he turned back her fur and injected the serum. He put the earpieces of his stethoscope in his ears and bent forward to press the metal disk near her heart.

Seconds later those golden eyes closed. Her head became leaden in my hands. I eased it down on her paws and stroked her head, my throat aching. It was quiet in the room. The vet listened awhile longer, then looked up at me and nodded. I was still stroking her.

He let me out the back door to fetch the blanket I'd brought along; the brown blanket that had lined Shannon's bed for twelve years. He helped me wrap her in it and he carried the heavy burden to the truck. I held myself together until I pulled out of the parking lot, then disintegrated.

On the bank of the stream in the woods behind the house, fresh earth mounded among the trees. Like a silent movie, scene after scene of my gentle, comical companion wound past my unfocussed eyes. *Good night, puppy. No more cold and lonely nights for you.* Ben straightened, the spade resting upright in his grasp. With his other arm, he pulled me to his side. I pressed my damp cheek against the soft flannel of his shirt. It felt different from the silk of Shannon's coat, but comforting all the same.

February 1986

In vain, I tried to block out her voice but the malignant snipes dripped like beads of molten wax on my back. Through the open French doors, Mother's end of a phone conversation intruded on my visit with Dad. I hung over the back of his recliner as he slowly turned the glossy pages of a book across his lap. His veined hand tenderly smoothed each new page as if enjoying the polished feel.

The volume from the hallway rose a notch. Mother expelled her breath on certain words, hardening them in spasms. "That's *right*. She doesn't know a *thing* about it." It occurred to me that gossiping was her substitute for sex. She sounded like she was working up to orgasm. "I told her she had *no* business taking those home." Pause. "That's *right*." Pause. "They're for *everyone's* use." She was reaching a plateau, speaking in paroxysms.

Dad turned another page. "Oh now that's a nice one," he said. "What kind of bird lives in this house?"

"Purple Martins," I answered. "See, it shows you the male and female on the opposite page."

"They must be kings and queens to live in a palace like that."

I chuckled "No Dad. They're communal birds. They live in colonies."

"You think I could build something like this?"

"Of course you can. That's why I bought you this book. All the plans are at the back."

An abrupt hush in Mother's speech signalled that the topic had shifted to something either Dad or I wasn't supposed to hear. Dad seemed oblivious. I wondered for the gazillionth time whether he just pretended not to get it or if he'd long ago cloaked his mind in denial in order not to see how she treated him. This time the thought gave me a twinge. Was I like him, settling for "half a loaf" in staying with a man who didn't love me?

"Well Vera, I should get off the phone," Mom's pitch returned to normal. "My daughter's visiting. Brought Calvin his birthday present." Pause. "No, not yet, I'm afraid." A few wind up phrases and she hung up.

She bustled in and sat in a stiff-backed French Provincial imitation, her own back not touching it.

"That was Vera Hanlon. She asked after you, Shelley."

"Who's Vera Hanlon?"

"Well *you* know Vera. She's been a member of my quilters' guild for years." I gave a non-committal nod, bracing myself. Mother had that look of taut expectancy. Something, I sensed, was coming.

"Vera's daughter's getting married in May. They're having a big wedding out at Christchurch." She leaned forward a fraction. "When are you getting married, Shelley?"

I looked her in the teeth. "I'm not."

"Well!" she huffed. "Why not?"

"I don't want to, Mother."

She sniffed contemptuously. "I'll just bet he never proposed. I'll bet that's the truth of it."

My spine stiffened. "He has a name. It's Ben," I said icily. "And I have no interest in being married. I'm fine the way things are." I felt angry tears behind my eyes, tears I refused to let her see.

"He'll leave you high and dry, Shelley. Mark my words. He won't marry you because you're not one of his kind."

That sparked a flashpoint in my chest and a second later, in my head. Anger so hot it felt like lava boiled in both places. "His ex-wife wasn't Jewish either," I retorted though I knew that it wasn't strictly the truth. She'd converted to marry him.

"Well," she snorted, in a voice rich in self-righteousness, "He's not married to her now, is he."

I held my tongue till I felt reasonably sure no steam was escaping my nostrils, then I looked at my watch. "I have to go if I'm going to miss the rush hour traffic."

Pyrotechnics kept going off in my head as I drove toward the freeway. I wanted to believe it was just her bigotry that had fired me up. But in some dark recess of my mind I knew it went deeper. *He'll leave you high and dry, Shelley.* Having botched my attempts to learn about men years earlier, I had avoided exposing myself to life's possibilities of rejection—until Ben. I had loved with total abandon only that which couldn't reject me. My mountains, Shannon, and Shangri-La.

A sign in a strip plaza caught my eye. The wheel turned seemingly of its own accord and I found myself parked in front of Linda's Love Lace. I sat unmoving, staring at the mannequins in the window. I hated these places. Looking through racks of lingerie wasn't so bad, but inevitably one wall was always lined with plastic penises. They mortified me. *Thank God none of my feminist colleagues can see me now.* Mother's face, with its pinched mouth, floated before my eyes. I got out of the truck slamming the door and marched into the store.

Ben turned the key, pushed open the door to the five-star hotel suite and stood aside for me to enter. On a marble sideboard, champagne sat chilling on ice and someone had arranged roses in a crystal vase. I plucked the tiny white envelope pinned to them, finding my name written there. I withdrew and read the card inside. *My Treasured Valentine, You are becoming more precious to me with the passage of time—two years, two months and one day. Ben*

"How do you do this, Ben?"

"Do what?"

"Stage everything."

He took me in his arms, putting his forehead to mine. "I do it. Do you want me to stop?"

I bit my lower lip in a coquettish smile. "No."

"Then don't ask questions." He released me and poured champagne. I sipped from my glass, admiring the panorama of city lights from the window of our top-floor vantage-point. Ben arranged a cassette player on the sideboard and stretched out on the bed with his glass. Shortly, I shouldered my overnight bag and headed for the washroom. "I'm going to freshen up a bit."

The zipper on my suitcase purred as I pulled it. I withdrew several ivory coloured paper bags inscribed Linda's Love Lace and removed the contents, each wrapped with care, in tissue paper. They were all lustrous red, for the occasion. I fingered the textures, silky chemise, feather boa, satin over-the-elbow gloves, lacy garter belt. Feminist contraband, all.

I set them aside and began applying a heavier layer of eye shadow, mascara and blush. Satisfied with the look, I stripped to the skin and put on the red nothings. I smoothed a stocking up my leg and stretched the tops to hook into the stays, front and back. Red spiked five-inch heels lifted me to a new height and I wondered where else I would ever wear them. I gathered my hair into a red satin bow that let its fullness tumble down my neck. I shook my head, luxuriating in the sensation of my hair sweeping my back.

The fresh lipstick tube in my hand was about to touch my lips when a voice barked in my head. *You look like a tart!* My hand shook. The painted eyes in the mirror clouded in confusion and I set the lipstick back on the vanity.

As a child, I'd loved red. But Florence Gallagher had impressed on that child that it was the trademark of harlots and hussies. *Well Mother, I'm definitely a scarlet woman now.*

To distract myself, I read again the silver card bedecked with tiny raised hearts and I mouthed the words, *My Treasured Valentine.* Another voice, more intellectual but just as critical, chastened. *Shame on you! Trafficking in the sex trade that enslaves and degrades women.*

Shut up! The hussy in the mirror hissed back, her mouth pressed in a determined line. Calmer now, I picked up the tube on the vanity, raised the smooth red erection and stained my lips.

The room was in darkness when I opened the door. The only sounds that reached me were the strains of violins coming from the cassette player, then, the distinctive zip of a match. A flame blossomed across the room. Touching the wick of a taper on the dresser, it bloomed brighter, repeating itself in the mirror beyond. Almost holographic, Ben's image floated behind the reflected flame. The light caught his eyes as he looked up. His body tightened in response to the image he saw deeper in the mirror.

He turned toward my approach, his face in shadow. He slipped his arm around my waist, drawing me into a slow dance. His lips brushed my ear, then my neck where it curves into the shoulder. He went down on his knees pushing up the chemise to kiss my belly and I moaned. I sank my fingers in his hair; his hands slid down to find the exposed skin at the back of my thighs. As his mouth crept lower, I threw back my head; my eyes closed. I felt myself pressed back onto the bed. His tongue traced my skin along the panty line and a series of kitten-mews escaped me. Needy, hungry now, I reached for him and tore at the buttons of his shirt.

"Oh no, my little minx," he grinned with villainous satisfaction. "Not so fast." Pulling up the chemise, he took a nipple in his teeth. He began removing the slinky garments from my body. Reaching under me, he lifted my pelvis into his. He was utterly stiff. His own need overtook him then and he hurried to shuck out of his clothes. But when he was naked, I asserted myself.

"My turn now," I said with a vixen smile. I pressed my hand hard against his chest, pushing him onto his back. He protested and tried to sit up but I began planting a row of kisses down his torso till he surrendered in his own deeper groans. Then suddenly his hand clamped my wrist with strength not to be denied, pulling me to him. In a single motion, he rolled and flipped me onto my back. He was in so quickly it caught my breath. He came in a rush and my own convulsions followed.

The scent of roses and hot wax lingered in the darkened room. I lay awake, thinking without regret, of the swatches of red strewn haphazardly across the floor. What was it he said? "I'm trapped in a by-gone era. You can teach my brain to respect women as equals, Shelley, but other parts of my anatomy have ideas of their own."

A small miracle was unfolding on my belly. Resting there, his head rose and fell with my breathing. His own breathing deepened while the last vestiges of tension drained from his body and he slept.

Two hours north of Toronto, snow fell thickly. The weather report implied we'd encounter it all the way into Sudbury. Jamie invited us up to ski but the real reason for the trip was to meet his new girlfriend. I wondered aloud what she was like.

"I'll bet she boring," Ben answered."

"What makes you say *that*?"

"Didn't you say she's the loans officer in the bank where he set up his student loan? We accounting types, we're notorious bores."

"Right. You're so boring that you nod off in the arms of your *Treasured Valentine*." I quipped.

"I was NOT bored!"

He picked up my hand and brought my fingers to his lips. "I still can't believe I did that," he said softly.

"Next thing, you'll be saying you trust me or some crazy thing," I joked. But he didn't laugh.

"I still hard find it hard to believe I could trust *anybody* enough to really open up to them."

I squeezed his hand. "You know I wouldn't hurt you."

"I know."

"Then what's not to trust?" He shrugged. "You afraid I might leave?" He didn't answer. "It's been more than two years. If I haven't found anything by now to make me want to leave you, what are the chances?"

"Everybody has secrets."

"Do they?"

He shot a glance at me but his expression was guarded. "Well, maybe you're the exception."

"What secrets do *you* have?"

A long pause ensued. "Are you asking me to take a risk?"

Instinctively, I wanted to retreat. Something was about to happen. But I felt that if I pushed away this implied offer now, it might never come round again. "Will I hate you?"

"You might."

My heart pounded. I stared straight ahead and said in deliberate, measured words, "If your secret could blow us apart, then so be it. It's also keeping us from being fully together. Take the plunge, Benjamin. Let's see where we end up."

He let the air in his lungs escape slowly. "Well, you know the trips we've taken since you've been with me—Disneyland, British Columbia, Vegas—some of the frills, like last weekend at the Inn On The Park; the ring I bought you last December?" I nodded, afraid to speak. "The money came from my employer, Revenue Canada, but not exactly in a way that's kosher. I guess you could say I've been giving myself my own raise."

My eyes closed. I felt myself falling—falling. *Oh God. Ohgodohgodohgod.*

CHAPTER FIVE

Jamie hung up the phone and began pulling on his parka. "Who's coming with me to pick up the pizza?"

"I will," I said, glad for the chance to escape. At opposite ends of the sofa, Ben and Melanie chatted about investments. A sweet, soft cadence in her voice hinted at a giving nature, while her articulate grasp of finances signalled intelligence. In a cerise angora turtleneck and jeans, she sat sideways on the sofa, hugging her knees. Glistening chestnut hair framed chiseled cheekbones and brushed her shoulders. It was natural that those two would be talking money, both having careers in the financial world. But under the circumstances I found it torturous.

In the car, I leaned my head back on the headrest and closed my eyes, letting Jamie navigate the hills of Sudbury. It was dark and my body throbbed from the miles of ski trails we'd done that day. "The pizza won't be ready for twenty minutes," he said. "I'm gonna drive by the college to show you where I go to school."

I smiled. "You should be proud. I know you'll do well. You're a natural at cabinet making."

"You're the one who gave me the push I needed, Shel. I knew if you came back to Ontario, you'd get me on the right track."

"You got yourself on the right track, kiddo."

"I hope so. I don't want to screw up this time. Not with the course and not with Melanie. What do you think of her, anyway?"

"I like her," I said, meaning it. His chest swelled a little. "What's more important," I added, "is that you seem to really like her."

"She's special. Not like the rest. She's honest, y'know what I mean?"

"Yeah, I know what you mean." The sick feeling came back.

I heard him ramble on as if from a distance. "She'll be a big help to me in the financial planning department. I've always been over my head when it comes to finances."

"Take it slow, Jamie. Don't jump in with both feet. I know it seems like I did with Ben, but..." I stopped. What could I say? I had no advice.

"Don't worry, Sis. I told you, I'm not gonna to screw up. My priorities now are school and Melanie. And not necessarily in that order," he grinned.

The water drove over the edge of the falls creating enough power to illuminate southern Ontario and half of New York State. From my vantage point on the parapet, I stared at the place a few feet below me where the Niagara River takes its spectacular plunge. Mesmerizing in its constancy, it awakened in me an appreciation for how it pulled many a lost soul to a watery grave. It wasn't death's attraction though, that drew me to the border town this dismal afternoon, but the river itself.

I'd been a young girl when the story of a boating accident had broken. A boy in a boat swept over the falls and miraculously survived. He'd been wearing a life jacket. The incident made a lasting impression on me; was perhaps the source of my metaphorical philosophy of ethics.

Ben, what have you done? I could visualize how it had unfolded; could fathom his perverse logic. He chose work that used his penchant for sleuthing, yet gave him time to devote to his children. But Revenue Canada is not a rewarding employer. It exacts a drudging workhorse mentality. The disparity between salaries as a government auditor and accountants in business insulted Ben's creative genius.

Catching liars and cheaters for a living reinforced his early life perspective that people were basically untrustworthy. The rhetoric of wealthy public figures soured him in light of the tax department's knowledge that they were often the biggest cheaters. Yet the department left them alone to bilk the public while it subjected its own employees' tax returns to intensive scrutiny. What was there left to believe in? Rules were made for the naive and the powerless—other people, in Ben's ethical ledger.

Intellectually stifled and morally indignant, he dreamed of the perfect revenge. "At first it was a game," he told me. "I did it just to see if I could. It was how I coped with my frustration. Then I saw how lucrative it was."

He argued that it was a victimless crime. But I felt sick at my unwitting involvement. 'Living off the avails.' *Well I can't continue. But what am I to do? What's right? Turn him in? That's what Mother would do, self-appointed judge, jury and executioner. I can't do that. Maybe it is finally time for me to leave.*

But what of the children? Sara, with her acting up and Ari, so removed from his feelings, needed continuity. And quite simply, I loved them. On the other hand, I yearned for my mountains, felt bereft without them. The damp cold of the falls' winter mist chilled me to the bone. The plunging water thundered its imperative to decide. Still I vacillated.

Ben and I sat facing each other across the living room. The fire crackled, suggesting a coziness that defied the grim melancholy that hung between us. "Did you consider what would happen if you get caught?" I asked.

"They won't catch me."

"Every criminal can be caught. You're clever, but you're not infallible. And if you are caught, make no mistake, you *will* go to jail. What'll that do to your kids? Sara's already messed up and things with her aren't improving. If anything, she's getting worse. She lies. She manipulates. She steals from us. I don't mean to be cruel, Ben, but she's doing everything you've been doing." The arrow hit its mark. He looked heartsick. I shifted my gaze to the fire.

"Wait here," he said, getting up. He disappeared down the stairwell to the basement. In a few minutes, he emerged bearing a cardboard box, set it on the coffee table and left again. He returned momentarily with a second.

He opened the screen to the fireplace and began to toss the contents into the flames a little at a time. It was mostly paper and envelopes. He said nothing and did not look at me. It was a long time ago, but I remembered the boxes he'd told me to burn on the frozen pond when he had cancer. When they were empty, he turned to me.

"It's over," he said. "Those were the tools I needed to collect the money. I can't re-create them without leaving a paper trail that will lead them to me."

March 1987

The hammer tap-tapped. Then Ben handed it to me and picked up the framed print from the bed. I stepped back to the middle of the room as he eased it on the hook on the recently painted wall. "Straight?"

"Mmmm, the left is a trifle high. There, that's good." I set the hammer down and folded my arms, smiling.

He turned. "What are you grinning about?"

"I don't know, it's just that it's finally coming together. The house is starting to feel like a home." He unfolded my arms, tucking his own under them.

"Like *our* home. Come here." He took my wrist and pulled me toward the bed. "I want to talk to you." He propped himself on his elbow beside me where I lay on my back, the palm of his free hand tracing circles on my midriff.

"Shelley, go back to school. Get your Master's degree. If you apply now, you might get in this fall."

I frowned. "What brought this on?"

"You always said you wanted to get your Masters degree."

"Yes, but—"

"Then do it. Do it now. You could finish in a year or two. I'll support you while you go." My countenance must have shown reluctance. "Look, we both know you don't have a lot of business acumen. The investments I've suggested for you have done well and it's a nest egg for you. But it's not a fortune. If anything ever happened to me, you wouldn't be able to maintain the lifestyle we have on the salary you make now. I want you to be able to command what I know you're worth. To do that you'll need a graduate degree."

"And just what do you think is going to happen to you?" I challenged.

He arched an eyebrow. "Oh probably gunned down by a jealous husband."

"Yeah, right," I laughed. I reached behind his head and pulled his mouth down to mine.

Sara's exasperated voice from down the hall cut across my awareness. "Caitlyn! Pay attention. We'll never get through this chapter if you keep fooling around."

I pushed on Ben's shoulder, our mouths separating with the sound of suction cups coming apart. "Wait a minute," I said, sitting up and swinging my legs over the side of the bed. I put my forefinger to my lips and tiptoed down the hall. I stopped short of Sara's open bedroom door.

"Where'd you get this poster?" That was Caitlyn. "I want one. It's so-o cute."

"Shelley sent away for it for me."

The Kodak babies. The instant I'd seen the ad for the offer, I knew I had to get it for Sara. The poster of fifteen infants in pink, yellow and blue sleepers, propped up side by side on a sofa had been a hit. She and I scrutinized it on her wall many times, guessing at the babies' names and speculating what they were thinking and saying to each other.

"Come on, Caitlyn. What's the answer to number nine?" This was followed by such intense silence that I dared not move for fear the floor would creak and give me away.

Finally, Caitlyn spoke uncertainly. "X squared minus x?" There was silence again and I cocked my head, wishing I could see Sara's expression. She excelled in math. In fact, she excelled in everything at school—except art and physical education. Caitlyn, on the other hand, had a flair for modern dance, gymnastics and drama. But she came to Sara to tutor her in her academics.

I ventured to the door and peeked in. Leaning against the headboard with a text on her lap, Sara noted my appearance with a quick movement of her eyes. She then went back to peering sternly at Caitlyn over her glasses. Caitlyn hunched cross-legged on the bed, her chin poised on her forefinger. "I don't know. I just don't get algebra."

Sara's shoulders lifted in a silent sigh. "Okay Caitlyn, I'll go over it again. You've got to get this, you know. It's sure to be on your exam."

"How's it going, girls?" I interrupted.

"Okay," Sara said, but with a trace of despair.

"Oh hi," Caitlyn enthused. "Where'd you get the neat baby poster? I *want* one."

"It was a special offer. You have write to Kodak to request it." I knew she never would. "When do you expect your Mom to come for you?"

"Soon, I hope. My *brain* needs a rest." I chuckled. No guile there. Perhaps it was the contrast in their characters that bonded these two together, kind of like Ben and me.

"I understand," I agreed. "Algebra wasn't my cup of tea either. Well, have fun." I waved and retraced my steps.

"So?" Ben said when I lay back down beside him.

"Poor Sara. She looks shagged out from trying to get anything to go into Caitlyn's head."

"Never mind about Caitlyn's schooling. It's yours I'm interested in."

I thought for a moment. "It's true I want to get my Master's. But now? Coordinating my own family violence treatment program is what I always wanted. The agency's not going to give me a leave of absence so soon after hiring me." I'd designed the program, secured the funding and negotiated with the agency to house it. "Besides, it's close to home. No more commuting. I don't want to quit."

"Just think about it, okay?" he finished.

I agreed to look into it.

As it turned out, after some exploring, I found a Master's program designed for people who continue working while they studied. My boss was accommodating and willing to allow me to work a flexible schedule. I submitted my application.

Sulphur singed my nostrils as Ben struck a match. The wick of a candle caught. "Baruch ata Adonai" his deep voice intoned in Hebrew. The Shabbes ritual normally performed by a Jewish wife fell by default to him. The second candle flowered. He held the flame in front of Ari, whose turn it was to blow it out, a Volski ritual. We had scarcely sat down when Sara spoke.

"Daddy, can we go to the mall tonight?"

"Whose 'we'?"

"Me. I mean will you take me."

Ben turned to his son and asked with a trace of sarcasm, "Ari, you want to go to the mall?" Ari shrugged, indifferent.

"Daddy," Sara whined. "I need a three-ring binder."

"For what?"

"For *school*."

"I see." He shot me a questioning look. *Am I getting conned again?* I, too, shrugged.

"All right, I guess so," he said. "Maybe we'll all go and get an ice cream."

"I need nail polish, too," she announced.

"I can accept that you need a binder for school but how does one *need* nail polish?"

"DADDY! My recital is on Saturday. Everybody will be looking at my hands when I play my harp."

"They will care about what your fingers do, Sara, not the way they look." She pouted, slouching in her chair. "All right," he conceded, "we'll get you nail polish, too."

She leaned forward. "Can I get my allowance?"

"Your allowance isn't due until Thursday."

"I'll pay you back."

Ben scowled. "What do you want it for?"

"There's a special on at the mall. It only costs eight dollars to get your ears pierced?"

"Absolutely not."

Her spine stiffened ready for battle. "Why?" she protested, jutting out her chin.

"You're *not* getting your ears pierced. I don't approve of that in someone your age."

"Caitlyn has her ears pierced."

"Caitlyn isn't my daughter."

"You *NEVER* let me have *ANYTHING*!" She lunged up and bolted from the room.

He turned to Ari. "Well, I don't see why *we* shouldn't still have some ice cream." I got up to clear the table, Sara's scream still ringing in my ears.

A while later as I scrubbed the few things that wouldn't go in the dishwasher, headlights turning in the lane caught my attention. "Ben," I called, "someone's coming down the drive." He went to the front entrance and turned on the outside lights. I recognized Margaret's car.

I heard the front door open and close. Ben emerged into my line of vision. Margaret met him at the end of the walk. Suddenly the front door opened again and slammed. Sara ran out. She had her coat and book bag. She hovered by them. Ben hunched his shoulders and stuffed his hands in his pockets, perhaps against the cold. Beside him, Margaret looked small. She never looked directly at him. Her arm fluttered in nervous little gestures as she talked. Sara got into her car. Ben pulled his hands from his pockets and began waving them around. Margaret's lips moved occasionally but she still didn't look up at him. She looked off into space or at his chest or, I thought, tracked his hands.

He must have cranked up the volume, because now I could hear his voice, though the words were still inarticulate to me. The oval of Sara's face in the open passenger window was pale and somber. One of her parent's must have spoken to her because she shook her head. It had to be Margaret; Ben's mouth was clamped shut, his jaw set.

Sara shook her head again, this time more fiercely. I couldn't tell at this distance and in this light, but it looked as though she might be crying. Then the car door opened and Sara stormed past them, shrugging off her mother's hand that went to her shoulder. The front door opened again and slammed with a vengeance. There was thumping down the hall, then another door slammed.

A minute later, Margaret got in her car and pulled away. Ben walked toward the front door. I wondered where Ari was. I dried my hands and turned to Ben where he leaned in the kitchen doorway. "What was that all about?" I asked.

He sighed and muttered something but all I caught was 'bitch'.

I went to him and put my arms around his waist. "Who are you mad at?"

"Pff" he exploded "If it's not one female it's another."

"Me?" I teased, pretty sure I was immune. He put his hand to the side of my head and threaded his fingers through my hair.

"No, not you," he said softening. I cocked my head inviting him to explain. He snorted again dropping his hand. "Sara. She can't get what she wants so she sneaks off and phones her mother, telling wild tales about how mean I'm being to her. Margaret storms up here thinking Sara's getting murdered. Why the hell couldn't she just call me? Why does she have to rush to Sara's rescue? It encourages her and undermines me."

"What did you tell Margaret?"

"I told her what happened."

"Did she believe you?"

"Hell, I don't know. I guess so."

"Who told Sara she had to stay here."

"I didn't want her leaving. I don't want her to think these little tricks will work and she won't have to deal with me."

"Did Margaret agree?"

"She would have gone either way. But she cooperated, this time."

I studied his face. "Ben, have you ever hit Margaret?"

"No!" He stared wide-eyed at me. "Where did *that* come from?"

"She looks afraid of you."

"I've never hit anyone, not since I was a kid anyway. You should know by now that I'm not violent."

"I didn't think so. But you can be scary. You're big and when you're angry you convey the impression that people better not mess with you."

"Well, it's true! But I don't hit."

"Are you going to talk to Sara?"

"What's the point?" he said sourly.

"Tell her what you expect."

"No! Leave her here while we go for ice cream. She'll get the point."

"What *point*, Ben? That you hold all the cards, that you have the power to punish? *Talk* to her. Tell her how you feel; find out how she feels."

"No. I don't want to be in the same room with her till I calm down. I'm taking Ari out. You gonna come?" I studied him. He wasn't going to budge.

"Not a chance," I said. "The house might be burned to the ground in our absence. You go. I'll stay and hold the fort."

––––––––––––––––

I picked up my messages from the front office. Agnes, on the phone, waved me to wait. "Hang on, Terri, let me ask her," she said, pushing the 'Hold' button. "It's Terri Moffat. She's in a bad way. She wants to know if it's possible to see you."

"Now?" I asked, glancing at my watch. It was almost quitting time.

"I know," she said, reading my mind. "But she's crying so hard I could hardly understand her."

"Crying? That's a first. I better see her."

Terri Moffat was a leggy blonde, with huge fawn eyes. At twenty-six she might have been at the height of her modelling career if she hadn't quit after marrying fashion mogul, Jarrod Moffat. She was one of my first clients from general counselling after I'd agreed to take on some non-domestic violence cases.

Her problem, she'd explained, was that she was having trouble "keeping up appearances anymore." She couldn't get out of bed in the morning and once she did rise, she went about with a black cloud over her. Recently, she became so profoundly anxious in social situations that she would hyperventilate. Twice she'd fled unceremoniously; once from a dinner party with friends and once from a fashion show her husband was hosting.

I had taken some history both recent and childhood, alert for typical themes: grief, abuse, conflicted relationships, psychiatric problems. I had unearthed nothing remarkable other than the fact that she'd been adopted at birth by a childless couple. When I wondered aloud if her depression might have a biological component, she'd reacted with a vehement protest. She would *not* see a doctor, was not about to let anyone prescribe medication for her.

It was just five when Terri arrived. As soon as she sat down in my office, she burst into sobs. I waited for the storm to blow out, noting the blotchy redness of her face. When her tears abated a little, I asked what had happened.

"We were supposed to go this big affair tonight in Toronto at the Royal York. Jarrod's trying to secure a contract with this sponsor. He expects me to attend these things to, you know, make a good impression. I'm supposed to chat people up, be charming and glamorous, make him look successful." Her voice trailed off.

"Go on."

"He was counting on me, bought me a gown for the occasion. But I just couldn't face going. I told him I was sick but he saw through my fib. I don't blame him for being so furious. I really let him down."

"What did he do?"

"He yelled. He was so disappointed in me, but I made things worse, becoming hysterical and begging him not to make me go."

"Is that when he hit you?"

She shot an incredulous look at me. "How...how did you know?"

"The mark on your face."

Her hand went to her cheek. She hung her head as if she'd done something wrong. "He's never hit me before."

"But he's hit you now." She sat frozen, staring into her lap. "What happened to your arm?" She lifted her hand and turned it palm up and examined the small bruises I'd noticed when she'd been dabbing her eyes with a tissue.

"He grabbed my wrist to pull me out of bed. I told him he was hurting me but he just squeezed tighter. He was so *angry*."

"Where is he now?"

"He went to the banquet. That's when I called you. I needed to talk to someone."

"I'm glad you called. It's not your fault Jarrod hit you. He was wrong."

"But he was upset."

"Then he can talk to you about his feelings. To hit you or grab you like that is assault; a crime."

She stared at me, wide-eyed. "But surely he has a right to expect me to help promote his work?"

I hesitated, unsure about how much confrontation she was ready for. "When you say Jarrod expects you to make a good impression for him, make him look successful, isn't he using your looks and sexuality to sort of seduce his customers?" The anguished look told me I'd struck a chord.

"It's true," she whispered, "sometimes I feel like a prostitute."
"And when you wouldn't do what he wanted, he hit you."
"What am I to do?"
"What do you want to do?"
"I don't know."
I nodded. "You'll figure out what you want in time. Let's talk about what you can do in the meantime to be safe."

The roar of the vacuum drowned out the sounds of my entrance. Ben was pushing it around the living room when he noticed me and shut it off. "Hi," he said. "Rough day at work?"
"Mm. Somebody in crisis. You got my message that I'd be late?"
"Yeah. Dinner's in the oven."
I grabbed him in a heartfelt hug. "I thank my lucky stars for you."
"What brought this on?"
"You remind me that there are men in this world who are not abusers. Some days, I really need to remember that." I laid my head against his chest, closing my eyes, and murmured, "I love you."
"I love you too."
My head snapped back as if zapped by electricity. "I thought I'd never hear you say those words." I expected him to disappear behind his clown face. But he didn't. "Would you it say again?"
"I love you, Shelley."

From my perch on the roof's apex I admired the assurance in my brother as he worked. You could tell to watch him that this was *his* house he was building, the squared shoulders, purpose in his movements. Ben was a mere assistant. Applying shingles, their hammers pounded out an ascending musical scale, driving home nail after nail into timber.
The lot sloped down to the Nottawasaga River drifting by, wide and shallow. Ari waded up to his knees. Sara leaned against a stately willow on the bank, a book resting in her lap. Facing her, cross-legged on the grass, sat Melanie. Her soft soprano floated up to the rooftop accompanied by an occasional giggle from Sara. Affection welled inside me for my petite new sister-in-law. Afraid that Jamie would again sabotage his relationship with a woman, I hadn't permitted myself to grow attached to her until the wedding. When they bought this acre lot here near Angus, halfway between their respective childhood homes, I felt a new optimism. Maybe my brother was finally growing up. Watching Melanie with Sara I thought, *she'll make a good mother.* Fatherhood will season Jamie too. He'll adore his own children.

"We're low on nails," he announced. "We could use a few other supplies too. I'm going to have to run in to Barrie." We climbed down from the roof. "Need anything in town, Hon," he asked Melanie.

"Would you pick up something for dessert."

"Okay." He bent to kiss her lips and invited Sara and Ari to come along. Ben took advantage of the quiet to grab a siesta in the construction trailer while Melanie and I lay back in the shade on lounge chairs and talked.

When Jamie's van returned, Ari climbed out with a small paper bag in hand and wandered over munching jujubes. Sara slipped away to the tent-trailer she and Ari had set up as their sleeping quarters. She hugged her satchel under her arm.

"Did Jamie buy you the treats, Ari?" I asked as he wiggled into my lap.

"Uh uhn. Sara."

"That was generous of her. What's the occasion?" He shrugged and held a green jujube to my lips. I opened my mouth. He popped it in then held out the bag to Melanie.

Shadows were lengthening across the yard when Ben climbed down from the roof and came over to where I was tossing a salad on the picnic table. A piece of paper blew across his path and he stooped to pick it up. It was a chocolate bar wrapper. "Sara seems to have quite a stash of candy," he said. "I've watched her reach into her bag when she thinks I'm not looking. Jamie says she bought a load of junk at the store. He asked her if it was okay with me and she said yes. But she never asked me. Did she ask you?"

I shook my head. "She bought for Ari too."

"It's not like her to part with her money or her candy," Ben said. He wheeled around and climbed into the construction trailer where I'd set up sleeping quarters for the two of us. He emerged a moment later. "I was afraid of that," he said. "A twenty dollar bill is missing from my wallet." A heavy silence hung between us as he stood clenching his hands by his sides.

"Maybe you should talk to her, say what you suspect."

"I don't know. Jesus, it never ends. I'm tired of fighting with her. She slept poorly last night too," he added. "Between that and the junk food, she's going to make herself sick."

"You could take it away from her."

"And invite World War III? No thanks. She's almost thirteen. She's got to start taking responsibility for her health. As for the money, there's no point in asking her. She never owns up to her crimes."

By suppertime, Sara was wheezing heavily. By dark, her cough grew persistent. I bedded the kids down early in the tent trailer. Before I left, Sara threw up. I helped her clean up and tucked her in, hoping rest would help.

"Damn!" Ben swore. He rooted around the overnight bag by the light of the kerosene lantern on the picnic table.

"What is it?" I asked.

"The little devil must have got hold of the spare puffer I packed, too. Why can't she just ask for it when she runs out? I wouldn't withhold medication from her, for Pete's sake."

I pulled him down on the bench beside me. "It wouldn't be nearly as much fun for her to ask," I humoured him. "Don't lose your perspective, Ben. Even if she acts like you're the enemy, you've gotta remember that you're not."

It was murky when I roused. I wasn't sure at first, why I had awakened. Then I heard it again, a dry hacking cough, weak and distant. I strained my ears. There... again. I swung my feet over the edge of the bed. The floor was cold. I found my clothes and put them on. I slipped into running shoes without socks and tiptoed out of the construction trailer into the grey dawn.

The zipper of the tent trailer as I tugged on it rent the early morning stillness. Sara sat hunched in the tangle of blankets on her bed, fighting for breath. She coughed incessantly. I sat behind her and rubbed her back. Her body burned; her shoulders heaved.

"Sara, how long have you been awake?"

She sucked at the air like a fish, once, twice, three times. "All night."

All night! I looked at my watch but couldn't see the hands. "Come on, Kiddo. Let's get you outside. Maybe fresh air will help." She didn't respond. I tugged her nightgown over her head and pulled on her jersey. She was like a rag doll, passively accepting the help to put on jeans, socks and shoes. I dragged her to her feet and something fell to the floor. A puffer. I picked it up and shook it. *Empty.* In a sudden inspiration, I lifted her pillow. A second puffer lay there, also empty. *Oh God, a whole puffer in a few hours!*

I climbed out of the tent trailer first and lifted Sara to the ground. She staggered and sagged against me. I swept a damp lock of hair from her forehead. Her eyes were glazed, her face grey. I helped her to the nearby car and half pushed, half lifted her into the back seat. "Wait here, Honey. I'll be right back."

Ben came awake with a violent start when I touched him through the blankets. "Huh? What is it?"

"Sara's sick, really sick. You have to take her to a hospital."

He leapt up, galvanized. "What time is it?" he asked reaching for his pants.

"I don't know. I'll wake Jamie. He'll take you. He'll know where the hospital is."

The van's engine seemed obscenely loud in the dawn. In the back seat, Sara looked so slender in Ben's arms, like a limp stork. I slid the door on its rollers and slammed it shut. The red taillights as Jamie pulled away, made me think of an ambulance. I whispered a silent prayer as they disappeared in the mist, and looked again at my watch. Four twenty.

CHAPTER SIX

"I want to go H-O-O-OME!" Sara's vocal chords strained. I hunched my shoulder around my ears against the penetrating scream.

Ben sounded absurdly patient and reasonable by contrast. "Sara, Mommy is still away. I've been trying to reach her ever since we got home."

"I don't CARE! I can stay by myself."

"No. I can't allow that. Not when you just spent the night in a hospital." Wailing, heavy footfalls, a door slamming, muffled wailing, a few thumps of something hitting a wall. I peered out the kitchen door to survey the war zone. Both combatants had withdrawn. I scouted for Ben and found him standing in the middle of our bedroom, breathing heavily. "God, she tries me," he exclaimed. "I know I shouldn't say this," he addressed the wall, "but I can understand why some parents lambaste their kids."

I pressed my lips together in an effort not to smile. He noticed.

"Come on, Shelley. Just once, let me indulge in a little child abuse, huh? Just one good one."

"Now, Ben, that won't improve relations."

"No. But one of us will feel better."

He began unbuttoning his shirt. "For real, I'm going to read in bed. Maybe that will help restore my sweet, loveable disposition."

"I'll join you after I see that Ari is down for the night."

Domestic tranquility seemed to have returned. I snuggled deeper under the covers beside Ben, each with our own book. Down the hall, a door opened. Bare feet stomped toward us. I stiffened and felt Ben do the same. The bedroom door flung open and Sara strode in hauling a wastebasket. She dumped the contents on the foot of the bed and stalked out slamming the door behind her.

For a moment, we stared at the pile of postage stamp-sized bits of paper. I crawled toward it and picked up a couple of pieces. "Oh Ben, it's the Kodak babies."

This was my favourite place, in the shade of the latticed porch Jamie had helped us build last fall. Leaning on the railing, I could peer into a small reflecting pool, the centrepiece of my spring landscaping project. Goldfish darted to and fro in aimless loops and circles. But for once, the patter from the miniature waterfall didn't buoy my spirits. I'd just said goodbye to the best friend I'd made since leaving my mountains.

Daphne had spent the afternoon. "I'm nervous about moving to Italy when things are so rocky between me and Eddie," she'd said. "But when his father called and said he couldn't manage on his own anymore, I saw something in Eddie's eyes I've never seen before. He's always felt that his father disapproved of him. I think it's what made him so defiant. He'll be taking over the family business, but I don't think that's his motivation. I think he saw a chance to finally get close to his dad."

I told her about starting grad school next week and I confided in her about Sara. As I recounted some of Sara's escapades, Daphne chuckled in that easy way of hers. "She's what, thirteen now?"

"In three weeks."

"Puberty's the worst. Sometimes you think you just won't survive it. Robin was my nemesis last year. Did that girl have a temper? Lord! She just couldn't verbalize her feelings, but now at fourteen, the hormones seem to have settled down and she's more able to talk things out."

"It's true. Sara can't seem to say what's on her mind either. That's why I chose the birthday present for her that I did." I disappeared inside to retrieve it.

She took it from me. "The Judy Blume diary!" she exclaimed.

"Blume is Sara's favourite author."

I sat with it now in my lap, smoothing the cover as I watched the dust billow behind Daphne's retreating car. When she disappeared from sight, I looked down at the rainbow coloured cover. That should be a hit too; Sara loves rainbows.

February 1988

Ben massaged the back of my neck as I stood at the sink cleaning the frying pan from brunch. He swept aside my hair and kissed the place where my neck curved into my shoulder. I shivered. "Mmm, that feels nice."

"I won't be long," he murmured. "How convenient that Sara wants to go home to practice harp for the kid's recital tonight. I'd sure like to spend the afternoon in bed with my Valentine."

As he walked away to round up the kids and get his coat, I gave him a meaningful look. "Hurry back."

I noticed Sara slip down the stairs to the basement, thinking that was curious. She came up just as he came round the corner in his coat. She hefted a ski boot in each hand.

"What are you doing with those?" he asked.

"They're too small for me."

"Yes, I know, but what are you doing with them?"

She glowered at his chest, refusing to look him in the eye. "Mommy is taking the old stuff to the ski swap."

Ben's voice turned grave. "Sara, you know the drill. Your mother and I alternate. Whoever took you to Snowbird last upgrades your equipment if you need it and gets to sell the old stuff. *I* took you last year." Her face was a black scowl. "I'll be selling the old equipment. The boots stay here."

She whipped her head back to glare at him. "You *said* I could have them."

He paused. I wondered if it were to bridle his temper or do a reality check. Her claim was a bald-faced lie. "No, Sara. I did not."

I heard her exhale, sensed the volcanic explosion. Boots hurtled down the stairs. "You LIE!" she screamed. "You're always picking on me. I hate you! I'm not coming back here, ever. E-V-E-RRR!" She shoved past him, stomping. The back door slammed.

Ben's eyes as he turned to meet mine were shot with pain. Neither of us spoke. He turned and walked away. A moment later, I was alone in the house.

I draped the tea towel, still in my hands, over the stove handle and went to Sara's room. Standing in the doorway, I felt an emptiness wash over me, emptiness reflected in the room. There was nothing left to suggest that Sara lived here one-third of her life. I never actually saw her remove anything, but over a period of months, her room had been striped of every article and possession that identified it as her space. *I'm not coming back here, ever. EVER!* I shivered. It was no impulsive threat; Sara had planned this exodus. I never got to say goodbye.

April 1988

I was exhausted. I'd slaved till nearly 3:00 a.m. on a paper for school. From inside my warm cocoon, I heard Ben leave for work, the back door close. Heard his car drone past the bedroom window, fade and evaporate in the cool, spring morning. Hungry for another twenty minutes' sleep before it was my turn to get up, I burrowed deeper into the blankets drifting toward oblivion once more. Almost there, something dragged at me. Something... sounds. I resisted them but they probed, prodded. A car's engine again, the back door, voices. Voices? Footsteps in the hall, in the bedroom.

"Shelley, you have to wake up." Ben's voice was ragged, shaky. "Police are here." I struggled to open my eyes. "They have a search warrant."

Like silk collapsing over a lifeless parachutist, a deadly stillness settled over me.

"There's a female officer here," he nodded toward the bedroom door. "She says she has to remain with you." Then he was gone and a stout woman in uniform stared down at me.

Heavy boots sounded down the hall on the parquet floor. Self-conscious, I got out of bed and reached for my robe. Wrapping it around me, I squeezed past her and padded down the hall. She followed me.

The house swarmed with towering men in plain clothes. One or two glanced at me mutely. Another snapped photographs here, there and everywhere in our house... OUR house.

One, smaller than the rest, dressed in a trench coat, approached me and thrust a badge under my nose. "I'm Corporal Parker of the R.C.M.P." He repeated what Ben had said, that they had a search warrant.

Parker's words, spoken softly and sounding polite, carried a funereal sobriety. He was barely taller than me, with a baby face; I couldn't help notice his gorgeous long eye lashes. But his eyes were steely blue and I imagined his stare could pin a living butterfly to an exhibit mat. He said I was not required to stay but I had no intention of leaving. I called Agnes at the office and concocted an excuse for being delayed.

Men clumped up and down the basement stairs, lugging boxes and pawing through them. In the den, one scrambled up onto the file cabinet in the closet and disappeared through the opening into the rafters. I thought irrelevantly, *I've never even been up there.* Only the female officer stood idle. But wherever I went, she dogged my heels like a shadow. Rankled, I retreated to the bedroom to put on clothes but she followed me there too and coldly watched me dress.

When I returned to the dining room, Parker had claimed Ben's customary place at the table, while Ben sat on the edge of a chair at the table's corner. Parker addressed him. "It is my duty to inform you that you have a right to retain and instruct counsel without delay. You need not say anything. Anything you do say may be used as evidence." Ben looked up and locked eyes with me. Parker finished his speech and went back to directing the search, ignoring us.

Ben whispered to me, "Come outside."

The gravel of the driveway crunched underfoot. We ambled away from the house. He hunched his shoulders, his eyes downcast.

I trembled as if in the grip of hypothermia. "Did he charge you?"

"Yes."

"With?"

"Fraud and breach of trust."

"Are you under arrest now?" I asked.

"No. I'm on my own recognizance to appear at the station in a day or so, to be fingerprinted and photographed."

I moaned, unable to know what to say.

"I know. Listen, you might as well go to work. There's nothing for you to do here. This will take hours." He sounded spaced out.

"I think I should stay with you."

"I'll be all right. You go."

"Will you be here when I get home?"

"It's Thursday. I have to pick up Ari."

When I came out to the garage to leave, I encountered Parker rooting through containers, tools and junk. I opened the truck door to climb in. He took a step toward me. "Where are you going?"

"I'm going to work," I answered tersely.

"Then I need to search your purse and vehicle."

"Very well." I deposited my purse on the hood of the truck and stepped back with arms folded while he went through both thoroughly. He let me go.

Agnes barely looked up from her typing when I came in. I grabbed my messages, fled to my office and closed the door. I sat down heavily, dropping my forehead to the desk. Through the walls, I could hear the sounds of a typical day; the tap-tapping of Agnes' typewriter keys, a muffled conversation in the next room. Somewhere a phone rang. I had just experienced an earthquake, yet life carried on around me. I sat up. My eyes fell on the poster I kept on my wall, the Vancouver skyline. I groaned and let my head fall to the desk again.

Ari greeted me when I came through the back door with his familiar cheery "Hello" and a hug. In the kitchen, Ben prepared dinner. The house betrayed no sign that an army of police officers had ransacked it earlier. After dinner, Ben set Ari to playing games on my computer. Returning to the kitchen where I was cleaning up, he said, "Leave that, come outside."

We meandered down the driveway again, he with his hands stuffed in his pockets, neither of us speaking. Finally, he broke the silence.

"I guess you'll be leaving now."

His quiet statement stunned me, stopped me in my tracks. I whirled toward him. His face was a mask of hollow resignation. Speechless for the moment, I just stared.

"I'm not going anywhere." I said finding my voice at last.

His eyes failed to register my meaning.

"I knew when you first told me about this, that it could come to this. I would have left you right after you told me, if you'd carried on. But you stopped."

Something seemed to drain from him then. He reached for me and held me tight. When at last he released me, we wandered aimlessly, like lost souls. "What happened after I left?" I asked.

"They removed several items, a set of typewriter balls, a couple of unregistered guns... a handgun and an Uzi."

"A handg... an Uzi!" I echoed, stunned, "Why did you have them?"

"To tell the truth, I'd forgotten them. I've had them since long before I was married, even before I knew you. I kept them in a trunk. When I separated from Margaret, I moved it without even opening it."

"But why?" I repeated. "What did you want them for?"

"When the Six Day War broke out between Israel and Egypt, I planned to join the Israeli army. I thought they'd be happy to take a Jew who had guns and knew how to use them. But before I could get on a plane the whole thing was over."

I shook my head, trying to dispel this new shock. "I'm always learning something new about you."

"It was a long time ago. I guess I'm not very good at housecleaning. Like those two boxes I burned..." He looked at me with miserable eyes. "I thought I'd gotten rid of everything. I had two sets of typewriter balls; one for normal use and the other for... well, for the other. The police took the set I kept for normal use. They didn't find the other, and they won't now. I got rid of them after they left."

I wondered if they were at the bottom of the pond but I didn't ask.

"I always kept them separate. I think."

"What do you mean, you think!"

"Well..." he grimaced. "It gets worse. They have my fingerprints on a postal box application form." The crime was beginning to take shape in my mind. I wished he wouldn't tell me so much. What I didn't know, I couldn't be asked to repeat.

———————————

A little while later, I bent over Ari's bed in the dim light from the hall and kissed his forehead. "Good night Ari."

"Good night."

In the living room, Ben sat on the sofa, elbows on his knees. I sat beside him. He looked like he could cry—needed to cry.

"Well, I guess my job is gone," he said, not looking up.

"I guess it is."

"I can't believe you're still here."

"You haven't done anything to me. We'll get through this."

"I'm going to need a lawyer." A knowing look passed between us. "Guess I'm gonna have to tell to my brother."

"Martin will refer you to a good criminal lawyer."

"If he doesn't disown me," he sighed. "My job, my friends, my children, will there be anything left after this is over?"

He sank toward me and lay his head in my lap. "I'm glad Parker took the guns."

I stroked his hair and shivered inside.

The red neon numbers on the clock radio showed two twenty a.m. The rise and fall in Ben's breathing confirmed that he had at last drifted off. Thursday morning seemed a lifetime ago.

When I'd started school I adjusted my schedule to give me Fridays off to study. So I was home when Ben left for his office, knowing full well he faced certain suspension. I imagined him walking across the open office pool to his desk before the silent, intruding eyes of co-workers. I hugged him to give him courage and waited for his return. It took less than an hour. "Thank God my father's not around to see this," was all he said.

Only outside did we discuss things, paranoid that the police may have bugged the house, the phone, the vehicles.

"If I plead guilty and make full restitution," he ventured, "maybe I'll just get a fine and probation." I was dubious, but dared not destroy his hope. I thought of the gun the police had failed to remove, stuffed in the back of the closet, an ancient double-barrelled shotgun. Ben kept shells, I knew, to drive away starlings that try to roost in the chimney. I didn't like guns and he never brought it out when I was around. I wondered where he kept the shells. Asking him now would be too obvious.

The evening dragged by seemingly endless, with neither of us able to turn our minds or hands to distractions. We went to bed and lay close, but sleep refused to come. I watched the numbers on the bedside clock flip over to three a.m.

It scared me to leave him alone for the day, but I had to go to work. I called from the office. Twice. The deadness in his voice played havoc with my heartbeat. The hours stretched like a rubber band, my body pulled taut with it. Time and space were viscous, sucking my limbs in a slow-motion race. *Don't do anything rash, Ben. Don't go to the closet.*

The hands of the wall clock dragged around its face, labouring its way to five o'clock. Tentacles clung to me, holding me back, a phone call, an interruption, the very room clutching at my clothes. *Oh, hurry!* In my mind's eye, I saw a shell, red plastic and scuffed brass, thumbed into a chamber. And a second shell. *No, Ben! Wait. I'm coming.*

I gunned the truck out of the parking lot, terror shooting through me turning my arms to lead on the wheel. Taillights glared red. Traffic snarled in a Gordian knot. Down a side street I streaked, nearly ramming a moving van that breached the road. My tires screamed in reverse. I could swear I heard a shotgun blast rip through my head. Finally...finally I reached home.

Silence choked a darkened garage. My heart thudded like a gong. "Ben!" My cry echoed through the house. "BE-E-EN!" Heart-stopping silence.

I crept down the hall, heart hammering my sternum. A stench rolled from the bedroom. My fingers felt for the switch; I forced myself to look. Something black and liquid congealed on the floor. No, not black... *Oh God, it's blood!* A hand...limp...

I jerked upright in bed, gasping for air. Sweat beaded on my forehead. My eyes probed the blackness. Red numbers on the clock radio showed four oh six. I strained my ears. *There!* Ben's slow, rhythmic breathing. *Dear God, he's safe! It was a dream.*

Terri's call came Monday morning. She wasn't due for her appointment till Wednesday.

"Would be possible to see you today, Shelley."

"What's up, Terri?"

"I'm in the shelter."

"What happened?"

"He beat me up—really bad this time. He just went nuts. I got away from him and locked myself in the bedroom. He kicked the door in and hung up the phone after I dialled 911. But they called right back. When he realized the police were going to come, he settled down.

"I was so scared to call the police, but they were great. This one officer was *so* nice. He brought me here and kept saying I did the right thing and I shouldn't have to put up with this. He was just so nice," she repeated.

I told her to come right away. While I waited, I reviewed my case notes, made over the eleven months I'd been seeing her. For the first four or five months my recording was peppered with phrases like, "Extremely guarded" and "vague in her answers to my questions". Eventually, she admitted that she was lying to her husband about seeing a social worker. "He thinks I'm seeing a psychiatrist. He figures the problems are all in my head and that I should be on medication. I haven't told him I quit taking the drugs long ago."

By the time she revealed this, Terri was beginning to acknowledge the many ways in which Jarrod controlled and belittled her. Her agoraphobia diminished. She re-established contact with friends and told Jarrod she was not willing to act as his trophy. But progress was not smooth. He reacted to her newfound assertiveness with contempt. An entry in the winter recorded an escalation in the conflict; "Today Terri reported a serious incident. Stated that her husband wanted her to fly with him on short notice to a business meeting in Montreal. When she refused, he became enraged, yelling, throwing and smashing things and finally hitting the wall by her head with his fist. She was badly frightened by the incident and gave in to his wishes."

For the next several months, I witnessed Terri's body manifest the contest of wills. She lost nineteen pounds. Anorexia, she acknowledged had plagued her since adolescence.

I thought she'd sounded remarkably composed on the telephone, determined, even. But the jittery creature that paced the waiting room was anything but composed. In my office she perched on the edge of the chair, her hands fluttering like butterflies. Her left cheekbone sported a black bruise the size of a baseball. Blood shot through the white of her eye. The right side of her jaw exhibited another bruise, the size and colour of a ripe plum. She rolled up her sleeves to show more marks on her upper arms. She even pulled up her skirt to reveal a huge blackened area on her leg, near her hip.

"He wanted sex," she explained. "When I said no, he got nasty, calling me frigid and neurotic. He asked if I'd told my psychiatrist about my sexual hang-ups, if I was taking my medication. I said I didn't need drugs, just to be treated respectfully. His insults became more vicious. I kept calm, but that seemed to infuriate him. He started to hit me and this time he just didn't stop." She hunched over her hands, clenched in her lap, rocking slightly. "Shelley, if someone called here and asked about me, would anyone tell them anything?"

"Not without your signed consent."

"That's what I thought."

"Are you worried Jarrod may try to track you down?"

"Not Jarrod. My father."

"Your... father?"

"Jarrod called him, thinking I might have gone there. My father knew enough to call the local shelter. The staff didn't let on I was there of course, but they told me he called. I called him back. He told me Jarrod said that I've been more temperamental than usual lately and nobody knows what he has to put up with. Jarrod made it sound like I attacked *him* and then called the police. He complained that the police always take the woman's side."

"Did your father believe Jarrod's version?"

"Kind of. My parents have always considered me to be mentally unbalanced. Jarrod picked up on that very quickly. In the early days of our marriage, he would make teasing remarks to my parents about his 'dizzy little wife' and how 'cute' I was when I would get agitated. My parents sympathized and Dad would laugh along with him.

"I never told them how he treats me or that he hits me. They thought he was such a good catch, someone to take care of crazy little Terri. This morning when I told Dad how severely Jarrod beat me, he was shocked but he still thinks Jarrod just lost control because he was at the end of his rope with me. Dad wanted me to just go home, kiss and make up. When I told him I wasn't about to go home, he wanted me to come to stay with him and Mom."

"Do you want to?"

"I don't know," she moaned in a decidedly ambivalent tone. "I don't want to alienate him."

"At the moment you're safe in the shelter. Whether you go to your parents or not neither Jarrod nor your father will get information from here." I assured her again.

Terri's sigh had a despairing sound. "My father is a powerful man. He has a lot of influence, connections. He can find out anything he wants to."

"What makes him so powerful?"

"He's a Criminal Court judge."

"Judge!" I echoed stupidly. My mind short-circuited to Ben. What if he appeared before my client's father? How was I ever going keep my private life and professional life separate once his case hit the public arena? A shadow would most certainly be cast upon my own ethics. What would happen to my career?

"Yes." Terri went on. "Judge Gordon Stone. I'm sure he's mortified that his son-in-law is going to appear in a courtroom in his jurisdiction."

Right! In Halton County. Thank God! Ben will be tried in Hamilton court. Come on Shelley, get a grip. Focus on your client.

"You're under a lot of pressure from your parents in regard to Jarrod. What do *you* want to do?"

"I'm not going to let them talk me into going back to him," she said with conviction. "That's for sure."

———————

A pair of Canada geese coasted overhead, honking and descending toward a field of stubble on the neighbouring farm. Standing on the bank that sloped to the pond behind the house, Ben and I followed their progress.

"So you want steps down to the pond," he said, shifting his gaze to the dozen or so feet of slope below us. It wasn't a pretty pond, brackish with a clay bottom, but I loved it for the wildlife it attracted; herons, muskrat, deer and a monster turtle. "It would make it easier on me to fetch water for my flowers," I said.

"Okay. It'll give me something to do. Where do you want them?"

"I don't want to talk about steps," I said irritably. "I want to know what happened with your brother today."

Ben tossed a stone into the water. It made a thunk and sent ripples out in ever widening circles. "Martin took it better than I expected. Told me that when this is all over, he's going to kick my butt. Guess that's better than telling me to get the hell out of his office—or cutting his clothing."

I envisioned the scene he must have feared. Ben had taught me about the Jewish custom; slashing the fabric of one's clothing to signify the loss of a family member, usually due to death, but sometimes to disown someone, as if they had died. "Did he recommend a criminal lawyer?"

"Yes. I have an appointment for Wednesday."

I sighed. Wednesday seemed so far off.

"Shelley?"

"Mm hmm."

"Martin says this thing carries a maximum of ten years."

A trap door opened beneath me. I couldn't look at him. No one could be the same after ten years in a penitentiary. I knew lots about prison, had worked inside them, looked into the eyes of lifers. Ten years, six, even three or four would destroy everything I loved in Ben.

"They won't give you the maximum," I said, as much to reassure myself as him. "Not if you plead guilty, make restitution."

"He thinks they'll make an example of me. The 'breach of trust' charge complicates things. Being a government employee will go hard for me."

I stood up suddenly, not wanting to think about it. "Let's wait to see what the lawyer says on Wednesday." I held out my hand. He took it and let me lead him into the house down the hall to the bedroom. I needed to lie next to him, absorb his scent, close and real.

The moment I turned into our lane, I spotted the contractor's blue pick-up. Late last fall he'd erected a barn for us that sheltered the tractor and other farm equipment. Behind the house, Ben conversed with him. I parked and exchanged greetings as he headed to his truck to leave. "What's up?" I asked Ben.

"He's ready to pour the floor, but the ground slopes a lot to one end of the barn. I told him I'd take care of it, move some dirt from another part of the property."

"How? You don't have a shovel for the tractor."

"Spade and wheelbarrow."

"That's nuts! It's tons of earth and ours is hardpan. You'll break your back."

"I've nothing else to do." He kicked the dirt despondently.

I sighed and shook my head. "Never mind. Tell me about the lawyer."

"His name is Adam Ginsberg."

"Yes?"

He paused as if reluctant to elucidate. "He told me if I plan to plead guilty to find another lawyer."

"Why?"

"Ginsberg doesn't come cheap. He says I'd be wasting my money on him." I waited for the other shoe to fall. "Whether I plead guilty or I'm convicted in a trial, it's jail either way. With a record, I'll have trouble finding work in the field for which I'm educated. I might not be able to cross the border, to Snowbird, for instance. The state has to *prove* their case. Shelley, he made me re-think this thing. He suggested that I at least wait to see what they've got for evidence. The forensics might not turn up anything. If they don't, there might not be a strong case against me. I could beat this thing."

My stomach pitched. *You did it Ben,* I wanted to say. *You're guilty. You got caught. Why can't you take your lumps?* And then, *What the hell am I supposed to tell people?* Tears smarted my eyes, but I blinked them away. I needed strength now, not tears.

He took me by the shoulders and peered intently at me. I didn't want to meet his eyes, but he waited till I did. "I know what this must mean to you, keeping quiet, keeping secrets. But I stand to lose so much. I have this one chance. It's not just for me; it's for my kids. If I can't work, I can't support them. I have to try."

A raging current was sweeping me along to who-knew-where? Convictions. Following them had always seemed so simple. But now? What was right? I believed in the system. A person *did* have the right to a trial; that's how it worked. I looked away and nodded.

———————

My intercom buzzed. My client wasn't due for another ten minutes. "Yes, Agnes."

"A man in the waiting room is asking for you."

"Did he give his name?"

"No. But he said you were expecting him."

"My next client is a woman. Ask him... Never mind, I'll come out."

The waiting room at nine minutes to two was half full with clients waiting for their session. A man in a trench coat stood in the middle of the room, holding a brief case. With a shock I realized I was face to face with Corporal Parker. A quiet fury ignited inside me. *How dare he come here!* I couldn't ask him what he wanted in front of all these people. To get rid of him, I'd have to take him into my office. I recognized the female officer who had invaded my bedroom that morning too. Coolly, I signalled Parker to follow me. The woman came too.

I didn't wait for them to sit down. Closing the door, I demanded, "What do you want?"

"I'd like to interview you," he said in a dulcet voice. Under other circumstances, I would have found him attractive. I remembered him being small but now he seemed to take up so much space in my office.

"I'm afraid I have a client in a few minutes."

"I will only take a few minutes of your time."

I wavered. Though I didn't want to give him an interview, I also didn't want to appear hostile or that I had anything to hide. "Very well, but I must stop when my client comes." I sat at my desk, not inviting them to sit down. They did anyway.

"I would like to tape the interview," he said, pulling a recorder from his briefcase.

"I don't know about that."

"It's just to help me make accurate notes."

I hesitated. "I think I should be speaking with a lawyer," I said, feeling my temple start to throb.

"You do not need a lawyer. You are not a suspect." He spoke very precisely while he continued to set up the audiotape. I didn't want to be taped. I wished I could talk to a lawyer. "May I turn on the recorder?"

His voice sounded so polite, genteel almost. Seconds ticked by. I shrugged helplessly. "I suppose."

He pressed the 'On' button.

"Ms. Gallagher," he addressed me formally, "did Ben Volski explain to you what this is all about."

"Not specifically."

"He is suspected of filing income tax returns under false names. Do you know if he has any postal box numbers?"

"Yes, one."

"Do you know the number?"

I gave it.

"Any others?"

"No." So far, so good, I thought. From the corner of my eye, I observed the female officer, resenting her additional presence.

"Did he open any postal boxes under assumed names?"

"Not that I know of."

"I'm going to read you some names of people. I want you to tell me if you have ever heard any of these names."

He said a man's name. I shook my head.

"Please, Ms. Gallagher, can you speak, for the tape recorder."

"I don't know that name." He said another. "No." Then three women's names. The last was another man. I didn't know any of them.

He took a blank writing pad from his briefcase and put it near me on my desk. "I would like you to give me a sample of your handwriting."

"Why?"

"There is some indication that two people were involved. I need samples of your handwriting to eliminate you as a suspect."

I could feel my blood pulsing through my ears and chest. I tried to keep my hands from trembling. "You said I wasn't a suspect. Now you're saying I am."

"Not actually, no. We have no indication that you were involved."

"Then why do you need my handwriting?" I glowered at him. He maintained his quiet, soft-spoken demeanour.

"We are just checking out every possibility."

"It sounds like I need a lawyer."

"No Ma'am."

"Look, Corporal Parker, I've done nothing wrong. I don't mean to give you a hard time but I think my rights are being violated."

"I can assure you that you do not need a lawyer. You are not under suspicion. It would be helpful if you would provide me with these samples so I can prove that you have done nothing wrong. This will clear you."

What a load of bull, I thought.

I glanced at the clock. It was already twenty past the hour. Was my client in the waiting room? Maybe Agnes thought she should not buzz in, knowing I had someone in my office.

"I'm late for my client, Corporal."

"I don't need anything more from you. If you just give me the samples, we can be finished."

My handwriting could not harm me *or* Ben. But it made me boil to be bullied like this. "Very well," I snapped.

He placed the list of names he had read beside the writing pad. "Write each, five times." My pen scratched across the paper for the next couple of minutes. I wondered if these names belonged to real people or were fictitious. I handed Parker the pad. He had turned off the tape recorder while I wrote and returned it to his briefcase.

"Is that all," I asked.

"For now."

I stood up. I didn't offer to show him the way out.

———————————

Ben told me I needn't take time off work to attend court with him.

It was only to set a date for trial. He seemed grateful however when I insisted that I accompany him all the same.

A misty rain accentuated the grimy appearance of downtown Hamilton. Ben parked across the street from the Provincial Court, an ugly, antiquated building that appeared to be constructed of a hodgepodge of leftover materials. He held an umbrella over me till we got to the door. My pumps clicked on the terrazzo floor. "I don't see Adam. Let's wait here." He motioned to an unoccupied place on the crude benches lining the walls.

"I'm going to the washroom," I said. When I returned he was talking with a small bearded man in an expensive looking grey suit, toting a briefcase. Ben broke off in mid-sentence and introduced me to his lawyer.

Intense blue-grey eyes looked squarely into mine, on the same level, as Ginsberg extended his hand. He nodded, as if approving of me. "Hello, Shelley. Ben speaks highly of you. I'm glad to meet you and to see that you have come with him today. Your support for him will be important." I liked him immediately and couldn't help thinking that he reminded me of a mature grey squirrel.

"Adam wants a few minutes in a private room to talk before we go inside," Ben said. "Do you want to come along?"

I looked questioningly at the lawyer. "Perhaps," he interjected, immediately seeming to grasp my question, "you might wish to sit out while Ben and I discuss matters directly pertaining to the case. You may also have some questions, however, and if Ben has no objections to you joining us in a few minutes, I would be happy to include you."

"I think that would be best," I agreed, relieved. As it turned out, there was not time for me to join them before Ben's case was called. Less than five minutes after we entered the courtroom, we exited again. The police forensics were not complete yet. The Crown requested the matter be set over to another time to set a date for trial.

Adam shepherded us back across the now crowded corridor into a closet-sized interview room. He immediately turned his attention to me.

"Shelley, I have explained to Ben that it is important that he try to find work, any work. While it is my job to defend him, if he *is* convicted, it will help his situation if he can demonstrate that he is gainfully employed and meeting his financial responsibilities. That includes supporting his two children."

"I understand."

"It is also important that Ben keep up his spirits. These will not be easy times for either of you. From what he has told me already, I understand that you have been very generous in your support for him. He is going to continue to need it." I nodded, feeling complimented by this grey squirrel of a man. "Ben told me that Corporal Parker paid a visit to you at your place of employment."

"Yes. I was upset that he showed up there. I had no warning. Obviously, I don't want to have to be explaining to anyone at work why the police are there to talk to me."

"I can appreciate that. Do you mind telling me about his conversation with you?" I recounted everything I could remember. Ginsberg listened intently, without interrupting. When I finished, he said, "You were correct in believing that you were not required to give samples of your handwriting. You are under no obligation to speak with him."

The tines of the garden fork penetrated barely three inches of baked clay. I strained to turn the clod over, then stooped to shake loose the weeds, tossing them into a wheelbarrow. The labor felt good. The earth was a worthy opponent; a target for the tension I had held in check all week.

The first report had come from one of Ben's closest friends. Corporal Parker had contacted and interviewed him. Then another friend related a similar encounter. Still wary of talking on the phone from home, Ben limited his questions and explanations. By the end of the week, he learned of two more acquaintances who had been approached.

Each report added another stone to the invisible burden he appeared to carry. I watched helplessly as he sagged under the strain. This morning, he left early for Toronto to link up with a few friends to find out what Parker was talking with them about.

The sun blazed unusually hot for this early in the year. I drew my sleeve across my beaded forehead. My back ached. When I straightened, arching at the waist to relieve the tension, I noticed Ben's car turn into the lane. Leaving the fork in the earth, I retreated to a patch of shade on a grassy berm beside the house.

Minutes later, he emerged through the patio door bearing two tall glasses of lemonade. "Thanks," I said, gratefully accepting one. We sat not speaking, sipping lemonade. When he drained his glass he set it aside.

"I'm glad you're with me," he said at last.

"What about your friends? Are they still with you?"

"So far—no thanks to Parker. He seems to be doing his level best to alienate my friends from me. He told them what I was charged with. Well, okay, so what? But he also told them I was suspected of a lot more. Is he bluffing, I wonder, hoping it will get back to me and make me say something stupid? Maybe he's trying to put pressure on me by trying to undermine my friendships, or maybe he just can't resist embellishing a story to pump up his own ego. I know you don't like me to tell you details, Shelley, but listen to this. He told one person that I was suspected of filing up to a thousand false income tax files. A thousand!"

I smirked. "You're a regular workaholic, aren't you."

He snorted. "No kidding."

"What is he asking them?" I asked. "No wait! Don't tell me. I don't want to know."

The sound of tires on gravel caught our attention. A van rolled down the lane toward us. "Oh crap," I blurted. "It's Jamie and Melanie. I'm not ready for this! Not to deal with my family."

The van turned into the circular drive in front of the house. Grinning broadly, Jamie leapt down and bounded toward me, swooping me into a great hug. "Hi, Sis! It's been ages since I last saw you."

When he let me go, Melanie embraced me warmly though more gently. "I told Jamie, I thought we should call first but..."

"Come on Mel, she's family. What's she gonna do? Tell Ben to throw the bum out? She's glad to see me. You're glad to see me, aren't you Shelley."

"Sure, Jamie," I said, hooking my arm through his and rolling my eyes at Melanie, "I'm glad to see you. Both of you."

Ben asked, "Did you two make a special trip or were you in the neighbourhood?"

"I guess you could say we were in the neighbourhood," Jamie answered. He gazed at his wife and an intimate smile passed between them.

Melanie elaborated, "We spent a lovely weekend in Niagara-on-the-Lake."

Jamie put his arm around her and kissed her temple. "The real reason we came by," he said, "is that we wanted to share our news with you." He paused dramatically and grinned. "Melanie's pregnant."

———————————

Ben invited Jamie to inspect his work on the steps to the pond. Melanie wanted to take advantage of the chance to buy fresh eggs from our neighbour, a farmer older than God. She and I strolled along the country road.

"I'm glad to have a few minutes alone with you," she said. "There's something I wanted to ask you. To ask your advice."

"If it's anything to do with having babies," I observed, "you've come to the wrong person. Try Gayle."

"No. It's you I want to talk to." She sounded solemn. "I know *you* see the good in Jamie." I caught her oblique reference to how critical other family members could be of him. "I'm hoping you can give me some ideas on how to talk to him. Or rather to get him to talk to me."

I felt a sinking sensation in my stomach. *Jamie, don't screw up now. You're a husband. You're going to be a father.* "What's happening, Mel?"

"I don't know if you know that Jamie bought a backhoe in March in partnership with a fellow in our neighbourhood."

"No, I hadn't heard."

"Well, his idea was that it would be a good sideline to his carpentry. They would hire themselves out to do private work. The other guy has experience operating this kind of equipment and would do most of the jobs. And Jamie could do it part time when he isn't working at his full time job."

"Okay."

"Jamie's a hard worker, but," She hesitated.

"Go on."

"He's not so strong on thinking things through. He's an ideas person, not a facts and figures person."

"That's why you're good for him."

"I know, but he has to talk to me if we're going to work together."

I groaned. "Don't tell me; let me guess. He didn't discuss this plan with you. He bought in and told you later."

She didn't answer. I looked over and caught a glistening in her eyes. I took her by the elbow. "Come here," I said, steering her to a boulder nudged against an ancient maple at the roadside. We sat. "Is his enterprise a bad idea?" I asked.

"The *idea* isn't bad but I'm worried. For one thing, he doesn't know the other guy that well and I strongly suspect the man has a drinking problem. He was out of work most of last year. I think he may have been fired from his job. I think he talked Jamie into this, convincing him they would make tons of money."

"Did Jamie put up a lot of money?"

"I don't know."

"You don't know?" I echoed.

She looked embarrassed, and anxious. "I can't get a straight answer out of him. Every time I try to talk to him, he jumps all over the place. He'll make a joke or get silly...like a little kid. If I persist, he says, '*Trust me, don't worry, I know what I'm doing*'. If I keep pushing, he just puts up a solid wall. He got mad a time or two, raised his voice and told me not to hassle him. I don't want to fight with him and I don't want to nag, so I back off."

I sighed gazing into the distance. Sheep grazed in a field across the road; black lambs shadowed woolly white ewes.

"He so wants to be a success. He wants to please you, Melanie."

"I *know* he does. Those times he got angry, I got the feeling that he was scared, afraid I'll challenge or criticize him. I don't want to put him down; I just want to plan and decide things *with* him. I wish he would trust me."

"He has a hard time trusting that women won't put him down. I guess you know the origin of *that* fear." She remained silent but I knew she knew. "Did he know about the baby coming when he got involved in this venture?"

"No. It was very shortly afterward that we found out. Actually the pregnancy is sort of an accident. We're a statistic; the birth control failed. We both want children of course but we intended to wait a while, to be more financially secure. Jamie argues it's all the more reason to have extra money coming in. I hope it works out that way, but I'm worried?"

I suddenly felt very weary. *Problems. Everybody expects me to help them with their problems. If you only knew. I don't even know how to solve my own.* I regarded my sister-in-law sympathetically. "He needs to learn to communicate with you, Mel, if he's going to make your relationship work. I think you're right, that he's scared. Let him know it's safe to talk to you and don't relax your expectations that he do so. That's all I can suggest. If you don't get anywhere, get counselling."

The office intercom intruded on my efforts to write a synopsis of the previous hour's counselling session. Distractedly, I picked up the phone. "Yes, Agnes."

"There's a police officer here asking to speak with you. Are you free?" I jerked, nearly dropping the receiver.

"Did he tell you his name?"

I could hear muffled voices over the wire. Then, "Constable Sparks," she said. *Sparks? Does she mean Parker? Corporal Parker? Lord, what now?*

"Shelley? Are you still there?"

"Yes, Agnes, I'll come out."

Rounding the corner to the waiting room, I confronted a young officer in uniform. He shuffled from one foot to the other, turning his cap in circles with both hands. He stood over me, blond, slender and athletic. The insignia on his shoulder said Halton Regional Police. *Not RCMP.*

He rushed toward me extending his hand. "Miss Gallagher?"

"Yes."

"I'm Constable Brad Sparks. Would it be possible to speak with you for a few minutes?"

Eyeing him guardedly, I scrambled for a clue to his agenda. "Is it about a client?"

"Oh. Here," he offered, pulling a folded piece of paper from his pocket. "I'm supposed to give you this."

I took it. *To the attention of Shelley Gallagher: This is my permission for Brad Sparks to speak with you about me.* It was signed, Terri Moffat. I relaxed. "Ah, you're the officer who took Terri to the shelter in April. I've heard nice things about you." He lowered his head, tipping forward on his toes like he was checking his boots. "Come in," I said, leading the way.

When we sat down, I gestured with my hand inviting him to speak.

"When Ms. Moffat went to stay with her parents after we charged her husband, I thought that would be helpful. Now I'm not so sure. She's in the hospital," he said. "I took her there this morning." My consternation must have showed. "I've kept in touch with her," he explained, "to be sure her husband wasn't bothering her. A lot of these guys harass the shit out of their wives so the women will try to get the charges against them dropped."

"I know," I said.

He laughed and looked embarrassed. "Yeah, I guess you *would* know. Anyway, I hope she doesn't give in and go back to this jerk, pardon my language. Several times I called around at the house; her mother always answered the door. She would say Terri wasn't there, or was busy or sleeping. I suspected she might not be giving Terri the message. I stopped by again today. Her mother answered again and told me Terri was ill but Terri herself called from another room asking who was at the door and then came out. I'll grant you, she didn't look well, but if she hadn't been right there, I don't think her mother would've told her I'd come. I couldn't help but notice how wary she seemed around her mother, too. I thought the only way I was going to be able to have a candid conversation with her would be away from there, so I asked her out for coffee. She seemed eager to come along."

The officer leaned forward on his knees. His sidearm, flashlight and other leather-encased items seemed bulky around his trim waist. He twirled his cap. The bunching of his shoulders betrayed emotion. I found myself as absorbed in him as in the news he brought of my client.

"Her parents have been urging her to patch things up with her husband. I don't think they appreciate how badly he beat her up. She levelled with me about the anorexia too. She's hardly eaten in weeks. I tried to get her to eat something at the donut shop but she wouldn't. I 'spose that's not very healthy food anyway. When we got up to leave, she pitched forward in a faint, would have fallen down if I hadn't caught her. When I left her at the hospital, she asked me to let her parents know, and you too."

At the door, when I ushered him out, he said, "I hope you can help her, Ms. Gallagher. She's a good person."

The doorbell sounded. I opened one eye and checked the clock radio. Six-forty-five a.m. I nudged Ben, still sleeping soundly. "Ben someone's at the door."

He staggered out, wrapping his robe around him. Soon he returned to the bedroom. "Guess who?" he said, with a lightness that sounded forced.

"Who?"

"The gendarme. They have another warrant. They're here to search again."

"Oh Lord," I groaned. "This is iniquitous!"

He shrugged, turning his palms up.

In a repeat performance, the same female officer from before entered the bedroom as Ben left. "Yeah, yeah, I know," I cut her off when she started to speak. "I don't need to hear it again." I proceeded to get dressed, ignoring her as best I could, given that I had to walk around her to assemble my clothes.

The now familiar routine was underway when I came down the hall. Men prowled the entire house. Parker greeted me with his familiar somber expression. I ignored him too.

Deciding to act as if a police search was an everyday occurrence, I wandered into the kitchen to get some breakfast. As soon as I opened the fridge Parker hustled in from the dining room. "You are not to break that seal," he ordered, motioning to the fridge. That's when I saw that the freezer compartment above the fridge was taped shut.

We sat side by side on the new steps to the pond. "Why are they back, Ben?"

"Damned if I know."

"Do you think they're on a fishing expedition?"

"I was wondering the same thing," he said.

"To get a warrant, don't they have to convince a JP that they'll find evidence for their case?"

"I think that's how it works," he replied. He picked up a stick and tossed it testily into the water. "I wonder if they're just trying to piss me off."

"Is it working?"

"It's beginning to."

I caught sight of movement out of the corner of my eye. "Watch what you say," I cautioned. "One of them is prowling around up there." An officer in a white shirt and tie skulked through the long grass behind the barn. We watched him zigzag through the field, scanning around, looking down at the ground. "He's looking for something."

"I bet I know what," Ben said.

I looked at him. "What?"

"Marijuana plants."

"Marijuana plants! Why?"

"They found some stuff."

"What *stuff*?" I exclaimed, my eyes bulging.

He sighed. "It's just garbage," he muttered. "Scraps from plants. Marijuana plants. A buddy of mine processed it here, ages ago. What's left is the part you don't smoke. They found it in a green garbage bag in the basement, covered with dust. I didn't know it was still there."

"Holy crap, Ben." He gave me a glum look. "What about the seal on the freezer? Are there drugs there?"

"Yeah, a joint or two wrapped in foil way at the back. Didn't you ever notice."

"Excuse me, but I don't smoke; I wasn't exactly looking," I retorted. "Anyway, I wouldn't know what I was looking at." A fresh anxiety gnawed at my stomach.

"I forgot about them. I can't remember when I last smoked up."

I wanted to yell, lecture, scold him but he would be punished enough. *Is this why they came back? Surely they saw this stuff the first time. Maybe they weren't interested then. But if they didn't care then and do now, maybe that means they don't have much of a case against Ben. Maybe, maybe, maybe.* I kept my thoughts to myself. "I might as well go to work," I said wearily.

I went back inside to retrieve my purse from the bedroom. Two officers occupied the room, one sitting at my desk, the other on the end of our bed. On the floor by his feet, I noticed a metal file box in which I kept documents, letters and other personal information. Horrified, I saw that he was leafing through my journal. No one had ever trespassed the sacred ground of my private journal writings. I flushed with rage and humiliation.

Looking more closely now at what the officer at my desk was doing, I realized he was perusing letters belonging to me, some written by Ben when I still lived in British Columbia. He had a stack he had set aside. Sticking out from the bottom of the pile, I noticed the corners of a couple of photographs. Tipping my head to decipher what they were, I could make out a bare shoulder and arm. Mine. *Oh man, not those pictures! What can they possibly have to do with the charges against Ben? Lecherous bastards! Damn Ben and his penchant for titillating snapshots.* I hurried out; it was too much to take. In the garage, Parker was rooting around, just as he had been during the first search when I'd been ready to leave.

"What are you doing?" he queried as I opened the truck door.

"I still have a job," I snapped. "I'm going to work."

"Someone will be coming to your office to talk to you."
I went rigid. "No," I growled. "I will not see anyone at my office."
"Then maybe you should stay here."
"Why?"
"Because you may be arrested."

CHAPTER SEVEN

My knees went weak. "What for!"

"I can't tell you but I don't think you should leave. There will be other police arriving soon." In a shocked haze, I lurched back into the house in search of Ben.

They arrived in a blue and white cruiser, Halton Regional Police, two men and a woman. In stark contrast to the R.C.M.P. in their suits and ties, the trio in long hair, flowered shirts and ragged jeans reminded me of the bad TV series, The Mod Squad. Ben let them in but Parker whisked them away into the kitchen. After a hasty consultation, the three clumped down the basement stairs after Parker.

In a few minutes they were back up. The Mod Squad grouped in the foyer by the front door. Parker and his men retreated to the living room conferring at close quarters. Ben and I stood in between surveying both groups. One member of the drug squad seemed to be griping to his colleagues. His two partners didn't look any happier. I took a step or two closer and strained to hear.

"Jesus Christ! They drag us out here for this piss-ant stuff. Damned anal retentive Mounties!" This one turned to us and asked us to follow him into the den. The second male officer trailed behind us and closed the door. The first fellow sat in Ben's desk chair, leaning back in a casual, easy posture. The other one perched sideways on a bookcase, with similar nonchalant body language. Even in this respect they distinguished themselves from the stiff and proper mannerisms of the Corporal and his men.

"You guys seem a little unhappy about being here," Ben said affably.

"Yeah," the one in the chair flashed a friendly smile. "We were out on a case until five a.m. I just collapsed into bed when the damn phone rings and we've got to come out here for this piddly stuff." He tossed a plastic bag with two joints on the desk.

"I can assure you," Ben grinned, "it wasn't my idea to call you."

The guy on the bookcase laughed. His partner continued. "Look, it's obvious that the stuff in the bag downstairs has been there a while but it does indicate movement of drugs. We have to establish who owns it."

123

Ben did not hesitate. "The joints are mine," he said. "Shelley has nothing to do with it."

"Fair enough. If you're claiming ownership, we will have to charge you. I do have to go through the procedures, though." He faced me. "You are under arrest." After reading my rights he said, "Do you own these drugs?"

"No." Then he turned back to Ben and repeated the procedure and Ben confessed again. Then he formally charged Ben with possession of an illegal drug.

"I'm also charging you with trafficking marijuana."

"I deny that charge," Ben said simply.

Trafficking! I thought I would faint.

"I'm going to have to ask you to come with us to the station for fingerprinting and photographing." Ben shrugged and said nothing.

They left in a mass exodus, the drug squad taking Ben and putting him in the back of their cruiser. The R.C.M.P. carried a couple more boxes of booty, my journals and the photographs among them. They climbed into four or five cars and drove off.

Silence and devastation collided. Feeling lost and defiled, I did what I heard so often in my office that violated women instinctively do. I cleaned. I scrubbed and swept and scoured.

———

My job involved participating in a regional task force on domestic violence to develop protocols between the justice system and support services for victims. Quite apart from the mess in my personal life, I dreaded the monthly meetings chaired by the Halton Chief of Police for other reasons. In the criminal justice system and in the police department in particular, attitudes about wife assault remained highly patriarchal and condescending.

Two of my best allies on the task force were absent today. The Chief took advantage of their absence and brought forward a motion to disband the committee. "We've accomplished our aims. There's no reason to continue meeting."

"A protocol on paper isn't enough," I protested. "We need to ensure it's working."

He bristled. "Miss Gallagher, our officers receive the finest training. Every case is monitored. The system in the police department is *flawless*. Wouldn't you agree?" he turned to the two flunkies he frequently brought with him. They nodded their allegiance.

"I'm not criticizing, Murray," I stated levelly. "It's just that some people are still falling through the cracks. I hear their stories in my office."

He harrumphed. "If you know of any situation you think is not being handled properly by my officers, you may speak to me directly. I will personally investigate it."

"Thank you, Murray. I'll be happy see you privately after this meeting." We adjourned. I told him of my session that very morning with Brigitte Kohut, a separated woman who had a restraining order against her husband. He'd been arrested following a battering three months ago that left her bruised, bleeding from the mouth and with two broken ribs. She'd gone from hospital to shelter before getting an order for exclusive possession of the home for herself and the children. Her husband's crank calls, threats and drunken nighttime appearances in defiance of a restraining order, paralyzed her with fear. The police responded to each incident in isolation but did nothing to curb his access to her. I had already obtained her permission to advocate with the police on her behalf. Murray promised to follow up.

───────────

I let the water sluice over my naked body. The encounters of the day even more that the searing heat left a feeling of filth clinging to my skin. I turned my face to the cool spray. The bathroom door opened and closed. I shut off the tap. When I pushed back the curtain, Ben enveloped me in a huge, fluffy towel. He plucked a second one from the rack as I stepped out, and began to tousle my hair. "Dinner's ready," he spoke softly. "Why don't you just put on your robe and come eat?"

At dinner he asked about my day, nodding as I griped, and jumped to get me the glass of water I wanted, and then the napkins. When my plate was empty, he bustled about clearing the table. He made me think of myself as a young girl; hustling to gain my mother's approval, bringing tea, cleaning the house, caring for Jamie, trying to anticipate her every whim. I took the dirty plates from Ben's hands, set them on the counter and clasped my arms around his waist.

"You want to talk?"

"It's not fair," he hedged. "You've had a rough day. And you still have to transcribe your latest interview for your thesis."

"Research can wait. What's eating you?"

He hesitated, then said, "It's just that...I talked to Margaret today. Parker went to her too. It's getting to me, him poking into every corner of my life."

It was all getting to him, I knew; the investigation, the boredom, the looming terrors of jail, of the violence there. "Let's sit. We'll talk."

"It isn't talking I need. I just want to lie down and hold you."

"Okay."

"But—"

I pressed my finger to his mouth. "I said okay."

It was dark in the bedroom. I lifted my head to read the numbers on the clock radio. Eleven fifteen. Ben's breathing was regular and deep. He slept a lot these days. I crept out of bed and slipped down the hall. In the den, I turned on the computer, plugged in the transcriber earphones and rubbed my weary eyes. The blue screen burned into life and I began to fill it with type.

A heat wave stalked the month of June, one sweltering day after another. Sun scorched the lawn and baked the clay brick-hard. Saturday found me installed at the dining room table, my papers and books spread over the surface. Sequestered in the air-conditioned interior, I noted the signs of the furnace outdoors. The thermometer tacked to the outside sill topped ninety-four degrees. Out there, a slow-motion drama distracted, and finally engrossed me.

The driveway looped in front of the house, enclosing a circular patch of scraped earth. A wretched figure wielding a pick hacked at the clay. Stripped to the waist, Ben moved with the indolence of a convict on a chain gang. Seven, eight, ten times the pick climbed above his head and fell to the earth. Each time, I heard the impact a split second later.

He dropped the pick to the side, swaying like a drunk and seized the spade. In short, jerky stabs of the shovel he loaded great lumps of heavy clay into a wheelbarrow. When it was piled high, he drove the spade spear-like, into the ground. He drew his bare arm across his forehead, then stooped to grip the handles of the barrow. He straightened with effort, staggered, the muscles of his back bunching, then leaned into his load. It yielded grudgingly and he trudged after it, disappearing around the corner of the house.

The scene disturbed me. *He's punishing himself,* I thought, *and he's avoiding!* Since April we had talked, examining his options, struggling to construct a plan to rebuild a future. Mindful of Adam's counsel, I urged Ben to look for a job, any job. But he didn't seem to know how to begin. I coached him, helping him to brainstorm ideas.

But my own job, classes and study consumed sixteen hours a day. He was left to his own devices for these long hours. Each morning, he dutifully composed lists of chores for the day. These I noted, included shopping, paying bills, cooking, doing laundry, repairs and home improvements—but no job hunting. Newspapers piled up unopened. An invisible barrier separated us, like the window through which I watched him work; I witnessed his struggle, unable to penetrate his remoteness. And every day he shovelled more clay.

I rolled over for the fifth time in as many minutes. The sleep for which my body ached fled before a maelstrom of aborted thoughts. *Where's the common thread in my research subjects' responses...must get Ben to show me again how to drain the wells into the cistern...can't keep track of all those valves and taps...what's happening to Sara?...haven't seen her in months...what will it do to the children if Ben is convicted?...why are the forensics taking so long?...will I be put on the stand at the trial?...how do I avoid both lying* and *convicting Ben...what if he never takes charge of his life again?*

I swung my legs over the side of the bed. He slept the sleep of a condemned man, with long, deep drafts. I reached for my robe and tiptoed down the darkened hall. On the couch I sat sideways, hugging my knees in the dark and for the first time since his arrest, tears spilled over.

Ben always slept through my nocturnal wanderings, yet tonight I heard his slippers rustle along the floor, whisper across the carpet. I felt the dip of the cushion as he sat beside me. While I wept, he waited, still and silent. After a while my sobs lessened.

"What is it?" he said finally, his own voice wrung with anguish.

I fumbled in my pocket for a tissue. "I love you."

"You're not crying because you love me."

"No." I drew a shaky breath. "Through all this trouble with the police, I've never given a thought to leaving you. I'd begun to think there was nothing that would ever again make me consider leaving you. But I'm afraid, Ben. I'm afraid now that you've been knocked off your feet you may never get up again. I watch you procrastinate day after day and I can't reach you. I'm willing to help you, support you, but I can't—I *won't* carry you."

The moon rose and streamed through the skylight. I could see him clearly now, staring fixedly at a spot in the middle of the floor. Then he lifted his eyes to me and in a voice flat with despair, he asked, "Are you leaving, then?" I began to cry afresh and again he waited.

"I don't want to leave. I don't want to *have* to. But, you *must* hear me; I cannot stay with a man I don't respect."

His chest rose and fell, like a person acutely ill, laboured and uneven. Finally he spoke. "I want to tell you how I feel. But not tonight. It's late. I want to hold you in my arms in bed. Will you let me do that?" I looked resolutely into a face that was achingly sorrowful, and nodded.

Finches and robins chirruped by turns outside the bedroom window.

Their chorus ushered me into wakefulness. Forgetful for a moment, of last night's grief, I stretched, reaching across the bed. The space beside me was empty. The time on the clock showed ten to ten. Startled, I sat up. I looked out the window to see if Ben was moving earth in the yard but he wasn't there. I discovered him at his desk bent over the newspaper. It was folded open to the classified section, the lists I'd helped him create, spread across the desktop. He turned to face me. "You looked like you could use the sleep so I tried to be quiet."

I pulled his head to my chest; he leaned willingly into me, smothering his face against me. He said something but it was muffled in my robe. "What?" I asked.

"I said, 'Are you hungry?'"

"No. I just want some coffee."

"Good. I'll get it. I want to talk to you. Go sit in the living room."

I nestled in a chair, tucking my feet under me. He handed me a steaming mug, sat on the sofa and waited for the caffeine to take effect. "I'm not good at this," he began, "but I have never needed to convey my feelings as I do now. Please, let me speak. Don't interrupt." I nodded, nursing the mug.

"I couldn't possibly ask more than you've given before and especially since my arrest. You've been loyal and loving. You've shown concern for the welfare of my children. And you've been incredibly strong. It was no surprise last night to see you cry. What surprised me is that it took so long to come. And it hurts to see, especially to know I'm the cause.

"When I was arrested, I assumed you'd leave, not because I think you are shallow but because it's what I've learned to expect of people. All my life I felt alone. When you told me you had no intention of leaving you blew me away. For the first time, I began to feel that I'm not alone. I began to trust in a way that I never thought possible.

"What you told me last night, goes beyond pain. Your message reached to the depth of my soul and threatened to rip it apart. The thought of you leaving caused a pit to open up inside me—a wound as deep as any I have ever felt."

As he spoke, my throat thickened but I kept my promise to listen. "I don't ever want to hurt like that again. If you were to leave me now, I would feel no malice. I know you have too much integrity to leave just because it's getting tough. I heard what you said. If you were to leave, it would be because I had failed. Failed at my own life. I would have no one to blame but myself.

"But I'm not prepared to lose you. I will not give up so easily and throw away what I've been looking for all my life. Someone who truly loves me. Someone I can trust completely."

My throat ached, the lump there swelling. He was silent now. I uncoiled myself and folded in beside him. It was not till I lay my head in his lap and let the tears flow again that the tension began to drain from my throat. He stroked my hair.

"Maybe later," he said, "if you don't mind, we could go over some of those lists again. I was looking at them this morning and I'd really like your thoughts on some things."

———————————

"I guess you heard the news," Agnes greeted me Monday morning. When I shook my head she shoved the morning's newspaper at me. The headlines leapt off the page.

> MAN HOLDS HIS FAMILY AT GUNPOINT
> In a tense hostage situation last night, a man armed
> with a handgun threatened to kill his wife, his children
> and himself in their home. Police were called to a
> house on Avon Court just after 11:00 p.m. Saturday.
> Neighbours, aware of ongoing domestic problems,
> tried to telephone Brigitte Kohut when they noticed
> her estranged husband's car in her drive. They
> became suspicious when she did not answer her
> telephone and alerted the police. Officers cordoned
> off the area and were able to establish contact with
> the gunman. Just after 1:00 a.m., he surrendered and
> was taken into custody. His wife and children were
> unharmed.

Distantly, I heard the phone ring and Agnes answer it. "It's the Chief of Police for you, Shelley." I went to my office to take the call.

"Murray?" The constriction in my throat made it hard to talk.

"I take it that you know what's happened."

"I just saw the morning paper." A long pause hung between us.

He broke it finally. "I can't tell you how sorry I am. At least we can be thankful that no one was hurt." The consummate remorse in his tone wasn't enough. My eyes smarted. I covered them with my hand. "What about the emotional wounds, Murray?" I countered. "Those kids were traumatized. Do you think they'll ever forget?"

"I suppose not." He sounded whipped.

"I feel like I'm running an emotional M.A.S.H. unit here, putting Band-Aids on women and children."

"I guess we need to keep the committee going." I swallowed hard. It was a hollow victory.

———————————

"Ar-r-r-rgh!" Ben lurched around the picnic table like Frankenstein. Ari squealed and cowered behind me where I sat on the bench. He seized the boy in outstretched claws, lifted him and laid him on the tabletop. Baring his teeth and growling, he pretended to devour him. Ari shrieked.

"Daddy, no!" he giggled. "I'll pee my pants."

"Oh *really*," Frankenstein replied in wide-eyed glee. He redoubled his efforts.

"Go easy, Dad" I laughed. "His feet are in the pizza box."

"Hmph! Boy eats with feet. Table manners of baboon!"

"The pizza's all gone," Ari retorted. Ben sat beside me. Ari sat up on the table, straddling his dad. "Can I ride the go-kart now?"

"Sure." Ben reached into his pocket and handed him a couple of bills. He watched the boy's retreating back and sighed heavily. "I have to tell him sometime. I guess this is as good a time as any." We watched Ari pay the attendant, strap on a helmet and climb into the low slung contraption. Before he edged out onto the track, he checked to see if Daddy was watching, and waved. "God give me strength," Ben muttered. "I'm about to terminate my son's innocence."

We'd decided to wait till school was out to tell the children. They didn't need a crisis at exam time. Ben had hoped Sara would relent in her cold war and come on vacation. He wanted to tell them away from home. There would be ten days to help them with their reactions, their questions, their feelings. But Sara refused to come.

Ari bounded back toward the picnic table, the quintessential eleven-year-old boy, I thought, carefree and trusting. Ben stood. "Ari, come here." He clasped his son's hand, reached for mine and led us to the shade of a spreading maple. I leaned against the trunk. Ben stretched out on the grass on his side leaning on an elbow. Ari crossed his legs and sat pulling up grass.

"Ari, I have something to tell you. It's very hard for me to have to share this with you." He paused and the boy went very still. "I lost my job, son. I did something I wasn't supposed to do and I was fired." Ari arched his eyebrows. Ben swallowed. "I may go to jail."

Still as stone, Ari rotated his eyes, seeking my face. I nodded. "It's true, Honey," For long seconds he sat motionless, then his face contorted in silent tears. Ben pulled him into his arms.

"I know, son. It's hard, it's har... ," his voice choked off. All colour and vitality bled from the child's face. I reached out my hand to him. He crawled over and curled into my lap, limp and weak. I rocked him and kissed his hair and exchanged anguished looks with Ben.

The rest of that day, he remained glassy-eyed and withdrawn. In the days that followed, he asked no questions, made no comment. Several times, Ben or I would invite talk, but he didn't respond. To the casual observer he would appear to be a playful, untroubled eleven-year-old. But I knew better.

———————

Ben pulled up to the mailbox at the end of the lane and hauled out a week's worth of mail. "Ari, when we get in the house, I'll be calling your Mommy. I'm going drop you off in a while. I am going to ask Sara to go out with me. I want to talk to her about what I told you. It is up to me to tell her, son. I don't want you to have to do it. Do you understand?"

"Yes, Daddy."

A few minutes later, Ben hung up the phone and emerged from the den with a scowl.

"Something wrong?" I asked.

"Kind of."

"Sara?"

"No, not Sara. Believe it or not, she agreed to come out with me."

"Margaret?"

He shook his head and hollered to Ari to get ready to go. A muffled response echoed down the hall. As Ben stooped to kiss me goodbye, he put an envelope in my hand. "Read this when I'm gone. I'll talk to you about it later."

I watched them go, then flopped down in an armchair. The envelope was addressed to Ben and contained a single page. The script was large and careless as if written in a hurry—or in anger. I dropped my eyes to the bottom. The signature was a woman's name I didn't know. The letter was a savage diatribe. The writer denounced Ben with a string of expletives, though it gave no explanation, as if none were needed. It concluded with a threat. "If you ever try to get in touch with me again I will contact my lawyer to get a restraining order."

Dusk fell before the headlights of Ben's car appeared at the end of the drive. He said hello when he came in but busied himself with unpacking and chores.

Later, we lay in the dark, my face in the curve of his neck. When he spoke, his voice sounded hollow, as if coming from out of a tunnel. "My daughter and I are strangers. We've forgotten how to talk to each other. How does that happen?" I twined my fingers in his and squeezed. I had no answer. "I took her for a drive," he continued. "Found a park where we could be alone. She said nothing when I told her. No tears. No questions. I wanted to know what she was thinking but I didn't know how to get inside her head."

"At least she went with you Ben. That's the first time in months."

"Maybe it's the last time."

"You can't think like that. Give her time. Keep reaching out to her."

He sighed and turned to nuzzle my face. "You still love me?"

"Silly question."

"Even after reading that letter?"

"Mm. Guess you got some 'splainin' to do."

He sighed again as if to summon strength. "I knew the woman a long time ago, in my twenties. Over the years, I'd call her now and then and talk on the phone, you know, typical flirty stuff I used to do. And she'd dish it right back; she enjoyed it, or if not she's a great actress. It's been a few years since I talked to her. Nothing that ever happened between us could explain that letter. Especially coming now, out of the blue. It's got to be that bastard, Parker. Her phone number would have been among those he took. He must have revved her up with some cockamamie bullshit. What the hell is he telling people about me?"

I glanced at the clock in my office. A new client was scheduled at three, a mystery client. Two days ago, Agnes had taken a call from a man who requested an appointment with me on behalf of a woman. I was used to female clients being guarded and secretive since many feared vigilant, violent husbands. I wondered who had called on her behalf. A brother? A friend?

At three, I put down my pen and went out to the waiting room. At the far end sat a stout woman in a skirt and blouse. I struggled to remember where I had seen her before. A man bent over a briefcase on the floor. He looked up with baby blues and long lashes. A rush of cold fury flooded me.

"I thought you were *investigating* fraud, Corporal, not practicing it."

"You wouldn't respond to my calls."

It was true; I hadn't. He'd called twice in the past few weeks.

"This is company time you are using," I said, deflecting his remark. "We charge by the hour."

"I didn't want to talk with you at your home. Can we speak in your office?"

"No."

"Do you have a reason not to talk to me?" I'd come to loathe the silk in his voice.

"We've been through this."

"There are some new developments. I have information I think you will want to know."

I vacillated. Was he lying? He was so smooth but I sensed a threat behind his manner. Yet maybe he did have information. Maybe I should hear it, just listen. "Very well." He followed me, the woman on his heels. In her civvies, the female officer appeared innocuous and feminine.

"How long have you known Ben," he asked as soon as we all sat down.

"You said you had information," I countered.

"What I'm trying to say to you, Ms. Gallagher, is that there may be a side of Mr. Volski that you don't know." I looked at him unblinking till he went on. "Our investigation suggests that he used his access to information at Revenue Canada to gain sexual favours from women."

I stifled the urge to laugh. *You ass. Ben's been a Casanova...an incorrigible flirt. But he's not capable of what you're suggesting.* I kept my face impassive though and thought I detected a shadow cross his. "I'm afraid I won't be able to keep this out of the papers," he said, his voice too soft. "There will be a lot of publicity."

"Why are you telling me this?" I said, feeling nauseous at the menace I suspected behind those baby blues.

"In your position, with your line of work, you won't want that." There it was—the raw threat. He looked smug.

"Why are you telling me this?" I repeated.

"To prepare you. You'll be called as a witness."

I thought of my journal in his hands. *What could he possibly construe from it?* "If you have conveyed everything you wanted to, Corporal Parker, I have work to do." He nodded to the other officer. They rose and left.

––––––––––––––

In my sister's backyard, the Gallagher family gathered to celebrate my youngest niece's third birthday. Sara knelt on the grass in a tight denim skirt and pink jersey, plaiting Chantal's hair into a French braid. I'd seen so little of Sara this last year. She had metamorphosed into a petite, pretty, almost-fourteen year old. Ben and I felt grateful for the ebbing of the pre-adolescent storms of earlier years and ecstatic that she'd agreed to come to this gathering.

The patio door opened with a soft rumble and Mom lumbered out with a tray of tumblers filled with punch. Melanie lurched upward from her recliner. "Mrs. Gallagher, let me help you."

Gayle half rose and grasped Melanie's arm. "You stay put, Missy! The doctor said you shouldn't be lifting. Here you are only five months along and having all these problems!"

"Where's Tom, Gayle?" Ben asked, accepting a glass from the tray.

"Jamie hauled him off to the pool hall for a few beers. They'll be back soon. Trust me, Tom won't miss cake and ice cream." As if on cue, Tom and Jamie sauntered in.

"How's my birthday girl!" Tom bellowed as Chantal leapt at him. Jamie stooped to kiss Melanie but she turned away so that his lips barely brushed her cheek. The hunch of his shoulders suggested a guilty conscience. Then I saw the bandages swaddling his hand. "Jamie! What did you do to your hand?"

Tom guffawed. "Didn't you hear?"

Jamie coloured. "Shut up, Tom," he muttered.

Tom laughed again. "Jamie's been building this million dollar doll-house for his kid? Had to take out a second mortgage on his own house to pay for it."

"Did not," Jamie sulked.

"How much have you had to drink, Tom?" Gayle admonished him but he ignored her and forged on.

"He turned out these miniature spindles on a lathe and made ginger-bread trim in exotic woods. A be-oo-tiful work of art." Melanie gripped her glass and stared off into space. "He's some master carpenter all right," Tom rolled along, oblivious to the strained silence around him. "Figures he can do the electrical work for the wee chandeliers. He wired it all right. *Hot*-wired it. Goes in to wash up and next thing, the little wife is screaming that smoke's comin' from the garage. He tries to put it out while she calls the fire department. Damn near burned down his own house. Biggest little house fire the Angus volunteers ever seen."

Gayle cast a dark look at her husband. "You're an asshole, Tom. Why don't you go soak in the pool awhile?"

"For heaven sakes, Jamie," Mother scolded. "Why on earth were you building a dollhouse anyway? You don't know if the baby's going to be a boy or a girl. You ought to be buying things the baby will *need*, not wasting your money on these foolish projects."

"How bad is the burn?" I interjected to cut her off.

"S'no big deal," he muttered.

Melanie whispered, "Third degree burns from his fingers to his wrist."

"Hey Melly," Tom bawled, swaying slightly, "You're awful quiet today."

"Leave her alone," Gayle snapped. "She's not feeling well."

He raised his eyebrows at Melanie. "Is it the baby, Mel?"

"Well for goodness sake, Tom. She *is* pregnant. You men have no idea what a woman goes through."

"I understand, Babe, sure I do. Women are fragile when they're preggies. Ain't that right Jamie? You gotta take extra special care of 'em. If you don't, you're in hot water every time you turn around. Yup, pregnant women are real emotional yo-yo's."

"Shut *up*, Tom." The bite in Gayle's voice did the trick this time. Tom cut his palm to his forehead in a salute, and clammed up.

Talk turned to other topics. I saw Jamie's forlorn expression as he watched his wife disappear through the patio door into the house.

I found her downstairs in the darkened rec room on the sofa. She was turned away from me. I heard a sniffle. "Mel?" I reached out and touched the hunched shoulder. She spun and flung her arms round my neck. Tears splashed my skin.

After a moment she released her hold, fished a tissue from her pocket and blew her nose. "It's hard," she began, but her voice cracked. She inhaled and resumed. "I love him. I really do. But this stupid backhoe thing; it's killing us. Jamie led me to believe he went into this deal fifty-fifty. But I don't think the other guy had that kind of money. Since I've had to stay home because of problems with my pregnancy, I started getting the phone calls. The bank—not the one where I work, bill collectors, people complaining about Jamie's partner not showing up to do the work. I think the man goes off drinking somewhere. When I ask Jamie anything, he brushes me off. He told me to stay out of it and let him take care of things. Yesterday, I found a drawer *full* of unpaid bills. Shelley, we're in debt up to our teeth. We had a terrible quarrel. I ended up by getting sick to my stomach. He felt bad then, and took care of me. But neither of us have had the courage to talk about it since."

I listened with a mixture of anguish and anger; anguish for both her and my hapless brother and anger that Jamie's bumbling and lies were destroying his wife, his marriage.

"Have you talked to him about getting counselling with you?"

"Not yet."

"Do you want me to?"

She smiled sweetly. "No. I'll ask him now. I'm sure he'll be willing. If we hadn't been here today, we'd probably be sorting things out right now."

"You're sure you don't want me to talk to him?"

"Yeah, thanks. I just needed a good cry."

———————————

I turned off the highway north of the city and bounced through potholes in a gravel lot that was rapidly filling up with orange and black buses. I nosed the truck up to the hut in the far corner, parked and climbed the wooden steps to the dim interior.

Two men drinking coffee out of paper cups looked up when the screen door squeaked open. "Can I help you?" one asked.

"Has Ben Volski brought his bus in yet?"

"Don't think so, ma'am. Should be along any minute though."

"Okay. Thanks."

I wandered down a corridor between rows of parked buses, dodging more that were barreling in from the highway. It was just four thirty and the Halton Board of Education school fleet was herding back to base after discharging its loads of students. In late August, Ben took the driving test and began the morning and afternoon rounds right after Labor Day. He called me this morning, asking me to meet him here on my way from work to class at the university. I walked toward the highway entrance so I could scan each big front window as buses passed. The beep, beep, beep of the back-up signal from a new arrival warned me to step aside. It stopped beside me and the door swung open. Behind his sunglasses, Ben grinned down at me.

"Hey lady, can I offer you a lift?" Grinning back, I clambered aboard. He pulled the lever to close the door behind me and the bus pitched forward toward the far side of the lot. "This bus gives preference to school children, Ma'am," he said. "You'll have to ride at the back."

"Is that so?" I tossed my head archly. I lurched down the aisle steadying myself on the backs of the seats, while Ben eased the bus into its berth for the night. I sat in the last seat, the one that spanned the width of the bus. The engine fell silent.

Ben stood and honed in on me down the passageway. When he towered over me, he removed his sunglasses and pocketed them with a deliberate stare. He placed his hands on the backs of the last two split seats, blocking me in. Feeling slightly claustrophobic, I tipped my head back to look up at him. His eyes narrowed salaciously. I giggled. Then his hands were on my shoulders, pushing me down on the seat. "Hey Baby, how'd you like to do it in the back of a school bus?" The orange roof curved overhead and his body pressed full length against me.

"But Mr. Bus Driver, I'll be late for my class," I protested.

"I'll write you a note," he grinned.

"You fiend. I think you should let me up."

"Why?"

Just then a blast from a horn a few feet away sent a shock through my body. "That's why!"

He did a push-up on his arms and peered out the window. I shoved him off me and craned around to see. In a bus that sat nose to tail to ours, the driver eyeballed us. He opened his door and motioned that he wanted to speak. Ben stood up and pushed down the nearest window. "Hey Volski," the fellow shouted. "I hope that isn't a student you're banging."

"As a matter of fact, it is," he grinned. I averted my eyes, feeling sheepish. "Jim, I'd like you to meet the woman who sleeps with me," Ben said. "This is Shelley. She's a co-ed at York University. *And* a social worker. We were just practicing a little social work."

The other man laughed, "How do you do, Ma'am? Ain't he a corker?"

"You're telling me! I have to live with him."

The driver dismounted and pushed closed the door to his bus. "Have fun you kids," he said and waved as he strolled off.

Ben sighed then, letting his smile slip. "Sit down, Shelley. I want to talk to you." I took the second last seat and faced the aisle. He sat opposite, our knees almost touching. "Adam called me today. The forensics are back. I figured they would determine conclusively whether or not the typewriter balls the police took were used in any of the tax returns. The report claims a sixty per cent probability that they were."

"What does *that* mean?"

"How the hell do I know? It's so frustrating. All these months we waited so I could decide how to plead. The evidence seems no clearer now than in April.

"I've thought it over. The trial date isn't until late May, more than a year since this started. If it goes against me and I'm convicted, Adam figures I'll get a year, maybe two; that means four or eight months on the inside if I behave myself. It would be a year or two before we could start to put our lives back together.

"Even if I'm found not guilty, it won't be easy. Finding work will be hard. There'd always be a shadow over me. And I *know* how you'd feel if I'm found not guilty. But if I enter a guilty plea, I don't have to wait till May for a court date. With luck, I could serve my time inside and be home before May even rolls around."

He paused and held my gaze, letting his meaning sink in.

"That's it then," I whispered.

He nodded. "I told Adam to get me into court. All I asked is for three days notice."

Air escaped from my lungs like from a balloon with a small hole. "I'm glad," I said, but a desolation left my insides feeling desiccated.

After the staff meeting, I collected my messages in the front office. One was from Terri Moffat. I'd half expected it. The assault charge against Jarrod was scheduled for this morning. I dialled the apartment that she took at the first of August. A male voice answered. Suddenly on guard, I asked for her. "Ms. Gallagher?" the man asked.

"That sounds like Brad?"

"Yes, Ma'am," he said. "Hold on."

Terri came on the line. She sounded despondent "I'd got myself psyched up to testify but they reduced the charge from assault causing bodily harm to common assault and Jarrod pleaded guilty. He was given an unconditional discharge. He doesn't even have to report to a probation officer. I had no say in anything. It hardly seems fair."

After I hung up, I pondered the wife assault poster on my wall that encouraged victims to call the police. *Whoever claimed that Justice is a lady,* I thought, *must have been a man.* Terri's despondency echoed my own depression. It was all getting to me, the months of enforced silence, the isolation, the violation and intimidation from the police, the worry and uncertainty about the future.

I left work and got into my truck. I turned down the visor. "I'm not a bad person," I said aloud to the mirror. "I work hard. I follow the rules. I try to make the world a better place." The visage looked unconvinced. "I'm *not* a bad person." Parker's steely blue eyes seemed to stare back. "Am I?" I turned the key in the ignition and eased the truck out into traffic.

———————

The hotel dining room was filling up. The hostess seated me by the window at a table for two, lit the candle and left two menus. Etched along the far shore of my north-facing view of Lake Ontario was Toronto's geometric skyline with its signature CN Tower. Scarcely settled, I caught sight of a figure surging toward me from the entrance. A dozen paces away, the woman's familiar singsong chuckle gave me a catch in my throat. I rose to be swept into Daphne's exuberant squeeze.

"How was your parents' anniversary party?" I asked, over the appetizers.

"The usual insanity," she said, waving her fork. "My parents whining about how I've deprived them of their grandchildren; my dear brother crowing about what a great job he'd done organizing everything. I know perfectly well he delegated the work to his secretary. Poor Richard needs to feel important. Politics suits him. Trust me, attending was more of a duty than a pleasure."

"Italy is a long way to come for duty."

"I did it to please Eddie, really."

"Eddie? What? He needed a break from you?" I deadpanned her.

"Touché," she chuckled. "He probably does. But truth be told he seems to be undergoing some kind of redemption. Family has become awfully important to him lately. He insisted I come." A waitress topped up our wine glasses and retreated. Daphne leaned back and eyed me steadily. "When I called you, you said you had a story to tell me."

I ran my thumb and finger up and down the stem of the glass, unable to look up. "I do," I said, dread welling up in me. I forced myself to meet her gaze. "I hope we'll still be friends afterward." For the next hour, I recounted the events of the past many months, how I'd learned of Ben's criminal activity, my struggle over how to respond, how he had stopped. I gave an account of the police raids, Ben's arrest, the impact on him, on me and on the children. I spoke of his imminent incarceration and my hopes and fears for the future.

She listened intently, interrupting only to ask a question or two. When I finished, I fell silent. I felt spent but at the same time a terrible anxiety, as if I were a condemned person awaiting sentencing. I picked up my glass and drained it.

Daphne maintained a hard stare. I wondered if there would be a scene. Or perhaps she would wade gracefully through the meal and leave, never to communicate with me again. Or would she withdraw her friendship slowly, sending perfunctory cards at Christmas for a year or two, then drifting away?

"You underestimate me, Shelley," she finally spoke, "if you think this would cause me to end my friendship with you." She lowered her head, forcing eye contact with my down-turned face. "After all," she said, "what have you done wrong?"

I felt my mouth pull into a wistful smile. "You can't imagine how paranoid a person can feel, not to be able to talk to anyone about your life being turned upside down and shaken. I can't even *write* my thoughts. They took my journal, for God sake." She made a sympathetic sound. "I can handle the problems and the pressure," I said, "but I've been so cut off from people, at least people who care. I'm starting to lose sense of who I am and of what's right or wrong."

"Can't you talk to your family?"

"Pfft! Telling my parents would only add to my stress. If Ben isn't in jail long, they may never have to know."

"Your brother? Aren't you close to him?"

"If I were to ask Jamie to keep it from the rest of the family, I'd be putting him in the same predicament we grew up with—keeping secrets. I don't want to do that to him. Besides, right now he's got his own problems."

"What will you do at Christmas?"

"I've already told my folks I have other plans."

"You must feel pretty alone."

I shrugged, not wanting to succumb to the well of depression again. "It's not all bad," I countered. "Sara is beginning to warm up. She's come out with us a few times. It means so much to Ben—and to me."

She smiled broadly. "You see! I told you. You just have to wait till they turn fourteen and all those little hormones settle down."

Silvery notes cascaded into the auditorium from the harp on stage. From my seat six rows back, I thought ruefully, *Sara was right. One does watch a harpist's fingers.* Even from here, I could pick out the pearl polish on her nails.

She finished the score and bobbed the obligatory bow, her eyes glued to the floor in front of her. Above the general applause, Caitlyn clapped with the fervour of a groupie. Now that they were old enough to navigate the cross-town buses to call at each other's homes, the girls were often together.

When the recital ended, Caitlyn dashed to the front and dragged Sara through the crowd. Ben spotted them in the foyer. Animated and laughing, Caitlyn had cornered a lanky teen-aged boy, touching his arm as she talked. In stark contrast, Sara, cheeks aflame and tongue-tied, stood twisting her sheet music into a scroll.

We dropped the girls off at Caitlyn's house. When Ben pulled away, he sighed heavily. "Tell me, Shelley, why does a talented girl like my daughter lack self-confidence while her friend, who's hardly the sharpest tool in the shed, exudes it?"

I considered the teens I see in counselling. "Being accepted is so important at their age," I said. "I imagine her asthma and coughing embarrass her. Her arms and legs are so slender; I notice that she always keeps them covered. She won't wear her glasses in public. It wouldn't surprise me if she thinks she's ugly and that no one will like her, especially boys."

"Anything a Dad can do?"

"Sure! Sara *is* pretty—and feminine. She *knows* she's intelligent but just doesn't know she's attractive. When she makes an effort to look nice, tell her. Adolescent girls need their daddy's admiration."

He clasped my hand. "Thanks. I need you for things like that," he said. "To explain young girls to me. By the way," he arched his eyebrows at me, "you look rather luscious, yourself."

––––––––––––––

The phone jangled the moment I opened the back door. I bolted for it, puffing into the receiver. "Hello."

"Shelley, is that you? Thank God!"

"Gayle? What is it? What's wrong?"

"Is Jamie there?"

"Jamie! No. Why?"

"Melanie lost the baby."

I slumped into a kitchen chair, my "Oh no" involuntary. I reached for Ben's hand and repeated the message to him.

"I'm at the hospital with Melanie. She called me from here and I came right away," Gayle said. "She was in labor and I stayed with her throughout. The baby was too premature. It didn't have a chance, poor wee soul. It was a girl. Jamie was right on that score, the stupid little twerp"

"What *about* Jamie, Gayle? What's he done?"

"Guess you know he got them into a pile of debt. He's been sneaking around spending money they don't have and lying to her about it." I flinched at her rancour. For once, I felt helpless to defend him. "They got into a terrible argument. After all the ribbing Jamie got over sinking big bucks into that extravagant dollhouse and burning it, the dumb cluck went out after that and spent *more* money on materials to repair it. They don't even have a crib, for Pete's sake! When Melanie found out, she told him to take the material back to the store but he refused. Damned fool! He had a tantrum and took off. He left her upset and cryin' and all stressed out. Shortly after he left, she went into labor and now he's nowhere to be found. She had to call a taxi to get to the hospital. Melanie tried calling you when she went into labor thinking Jamie might go there but she just got your answering machine."

I leaned on the table, head heavy in my hand. "We just got in. We didn't even have a chance to listen to the mes..."

"I'll bet he went drinking," Gayle interrupted. "If he comes home and finds her note and tries to drive here, it's just like him to get in an accident. Shelley, will you drive up to Angus, go to the house and wait for him? Don't let him do anything stupid."

"I'll do it. I'll leave right now."

"I'll stay with Melanie. If the hospital discharges her and Jamie hasn't shown up, I can bring her home. Don't let him come to the hospital without calling first to see if we're still here."

"Okay, Gayle. I'm on my way."

The house lay in darkness when I pulled into Jamie's driveway. The parted living room curtains suggested that no one had been home since daylight. Melancholy cloaked the place that only a year ago had given Jamie such pride. The barren lot and un-sodded front yard had grown up in weeds. The disgraced backhoe skulked in the shadows beside the house. In the dark at the front entrance, I crouched to the ground and groped blindly with my hand. I was rewarded almost immediately by the cold touch of a flat rock the size of a small frying pan, just as Gayle had described. I tipped it on its side.

"Aha," I exclaimed, closing my fist around a key. I let myself in, flicking on lights to disperse the shadows and my jitters. I pulled the drapes and roamed from room to room. By contrast with the neglected look of the yard, warmth and orderliness prevailed inside. The furnishings were neither new nor lavish but through subtle mixing of colour and fabric, Melanie's aesthetic touch graced each room.

I opened the door from the kitchen leading to the garage. Here, Jamie had created his own orderly sanctuary. A workbench ran the length of one wall, with tools neatly arranged on hooks in pegboard. Braces on the opposite wall stored an assortment of lumber. A table saw, band saw and lathe each occupied its own distinct work centre. In the middle of the workshop, a makeshift platform supported a massive Victorian dollhouse. I descended the two steps to the garage floor for a closer look.

Elaborate ginger-breading decorated the exterior. I marvelled at the hundreds of tiny shakes covering the roof. A staircase joined the floors with miniature spindles in the railing. Tiny light fixtures suspended from ceilings.

About one quarter of the house was scorched, two rooms badly charred. Tom had exaggerated the damage done, since obviously the fire had been confined to the dollhouse itself. Beside it were stacked lengths of exotic wood of varying colours—ebony, rose, yellow and mahogany.

I returned to the kitchen and called the number at the hospital that Gayle had given me. Gayle herself answered. I told her Jamie had not come home yet. "Well, it can't be helped," she said. "The doctor is releasing Melanie. We should be there in half an hour."

I hung up. I sat on the couch to wait. After a while lights splashed across the drapes. When he opened the door, Jamie's face registered surprise. "I saw your car. Where's Mel? She in the kitchen?"

"Melanie's not here, Jamie. You better come and sit down."

He frowned, sitting down obediently. "I guess I'm in the doghouse, huh."

I studied him. "I have to ask you something. Have you been drinking?"

"No!"

"I hope you're telling me the truth."

"Hey," he flashed a charming smile. "I don't lie to my sister."

"No? Only to your wife."

His eyes flared wide and a muscle rippled in his jaw. "Who said I lied? Melanie?"

"Slow down, Jamie. I'm not here because you and she had a fight." The defiance in his face gave way to guarded curiosity. "She's in the hospital."

He jerked forward. "The hospital! What's wrong?"

"She's alright. She's going to be alright but...she lost the baby." He froze on the edge of his seat. His eyes closed and pain creased his forehead. There was nothing I could say to ease this hurt for him.

"I gotta go to her," he whispered.

"They're sending her home. Gayle's bringing her right now."

"Gayle?" he exploded. "What's that bitch here for?"

"Come on, knock it off. Melanie called her."

"Swell! So Gayle knows about the fight me and Mel had this morning." I didn't answer him. He snorted. "Was it Gayle who said I lied?" My look gave him his answer.

"Damn her superiority!"

"Quit it. Melanie couldn't find anyone else to help her. Gayle's been with her most of the day. She was with her when the baby came."

He covered his face with his hands, elbows resting on his knees. After a moment he got up, faltered into the kitchen and stood with his back to me. I came up behind him touching his arm but he shook my hand away.

"Leave me alone," he croaked. He went into the garage. The door slammed shutting me out. I hugged myself trying to stop the shaking. For several moments, the only thing I could hear was the sound of my own breathing. A sudden crash electrified me. A second crash followed, the sound of wood splintering. I threw open the door. An axe hovered in the air above Jamie's head. He flung it full force into the mangled shell of the dollhouse.

I did not try to stop him but withdrew into the kitchen, closing the door on the hacking, shattering sounds.

It stopped. I strained to hear something, anything. I was on the brink of deciding to investigate when I heard the front door open. Melanie shuffled in on Gayle's arm. Her face was chalky and dark rings underscored her eyes. I went to her and took her in my arms. Strands of her dark hair clung to her neck as if she'd been exercising heavily.

"Where's Jamie?" she murmured. "I saw the van." She pulled back as she said it and looked over my shoulder. Jamie had come quietly into the kitchen. The two looked searchingly at each other for a long moment then he lurched toward her. She wrapped her arms round his neck, her face buried there.

"Help me to the bedroom," she groaned. "I need to lie down." She clung to his arm as he led her toward the hall.

"You two gonna be okay?" Gayle called after them. "You need anything, Melly dear?"

She turned and smiled wanly. "No. Thanks, for everything, Gayle. You too, Shelley. Jamie and I will be fine."

Gayle and I exchanged glances, waved our good-byes and let ourselves out. On the front steps, Gayle reflected, "I guess it's best to leave them be now. They'll work it out themselves."

I kept my doubts to myself.

———————

Ben leaned on the kitchen doorframe engrossed in a rare scene. The kids had taken over the living room the way only teen-agers can. I crept to his elbow and we exchanged a glance of pleasure. Caitlyn was mixing things up. She had Ari manning the sound system, cranking up the volume till the sultry voice of teen idol Rick Astley reverberated from the rafters. *It would take a strong, strong man, to ever let you go.* She lip-synced to a choreographed routine with her hands, directing a hopelessly uncoordinated Sara who followed along, her shyness evident. But she began to get the hang of it and was visibly enjoying herself. I wanted to freeze-frame this moment in my mind. We'd had so little of the children's joy and I feared for the toll from what still lay ahead.

When the song ended I reluctantly announced dinner. Ben put a yarmulke on his head and motioned to Ari to do the same. He struck a match and lit the first candle on the silver menorah. In a voice deep and rich he recited in Hebrew. "Baruch ata Adonai Elohenu melech ha-olam, asher kid'shanu b'mitsvotav 'tsivanu 'hadlik ner shel Hanukkah." As flame after flame caught, the candlelight softened the circle of faces. Ben held the match for Caitlyn to blow out.

Hanukkah wrap lay scattered about. All gifts had been exchanged but one. Sara turned an expectant look to Ben. "I suppose you think there should be one more for you," he teased.

In a pink sweatshirt and powder blue jeans she sat leaning against one end of the sofa with her knees up and stockinged feet pointed toward Caitlyn at the other end. Her hair, fastened at the back in a barrette, fell in a blond wave down her neck exposing gold studded ear lobes, still slightly pink from the recent piercing. She lifted her chin with a hint of vanity and more than a hint of expectation.

"Yes."

He smiled at her answer and handed her a package the size of a large ice cube. "Happy Hanukkah, Sara."

She held it close to her, possessively, working at the tape with her painted fingernails. She peered up at Ben a time or two, her eyes dancing. The wrapping gone she held a black velvet case. She tipped back the lid. "O-o-o-h, Daddy." Her cheeks dimpled. "They're beautiful."

"Lemme see. What is it?" Caitlyn craned forward. "Pearl earrings! Oh you lucky dog. They're gorgeous. You'll be able to wear them when your keepers come out."

Sara beamed.

"Every young lady should have pearls," he conceded.

My phone buzzed. "Line three for you," Agnes said.

It was Ben. "Adam called." His voice was leaden. "Court is tomorrow."

"Tomorrow! He was supposed to give you three days notice."

"He would have but Adam just found out. Parker took his sweet time informing him." I thought I'd been prepared. Instead I felt hit by a truck. I glanced at today's date on my desk calendar. December twentieth. We cradled a silence between us. Whatever there was to say had been said in the long months since April. Finally Ben asked, "How soon can you finish work?"

"I've one more appointment."

"Can you meet me at Margaret's house at five? I'll pick up the kids. I want to spend the last night on the outside with the three people I love most."

CHAPTER EIGHT

My last client was Terri Moffat. Over the fall, I'd seen her only two or three times. With court behind her, Terri had applied to, and been accepted in a fashion design program and already impressed her teachers with her natural talent, getting A's in all her assignments. She revelled in her newfound freedom and stabilized emotionally. It had not surprised me that a romance had sprung up between her and Brad Sparks. He celebrated her growing strength and independence and supported her aspirations.

For the first ten minutes of her session, Terri extolled his many virtues, how he would coax her outdoors for a walk when she was blue, bring her a treat when she was studying, leave her inspirational notes to find when their schedules prohibited seeing each other for several days.

"So what's the 'But', Terri?"

She came to a full stop and glared at me. "How do you always know? Sometimes I think you can see right inside me and read my thoughts."

"You just don't look as contented as your words would have me believe."

She grimaced and let her shoulders, where I'd seen the telltale tension, slump. "It's...intimacy." I had to wait for a moment for her to elucidate. "Jarrod used to accuse me of being frigid. I thought I disliked sex because he was so mean and demanding. But Brad isn't like that and still I'm..." She looked up with an agonized expression. "I just can't."

She exhaled. "You asked me a long time ago Shelley, but I never told you the truth. You asked me if anyone ever molested me when I was a child. Well, someone did." She bowed her head. "My father."

There it was, the suspicion I'd held for many months, confirmed.

"His Honour, the Judge," she said, her tone acerbic. "Of course he was a criminal lawyer then, in a large, prestigious firm. I bet he defended men doing the same thing he was doing to me at home."

She sat with me in a gentle silence as if resting a heavy load she'd been shouldering a long time. When she spoke, it was with infinite sadness. "Sometimes I feel so damaged."

"But you lived through it."

"I guess."

"Well,... you did. How did you do that?"

She sat contemplating for a long moment, then her cheeks dimpled and she gave a stifled giggle. "Buttons!"

"Buttons?" I echoed, more than a little mystified.

She nodded, with a ghost of an impish grin. "I discovered how to drive Daddy mad!"

I frowned, puzzled. "You pushed his buttons?"

"Not pushed, cut. I got the idea by watching him primp in front of the mirror. He's very vain; a typical lawyer so full of himself. He wore expensive suits and immaculate shirts. I got back at him by cutting a button off one of his jackets or shirts on a regular basis. Later I got more creative. I would cut a few threads so it would pop off unexpectedly. Sometimes it happened as he was getting dressed. Other times, during the day when he was at the office or even in court. He started complaining to my mother, as if it was her fault. I remember one time when he was entertaining some big time politician he came into the kitchen where I was doing my homework. The button I had loosed popped off just as he opened the fridge for the mixer. Fell to the floor with a clatter. He swore and muttered to himself something about 'damned bedevilled buttons'. He must have thought he was jinxed. It was all I could do to keep from laughing out loud."

She laughed aloud now. I laughed with her. "Your flair for fashion design has interesting roots, Terri."

Sara and Ari took the news with equanimity. The lamp above our table pulled the four of us into its sanctum, away from the other restaurant patrons in the shadows. Looking deliberately from one face to another Ben said, "There's nothing we can do about the hard times ahead. But tonight we can make a happy time."

Heroically, Ari and Sara rose to his bidding. If they shared our sorrow, they did not let it interfere with their appetite. They made an enterprise out of running up Daddy's bill, ordering appetizers and kiddy cocktails, huge entrees and desserts. Ben told jokes and Sara teased Ari, for once without rancour. Halfway through his order of ribs, Ben yelped and spit into his napkin. "What is it Daddy?" Ari asked.

Ben groaned. "I broke a filling," he said holding amalgam up to the light. Sara dissolved into giggles which set off Ari. I couldn't help myself and followed suit.

"You guys are sadistic," he grumbled. That just made Sara laugh all the harder till a spasm of coughing caught her and she had to draw a puff from her inhaler.

It was dark under a moonless sky when we pulled in beside the truck, where I'd parked earlier in Margaret's driveway. We all got out. Ari and Sara stood silent and awkward, neither leaving nor saying goodbye.

"I don't know when I'll see you again," Ben said. Ari threw himself at him, hugging his waist. Ben held him close. "Be good, Ari." The boy backed up brushing the back of his hand across his eyes.

Sara stood rooted to the spot while Ben regarded her. "Goodbye, Sara," he said softly. In a sudden motion, she stepped forward and flung her arms round his neck. "Goodbye Daddy, goodbye."

When we arrived at the courthouse the next morning, Adam had not yet arrived. Ben's case was second on the roster. We slid into a bench near the back of the gallery and watched a trial in progress. The court clerk read the particulars. Ironically, it was a domestic violence case.

Lean and scruffy, the accused slouched in the prisoners' box. When his wife was called to the stand, she approached with a look of terror and he curled his lip at her in a sneer. A hint of a large bruise still lingered around one eye. She spoke so timidly I couldn't hear her words. The prosecutor told her to speak up. She described a scene commonplace in my storehouse of victims' stories.

On cross-examination, defence lost no time in challenging her role in the incident. He suggested that she had initiated the fight and perpetrated violence more severe than that of the accused. Her responses were no longer hard to hear. Defence pounded at her. She became confused. He had her contradicting herself. After her, defence counsel put the investigating officer on the stand, exposing a careless report full of holes and errors.

"He'll get off," I whispered.

"No way!" Ben countered. "He's guilty. It's obvious."

"Of course. But the judge has no choice. She's lost credibility and the officer screwed up. The guy will get off."

The judge was not fooled and said as much. "However," he said, regret lacing his voice, "I cannot in law make a finding of guilty." A yelp from the back of the room drowned the rest of his words. Clutching her coat, the woman blasted out through the door. Her husband stepped down from the box and swaggered out through the same exit.

Suddenly it was Ben's turn. Adam materialized at his elbow and chaperoned him to the prisoners' box. A sheriff stood by, feet planted wide, arms folded. In his navy suit, Ben looked defenceless somehow and out of place in the box so recently occupied by a wife beater.

The clerk read the charges and Corporal Parker took the stand. He gave his information not failing to insinuate that Ben's character was that of sexual predator and that his motive for breach of trust was to extort sex. He stepped down.

The judge ordered Ben to stand. "Mr. Volski, how do you plead?"

His baritone carried across the courtroom. "Guilty, Your Honour."

Adam stood. "Your Honour," he began as Ben sat down, "my client, Mr. Volski, has pleaded guilty to the charges of fraud and breach of trust. I'd like to provide the court with some information about him." The Judge nodded his assent.

"Mr. Volski is forty-six years old. He is the father of two children, a daughter fourteen years of age and a son, twelve. He is devoted to them. He separated from his wife, the children's mother, six years ago and has been living with a lady for five years in a relationship he describes as stable and positive. His children spend a good deal of time with him. He involves himself to a high degree in their care."

"Mr. Volski is a member of Mensa," he continued, "an association of people who score in the top two percent of the population on IQ tests. He is a voracious reader, consuming two or three books a week. He possesses several degrees including a Master in Business Accounting. He worked for Revenue Canada for thirteen years as an income tax auditor.

"Mr. Volski probably possesses the talent for more challenging work than he encountered in this job. Indeed, he indicates that he was often bored and frustrated in his position. However, he made a conscious choice not to pursue a more challenging career in accounting because it would have taken him away from his children much more. He places a high priority upon being involved with them during their growing up years. The boredom and lack of challenge were perhaps his downfall.

"One of his interests on which he is extremely well read, is military intelligence. Some years ago, he read a book called *The Man Who Never Was*, written by Ewen Montagu. This is a chronicle of a fictitious character created by British military intelligence during the Second World War to confuse and mislead the enemy. Mr. Volski was intrigued by the concept and wondered if he could duplicate the feat. He set about doing this without initially having an intent to make personal gain."

It was as if Adam were reading aloud to me the final page of a mystery. Sherlock Holmes to my Watson, Adam assembled the missing pieces, weaving the fabric that had cloaked my life with Ben in mystery and confusion. He explained how Ben had accomplished his goal, creating some identifying documents and obtaining others from a real individual who was deceased. Not until later, when frustrated with his employers, did he file income tax returns for his invented character and receive rebates under that name. Then he duplicated the process, creating several more personae for which he also filed tax returns.

I wondered about the deceased. What would it be like for their loved ones to see the names quite literally resurrected in the newspaper? Had Parker contacted relatives in the course of his investigation? Would the shock reactivate grief, open new wounds? Ben had professed that his was a victimless crime. Did he even once consider the impact on the families of those whose names he had robbed? I observed him in the prisoner's box. He had his own pain now; he would pay for his thoughtlessness.

Adam's summation drew to a close. "Mr. Volski stopped his fraudulent activities of his own accord in 1985. He divested himself of the tools necessary to continue filing under these fictitious names. He has made full restitution of the monies he defrauded.

"As for the breach of trust charge, Your Honour, this refers to actions while he was employed with Revenue Canada. He used his position as an auditor to gain access to income tax files for which he was not authorized. Corporal Parker of the R.C.M.P. in his testimony earlier made statements suggesting that Mr. Volski had an insidious purpose for doing this, such as to seek out women for sexual favours. In fact, there is no evidence of an insidious purpose. The individuals, men and women, whose records he examined were well known to Mr. Volski. They were in fact, friends who he assisted with tax advice. It was for this purpose that he examined their records."

And to find me, I added silently.

"My client has already paid a high price for his criminal actions. He was fired from his position at Revenue Canada and has been unemployed for a period of time. Recently he has found temporary employment driving a school bus. It will be difficult for him to find employment which utilizes his education and talent."

Adam recommended a sentence, which by prior agreement, the Crown briefly echoed. The judge scribbled some notes. Then he again ordered Ben to stand. He peered down at him over his spectacles. "The offences to which you have pleaded guilty are of a serious nature, Mr. Volski. I sincerely hope that in future, you put your talents to more productive and law abiding pursuits. I find you guilty and sentence you to one year in a common gaol."

It was done. The sheriff led Ben out the back. In the last second before he exited, he turned. Meeting my eyes, he gave a shallow wave and departed. I sat unmoving, numb, a gaping hole growing inside. It wasn't till leaving with Adam I realized nothing had been said about the drug charges. They were dropped, Adam informed me. It made me think that Parker's insidious insinuations and second search were merely tactics after all, meant to break Ben because he'd had a weak case against him.

———————————

Prison widow. I'd learned the term as a third year social work student in Hamilton. On field placement to Elizabeth Fry Society, I visited wives whose men were incarcerated in the old Barton Street Gaol. As I left the courthouse, its meaning began to sink in. Now I would shoulder a double load at home, Ben's chores along with my own.

For months, he'd tutored me in managing the finances; banking, balancing a chequebook, tracking investments and financial statements. There'd be no slack to make mistakes. Mortgage, insurance, child support payments, repairs and maintenance to house and truck, food and sundries would have to be paid from my income.

Living in the country, we depended on two wells and a cistern to provide enough water. Mineral-hard, it also offered endless possibilities for corrosion and plumbing breakdown. The jumble of pipes, pumps, valves, gauges and taps in the basement confounded me. The mathematical and mechanical demands gave me a deeper appreciation for Ben's aptitude. Gradually I'd learned to calculate the flow, adjusting taps to rotate intake between wells to the cistern, cleanse tanks, dismantle parts to scrub them free of calcium build-up and reassemble them.

As dusk fell, I fought off night terrors. The daily fare of stories of abuse and violence nurtured an unhealthy sense of vulnerability normally assuaged by Ben's presence. But now the isolation of our house, far from the road and neighbours, pressed in on me with the dark and unrelieved quiet. I permitted myself a reasonable amount of precaution, then kept busy until exhaustion overtook me in the small hours of the morning. When I finally crawled between cold sheets, my thoughts returned to him. *Where are you, my love; trying to find a comfortable position on a hard prison bed? Do you share a cell with other inmates? What are their crimes? Do they frighten you? If I concentrate really hard, will you hear me telepathically? I love you.* I rolled over and drifted into a grey void.

———————————

My first full day alone. The computer screen crackled to life. The events of the past eight months had delayed my schedule for writing my thesis. Now I could finally focus on it.

After an hour, I got up to scrounge a cup of coffee. Just as I sank back into my chair with a cup, the phone rang, startling me and causing me to spill a little. Cursing softly, I reached for a tissue with one hand to mop up and with the other grabbed the phone.

"Collect call for anyone from Benjamin Volski. Will you accept the charges?"

"Yes!"

"Go ahead, please."

"Ben!"

"Hi kid." His voice reached through the wire and soothed an ache I'd been unwilling to acknowledge.

"Where *are* you?"

"Hamilton."

"Hamilton! Barton Street Gaol?"

"Hamilton Detention Centre."

"Oh...yeah. They tore down that old dinosaur."

"Yeah, lucky me, I've a room in the Hamilton Hilton. It's maximum security; they'll keep me here till they classify me according to the level I warrant. You can visit me, though."

"Really! When?"

"How 'bout tomorrow?"

I laughed, relief making me giddy. "Oh God, I can't tell you how much I want to see you."

"Me too," he said earnestly. "Listen, Shelley, I had to stand in line for the phone and there are others behind me. I can't stay on. Visiting hours are between two and four."

Hamilton sprawls along the south shore of Lake Ontario's V-shaped western end. The Skyway Bridge bisects the V carrying city-bound traffic into the ever-present yellow pall belching from the steel mills. From home, this shorter route wends through the east-end slums: warehouses, taverns, tattoo parlours and row houses with peeling paint and sagging porches.

I preferred the longer, more aesthetic route rounding the end of the lake. Approaching the slums from the opposite direction, I found Hamilton Detention Centre in the more seedy end of town. A contemporary red-brick structure nearly devoid of windows rose in tiers of two, four and six-storey blocks. It presented an antiseptic exterior to this human warehouse, shielding the public conscience from its interior misery. Its predecessor, a limestone monolith with heavily barred windows and walls several feet thick had been more honest.

I approached the main entrance, a glass breezeway honeycombed with a series of doors. I pulled on the first. It was locked. Beyond the last door, I could see a uniformed man at a desk. I found an intercom and pressed the button. Nothing happened. I peered at the man but he didn't react. Seconds passed. I was wondering if I should buzz again when a gruff "Yes" sounded through the intercom.

"I'm here to visit an inmate," I stated.

"Visiting's not till two." It was one-forty. I hadn't expected to have to wait outside. The damp chill coming off the lake seeped in around my neck. I adjusted my scarf, wishing I'd worn a hat. I'd left my gloves in the truck so I hitched my purse strap higher on my shoulder and stuffed my hands in my pockets.

Over the next twenty minutes, various characters collected around me, apparently knowing the ropes. They cursed, borrowed lights from one another for smokes and bad-mouthed the guards and a lawyer who was ushered in immediately.

"Who's first?" a voice barked over the intercom. The others gawked at me.

I shrugged, "Guess it's me. What do I do?"

"Press the button to talk," one women instructed.

I put my mouth close to the intercom. "I'm here to visit Benjamin Volski." I couldn't understand the staticky response. Confused, I looked to the woman for help.

"Just wait," she said. "They gotta check 'im out." A minute later, the voice ordered me to come in. A buzzer sounded and I pulled the door open. Ten steps down, I found the next door locked. Another uniformed guard appeared beyond the farther door and motioned me to try it again. This time it opened. I now stood in a glass cubicle with one more door to go. Beside me, a third guard opened a hatch and ordered me to push my purse through. I did. He opened it and peered inside, then shoved it back and waved me through. Another buzzer ushered me in.

The clerk at the desk pushed a large open book toward me. "Sign in." It had columns headed Date, Inmate, Visitor, Relationship to Inmate, Time In, Time Out, Number. I wrote: December 23, Ben Volski, Shelley Gallagher, common law wife, 2:10 p.m. I looked at him, puzzled. He handed me a slip of cardboard with a number on it, which I wrote in the last column.

"Bring that back here when you leave," he growled. "And be sure to sign out."

"Okay. Where to now?"

"Wait over there," he tossed his head toward rows of benches. "I'll let you know when you can go in." I chose a seat facing a mural across the back wall. It boasted of progress. Prisoners in black and white striped garb broke rocks against the backdrop of the old Gaol. By contrast, inmates wearing contemporary overalls appeared content at work in a shop in the new Detention Centre. The other visitors filed in one by one. The hands on the wall clock crept around to twenty-five minutes after two. At last the man behind the desk bawled, "Okay, go ahead."

I followed the herd to a set of bars that blocked the passageway at one end of the waiting room. We bunched up like cattle by the grill. Beyond it, a granite-faced guard leaned on a panel of toggle switches in a glassed-in control room, surrounded by TV monitors that exposed various locations in the jail. Just then a loud electronic hum sounded. The gate rolled aside and the herd jostled through.

The sun warmed the rock where I sat, lotus style. My perch, a promontory atop the escarpment afforded a panoramic view. I looked down on the tops of trees. In the middle distance, fields, farms and woodlands stretched away in pastoral orderliness. On this exceptionally clear day, the Toronto skyline was visible on the horizon, sixty-five kilometres to the east.

Nothing moved in the valley. About now, the Gallagher clan would be gathering. Strange to spend Christmas Day without seeing another living soul. Peaceful really. I closed my eyes and felt the wintry sun bathe my face.

I can do this, I thought. Ben's image as I last saw him rose vividly before me.

I'd waited on a stool in the visitation room. Shallow partitions afforded an illusion of privacy from visitors on either side of me. A telephone receiver hung to my left. Mirror-image booths lined the prisoner's side of the glass where inmates arrived at intervals. My heart somersaulted when Ben appeared. We sat grinning idiotically till I pointed to the phones.

"Hi kid," his voice resonated over the wire. It was physically ache not to be able to touch him. I put my palm on the glass, a little fearful a guard would come along and tell me that was forbidden. Ben put his hand over mine. I asked questions in a torrent. How was he faring? What were the conditions? The routine? How was he treated?

They were kept in a common area called a range during the day, he said. Offenders of anything from unpaid parking fines to murder shared the range. "We're lined up several times a day to be counted."

"Are you scared?"

He shrugged. "I try to keep out of their way. It's the incessant noise that gets to me, television and radio blasting both at once from morning till night. It's an exquisite form of torture. And the smoke..." He shared a cell with smokers, three men in a space meant for two. As the newby, Ben got the mattress on the floor.

He explained about prison issue 'uniforms'. Twice a week, inmates pick up a 'roll'—a towel, T-shirt, socks and underwear. "You can trade in your jeans at this time too. But once a guy gets something in decent repair that fits, he hangs on to them. I want to go for a pair that zips up." He stood up, revealing a fly that gaped open. I flushed, embarrassed for him but he grinned, unfazed.

"You can't let stuff like that get to you in here. Don't worry; I'll get a better pair."

Always the information ferret, he already knew how to barter with the inmate on laundry detail to secure a better T-shirt or jeans.

It seemed we'd just begun when a voice came over the wire directing us to end the conversation. Dismayed, I looked at my watch. "Twenty minutes? Is this all the time we're allowed?"

"I don't know, Babe. But if they say I have to go, I have to go."

"When can I come back?"

"I'm allowed two visits a week."

A guard appeared and tapped him on the shoulder. Ben hung up. Just before he passed through the door, he turned with a winsome shrug of acquiescence and flashed a grin.

I can do this, I thought then. *If Ben can submit, then I can endure.*

———

Christmas week at the office could be either very quiet or crisis-ridden. Having no other plans, I volunteered to provide coverage so other workers could take holiday time. The sudden squawk from my intercom startled me. "Yes, Agnes."

"Constable Parks on line one." Confusion again. Which officer was it?

I picked up the line with thudding heart. "Shelley Gallagher speaking."

"Shelley, it's Brad." I sighed with relief. "I'm so glad you're there. Would it be possible for you to see Terri and me today?"

"You sound concerned. What's happening?"

"Well,... I don't know exactly. I mean, I don't understand it. Terri's sort of, well, flipping out. She's been crying all morning. One minute she's mad at me and the next she's apologizing and saying it's not me."

"Does *she* want to see me?"

"Yes."

"Okay. Come right away."

It was the first time I'd seen them as a couple. Brad watched Terri, worry lines rippling his forehead. Her breath came in shudders—hiccups really, from crying hard.

"What's happened," I asked.

Each prompted the other to go first. Finally he took the initiative. "Yesterday, Terri's parents had us over for drinks. When she was out of the room, her father invited me—that is, invited us to his New Year's Eve party. Judge Stone's New Year's bash is famous around the police department. A bunch of the high-ranking officers always attend. I thought it was a good sign... that he'd accepted me." Terri looked daggers at him. He winced and continued. "We were on our way back to her place when I mentioned his invitation. She seemed kind of mad but she wouldn't talk."

"I wasn't mad," she countered.

He dropped his head and exhaled softly. "I asked her if she wanted me to stay the night and she said yes. But then she wouldn't let me come near her. It was stupid of me, thoughtless really, to say yes to New Year's Eve without finding out her feelings on it. I just didn't think."

"Dad was drunk," she said sourly. "If he'd been sober, he would never have extended the invitation."

"We don't have to go, Terri." He appealed to me. "I told her that. It doesn't mean anything to me."

"Oh ho, no-o-o," she interjected. "No way. One does *not* spurn Judge Stone's invitations."

Brad sat back turning up his palms in a gesture of helplessness. "That's the circle we got into this morning." He turned to her again. "I'll do whatever you want, Hon. Just tell me." She covered her face with her hands and doubled over, moaning.

I looked from one to the other. "Terri, is there something you want to say to Brad?" She made no response. "Would it be okay if I have him sit out in the waiting room and you and I talk?" Seconds passed before her head nodded slightly. I made eye contact with Brad; he stood up willingly and closed the door behind him.

"I know I'm being impossible," she admitted.

"Brad doesn't know what you shared with me last week?"

"No."

"You seem caught on the horns of a dilemma."

She nodded slowly. "When I think of my father cozying up to him, it makes me sick. He did that with Jarrod. They would gang up on me, teasing me meanly. It made me crazy that he accepted Dad's invitation without consulting me. That's exactly what Jarrod would have done. If I had tried to tell Jarrod I didn't want to go, he would make me out to be a neurotic spoil-sport."

"Do you think Brad would do that?"

"I know he wouldn't. I believe him when he says it doesn't mean anything to him."

I nodded. "Hence your apology to him."

"Yes."

"So what's the other horn?"

Tension bunched her shoulders again. She rocked in the chair answering obliquely. "I'm scared. I can't tell him, Shelley."

"Except for me, have you ever told anyone?"

She stopped rocking. "I told my mother when I was fourteen. She called Dad into the room and told him what I'd said. He put on this huge act like he was so disappointed in me, so hurt. He convinced her that I was neurotic and malicious. Said only an adopted daughter could make up such lies about her father." Her knuckles whitened where she dug her nails in around her knees.

She took on a faraway look. "They had me committed to a private psychiatric facility. The doctor there tried to get me to say that it was a Freudian fantasy, that I wanted to get rid of my mother and have my father all to myself. They used drugs on me that made me dopey and passive. After I was allowed home, I had to continue to see the psychiatrist and take the medications." She blinked and looked at me. "That's why I'm so against drugs."

"Did you ever tell anyone else?"

Instantly, she went back to rocking. "You've come this far, Terri. Why don't you tell me the rest?"

When she spoke again, her voice took on a hypnotic cadence. "I had a boyfriend, Billy. He really cared for me, but Daddy didn't like him; claimed he wasn't good enough for his little girl. Billy's father worked in the steel mill. Dad looked down on them for being working class.

"I told Billy. He went ballistic. He wanted to confront my father but I begged him not to. After that though, he could barely be civil to him. I think Dad suspected that I'd confided in him.

"Billy started getting harassed by the police. He drove an old beater of a car. They'd follow him around, stop him, give him tickets. He told me they started threatening him with violence and once they even tried to force him off the road. He was convinced my father put them up to it."

"On New Year's Eve, Billy drove up to our house in the midst of Dad's party." Her speech sounded youthful, as if she were a teenager again. "He started yelling from the front yard. I saw him from my bedroom window. Daddy went out on the porch to get rid of him. Some of his guests—police officers—went with him. He threatened to have him arrested but Billy didn't give two hoots. He shouted out for everyone to hear what Dad had done to me. I thought I would die. I was so scared and humiliated. In a way I was mad at Billy and in another way, I loved his bravado." Terri stopped talking. She stared, catatonic, at the far wall, reliving something.

I prompted her. "What happened after that?"

She buried her face in her hands, moaning softly. "Oh Billy, why did you have to say anything?" For a moment, she seemed unaware of me. Then, "Later that night, Billy's car was found wrapped around a tree. He was dead." She sat silent a long time, before continuing.

"I went berserk when I found out. My parents put me back in the hospital and I was doped up again. My mother told me Billy had been drunk when he came to our house but I never believed her. That wasn't like him. My father refused to ever talk about it, as if he wanted to cover up something. I think Daddy sicked the police on him and they ran him off the road."

When I called the children's home, Ari's wavering pubertal voice answered.

"Hi ya, Munchkin," I said. "How's your vacation going?"

"Okay."

"Just okay?"

"Yeah."

"Hmm. Your sister and Mommy home with you?"

"Sara. Mommy's at work."

"I see. What day is today?"

"Thursday." Morosely, he added, "The day we usually spend with you and Daddy."

"Mm hmm. I wondered if you and Sara would like to go out for lunch with me."

"Sure!" he said, perking up.

"Why don't you ask Sara?" I heard a clunk as he dropped the phone.

"She says yes," he puffed when he came back on.

"Super. I'll pick you up at noon."

Sara rearranged the condiments in the centre of the table squirming under my gaze. Ari leaned his head on his hand, his elbow pushed far out on the table-top.

The waitress had taken our order and I'd exhausted my 'small-talk' questions. To break the awkward silence, I announced, "I've seen your Dad." Two pairs of eyes riveted on me. "For now, he's in a place in Hamilton. He'll be moved in a while. We don't know where yet." What thoughts were tumbling behind those sober expressions?

Lowering my voice to speak confidentially, I asked, "Do any of your friends know your Daddy's in jail?" They shook their heads. "Listen, you two. I know this must be very hard for you but it helps to talk. You can talk to me but I'm not with you everyday. It's a good idea to talk to people you trust, your Mommy, a friend." They looked so sad I wanted to sweep them into my arms but I sensed it would embarrass them.

"Do you want to see your Dad?"

Ari sparked to life. "Yes!" I had expected that. But Sara? Would the prospect of entering a prison to visit the father so recently estranged be too daunting?

She met my gaze and whispered a soft "Yes." I felt a rush of endearment. I explained the rules, that only two people were allowed per visit and an adult must be with a child. "So you'll have to go on separate days. The next day he's allowed visitors is Monday. That's the last day of your vacation. One of you could go with me then. You two can decide who goes first. I'll call Monday morning and you can tell me then."

January 2, 1989

I was feeling pleased with myself. It was Monday morning and in spite of the emotional roller coaster of the past twelve days, I had forged ahead on my thesis. Ben seemed to be coping. A dentist had attended to his broken tooth. I'd managed to keep my family unaware of our situation. The anticipated publicity had not materialized. I was handling the solitude and routine chores.

I picked up the phone and dialled. Margaret answered. I wished her Happy New Year and asked for the children. "They're both still sleeping, Shelley. They were up late last night."

"I understand. Would you have them call when they get up?" I hung up and went back to keying. One and a half pages later the phone rang.

"Shelley…" It was Margaret, her voice odd—flat. "I went in to wake Sara." There was a long leaden pause.

"She's dead."

"What?" No. I misheard.

"She's dead."

I was lightening-struck, blind-sided, weightless.

"I don't know what to do," she added plaintively.

"Call 911. I'm on my way."

CHAPTER NINE

*I*t *can't be true! Margaret's mistaken; playing a cruel game. I have to have misunderstood!* I careened down near-empty roads, slowed for a red light, ran it. At their house, I skidded into the driveway, hammered on the door, tried the knob, found it locked, pounded harder. At last I heard the bolt slipped. The door swung open on Margaret's ashen face. "I just called the ambulance now. I couldn't let Ari wake up to sirens; I had to tell him."

"Where is he?"

"In his room."

"I'd like to go to him."

She nodded dumbly. "I'll wait for the paramedics," she whispered. I laid my hand on her arm, then hurried past. I'd never been on the second floor of the house. I found the stairs and flew them two at a time. At the top I wavered. Rooms opened along the landing in both directions. I rushed to the right. At the first door, I froze. Crumpled on the carpet lay Sara's lifeless form. I ached to go in, to gather her in my arms and hold her, warm her. I teetered in the doorway gripping the frame.

"Ari, where are you?"

A muted whimper, "Here." He hunched on his bed, blankets rumpled over his lap, his face wet with tears. I sat and pulled him to me, rocking him, brushed his bangs off his forehead and kissed it. Muffled sounds stuck in his throat.

A mournful, undulating wail violated the morning, swelling in the distance. "The ambulance is coming," I whispered. His window overlooked the secluded front yard and driveway and we watched it halt beside my truck. Paramedics with black bags approached without haste, apparently aware that they were redundant.

A moment or so later, a rustling sound passed by the head of the stairs, accompanied by voices hushed and solemn. Outside, a police cruiser arrived. More footsteps on the stairs and down the hall.

"Do you want to go downstairs?" I asked Ari. He shook his head. "I'll stay with you then." The paramedics returned to the ambulance and put away their cases. Time hung. I had no sense of how much had passed. A dark sedan arrived.

I asked Ari again if he wouldn't like to go down to be with his mother. He shook his head. "I want to find out what's happening," I said. "Are you sure you want to stay here?" He nodded. When I stepped out of his room, I encountered a police officer shadowing the door to Sara's room.

"Who are you?" he asked in a voice that was deferential, yet official. I explained. "Did the mother call you?"

"Yes."

"You're on good terms then," he observed.

"Reasonable." The still form on the floor drew my eyes compellingly. "I'd like to go in and be with her for a few minutes," I said.

"Go ahead."

I tiptoed in and knelt beside her. She lay on her stomach, face turned away to the side, an arm curled up by her head. I thought of all the times that her coughing overheated her, exacerbating the cough. Had she had sought relief in the coolness of the floor? She wore a pink nightshirt. I knew the one; it had a white kitten on the front. Her face was ice blue. Her hand closed over an inhaler.

I yearned to brush away the strands of hair that lay pasted against the hollow cheek. With the officer watching though, I didn't dare disturb anything. I surveyed the room, examining it for the first time. On her bed, unicorns pranced across the fabric of a rumpled quilt. Clouds dusted a sky blue ceiling. Rainbows arced across the wallpaper. Books neatly lined a white painted bookshelf and here and there, more unicorns in crystal, china and plush adorned the ledges. A small desk bore an assortment of pens and coloured pencils, a writing pad with a rainbow in the upper corner, a unicorn ink-stamp and another inhaler. When I stood up to leave, I noticed a third inhaler among the make-up cluttering the surface of her dresser. I stepped back into the hall.

"Does the father know?" the officer asked.

"No. I have to go and tell him."

"Is he at work?" I groaned inwardly and told him where Ben was. The officer raised his eyebrows and asked about the circumstances. When I explained, he offered to call the supervisor at the Detention Centre, to prepare them for my arrival.

I entered the kitchen just as the paramedics, who had returned, led a man in a suit toward the stairs. "The coroner," Margaret whispered to me. A soft rap sounded on the door and a woman peered around it, her face a cameo of concern and compassion. She folded Margaret in her arms. Footsteps of several people shuffled down the stairs. I steered Margaret and her friend toward the back door, letting the cortege with its burden, pass unseen.

Ari appeared soon after, barefoot and in his pyjamas. Margaret held out her arms and he clung to her. Then he curled up on the couch, thumb in his mouth. I touched Margaret's elbow. "I've got to go to Ben. I've got to tell him."

She gave me a puzzled look. "Where is he?"

I gaped. "You don't know?" She shook her head, looking blank. "Margaret, he's in jail."

She closed her eyes. "Oh my God. No. I knew it was coming but... How awful!" I turned to Ari with shocked realization but the boy stared into space, insensible. *I should have* known *the children wouldn't tell.* How could I miss the cues? Why had I left them alone with it? *I* should have told Margaret. Sara, Sara... I left you alone to cope. You kept your secret, your terrible, shameful secret. Kept it to your death.

I drove in a trance. *How do I tell Ben? How? How?* Emotions with no name flooded me. Disjointed images slashed my mind. Sara fighting for breath, gasping, lungs clawing for air, slipping from consciousness alone in the dark. My own lungs felt near to bursting.

In a daze, I overshot the cut-off for the north-shore route. I'd have to go through the slums. I crossed the bridge and descended into the labyrinth of factories and warehouses. Nothing looked familiar. I was lost.

Anxiety ballooned within me. I turned down one dead end after another in a surreal nightmare, slipping toward full-blown panic.

Then on a light standard, I saw a familiar sign, Barton Street. I hung a left and five minutes later pulled into the lot at the Detention Centre. As soon as I gave my name, the guard let me in. The police officer had kept his word. I asked to speak to the person in charge. "That'll be Sherman Henshaw," the guard said.

Sherman Henshaw personified the tank that was his namesake. He bore down on me in the waiting area. I leapt to my feet but he spoke before I could open my mouth. "I'll keep other visitors out of the regular visitation room."

"Visitation room?" I stared in disbelief. "Can't I be in a room with him?"

"No, Ma'am, I can't allow that."

I felt the wind knocked out of me. "You can't mean that. I can't tell him through glass that his daughter has died."

"No personal contact. Those are the rules."

I pleaded but he folded his arms, immutable. "You may have as much time as you wish. That's the best I can do." The room reeled. I wanted to beat on this insouciant hulk with my fists but he pointed to the gate, dismissing me. I stumbled toward the grill at the end of the hall.

While I sat in the visitor's room I trembled so much my teeth chattered. An eternity seemed to pass and then, quite suddenly, he was there. He gave me a quizzical smile, gesturing at the empty room. "How'd you manage to arrange this?" he said into the phone.

"Oh Ben—" My throat closed up, the words strangled there. My mouth opened but nothing came out. He gave a slight shake to his head registering bewilderment.

"Sara." I choked. "She died, Ben."

As if a bullet had slammed into him, he recoiled violently. In slow motion, he crumpled onto the counter. The receiver clattered over the edge, dangling by its cord.

Remote, unreachable, he lay like a stone. Sobs wracked me. I stroked the unyielding glass where his head touched it. But he could not feel me; could not hear me. Time hung in suspension. I tapped the window, calling out to him, but he gave no sign of hearing. "*Please*, Ben," I implored, "please pick up the phone."

Finally, with agonizing effort, he roused, drawing himself up as if mortally wounded. He fumbled for the receiver and lifted his head like a man drugged. I pressed my palm to the glass, but he stared past me unseeing.

"How...how did she die?"

I swallowed a lump. "It was her asthma." He went down again.

He was drowning and I could only watch, helpless. My arms ached to hold him but the glass was an impenetrable wall of ice. I tasted my tears.

After what felt like infinity, he raised himself with supreme effort. He leaned on the counter, head in his hand as if it were a very great weight. Deep sighs whooshed through the telephone line. But the only tears were mine.

In sporadic spurts, he asked for details. Gradually, his eyes lost their glaze, though not the dullness. "I need your help," he pleaded. He wanted a Jewish funeral for Sara. Margaret had converted when they married but abandoned Judaism when they split. "She won't know what arrangements to make and I can't make them from here."

"Tell me what to do."

"Contact the rabbi. You'll have to tell him where I am."

I nodded. "What else?"

"I need you to call people. I'll give you a list." I scrabbled through my purse for something to write on. When he finished with instructions, I touched the glass again. This time, he put his own hand against mine, then leaned his head against it. "You'd better go," he groaned. "There's much to do and I'll have to find out how I get a pass to attend the funeral. I'll call you tonight."

"In my mind, I'm holding you."

"Thanks. I need that." He staggered to his feet, having aged before my eyes and left the room.

I hung up the phone in the den, drained. My head ached. I wished I could cry but once I left Ben I felt desiccated inside. In a seven-hour marathon, I'd communicated the news to one after another of Ben's relatives and friends. Since they all knew of the police investigation, I was spared the awkwardness of explaining why he was in jail. I shrank from facing my own family, not knowing how to begin. Finally I called Jamie. First I told him about Sara. After all the calls I'd made, I knew to allow time for the shock. I answered his questions and accepted his condolences.

"Jamie," I said, "there's more." As simply and briefly as I could, I explained the situation with Ben. When I finished, he was silent a long time. When he spoke it was with such tenderness, I felt again the pressure of tears that would not come.

"You could have talked to me, Shel. You didn't have to keep it from me. I love you, you know."

"I know," I answered miserably. "I don't want to get into my reasons right now but believe me, it was just easier. Anyway, I need your help. I can't cope with calling the rest of the family. Please, would you do it for me."

"Of course. I'll take care of it."

"Thanks."

"Are you alone?" he asked.

"Yeah."

"You shouldn't be."

"I'm alright. I still have some people to call."

I spent the evening like the day, on the phone, mostly with various call-backs. I called my office and left a message on the answering machine with news of Sara's death and that I would not be in all week.

Ben called. He'd submitted a request for a Temporary Absence Pass but the vacuum of information about what would happen only deepened his melancholy. As usual, his time on the shared phone was abbreviated.

It was after nine p.m. when the doorbell rang. It was Jamie. "You shouldn't be alone on such an evening," he said gently. He stepped inside and wrapped me in his arms.

A pale sun smudged the eastern horizon and gradually leached the darkness from my bedroom. Bleary-eyed, I gave up all hope for sleep. I could not rest until I knew Ben's request had been granted. I'd sent Jamie home at midnight. But now I was restless again and regretted sending him away. I calculated what time it was in Italy then dialled the fourteen-digit number. The cost would be exorbitant but I didn't care. I needed a friend.

"Ciao."

"Daphne Piccolo, please."

"This is Daphne."

By noon, no one else in my family had called. Margaret invited me over. In contrast to the emptiness in my home, hers brimmed with friends. After a while, most of them left. Ari sat on the floor aimlessly rotating the joystick on an Atari game. I was anxious to leave too. I told Margaret that visitation at the jail started in forty minutes and I wanted to be there.

Ari's head snapped up. "Can I come?" I looked to Margaret and she nodded.

———————

While we waited in the visiting room, he perched on my knee and chewed the inside of his cheek. On seeing him, Ben broke into a smile. I handed the phone to Ari. Though I couldn't read Ben's lips, from his animation I gathered that he was bantering. Ari smiled a smile that didn't reach his eyes.

I eased out from under him, stood behind him and waved for Ben's attention. I shook my head. His brow creased. I pointed to Ari and traced my fingers in two lines down from my eyes. Ben nodded and sobered. Scooping Ari into my lap once more, I tipped the receiver so we could both listen. "Ari," Ben said, "you spent more time with Sara than anyone else in the world. You knew her best of. . . " He broke off in mid-sentence, looked up at me and nodded toward Ari. The boy's face crumpled as tears spilled silently down his cheeks. Ben's face mirrored the boy's pain and laid bare his helplessness. All the same, I felt tension drain from the child. After a bit they conversed comfortably. Then Ari handed the phone to me. "Daddy wants to talk to you."

"As of today I'm back to the regular twenty minute visitation limit. I need to update you. I haven't been told anything yet about a pass. Parker was here this morning with a police officer from Halton. They asked me a lot of questions about how Margaret and I get along. I told them our relationship is civil. I have a bad feeling that Parker's appearance has put a monkey wrench into my request for a pass."

"A monkey . . . ?" I stopped myself because of Ari. "How?"

A muscle in his jaw rippled. "I don't put it past that bastard to stir up trouble for me. My gut says he's got people thinking I blame Margaret for Sara dying and that I'd be a threat to her at the funeral."

"What happens now?"

"Your guess is as good as mine. Nobody's banging down my door to give me information."

"Anything I can do?"

He shrugged while looking longingly at the boy in my lap. "Yeah," he said, "take care of my son for me."

Wet snow, the first of the season, pattered the windshield. As I spiralled down the tight ramp to the highway, I felt the tires slither. Beside me, Ari sat quiet and still. The truck settled into traffic and I relaxed my grip on the wheel.

"Ari, you okay, Hon?"

"Yeah," he said, but the word stretched out long and flat.

"You don't *sound* okay, Munchkin." I glanced over. He shrugged one shoulder, his body a question mark. His face worked but nothing came out, as if his thoughts were a breach birth. "Ari, I know you think about things and you have feelings. People aren't meant to keep those inside. They're harder to handle that way. Talking helps clear up a lot of misunderstanding. You mustn't go through life trying to work everything out yourself. Sara did that and I think it caused her a great deal of unnecessary pain. Your Mommy and Daddy and me, we love you. Talk to us. Talk to *me*."

A transport beside me forced me to keep my eyes on the road. Its drone all but drowned out the thin voice beside me. "You remember when you asked me yesterday if I wanted to go downstairs?" Remember! I could still *feel* him in my arms, the mind-numbing truth of Sara's death thick around us.

"I remember."

"I did want to."

I eased off the gas to let the transport pass me. "Why didn't you let me take you there?"

"Because I was afraid to see Sara's body."

For a foolish second, I closed my eyes as I felt an invisible fist punch my chest. "Oh Honey, I wish you could have told me then. You wouldn't have seen her." I ran my fingers through his hair, pushing it over his ear. "But you know what? I'm glad you told me now."

"*I'm* glad you phoned yesterday," he went on, the gate open now. "Mommy was gonna go out and let me and Sara sleep in. Because you called, she went to wake Sara up. If you hadn't phoned, it would have been me who found her."

I nodded slowly and deliberately. "That would have been very hard alright."

He exhaled and seemed to uncoil his body. The afternoon was darkening as I exited the highway, heading for Margaret's house. Five minutes later, the measured breathing beside me told me he had fallen asleep. Looking down on the top of the tousled head where he'd slid low in the seat, I felt a swelling in the vicinity of my heart.

Margaret met us at the door. "Caitlyn is here, Ari," she informed him with a hug. To me, she said, "I was hoping you'd go to the funeral home with me… to help make the arrangements."

"Of course I will."

Footsteps clattered on the stairs and Caitlyn rounded the corner. She swooped me in an emotional embrace. When she turned to Ari, I saw that her eyes were swollen and red-rimmed. "Hi Ari."

"Hi."

She slipped her arm through his and led him away.

By the time we finished at the funeral home, the mercury had fallen and snow fell thickly. I dropped Margaret off and headed home. When I pulled into our lane, my headlights swept across a vast sea of white. Only the stakes Ben had pounded into the ground every twenty yards late in the fall indicated where the lane should be. If this keeps up, I thought, I'll have to plough in the morning to get out. Before going inside, I trudged to the barn to plug in the tractor.

I counted six messages on the answering machine, all call-backs from Ben's friends. Too exhausted to talk to anyone, I ran a bath, ignoring the phone as it continued to ring intermittently while I soaked. It was too early for Ben's call. I would run for no one else.

Precisely at seven, he phoned.

"Has the funeral been set?" he asked straight away.

"Day after tomorrow, Thursday at one."

He needed me to do some errands. "I've lost weight in here. Any belts I own won't fit me now. Take one of mine and buy something two inches shorter. Take a shirt to the cleaners, too." Then he told me he'd broken his reading glasses. It was rotten luck. Reading was just about his only means of escapism. It would be weeks, he said, before he could get a repair. I reminded him that his friend and optometrist, Michael, l would be at the funeral.

"Right," Ben said. "I can give them to him to fix. If they let me out, that is." He'd heard nothing on his request for a pass. "The chaplain came to see me. She asked about my relationship with Margaret, how I feel about her now. For once, my compulsion about making lists paid off. I had a scrap of paper in my pocket where I'd been jotting down things I'll do if they let me out for the funeral. I showed her the list. The first thing on it was, 'Give Margaret a hug'."

"What'd she say to that?"

"She said, 'I guess that answers that.' She told me they were processing my request but by now all the professional staff will have left for the day."

"What's taking so *long*?" I fretted.

"I don't know, Shelley," he snapped testily. "They don't tell me anything. They ask the questions. I just try to give the right answers." After a pause he said, "I'm sorry. It's just that some weird stuff has been happening." He sounded grim.

"What kind of stuff?" I said, my heart thumping with alarm.

"I can't say over the phone."

"Are you in danger?"

He didn't answer. "Ben?"

"What?"

"Are you *safe*?"

"Let's just say my ignorance of prison etiquette is a liability."

He would say no more. Terrifying images bombarded me. I was sick with helplessness, sick of talking in code. Hour by hour, fear, grief, exhaustion and uncertainty ratcheted my muscles till my body became an over-wound spring. I leaned my head into my hand. "They just *have* to let you out." He didn't answer. "I'll pull strings if I have to."

"How?"

"Maybe Adam can help."

"Maybe," he sounded doubtful.

"Why don't I call him anyway? Perhaps he can get some motion through court or something."

"Sure, give it a try," he said without enthusiasm.

"I'll go political if you want me to."

"I hope we don't have to get to that. Maybe tomorrow morning, it'll come through."

It was after eleven when Gayle called. She'd been trying off and on all evening, she said, but either got a busy signal or no answer. "How you doing, Shelley? Do you need anything?"

"Actually, I *could* use someone here to answer the phone. I have to go out and run some errands but I'm reluctant to leave in case someone calls about Ben's request for a pass."

"I'll send Mom," she said. "I'd come myself but Chantal's come down with chicken pox. She's running a fever and I can't leave her." I groaned inwardly at the thought of having to cope with Florence Gallagher but at this point any help was better than none.

Sometime around midnight the snow stopped, leaving a six-inch blanket. Wednesday. By now I'd gone forty-eight hours without sleep. Ceaseless anxiety drove it beyond reach. Hoping to plough the driveway before the phone started ringing, I trudged to the barn in the pre-dawn dark. The diesel engine whined and protested but the battery was too weak to kick it over. I clamped the charger on to juice it up.

At eight I called Mother to tell her not to drive down the lane. "If you get stuck and I can't start the tractor, we'll both be stranded," I told her. "Wait in your car. I'll watch for you and come out to meet you."

At nine I called Adam. A legal remedy he said, would come too late to help Ben. He'd call the Detention Centre though and recommend Ben as a safe risk. "We'd be grateful for anything you can do, Adam."

At two, I sat at the kitchen table. Bone weary, I longed to lie down but had no choice but to keep watch by the window for Mother. When her car turned into the entrance of the lane, I jumped up and threw on my coat and scarf.

Mother bustled about the kitchen putting away foodstuffs we'd bundled in from her car. "Have you eaten lunch?" she asked.

"Lunch? Um...no. I haven't eaten, since, I don't know, Sunday, I guess."

"Hmph. You should eat. I brought a cooked chicken potpie. I'll heat it in the microwave." It was the only sign from her that anything was out of the ordinary. There'd been no condolences, no hugs, not even any questions. At least it was nice to have her do the 'mother thing' with food. The aroma three minutes later, aroused a grumble in my stomach. I *was* hungry after all. I wolfed it down piping hot.

Leaving her to mind the phone, I hurried out to plough, bring in her car, then to run the errands for Ben. I pulled back into the lane at four. Noticing the flag raised on the mailbox, I stopped to gather the mail. Back in the cab, I flipped through the pile, a newspaper, some bills and junk mail. I tossed the stack on the seat beside me. The newspaper fell open to the front page. The headlines jumped off the page. ***Catching the man who never was.*** I skimmed the first couple of paragraphs, my heart racing then started over and read more carefully.

Each year, Timothy Morgan dutifully reported his income on his tax return. For several years he received a refund. He supplied his social insurance number and date of birth from his birth certificate. Unfortunately, Timothy is a work of fiction, along with several more straw men and women who were issued refunds. Ewen Montagu's book about a bogus character British intelligence hatched during the Second World War to deceive the enemy, sparked an idea in the mind of a frustrated Revenue Canada auditor. The talented, entrepreneurial employee found a way to pay his own bonuses; he created Timothy and the others.

The story unfolded much as Adam had told it to the judge thirteen days ago. It went on to name Ben and give details of his sentence.

Why now? Why is this news today? A sudden hunch made me flip through the pages. Sure enough, Sara's name was among the death notices. Coincidence? Yesterday Parker accompanied the Halton Police to interview Ben. Had he thought it time that the newspapers pick up Ben's story? He'd got his pound of flesh. Wasn't that enough?

I barely shed my coat and boots before the phone rang. Wanting to pre-empt Mother, I ran to get it first. It was Ben.

"I just got back from seeing the Director of the Temporary Absence Program."

"And?"

"They haven't turned me down but they still haven't said yes either. She's a cool customer, that one. She wouldn't tell me why the decision keeps getting postponed. I get the impression, though, that a number of people have talked to them about me."

I heard a voice in the background at the other end of the line and Ben laughed. "Let me see," he said in an aside to someone nearby. "Hey Shelley, have you seen today's paper?"

"As a matter of fact, I just read it."

"Someone just handed it to me. Seems I'm some kind of hero in here. The guys just gave me a standing ovation."

"Wonderful," I said sardonically. "The idol of cons, crooks and miscreants." I didn't mention my suspicion about why thirteen days had elapsed before it hit the paper. He'd figure that out for himself soon enough.

The phone rang again as soon as I hung up. It was my boss. He expressed condolences "for all my troubles." Thankfully he was discreet. I hung up. Well, it was public now, just as Parker had warned.

I sequestered myself in my bedroom that evening, settling in for a sleepless vigil. With only hours left before the funeral, I racked my mind for some way to effect Ben's release. To fail was unthinkable. It would be heartless. I had dedicated my life to compassion and justice. If the so-called justice system could find within itself no compassion then that system was my enemy.

I'd been meditating with such intensity that I wondered if I made the phone ring when it did, at ten past six in the morning. I reached for it.

"Shelley? Is that you? It's Daphne, Honey."

"Daphne! I'm so glad you called."

"You sound awful. Did I wake you?"

"No. I can't sleep. I haven't slept since Sunday."

I described the tug-of-war over Ben's request since we'd spoken two mornings ago. "The funeral is in seven hours. If there's still no decision when I call the jail at nine, I'm going to phone our local Member of Parliament to see if he'll intercede. I don't know what else to do."

"Shelley, for goodness sake, why didn't you let me know. I'll call my brother Richard. He's the representative for Hamilton."

"Daphne, you can't stand your brother."

"So? It's about time he did something charitable. Besides, he owes me."

"Let me speak to someone at the jail once more after nine o'clock, first. If I get nowhere, I'll call you back."

"Okay. I'll be here."

At two minutes after nine, I rang the jail

"I want to speak to the Temporary Absence Pass Director?" The male receptionist grilled me and then put me on hold. The minute hand circled the bedside clock three times as I waited. Finally, he came back on. "They're in a meeting about Volski right now. Chaplain Bridges will call you when they are finished."

"When do they expect to be finished?"

"At ten." That was cutting it fine but maybe they were going to say yes after all. I crossed my fingers, deciding to wait. I dressed for the funeral and laid out Ben's clothes. I made breakfast for Mother, settling for a cup of coffee for myself. Ten o'clock came and went. I picked up the phone.

"May I speak with Chaplain Bridges, please?"

"She's gone for the day."

"How can she be gone?" I raged at him. "You told me she would call!"

"Well, she's gone." I slammed the phone down, snatched it up again and dialled Italy. I was on with Daphne less than a minute. Twenty minutes later, she called back and said Richard was working on it. At ten forty, Richard Cameron himself called.

"I'm on very friendly terms with the Deputy Minister of Corrections," he oozed. "I've just spoken with him and asked him to look into this matter. This is a tragic set of circumstances, Ms. Gallagher. I'm certain the Deputy Minister will see that things move speedily." Despite his pomposity, just then I could have kissed his feet. I thanked him and hung up. I paced like a caged tiger. At precisely eleven o'clock, the telephone rang once more.

"Ms. Gallagher, please."

"Yes! Speaking."

"This is Jerry Flynn. I'm the social worker at Hamilton Detention Centre. I know you've been anxiously waiting to hear from someone about Ben Volski's request for a temporary pass. You can come down now and pick him up."

Chapter Ten

Flynn had instructed me to deliver Ben's clothes to the rear entrance before coming to the front entrance to ask for him. I pushed the back door intercom and a gruff voice demanded my identity and ordered me to wait.

Prison warped time, I knew by now. Clocks on the 'outside' held no meaning. In the enforced idleness, questions beleaguered me. What had gone on behind the scenes while the institution kept Ben's fate dangling? Had Corporal Parker played a role? Had Richard Cameron? Would the door be opened for Ben or would administrators, resentful of outside interference, stonewall? My watch read a quarter to twelve. A sharp voice barked out of the intercom. The grate emitted a buzz, and I was in.

A husky guard produced a bag of clothing worn by Ben on his day in court. I had to barter my collection for his, item by item; shirt, suit jacket, pants, tie, socks, belt, underwear. With maddening slowness, he recorded each exchange while two other sullen fellows in uniform looked on. When we finished swapping the clothes, he thrust a paper and a pen across the counter, stabbing a spot with a fat forefinger.

"Sign."

I scratched my signature where he pointed and was summarily dismissed. Back outside, I checked my watch, twelve oh one. Wet snow sucked at my boots as I tramped to the front entrance. I asked for Flynn. The desk clerk let me in and issued the familiar command. Wait.

Soon, footsteps on the terrazzo announced the approach of two people, one with the squeak of flat leather shoes, the other a sharper click of a woman's narrow heels. A rotund man in a rumpled brown suit and thinning hair extended his hand, introducing himself as Jerry Flynn, the prison social worker. He turned to the woman. "This is Norma Guterson, Director of the Temporary Absence Program." The taller of the two, her scowl seemed set in cement on her square jaw. Her blunt-cut hair and navy suit matched her severe countenance. She cut to the chase.

"Mr. Volski is being released to your custody," she said in a brittle voice. "You will be responsible for him while he is on the temporary leave. He must be with you at all times. He is not allowed to drive a motor vehicle. He must be back inside the Detention Centre by sixteen hundred hours. If he is one minute late there will be a warrant for his arrest. Do you understand?" I nodded. "You must sign some documents. Mr. Flynn will go over them with you." She wheeled and strode away.

Flynn studied the floor until her footsteps faded, then looked up and said, not unkindly, "I'm sure you've been on pins and needles these last several days."

"To say the least."

"I can't give you details as to why it took so long but every time it seemed the way was clear, a new wrinkle would develop. I want you to know, as one social worker to another, you're the main reason that Ben was given the pass." I gaped at him, hoping he'd elaborate but all he said was, "You seem to have an excellent reputation in your community." I wondered whom they had talked to but he said no more about it.

He reviewed the requirements, stressing that they must be followed to the letter. I signed a seemingly endless series of documents binding me to meet them. He shook my hand and instructed me to return to the rear door to wait for Ben.

Outside, I slipped across the street first, to a phone booth. I punched in my home number. "I'm still waiting for Ben," I said, when Mother answered. "If they don't let him out, I'm going to stay here. I'll talk my way into sitting with him through visiting time even though we've used up his allotment."

"For heaven's sakes, Shelley, what's gotten into you. They've already told you he's being let out."

"I've been here over an hour, Mother. How complicated can it be?"

She didn't acknowledge my question or my frustration. I was ready to crack. "I have to go."

"What should I tell people if you don't show up?"

"Tell them," I blinked against the heat in my eyes, "tell them life sucks." I hung up before she could answer. I leaned my face into the back of my hand, still holding the receiver hung in its cradle and fought to get a grip on myself. Then I exited the booth and hurried back to my post, standing guard by the prison's back door.

I shivered in the January dampness. The minute hand on my watch crept past twelve thirty. Every fibre in my body, every muscle, every organ, every inch of flesh strained to hold on against something unseen that threatened to pull me apart. I clutched myself in my arms. Unable to stay still, I paced; ten steps away and ten back; ten steps away and turn. And there he was.

I flung myself at him. Holding him was the most real thing in those three endless days and nights. Through layers of winter apparel I felt his blood and bones, his ache and loss and longing.

The moment we crossed the threshold of the funeral home a throng enveloped him. He was borne through the room, delivered from hand to hand. People touched him, embraced him and murmured their sorrow for him and I was grateful. At last I could relinquish an immense load from my shoulders.

The crowd parted as if by design, opening a path between Ben and Margaret. They groped toward each other till Ben folded her in his arms. Ari squeezed through the throng and flung himself between them.

The rabbi shepherded us into the private wing of the L-shaped chapel; I took my place on Ben's left, Margaret on his right. Ari climbed onto his father's lap. A rose-colored coffin stationed in a bank of flowers obliterated everything else from my mind. The soft background organ music stopped. The rabbi's voice, compassionate yet strong, took possession of the hush.

"Sara Volski," he began, "held a passion for two remarkable motifs. One is symbolic of hope; the other of beauty. One comes from nature; the other from fable. Sara loved rainbows and unicorns."

His words hurtled me back into her bedroom, among mobiles and wallpaper, ink-stamp and ornaments. The torque in my muscles and emotions that had notched ever tighter over the past three days and nights snapped like a shattered clock-spring. I saw Sara running free, across a field of blowing grass. She took great gulps of air, painless and exhilarated. I heard the music of her laughter unimpeded by wheezing. I wept for a child I barely knew. I wept for grief that she never knew I loved her.

Later, I remembered Ben's rigid silence beside me. I remembered the deadness in his eyes as I faced him in the black limousine, how they smouldered as the cortege passed cruiser after cruiser, too many for the usual police escort. I remembered the bitter wind at the graveside, how it made the rabbi's coat billow.

The surrounding parking lot was dark and deserted. I extinguished the headlights, staring straight ahead at the dark wall of the Detention Centre. A single floodlight arced over the rear door through which Ben must soon re-enter.

"Did I do something wrong?" he asked.

I looked away, shaking my head. "No." Nothing moved outside the truck. Even in the dark with the recent snowfall, the city looked dirty, derelict. "I kept thinking you would give vent to your grief today, that you would cry."

"I can't cry."

"It's what funerals are for."

"I can't. I have to go back," he nodded toward the jail, "in there."

"But all day you've been among loved ones." He didn't answer. "Ben, it's not *healthy*."

Fury erupted from him. "What do you expect?" he shouted. The suddenness of his rage hurtled against me. I withdrew. The silence crackled between us. I waited.

"It's not safe," he said, sullen now.

"I don't understand." It was his turn to look away. "*Tell* me," I implored him.

"I don't want you to worry."

"Worry! For Christ sake, Ben! How can I *not* worry? You hint and speak in riddles. You start to tell me things and stop. I can't get organized around half-truths."

"Alright" he growled. "You want to know. I'll tell you." For several long seconds he remained mute, staring across the dark parking lot. "Remember I said that some weird stuff was happening." I braced against the fear I felt in the pit of my stomach. "I made some enemies. Seems it's not kosher in prison to admit your guilt, not to other criminals. It threatens the thugs who claim they were framed. That got me off on the wrong foot. Later, when I learned about Sara..." He broke off, swallowed, then whispered. "I just wanted to be alone. That pissed them off too. They didn't know about Sara and I didn't enlighten them. I coped by writing down my memories of her. Stupid illiterate clods get paranoid if you write. They think you're writing about them.

"On Tuesday when we filed back in after our outing in the yard, everyone else was directed down a different corridor from me. For a while, I was the only inmate on my range. A totally different group of inmates were brought in. One of the guards told me I'd better wise up. Some inmates had home-made weapons. They'd been planning to take me out.

"I can't cry in there, Shelley. I can't let down my guard or look weak." I reached for him. He neither reciprocated nor rejected my embrace. I didn't want to let go but he said hollowly, "Its time, Babe. I have to go."

I watched his retreating back as he crossed the street. When he reached the door, his hand went up to the intercom; the door opened. Without a backward look, he went through it.

A single parking space opened up on the busy coffee shop lot. I had to maneuver around a cruiser angled across two spaces to squeeze into it. Inside, a police officer's uniform stood out among the patrons. He noticed me and waved. I made my way over to where he was seated.

"Happy New Year, Brad."

"I understand yours wasn't so happy. My condolences, Shelley."

My heart missed a beat. "How did you know?"

"Terri got a call from your office last week to cancel her appointment. The receptionist told her you had a death in the family."

"Ah. Yes," I said without elaborating.

"Would you like to sit down?" he gestured toward the chair opposite him. I perched sideways on it.

"I can't stay long. Got to get to the office."

A waitress bustled over. "What can I get you?"

"A large black coffee to go, please."

Something caught Brad's attention outside the front window. "Great," he snorted. "Here comes trouble." I followed his line of vision to see two hefty officers strolling up the walk to the door.

"What! You're not afraid of the cops, are you Brad?" I grinned.

"Those two are a pain in the you-know-what."

They strutted in like they owned the joint. "Hey Sparky," bellowed the heavier of the two, "how ya' doin'." He clapped his large hand on Brad's shoulder and eased into the seat beside him, uninvited. The other officer grinned like a fool and took the chair by me.

"You tryin' pick up this peach, Sparky?" the first one said.

Brad gave him a baleful sideways look. "No Earl, I'm not."

Earl stretched out a hand to me. "M' friends call me Duke. Y'know, Duke of Earl?"

He held my hand overly long and winked at me.

"How do you do... Earl?" I said, pulling my hand out of his grip.

"Now Duke," the grinning fool interjected, "you know very well, Sparky's still taking out that anorexic model."

"She's not a model," Brad said, thin-lipped.

"Ri-i-ight," Earl lengthened the word, winking at his partner. "'Course she's not."

Brad bared his teeth. "Just what do you mean by that?"

Earl chortled and poked an elbow into Brad's ribcage. He leaned across the table toward his partner. "Eh, Bobby, do you know the difference between a counterfeit dollar and a skinny prostitute?" Bobby grinned and shook his head. Earl's upper lip curled in a salacious grin. "A counterfeit dollar is a phoney buck."

Brad blazed at him. "You're an asshole, Earl. Go find another table. Get the hell out of here before I do something stupid like assault a police officer." The two wheezed and convulsed but they got up and moved to the counter.

Brad sat gripping his coffee cup with both hands. "I'm sorry," he said. "I should exercise more self control. If you're not crass like them, they figure you're not tough. When I joined the force, I was prepared for the fact that you couldn't be soft. I just wasn't prepared for the fact that you not allowed to be civilized."

I shrugged. "Don't apologize. If I'd been in your place, I might have been upset enough to accidentally knock my coffee into his lap."

Brad sputtered. "Wish I'd thought of that."

"The police department needs more like you, Brad," I said sincerely. "Toughness and the ability to empathize aren't mutually exclusive. Social workers, in spite of the fact that people tend to think of us as a bunch of bleeding hearts, need a certain toughness too."

I noticed the waitress coming with my coffee.

"I wonder which of us has the harder job?" I speculated.

"I'm sure you do."

"You think so? Maybe we could play role reversal."

"How's that?"

"Is that your cruiser, out there?" I pointed to the one I'd had trouble getting around. He craned to look, as I stood up.

"Yeah."

"You're double parked. The fine is the price of my coffee." I took the paper cup from the waitress, smiled grandly at him and swept out of the cafe.

I found Ben morose as I faced him in the visiting booth once more. It was the third week in January and he'd heard nothing yet about being classified. He should have been moved on to another institution by now, with minimum or at least medium security. Detention was taking its toll, the inability to escape the incessant noise, the moronic music blaring on the radio, WWF on the television, the lack of mental stimulation or distraction of work, the inability to close a door or eat a meal with a fork and no doubt, his suppressed grief.

"It's taking a hell of a long time for them to decide whether or not I'm dangerous," he grumbled. "I think they're playing games with me, getting back at me for political interference in getting a pass for Sara's funeral." I didn't answer. Maybe it was true. Maybe it was just paranoia. He leaned on his hands and rubbed his eyes.

"You okay, Hon?" I asked.

"I've got a headache. Had it for days. I've been trying to read without my glasses."

"You haven't got them back yet? Michael should have sent them ages ago."

He shrugged.

"I'll call him tomorrow," I promised.

Terri sat white and rigid, her breathing shallow. Her nails dug into the fabric of the chair's armrests. Brad slumped forward in his seat in my office. A moan rose from behind his hands cupping his head. She had just told him her father had sexually abused her. "He...it started when I was about seven. He called me his little princess, gave me presents but I never wanted them. I wanted to please him, but not *that* way. At first he just fondled me." She spoke barely above a whisper. "Later it turned to...to intercourse," she finished in a whisper.

He lifted his eyes to her. "Honey, I'm so sorry." For a split second no one moved. Then she sprang into his lap and buried her face in his neck. Brad's face twitched and shifted through a rapid-fire series of emotions. "His own daughter! How could he do that to you?" he exploded. "I ought to give that bastard a piece of my mind."

"No!" she stiffened bolt upright. Her slender fingers covered his mouth. "No," she cried again, "you can't!" Her eyes flew wide, wild and panicked. She stumbled from his lap and backed up to the wall. When she could go no further, her hands searched behind her as if for an escape. Brad's own hand hung in mid-air following her retreat. She darted glances at the closed door.

"It's okay, Terri," I spoke, sensing her imminent flight. "You're safe here." She didn't respond; didn't seem to hear. "You're safe in my off—", but she bolted. Brad half rose from his chair but I arrested him with a flash of my palm. He looked truly alarmed himself now. I stepped into the hallway just as a door shut sharply down the hall. I went toward it, Brad hot on my heels. I paused outside a door that sported a black silhouette of a female figure. The lock clicked. I rapped lightly. "Terri?"

No answer. "Terri, can you talk to me?" I leaned my ear close to the door, listening.

"Tell him!" came the muffled response.

"Tell him what?"

"Tell him...about Billy."

I glanced at Brad. "Why don't you come out?" I coaxed. "I'll help you tell Brad."

"No! You tell him!"

"Alright. I just need to know you're okay."

"I'm okay. I want to stay here."

Back in my office Brad sat without speaking for several moments after I finished explaining, his face ashen. "You think Judge Stone really arranged this kid's death?"

"Who knows?" I answered. "Maybe. We know he had something to hide."

"Whew!" he leaned back, a far-away look glazing his eyes. "It's incredible."

"The point is, Terri thinks he might have. That fear has overshadowed her whole life."

Brad frowned. "It could be just a coincidence."

"Could be."

"After all, the kid was upset. Maybe he drove recklessly."

"Maybe."

"Do you believe it?"

"The objective truth of it is not my concern; Terri is. My job is to help her get her life on track." The door cracked open suddenly, lifting both of us from our seats in a startle. It crept wider until Terri revealed herself. Brad extended his hand to her. She took it and folded into the chair beside him.

"Promise me," she murmured, "promise you won't talk to Daddy." Gently, he drew his hand from hers and pushed a lock of her hair back off her face.

"I promise."

I woke with a start. Panting, my hand over my thudding heart. A nightmare again. A howling blizzard on a glacier. Footsteps in the snow leading to a deep crevasse. Sara's broken body at the bottom, her flesh ice-blue. Ben pursuing her footsteps deaf to my entreaties. I will lose them both.

Terror and sorrow brewed a crushing pain. It was cold in the house. I wrapped myself in my robe, stepped into slippers and scuffed down the darkened hall. At Sara's room, I clicked on the light. A bed, a desk, that was all. It was as if Sara had never been here. If only I had some tangible sign, some of her clothes, books, trinkets.

Sara, where did you go? Silence answered.

Desperate suddenly, for some proof that she once existed, I hastened to the living room, turning on a lamp. I yanked a photo album from the shelf, then two more. Hauling them onto my lap under the arc of the light, I turned back the cover of the first.

Two youngsters embraced by a white-gloved, giant-eared mouse grinned up at me. I turned the pages, trying to connect with the eyes of the skinny little girl. Mostly though, they evaded the camera lens. I recalled every place, every time. Most brought memories the photos did not reveal, battles and tantrums. But she was real.

The dream haunted me still. Back in my bedroom, I went to the closet, my fingers riffling through Ben's clothes. He was real too, but remote. I gathered an armful of sleeves and buried my nose in them. He felt closer then. I ran my fingers along the shoulders of jackets and shirts till I came to his old green flannel shirt, my favourite. I remembered the feel of it against my cheek when he hugged me the day we buried Shannon. Slipping it off the hanger, I carried it to bed. My last sensation before I fell into dreamless sleep was its fuzzy softness against my face.

I turned up my collar, shivering against the Arctic blast coming off the lake. At the jail's rear entrance, it lunged at me like a pack of hungry wolves, worrying the hem of my coat. I set the package between my feet and pulled back a sleeve to check my watch. Twenty minutes had gone by since I'd announced my arrival.

I'd called the optometrist office first thing Tuesday morning. Stunned, Michael told me he'd mailed Ben's glasses two weeks ago. He volunteered to put a trace on them but called me back yesterday saying they'd been returned with a card indicating that the Detention Centre had refused the package.

Knowing that Ben might be classified and moved without warning, I wanted to get them to him right away. After I hung up from talking to Michael and before I lost my nerve, I called the Detention Centre asking for the shift supervisor. Sherman Henshaw came on the line. "Mr. Henshaw, do you remember me?"

"Yes."

"Mr. Henshaw, is there any reason an inmate would be denied his prescription eyeglasses?"

"None whatever."

"Ben Volski's optometrist mailed his glasses to the Detention Centre. They were not accepted."

"They wouldn't be sent back if they were clearly marked," he maintained.

"But," I summoned all my self-control, "the package was labeled 'prescription eyeglasses'.

"Look Miss Gallagher. We have more important things to attend to."

I bit my lower lip to check the retort that hovered on my tongue. "How can I get Mr. Volski's glasses to him?"

"Bring 'em between two and three any weekday afternoon, rear door."

And so this morning for yet another day, I rearranged my schedule at work on Ben's behalf. I rose in the pre-dawn dark to drive seventy-five kilometres across metropolitan Toronto to Michael's office. The morning rush hour crawled.

Michael hastened to point out the label on the brown paper parcel. "You assume, Michael, that those baboons running the jail can read," I observed caustically.

I went to my office for a couple of hours, then left again after lunch, timing my arrival at the Detention Centre for two o'clock. When someone responded to my ring on the intercom, I explained that I had a package for Ben Volski. Through a tiny window in the door I could see the desk clerk.

"What is it?" he barked.

"Prescriptions glasses," I said, then added for good measure, "Mr. Henshaw instructed me to bring them here."

"Wait."

I burrowed my frozen hands deeper into my pockets. A woman in a duffel coat joined my wait. After a few minutes she was buzzed in.

With stiff fingers, I pulled my glove back from my wrist to check the time again. I balled one glove into a fist and smacked it into the palm of the other a few times, trying to beat feeling back in. I curled my toes inside my boots to do the same. Five minutes later, the woman reappeared and hurried away hugging herself against the cold.

I peered in the narrow window on the door. The desk clerk lounged against the counter. He seemed to be talking casually to someone out of my line of sight. He glanced my way, then turned his attention back to his hidden companion. *Well, so much for the theory that he's forgotten I'm out here.* Setting my parcel by the wall, I paced up and down to try and keep circulation in my limbs. I could feel a really bad cold coming on. My throat became raw; fever began to settle behind my eyes. An agonizing physical ache gripped my entire body.

Another twenty minutes elapsed. I was feeling sicker by the minute. My head grew stuffy; my chest rattled with each breath. *No way! Nothing can justify them keeping me waiting fifty minutes in this weather.*

Another individual appeared on the walk and announced herself at the intercom. Two minutes later, she gained entry. She reappeared shortly. As soon as she was out of sight, I leaned on the buzzer.

"Yeah, what is it."

"I've been here over an hour. How soon can I expect to be allowed in?"

"You'll be allowed in when it's time." *Bastard!* I glared at him through the narrow pane but he ignored me. *Come on Shelley, don't let these jerks get the better of you.* I began to think of leaving. My throat hurt terribly and there was a roar in my head like surf. I shivered uncontrollably. Ten more minutes elapsed.

"Gallagher."

"Yes."

"You're next."

I looked over my shoulder at the imaginary lineup of people waiting to gain entry. *'You're next.' Ha!* I knew I should have left well enough alone but by now I was in the mood for a fight. "Busy today, huh?" I stared him down. He glowered back without responding. I pressed on. "Is this the section that handles inmate property coming in and leaving the jail?"

"Yeah. You wanna leave something?"

"Yes, I believe I told you that over an hour ago." I thrust the parcel onto the counter. "Can you see where this package's contents are labeled, here on the outside."

"What's your point, lady?"

"Can you tell me why this would not be accepted and given to the inmate to whom it is addressed?"

He swaggered. "Can't accept packages in the mail for inmates."

"Not even prescription eyeglasses?"

"Nope."

"Funny. That's not what Mr. Henshaw said."

He bristled and leaned toward me over the counter. "You don't tell me how to do my job. See? You want to leave that, you open it and I'll see if I'll accept it." I held his stare a moment longer, then tore the wrapping off the box. He continued to stare at me even while I held out the glasses to him. He snatched them without looking at them and said, "You can leave. Now!"

"Have a nice day," I said curling my lips in a cold smile. I spun on my heel and stalked out.

Winter had turned the Nottawasaga River behind Jamie's house into a frozen highway. Tracks of deer and rabbit crisscrossed the linear tread of snowmobiles. A swish-swish sound kept time with the piston action of my skis. Scrub brush bordered the river on one side; snowy fields on the other. Slate grey clouds hid the noonday sun, leaving a depth-less glare.

Behind me, Jamie's whoop failed to penetrate my reverie until I took three more strides. I turned to see him strike out for the wooded bank. He waved his ski pole signalling me to follow. I step-turned out of the ruts I'd been following to glide through trackless powder till I fell in behind him. By the time I caught up, he'd halted by a large tree cut three feet above ground. The trunk lay where it fell. His skis stood upright in a snow-bank.

I snapped out of mine while he emptied his rucksack. He spread a clean, white handkerchief across the stump, unwrapped and set down two sub sandwiches.

"Dig in, Shel." Tendrils of lettuce, spots of tomato and corners of cheese slices draped out of the fresh torpedo buns. I helped myself to one, settled on the fallen trunk and bit into it.

"Mm, delicious," I mumbled with my mouth full. He poured two steaming mugs of hot liquid from a thermal jug. The tang of cider wafted my way.

"You seemed pretty distracted out there," he said, reaching into a breast pocket. "A penny for your thoughts." He tossed the copper onto the handkerchief. I gave him a Mona Lisa smile and pocketed it. "So?" he challenged.

"Hmm," I mused. "I was thinking about rivers."

He looked right and left and made a baleful face. "Is there some scholarly reason or are you just stating the obvious?"

"Philosophical actually. I've long regarded a river as a metaphor for the journey through life. I never thought of it as being frozen though. But even that fits. It matches how I feel right now, waiting for my real life to begin. I miss the ocean, the forests, my mountains. God, how I miss it all."

He pinched off a piece of bun and tossed it in the direction of a trio of curious chickadees. "You thinking of goin' back?" My answer was an ambiguous mix of a head shake and a shrug. The boldest of the chickadees flew down and worried at the bit of bread.

"I think I prefer the river when it's frozen," Jamie mused. "I don't especially like it otherwise."

Startled by this admission, I blurted, "But you built your house by it."

"Mel fell in love with the property."

"Why don't you like the river?"

"Gives me nightmares." I waited for him to elaborate. He watched as the other two birds joined the first, hoping for a morsel. His voice betrayed an edge when he spoke again. "After Mel lost the baby, I started having nightmares. I'd dream that I'd go down to the river and the baby would be floating face down in the water." His eyes glazed over. "It was just the way I used to dream about Davy after he drowned."

It was the first time I ever heard my brother refer to the tragedy he'd witnessed at the age of five. "Does Melanie know you have these dreams?" He shook his head. "Does she tell you *her* feelings about losing the baby?"

"We don't talk about it."

"You should, Jamie."

He was silent. "You haven't said why she's away," I observed.

"She took a vacation."

"To Sudbury? In January?"

"She's visiting her folks. She needed a break from everything, from all the... It's been a rough winter," he finished lamely.

"Are you separated?"

"No!" he protested, then capitulated some, saying, "Hell, I don't know."

I felt sick and wished I hadn't come. I didn't have the energy to deal with Jamie's problems.

"Did you ever go for counselling, James?"

"Yeah, I tried it. The guy was a dork. Even Melanie thought so."

"Was she willing to try someone else?" He didn't answer. "Jamie?"

"Aw Shelley. I can't talk to a stranger. You help me more than anybody. You always have."

My weary exasperation slipped out in a "Tsk."

He sipped from his mug and changed the subject. "Did Gayle get a hold of you about the party she's planning for Mom and Dad's fiftieth?"

"Yeah."

"You going?"

"Of course."

"Wanna go together. I could meet you at a car pool you have to pass going through Toronto."

"What's the matter? You scared to show up at a family gathering without your spouse?" I asked, not too kindly.

He gave an ironic smile. "Looks like we'd both be sans partner."

I reflected on Jamie's neat change of topic. "Fifty years of marriage. Do you think Dad got the life he hoped for?" I mused.

"Are you kidding? Married to *our* mother? She totally dominated him."

"He *let* himself be dominated. The question is why."

Jamie snorted. "'Cause he's weak, a total 'was-gonna'. Remember how he would regale us with grand stories about what he 'was-gonna' do. Never did any of it."

"That's a description, not an explanation."

"Okay Miss Social Worker, you explain it."

"Because he never dealt with his insecurities or confronted his part in his failure." I looked askance at my brother. "Don't be like him, Jamie." Silently, I admonished myself likewise.

He kept his eyes on the ground, his voice soft when next he spoke. The faint whine of an approaching snowmobile almost smothered his words. "You s'pose Dad wonders how he got to be this old? I wonder that about *my*self. I'm thirty-one and still don't feel grown up."

"There's the difference between you and me. I feel like I never got to be a child. I became a mother at seven years of age."

He shot a look of reproach at me mixed with something indecipherable. The engine of a snowmobile grew as the look hung between us. The roar reached a crescendo, whined past us and faded again.

The words on my computer screen swam in front of me. I tried to focus on my thesis but a sense of paranoia kept pressing through my consciousness. *Ben, where* are *you?* He had been transferred three days earlier. No one would tell me where.

"I don't think I'll be here tomorrow," he'd said Sunday night.

"Did you get word that you're being moved?"

"Not officially. They don't tell you in advance."

"So? Did you bribe a guard?"

"Of course!" he boasted.

"Same old Ben. Should I ask how?"

"The guard where I've been working in stores the last couple of days is fairly decent. I guess he knows my background 'cause he asked me about income tax. He had a few problems and I offered to help. I showed him how he could save some money…legally." The last word came out sarcastically. "Today he paid off; he let it slip that I shouldn't expect to be working for him anymore. Told me to eat light at breakfast."

"What does that mean?"

"They transport you in a van that does a milk run to jails, picking up and delivering prisoners. It usually takes hours; not many washroom breaks."

"Where are you going?"

"I regret to say I don't know my itinerary. Ontario Corrections makes a lousy travel agent."

The next day, I called Hamilton Detention. Sure enough, he was no longer there but they would not tell me his destination. As usual, I had to wait.

My fingers lay idle, the computer screen gaining nothing in ten minutes. I shut down and stared at the blackened screen and then at the blackened window where the late-January night had descended. Suddenly, I pushed back my chair and went into the washroom. Soon tubes and compacts cluttered the vanity. I began applying make-up, not the face I wore to the office but meticulously applied lines and brush-strokes. I finished by filling in the line that traced my mouth with deep red gloss.

From the bedroom closet, I chose a peignoir ensemble in mother-of-pearl pink. Opening drawers and cupboards, I draped accessories over my fingers and arm. I deposited these on the bed. From my dressing table, I withdrew a pair of wax tapers, crystal holders and a book of matches. I lit the candles, setting one on either side of the dressing table in front of the mirror and extinguished the electric lights.

I stripped out of my clothes, kicking aside my jeans and tossing my socks on the floor. I slipped into the peignoir outfit. Sitting on the end of the bed, I selected one of the oyster-coloured opaque silk stockings. Like a star in a movie, I drew it sensuously over my calf, knee and thigh, fastening it with a garter. The candlelight caught the shimmer of the stocking. I put on the second one and stepped into a pair of cream mules.

In front of the mirror, I clasped a string of pearls round my neck, fondling their smoothness as they lay against my cleavage. Tilting my head, I clipped on teardrop earrings to match the pearls. I reached for an amethyst-coloured glass spritzer and misted my throat with perfume. Giving my head a luxurious toss, I showered my shoulders with my full red mane.

I observed the gossamer sylph that blinked at me from the other side of the looking glass. Filmy fabric billowed about her like sea foam. The candlelight picked up highlights in her hair and a glow in her eyes. There, in the shadows, lived Ben's fantasy creation. Over time, with each piece, each accessory, he had sculpted and adorned this sensuous sprite. She had awakened shyly, reluctantly. It had taken time to accept and learn to enjoy this side of Ben, and this part of me.

The stridency of the telephone ringing beside the bed startled me. My quickened breath flickered the candle's flame. "Hello," I answered breathlessly.

"Collect call from Benjamin Volski. Will you accept the charge?"

"Yes!"

"Shelley?"

"Ben! I'm so happy to hear your voice. Are you alright?"

"Yeah, I'm alright. But, you sound upset. Is everything okay?"

"Yes, Darling, I'm fine." I answered, my voice husky with emotion. "I'm just...fine."

He cleared his throat. "God you turn me on when you talk like that. You sure some man isn't taking my place while I'm in here?"

"Only in spirit." The cheeks of the apparition in the mirror dimpled. "Where are you?"

"Mimico Correctional Centre."

"Mimico! Really?"

"Yeah. You know where it is?"

"Do I? I did my student placement there when I was an undergrad."

"Well, I'm sure the guys in here would love to have you back."

"No doubt," I retorted. "How is it?"

"Ramshackle, but the buildings are constructed of wood instead of that ghastly concrete and terrazzo at Hamilton. You can't imagine what a difference it makes to the noise level. Different type of inmate too. Most are short-timers who leave you alone. The first night was an education though. They warehoused us in transit at Toronto East Detention. A lot of inmates there were on their way to the pen, killers some of them. They know they aren't coming out for a long time and they pack a 'make my day' attitude. If you just look at a guy the wrong way, he's liable to jump you."

I shivered.

"Shelley, I have to let others use the phone, as usual. Visiting is on weekends here, from two to four. You can stay for a whole hour, though. Will I see you?"

I glanced in the mirror and murmured soft and low, "You bet, Baby."

"Hey, you're not playing fair with that voice."

———————————————

Terri rose the moment I poked my head into the waiting room. Thin-lipped and rigid, she swept past me toward my office.

"Hi Terri. I thought you were bringing Brad again today."

"Hmph!" she tossed her head. "I told him not to come."

O-kay, I mouthed to myself as I followed her down the hall. She flounced into a chair, a pout puckering her mouth.

"Men are all alike!" she spat. "Selfish, self-centred cads."

The regression to juvenile drama queen stirred a smile in me but I stifled it. "What happened?"

"We had a fight, an argument over sex." Her annoyance passed with the suddenness of a summer squall, giving way to something more vulnerable. "Not sex, really," she said. She collapsed with a huge sigh.

"Shelley, do you think I should charge my father with sexual abuse?"

"That's a complex question and not mine to answer. Is that what you and Brad argued over?"

She nodded. "He thinks I should."

"Did he say why?"

"He says if I don't stand up to Daddy, I'll always be a victim and act like one too."

"What do you think he meant?"

The haughty teenager returned. "It means he won't get his rocks off as often as he'd like." I gave her a deadpan look. Her face muscles worked as if to resist but then she laughed. "I guess I do sound kinda spiteful, huh."

I nodded with a wry smile and returned to her question. "What do *you* think? Will confronting your father help you to reclaim your body?"

"I don't know." She sighed again, deflating like a balloon. "Will I ever be normal?"

"There are two issues here, Terri. One is that you need to figure out what will bring you peace. The other is how you want to deal with your boyfriend's reactions to all this."

"Maybe he's right."

"Maybe. Maybe not. It's natural for him to have strong feelings; he cares for you. But they are *his* feelings. He can't know what's right for you. You're the expert on your needs."

"But I *don't* know," she wailed.

I smiled gently. "That's the work you and I need to do. In time, you'll know."

The borough of Mimico lies to the west of downtown Toronto along Lake Ontario's shore. I exited the highway amid a sprawl of industrial malls, rail yards, warehouses and transport loading docks. It was hauntingly familiar.

Soon after turning down Horner Avenue, I came to a high chain-link fence that surrounded a compound with drab green clapboard buildings. A sign affirmed that I had arrived at Mimico Correctional Centre. I turned the engine off and sat back with a sense of déjà vu. I remembered climbing those very steps, a steep, wooden half-flight that looked temporary and makeshift.

A starry-eyed social work student, barely twenty, I'd begun the placement eagerly. I enjoyed working with the inmates in the drug and alcohol program in this all-male institution. It was here, though that I first encountered the injustices that crop up in the so-called 'justice' system. The prison psychiatrist, an unlikely blond bombshell, contributed to my education, demonstrating the meaning of the term 'ball-crusher'. Her caustic remarks to inmates, withering characterizations in team meetings and punitive decisions went unchallenged by staff.

I learned about the treachery of prison guards, who bullied and tormented inmates with impunity. Twice I overheard officers bragging about how they had set prisoners up for punishment. If they didn't like someone in the treatment program and wanted him sent back to the regular prison population, they planted contraband in his belongings, then conducted a search.

I climbed out of the truck and stepped through the white powder that blanketed the parking lot. Inside was a narrow rectangular room split length-wise by a counter behind which a man in a blue shirt attended to two young Native women. A bank of cubbyholes at his back gave the room the look of a small postal station. But for the insignia on his shoulder, Mimico Correctional Centre, he could have been a mailman. He handed a key to one of the women and she and her companion proceeded into the next room. He turned to me. "Been here before?"

"No," I said, thinking ironically that it wasn't true.

"Sign in," he pushed an open logbook toward me. "Your name, who you're visiting and your relationship." He spoke in a matter-of-fact way, lacking the antagonism of the Detention Centre. When I put down the pen, he gave me a key and pointed in the direction the women had gone. "The number on the key corresponds to a locker. Put your purse, hat, coat and any other belongings in the locker."

"Then what?" I asked.

"You'll all go in together when it's time. In the meantime, just relax on a bench."

The next room was no larger than the first. I found the locker, stuffed in my belongings as instructed and locked it. I perched on the narrow bench that ran down the middle of the room.

The far door opened and a man in uniform droned, "Okay, come along." He led us down a dim corridor with peeling paint. Round a corner we spilled into a room with the look of a small gymnasium. Pebbled glass windows covered by wire mesh allowed light in from the open air compound that I vaguely remembered was out there. In the corner, adjacent to the guards' table, there appeared to be an antechamber. A second officer hovered there.

In spacious rows, small square wooden tables with four chairs each filled the room. A third guard at a larger wooden table directed me to "Row two, table four." I found it and chose the chair facing the antechamber.

The anticipation of soon being able to hold Ben made me jittery. It had only been a little more than a month, but the longest of my life. I smiled to myself thinking how deliberately I had arranged my appearance. I wore a blue silk blouse and black straight skirt with a pleat down the front. Black leather boots covered my legs to the knee. The tapered heels gave me extra height.

From the antechamber, a young, heavy-set Native man padded into the room wearing brown coveralls and slippers. He joined the women who had come in with me.

A minute later, another brown suited man entered. My heart skipped a beat. Ben strode across the space between us as I stood. He caught me in his arms and pressed me against him. I could feel every hollow and contour of his body beneath the thin fabric. I tipped my head back to let him kiss me. "Is it my imagination," I asked, "or are you 'au naturel' under that jumpsuit?"

He grinned lasciviously. "A wolf in sheep's clothing, my dear."

I leaned back on his arm, the back of my hand to my brow in a fake swoon. "Oh please don't eat me, Mr. Wolf."

Something in the direction of the guards' table caught his attention. "You're reprieved, Red. The goons are motioning us to sit down. They make us change into this outfit in that room over there just for visits," he explained. "Discourages contraband." He leaned back to check me out head to toe. "I like your CFM's"

I knit my brow. "CFM's?"

He squeezed my leg at the calf, ran his hand slowly up the leather, letting it come to rest above my knee. "Yeah, the boots—come-fuck-me boots."

I crossed my arms on the table leaning forward till my face was inches from his. "Listen, Buster, don't make suggestions you can't carry out."

A frustrated silence fell upon my office. Brad tore pieces of Styrofoam from his empty cup and dropped them into the shrinking remains. Terri flicked the nails of her middle finger and thumb together. I had to be missing something, I thought, a puzzle piece that would unscramble everything, dissolve the impasse. The conflict Terri had outlined in her last session had just been aired.

"How can you expect me to feel close to you," she renewed her challenge to Brad, "when I can't trust you? And how can I trust you, if you treat me like damaged goods?"

Brad let out an exasperated sigh. "I *don't* think of you like that. I wish you wouldn't put words in my mouth."

"You *said* I act like a victim," she hissed, stressing each word, "and I will until I confront my father."

"I just hate to see him intimidate you, that's all."

"No, that isn't all. Admit it, Brad, you're just like every other man on this planet. If you can't get your regular ration of sex, you think there's something wrong with the woman. It can never be your—"

"That's not fair," he shot back. They glared at each other. He ran his fingers through his hair, then leaned his elbows on his knees as if searching for answers on the floor. "I must be doing something wrong. I'm sure as hell not helping any. I don't mean to hurt you, but obviously I'm causing you additional pain. Maybe I should just—" He stopped.

Terri stared intently at the top of his head. "What? You should just do what?"

"Maybe I should back off," he muttered, "leave you alone for a while."

"Great. Why don't you?"

He looked up, searching her face. "Is that what you want?" She turned away, stony. "Terri," he pleaded, "I don't want to make you miserable. I just—"

"Leave," she said.

I held my breath, afraid that even the sound of breathing would ignite an explosion.

He blinked in confusion. "What?"

"I want you to leave. Right now. If you're not going to be here for me, I don't want you taking up any more of my counselling time." He gaped at her. Fury burned in her eyes.

"Leave!"

He flushed, then slowly stood up. I caught his eyes, saw the bewildered humiliation crinkling them. He pulled open the door and walked through it.

Terri examined an invisible spot on the wall, her face in profile. Moisture glistened on her lashes. "I don't think I really expected him to go," she said.

"Do you regret telling him to?"

"No. I can do it without him—heal. For the first time in my life, I realize I don't *need* a man, not enough to be dominated. I'm no longer willing to search for flaws in myself to explain another person's problems. You were right, Shelley. Brad has his own feelings about what my father did and he can't seem to separate his from mine. He won't take responsibility for his needs and I'll be damned if I'm going to let another man do that to me."

———————————

I yanked the vacuum hose from the wall socket, killing the roar. As I coiled it onto its holder in the kitchen closet, I noted that the dishwasher had also clicked off. With everything else to do these days, housework tended to fall behind. So too, had the maintenance of the water and heating systems. I removed the furnace filters from the dishwasher. In the basement, I shoved them back into place, topped up the salt in the water purifier and took out the testing kit. I filled both cells of a clear plastic container with water. I added five drops of yellow solution from a squeeze bottle to one side, five drops of red to the other. I capped the cells with two fingers, shook it and then examined the effect against the light. The reading was good; no need to add chlorine or pH to the water.

I checked my watch as I hurried back upstairs. *Better get a move on,* I thought. I had to meet Jamie in an hour at the north end of Toronto to go on to Mom and Dad's party. I picked up the phone and dialled his number. We'd agreed to synchronize our leaving to meet at the halfway point. While his phone rang, I looked toward the escarpment half a kilometre away. Murky weather shrouded the top. The thermometer hovered around zero Celsius. The wind blew rain and ice pellets against the windows in gusts.

By the fourth ring, I grew anxious. On the sixth, a very groggy male voice mumbled, "Hello". I thought I had a wrong number.

"Jamie?"

"Mmm hm." He sounded sick, his voice thick and leaden.

"Are you alright?" He didn't answer. "Jamie?"

After what seemed like forever, he replied woodenly, "I'm here."

"What's wrong?"

A heavy sigh whooshed through the receiver. "Nothin'."

"*Some*thing's wrong."

"Ah-mm okay."

"I'm ready to leave. Are you?"

"Mm not goin'."

"Have you been drinking?"

"No." The slight delay in his responses made him seem very far away. I heard a sound, muffled, as if he had his hand over the mouthpiece.

"You sound like you're crying."

"I can't do it anymore," His voice cracked. "I can't...handle it."

"Honey, what's happened?"

It took several moments for the answer to come back. "Melanie left. You were right. She's not coming back."

I sat down heavily in a chair at the table. "Oh Honey, I'm so sorry."

"It doesn't matter," he said flatly. "Nothing matters anymore."

Alarm buzzed through me. "Don't be alone. Come to the party. Meet me like we planned." There was no answer, just a small 'thuk', like the receiver knocking against something.

"Jamie?" Silence. "Jamie, talk to me!" Still no response. "Pick up the damn phone! JAMIE!" I couldn't hold back the sob in my own throat. "I know you can hear me," I yelled. "If you don't pick up that phone right now and talk to me, I'm sending the police."

I waited. Finally I heard fumbling.

"No police," he mumbled.

"Talk to me. Have you taken anything?"

"Like what?"

"Pills. Have you taken any pills?" No answer.

"For God's sake, tell me!"

He snorted. "That's not how I'd do it."

Oh God. I swallowed. "How would you do it?"

"They say with carbon monoxide you just go to sleep."

Taking a deep breath, I willed my body, my mind to become quiet. *It's just like any suicidal client, Shelley. Do your stuff. Establish a lifeline. Exact a promise.* "Okay Jamie, listen. I'm coming up there. I'm coming to you, okay?"

His voice came through the line with more strength. "Hey, I'll be alright. Don't come up here. Go to the party. I'll be fine." He sounded too bright...forced.

"I'm *coming*," I said firmly. "I need you to tell me you'll wait for me. You won't do anything to harm yourself." I waited for his answer. It was slow in coming.

"Don't call the police." There was a paranoid sound to his voice.

I exhaled. "Okay, okay no police. Promise me you won't hurt yourself."
Seconds ticked by.

"Okay," he whispered, crying again.

"I need you to promise."

"I promise. I won't do anything. Just come."

CHAPTER ELEVEN

The truck spit gravel as I hurtled down the driveway. I calculated how long it would take to get to Angus doing as much over the limit as I dared. I'd forgotten all kinds of things in my haste; a casserole sitting on the counter, my parents' present wrapped and waiting on the coffee table. And gas! Damn! I'd planned on gassing up on the way to Toronto. The fuel gauge showed less than a quarter of a tank.

Racing along the secondary highway, I fumbled for my wallet, pulling out bills, a five, a two and a one. I careened into the self-serve and leapt out leaving the door wide open. I pumped eight dollars worth in, raced inside the cashier's hut and threw the bills on the counter before an elderly man. "Where's the fire?" I heard him ask as I barrelled back out the door.

By the time I turned north on Highway 400, the weather had switched back and forth twice between rain and sleet. The wipers laboured to remove the slushy freeze on the windshield. Twenty minutes north of Toronto in an area of open rolling hills, the storm worsened. Snow gusted across the road. Sanders had preceded me, so I braved the fast lane, whistling past more cautious motorists. I bore down on the accelerator to overtake a transport in the middle lane. Suddenly my truck chugged and faltered.

No! Not now, dammit! I eased up on the gas pedal and edged over two lanes, the engine coughing. In desperation, I pressed my foot down again and the motor roared to life. I heaved a sigh. The image of Jamie's limp form crumpled over the van's steering wheel in his darkened garage loomed before me. *Stupid. I should have sent the police. Better to have played it safe; let him be mad at me. Dear God, don't let him die!*

Just south of Holland Marsh the engine cut out without warning. Before the truck rolled to a stop, I was keening my despair. I jumped out and hoisted the hood hoping to flag someone down. I'd leave the truck. I sidled toward the rear. That's when I noticed the flap open on the gas intake. The cap was missing. *Shit! I forgot it when I gassed up. No wonder. Probably moisture in the tank. Maybe ice pellets.*

In the cab, I scrambled through the emergency kit and found a toque.

It'll have to do. I stuffed it into the gaping mouth and closed the flap on it. Behind the wheel again, I tried the ignition. It whined but wouldn't catch. I tried again. Same thing. I hit the steering wheel with my fist. *Start dammit!* Maybe it was still best to flag down help. I turned the key once more; this time the engine roared to life. I whooped.

In Angus I thumped on Jamie's front door, tried the knob and found it unlocked. "Jamie?" I called out anxiously. I kicked off my boots and hastened through the living room to the kitchen. He wasn't there. On rubbery legs, I crept to the back door leading to the garage. Steeling myself for whatever was beyond, I opened it a crack. I could barely make out the side of the van in the dark. All was quiet and there were no fumes.

"Jamie?" I called again, stepping back into the kitchen.

I found him in the bedroom. He sat barefoot in a tight ball in the middle of his bed. Above his blue jeans, a thin khaki coloured T-shirt covered his upper body. Skin showed through a one-inch hole over his shoulder blade.

I crouched beside him, laying my hand on the middle of his back. It was hot. Little mewling sounds escaped from his throat. He looked so young and wounded. I ran my fingers through the hair at the nape of his neck. "Oh Honey."

His only response was a slight rocking. When he did speak, words tumbled out one after another, as if from a glass of spilt milk. "I'm so stupid; it's my own fault. I let her down. I let everybody down. I never learn; everyone is always going to leave me 'cause I'm so stupid... a stupid, useless screw-up."

"Don't beat yourself up like this. You're *not* stupid. Or useless." I paused, then chanced, "Those sound like Mom's words."

"Well, she's right," he retorted bitterly. "No wonder people leave. They get fed up. Even Davy."

Davy? Davy! It was the last thing I expected to hear from him right now. "Davy didn't *leave* you, Jamie. He drowned!"

"And I just stood there," he shouted, "stood there like a stupid little ninny. Stood and let it happen, watched him slip beneath the water."

With sudden clarity, I asked, "Is that what Mother said to you when Davy died?"

He nodded. "She screamed at me 'How could you let this happen?'" The words rasped his throat.

"She was wrong! Mom was wrong."

"But it's true! I just stood there!"

"You were *five years old!* You were scared. The responsibility for what happened belongs to adults—to the mothers. They should have kept an eye on you two. They let their five year old boys play unsupervised by a creek." He broke into racking sobs. I tried to gather him in my arms but he held his body rigid.

"Jamie, Mom must have felt terrible guilt… guilt and shock and grief. She displaced that guilt onto you. But a five-year-old can't be responsible for his friend, can't be expected to save him from drowning. You are not to blame for what happened."

"It *has* to be my fault."

"Why?"

"Because he *left*! Everyone leaves because I'm such a millstone. I drag them down till they're drowning."

"What you're saying is irrational. Davy didn't drown to get away from you?"

"*You* left to get away from me," he glared at me, looking up for the first time.

"Me?! When?"

"When you moved out west. Isn't that what you were trying to tell me two weeks ago? You left 'cause you were drowning under the weight of taking care of me. Say it! I was a Goddamn burden!"

My mouth fell open. I shook my head and lay my hand on his forearm but he wrenched away from me, rolling to the far side of the bed. With a sob, he slid down on the floor. I stared at the back of his head, as puzzle pieces fell into place. *'Everyone is always going to leave me because I'm so stupid… a stupid, useless screw-up.'* A self-fulfilling prophecy pronounced when a woman attacked a small boy for not acting like a man.

I crept around to his side but as soon as I sat on the bed, he jerked angrily away, turning his back again. I made no effort now, to conceal the pain in my own voice. "All these years, I knew you felt abandoned by me. Little things you said. Reproaches. But it never dawned on me for one second that you believed I *wanted* to get away from you, that you thought you had driven me away. Jamie, my leaving—going so far away, had *nothing* to do with you. It was never about you. If there was something I was trying to escape, it was the poison—*her* poison. I knew if I were ever going to have a life, I had to get away from her. She would have squeezed the life out of me, like she did with Dad. I told you two weeks ago that I felt like I never got to be a child. But you didn't do that to me, she did. She abandoned us both. I never blamed you. I never resented you. Leaving you was the hardest part. I felt guilty and sad. I missed you. You don't know how much I missed you."

He tipped his head back and his lungs tore at the air. He turned toward me at last and lay his head in my lap. I combed his hair with my fingers. "I thought you wanted to be rid of me," he choked.

"No," I whispered. "Never."

For a long time, we sat like that until gradually his muscles relaxed. After a while, he sniffed loudly. I squeezed his shoulder. "Now," I patted the bed beside me, "how about sitting up here and talking to me." He pulled a tissue from the box on the headboard and blew his nose noisily, then crawled up beside me. "Did Melanie talk to you today?" I asked.

He nodded.

"And she told you it was over?"

"Pretty much." He didn't look like a little boy anymore, just a sorrowful young man. "I've made such a mess of everything, Shelley. Melanie's a wonderful, loving wife. I was so afraid of failing that I tried to make a financial success single-handedly. I guess I wanted to impress her, to take care of her. But I never gave her credit for the intelligence and expertise she has, especially with money. I caused her so much worry. Maybe if she hadn't been so stressed, she wouldn't have lost the baby. I felt like I killed the baby, just like I felt I killed Davy. She needed me more than ever then, but I felt so guilty, so inadequate that I couldn't get it together to give her support. When my wife needed me the most, I wasn't there." He leaned his elbows on his knees, his face in his hands. "God, it was Davy all over again. Like watching him drown." This time, he let me wrap my arms around him "What should I do? Do you think there's anything I can do to get her to come back?"

"That's not a good focus for you, James. Trying to coax her or bargain with her will only increase her view of you as dependent and helpless. And if her mind is already made up, it will only make you feel more rejected."

"So what *should* I do?"

"What you should have done all along. Get counselling. Just for yourself, not to get her back. If the first person you go to doesn't seem to understand what you need, find someone else. Do it. But do it for you." He nodded thoughtfully. "You want to know what else I think you should do?"

"What?"

"Come with me to Mom and Dad's party."

"Aw no, Shelley. I can't face Mom and Gayle and the rest of them."

I glowered at him. "James Gallagher, if you're ever going to feel grown up, you're going to have to look people in the eye and stop hiding."

"Gayle's gonna be pissed at me for us being so late."

"So call her. Call her now. Tell her there was a problem and you'll explain later."

He gaped at me as if I were crazy, then broke into his familiar boyish grin. "Okay, I'll call her. But if she yells at me, I'm handing you the phone."

"You'll handle it."

Jamie set the receiver back in its cradle. "Guess what? She thanked me for calling. She wasn't mad at all. She just said, 'Get here when you can.'"

I gave him a wide grin, poked my finger through the hole in his T-shirt, stretching the fabric toward me. "I suggest you change your shirt."

Night's blackness and the exhaustion of another long day as I drove home from the office gave rise to a melancholy that was becoming my frequent visitor. In search of peace, I imagined myself driving the twisting mountain road to Shangri-La.

I had fallen into a life of parallel realities, one in which I aligned my future toward the day Ben would come home and we would build a life together, the other in which I waited for the day I would return to my real home. It was always there in the background, my mountains, my Shangri-La. An uncertain future with Ben, my loathing of Ontario's drab greyness, the bitter cold, the pollution and the population all contributed to my sense of exile from the mountains, the ocean, the forest and rivers.

At home, I picked up a message from Ben's brother on the answering machine, a cryptic request. "Would it be possible for you to call me tomorrow to discuss something about Ben?" At this late hour and with my mood, the mystery put a sinister twist on my thinking and I had trouble falling asleep.

I called Martin first thing in the morning, suggested lunch, since I'd be passing his office on my way to an afternoon class at the university. We agreed to meet at a restaurant on the top floor of his office tower. It was March first and it came in like the proverbial lion with a nasty wet snow squall that forced pedestrians to hide their faces in up-turned collars.

On the eighteenth floor solarium, I fastened my sights on the vested maitre d' zigzagging ahead of me through the luncheon crowd. He led me past an island of tropical growth. Water sprinkled down through limestone rockery into a pool whose shallow bottom glistened with coins. A plaque on a partly submerged stone thanked donors on behalf of the Lung Association. I almost collided with the maitre d' when he halted in the seclusion behind the waterfall.

A man rose from a table set for two. In black tie, crisp white shirt and grey suit, Martin evinced an understated grace that contrasted conspicuously with his brother's reckless flamboyance. Intelligent grey eyes enveloped me in their softness. "Nice to see you, Shelley. Thank you for meeting with me." He took my hand and executed a slight, but gracious bow.

In the time it took to be served, he asked insightful questions with compassion and solicitude, first about my circumstances and then about Ari. When I thanked him, he simply said, "Ari is family. You are now too."

His inclusion of me touched me but sparked a twinge of guilt too. I felt my rumination last night about returning to British Columbia disqualified me from membership in the Volski family.

"Martin, you wanted to talk to me about Ben. Has something happened?"

A flicker of something that looked like pain crossed his face. "No. Not yet anyway. I hope you may be able to assure me that I've no need to be concerned." I must have frowned for he apologized. "I'm being obscure. Allow me to explain.

"When the full extent of the holocaust broke upon the world's consciousness, I knew my parents' anguish over the fate of relatives. From then on, family became of primary importance to me. Ben was just a rambunctious kid at the time, needing firm, consistent discipline. Perhaps in their preoccupation, my parents were lax. Perhaps it is why he developed such contempt for rules.

"A year ago, when he told me what he'd done, I was appalled. I believed then that he was truly sorry and because of that, I was willing to help him. I did tell him however, that when things settled down I was going to give him a dressing down."

"Actually, Martin, I think he cited you as saying you were going to 'kick his butt'."

"Well, yes," he stammered, blushing. "But since then, he's lost Sara. I'd forget what I told him except..." He gave me a beseeching look. "Shelley, why did you stay with him after you knew he'd committed fraud?"

"He quit, Martin."

"For good?"

I stared at him in consternation.

"He calls me from jail," he went on. "An innocuous remark from me can trigger a stream of invective from him... about his situation, the treatment he receives, the duplicity he imagines from others. He blames his employer for his predicament and he has it in for the detective who caught him. He sounds so vengeful that I wonder if he's changed at all. It scares me. He's my brother and I love him. But I am a lawyer called to the bar. The law is my rod and staff. I cannot—I will not stand by him if he pulls a stunt like this again. If he commits another crime, I *will* disown him"

Martin's vow saddened me, for Ben's sake and I added, "That makes two of us." He held my gaze, as if we'd made a pact.

"I've been agonizing over whether to get into all this with him," he said. "One side of me says I should. Now is the time to make him think about his actions before he's out. Before it's too late. But I wonder if it would be overkill. You've been with him through all this. Tell me what you think?"

I looked at him a long time before responding. "If I knew the answer to that, Martin, I'd have the key to my own future. Still, before it comes to disowning him, I say talk to him."

The waiter came with the bill. Martin put his credit card on the tray and the waiter whisked it away. "The last time Ben got into that aggressive vein, I told him I still wanted to have a talk with him, when we could be alone without someone waiting for the phone and without a guard standing by. He called last night and said that tomorrow we'd have an opportunity, if I can get away from the office." I felt a stab of jealousy for the precious visiting hours but then Martin added, "He's being transferred today to a halfway house."

"Today! They're moving him from jail today?"

"Well, they don't actually transport him. He's required to get there under his own steam. It's about four kilometres from the jail to the halfway house. He's probably walking there as we speak"

I peered out at the storm; wet snow slapped against the glass solarium wall. Traffic slogged through thick slush. "He'll catch a hell of a cold," I observed. "He'll be in the clothes he wore to Sara's funeral" I pictured him shivering in his suit, Oxfords and thin black socks.

"From now on, he won't have to wear prison garb," Martin said. "He'll be allowed to come home to collect some clothes."

"Ben's coming home!" I gasped. "When?"

Martin shifted awkwardly. "Tomorrow. He asked me to drive him so we'll have privacy for that talk." Hurt must have registered in my eyes for he said, "I know," so softly that tears welled up in them. "Ben knew you'd have wanted to pick him up—to have the time together. He asked me to call you, to explain." I tried to blink back the moisture, ashamed of my jealousy, but not in time. He picked up his linen napkin laid on the table after the meal and caught the tear that got away. "Tomorrow's Friday. I understand that's your study day at home," he said gently.

I nodded. The waiter brought back the chit for Martin. He signed it and the waiter retreated. "I'll drop him off," Martin said. "You'll drive him back?" I nodded again, not trusting myself to speak. He stood and motioned for me to lead the way out of the restaurant. As we passed the fountain, the sound of something hitting the surface of the water with a sploosh caused me to glance back just as Martin withdrew his hand and coins sank to the bottom by the sign for the Lung Association. With a melancholy look, he said, "For Sara."

———————————

"I won't come in," Martin had said to me, tacitly promising to absent himself from our precious rendezvous. I kept watch down the lane from the dining room window. Anticipation stretched taut every fibre of my body. Over the weeks of separation I had become acutely aware of the primal need for touch, that drug that draws down pain, soothing battered nerves with its caressing, embracing, kneading narcotic. I was in acute withdrawal, denied my fix.

The straight-backed chair braced my aching back where I sat. My hands, locked in a death-grip, pressed into my lap. I let one spiked heel drop to the floor and leaned down to massage a cramp in my calf. In my short skirt and low neckline, I found it cool by the window and shivered.

Still rubbing my leg, I looked up just in time to see Martin's silver Skylark nose into the lane. I lurched up almost taking a dive as I scrabbled for balance on a single high heel. My stockinged foot gave frantic chase to the wayward shoe. With it only halfway on, I clopped toward the door, stopped, slipped my foot home. The sound of tires crunching on gravel reached my ears, an engine purred. A car door slammed, hurried footsteps scuffed across the porch, the front door swung open.

Halfway along the hall our bodies collided. He lifted me clean off the floor, his mouth crushing mine and I answered him, drinking him in. My feet found the floor again and he shrugged out of his suit jacket, buttons clacking on hardwood, his mouth still suctioned to mine. He gripped my head in his hands and kissed me hungrily, his fingers tangled in my hair. I tore at the buttons of his shirt, frantic and fumbling. He seized my waist hauling me against the hardness in the front of his slacks. Breaking free with a suddenness that left me dizzy, he lunged toward the bedroom, his hand clamped round my wrist.

We fell together, him on top, one of my spikes clattering to the floor, his hand hauling up my skirt and clawing at my panties, me pushing him aside and shimmying out of them, him wrenching at his belt and shoving down his trousers. For one brief second I was aware of the ropey muscles in his back, hardened from months of moving clay, before he injected me with his glorious drug and gave me sweet release.

––––––––––––––

I lay my head on his shoulder and moulded my body against the length of his. He spoke, his voice husky from the cold he had caught in the snowstorm, just as I had predicted.

With my finger, I traced a meandering path through the fur on his chest. "What's it like there?"

"Different from jail."

"Illuminating answer."

He kissed my forehead. "Things should be easier from now on. I'm expected to find some kind of job. I won't mind that. I'll be allowed out for short periods of time without supervision. Oh yeah, and I have to attend group counselling every night." He added, "They expect spouses or family members to attend some of them."

Good, I thought. *Maybe now you'll get down to the business of grieving.*

"I have to get up, Babe. I have to pack some clothes and get you to take me back." I moaned my protest. "I know," he said. "I hate to go"

I propped myself on an elbow, hooking my bare leg over his. "What did Martin say to you?"

"He told me I'm in deep shit with him for being a bad boy," he answered plainly. "And that if I screw up with you, he's going to hire a private detective to search out all the women I ever conned and sick them on me."

"He did not."

———————

When I returned Ben to the halfway house, it was suppertime and I didn't go in. Tonight I retraced the route. Following Lakeshore Road through blocks of commercial slum, the truck bounced in and out of streetcar tracks. He rode the streetcar weekdays to the cut-rate, assembly line tax preparation business where he'd found work.

Commerce gave way to large, once-fashionable dwellings now re-duced to run-down boarding homes. The halfway house commanded a corner lot. I rang the doorbell. Curtain-less panes of glass enclosed a rectangular porch. Boots cluttered the floor. Overcoats and jackets on hooks lined the walls.

A man in a flannel shirt and stockinged feet answered. He paid no mind to me standing there with a huge teddy bear in my arms. I asked for Ben. He retreated inside. A moment later, Ben appeared. "Hey great," he grinned. "You brought him!"

"As you requested." Beasley, the grizzly teddy Ben had bought for me in Banff, was a fixture of my office, comforting people of all ages and often drawing children out.

Ben took him. "Beasley! How ya doin' Buddy."

"Hyuk, not bad, Bawth," Beasley lisped in a baritone. "I unnerthtan' we're goin' to group therapy tonight."

"Yeah Beas. I thought it'd be good for you. You might learn some-thing."

"I doubt it."

I observed these shenanigans with folded arms. Ben took my elbow and tugged me in from the porch. "I'll show you around." Off the porch was a room dwarfed by a large pool table at which a game was underway. One of the spectators, a gaunt wizard who reminded me of a burnt out jockey, sucked on a cigarette. Spying Beasley, he rasped, "Ho, that your teddy bear, Ben?"

"I ain't a teddy. I'm a grithley." The wizard doubled over, wheezing out a laugh. Ben led me to the next room whispering over his shoulder, "That's Corky. He thinks everything is funny." Next was a large room crowded with a mishmash of shabby straight-backed and easy chairs, sofas and coffee tables. "The group session will be here."

Two couples, huddled in separate corners didn't bother looking up. I followed Ben into a hallway. "Whath the matter with thoth guyth?" Beasley muttered. "Thtuck up or thumpthin'?"

"Don't worry about it, Beas," Ben replied. "The guys are wrapped up in their girlfriends and the girls are just jealous of your fur coat."

"Oh."

I yanked the back of Ben's shirt. "You're a bad influence. He doesn't behave like this at work."

Ben paused in the doorway of an office. Two women of mirror-image chunky build lounged against desks on opposite walls, talking. One had frizzy brown hair; the other had hers pulled back in a ponytail though she looked too old for the style. "Oh what a cute bear," said the frizzy hair.

"Hey Doll," a deep voice answered her. "You're not a bad little cub yerthelf."

Ben clapped his palm over Beasley's snout. "Can it, Beasley! You'll get me in trouble. These two are staffers."

"Tho? I'm a thtuffer."

"Not stuffer. *Staffer*."

"Are you going to introduce us, Ben?" ponytail asked with a chastening smile.

"Sure. This is Beasley."

"I *mean* the lady."

In a startle response, he whirled around to look at the empty space behind him, then turned the other way, pointedly looking over my shoulder. "Lady? What lady? Oh! You mean her?" He sniggered. "That's no lady! She sleeps with me." I rolled my eyes.

"Ben..." the woman remonstrated, knuckles on her hip.

"Hilary, meet Shelley," he spoke formally. "Shelley this is Hilary and that," he nodded toward the other woman, "is Allison." I smiled weakly at them.

"Glad you could come," Hilary said. "In fact, I wonder if you would mind, Ben, if we talk to Shelley alone?"

He shrugged. "She already knows I'm a bad boy." Hilary laughed but moved to steer Ben out and close the door with me inside.

"He's quite the comedian," she noted. "Does he always hide behind a clown act?"

"Hide?" I hedged.

"Ben's a very intelligent individual but he doesn't like to deal with his feelings." I gave her my best Mona Lisa smile.

Allison asked, "What are Ben's plans for when he gets back home? For work, I mean."

I shrugged. "We haven't figured that out yet. The Society of Management Accountants revoked his CMA designation. It will be hard for him to work in accounting again."

"Has he ever thought of being a teacher?"

I stared stupidly at her. "I don't know. Why?" Allison and Hilary exchanged glances.

"From what we've heard and seen he'd be good at it," Hilary said. "One of the residents told us that when Ben was in Mimico he inspired an inmate who couldn't read and write to take a literacy course. We hear a lot of stories that don't amount to much but the fellow was in here for a short stay and he confirmed it. Even read a book while he was here."

"Since Ben's been here," Allison jumped in, "he's helped several fellows with reading or arithmetic and he has a way of helping them learn."

I looked back and forth between them. *A teacher? Who knew?* Hilary moved to the door, opening it for me. "Encourage him to think about it," she said. "See you at the meeting."

I found Ben sitting on the top step leading to the basement. Beasley straddled his shoulders. They led me down narrow, steep stairs. "Hey Bawth, I thmell thumpthin'. Ith there food around here?"

"Yeah. This is the kitchen. Watch your step, Shelley."

I looked down just in time to avoid tripping on a two-inch ledge between the landing at the bottom and a doorway into the next room. Ancient linoleum curled up from the edge. Cupboards, stove, refrigerator and freezer lined a cramped kitchen. Lacking a ceiling, greasy pipes crisscrossed overhead. At the far end, a tiny window high up looked like it hadn't been washed in twenty years.

"Yuck," I gagged. "This looks like one of those rat-infested holes beneath a skid row restaurant."

Ben shrugged. "Beats being in jail."

"Obviously rehabilitation isn't high on Corrections' list of priorities," I observed. "The government must pay a pittance to the people who contract to run this place." I wondered what caliber of staff they could afford to hire. Allison and Hilary seemed nice enough but they had that threadbare look of women who had lived too much life, and little of it in academia.

"Got any honey?" Beasley ventured.

"Forget it, Beas. I can't let you go to the group session with honey on your breath."

"How cum?"

"Well, you see, this place is for guys that got into trouble because of their substance abuse." In a whispered aside to me, he added, "Drinking actually."

"Really?" I queried. "Why are you here then? You don't drink."

"Maybe there isn't enough demand for a halfway house for ex-revenuers who rip off their employers." He motioned to me to head in the opposite direction. A few feet farther along a passageway, I stepped down six inches into a room with a large rectangular table covered in oilcloth. Chairs surrounding it squeezed up against the walls. I had to crawl over some to reach the inside. Two lamps failed to dispel the gloom; overhead lighting did not exist. Ben sat corner wise from me at the table. "What did Hilary want?"

"She wants me to tell you to become a school teacher."

"Why?"

I repeated what they told me. Ben laughed. "In jail I got the nickname of 'Professor'. Seems if you read books, people take you for a scholar."

"Tell me about this man you got reading."

"Oh him. One day this kid about twenty comes up to me and asks me to read his mail. So I do—to myself. Then he says, 'What does it say?' It didn't surprise me that he couldn't read. Jail's full of illiterates. What surprised me was that he didn't know what this particular letter said. It seems the judge who sentenced him figured he was getting involved in petty crime because he wasn't very employable, being illiterate. He told him that if he put his time in jail to good use and learned to read, it would be considered when he applied for early parole. Except, guess how he communicated this to him?"

"In writing." I responded.

"Bingo. Anyway, when I read it to him, he goes ballistic. He'd been toting it around for months, doing his time and not knowing what it said. He cursed the judge, the duty counsel, the jails and society in general. Said he wasn't 'going to be a good little boy and read kindergarten books to please a judge who screws him like that'."

"How'd you change his mind?"

He gave an evil grin.

"Ben...?"

"Asked him a few questions, how far he'd gone in school, if he could read anything at all. Comic books, he told me. Using the pictures, he could make out enough of the words to get the story. So I told him, there are books you can read that have no pictures at all that can really make the ol' flagpole stand straight up. He didn't believe me, so I made him do some research, ask people who were better educated. He signed up for classes the next day. The day he left to come here, he asked me where he could get some of those books. I suggested a few authors."

He looked like the cat that ate the mouse. "You *are* bad." I laughed.

"What's wrong? It worked didn't it."

———————————

The living room began to fill up. Seeing that there would not be enough chairs to go around, I slid onto the carpet by Ben's knee. He held Beasley on his lap. With a counsellor's practiced eye, I studied the men around the room. Each one had a story. Each face, each body provided clues to motivations and desires, to fears and character flaws. These clues help a therapist know what energy to harness and what to contain in the dynamics of group counselling.

Some men spoke furtively with their partners, others sat quietly withdrawn. The wizard had no partner and grinned vacantly about the room, making a bid for attention wherever he could. "Hey Ben, the bear comin' to group?"

Ben slowly manipulated Beasley's torso so he faced Corky. "Yeah. Tho?" Beasley challenged. Corky made snuffly, snorkelling sounds of mirth.

Allison and Hilary took their places side by side in two straight-backed chairs at one end of the room. When I lead groups, I always sit opposite my co-leader, so we can keep each other, and between us the whole group, in full view. These counsellors sought eye contact with no one. None of the residents looked at them either.

"Wellness promotion," Hilary announced, as if it was the prelude to a sermon. "Can anyone give a definition of what they think wellness promotion means?" Allison leaned over and whispered something to her.

"Oh yeah," Hilary said, "we should go around the circle and introduce ourselves. Who'd like to start?"

Silence. Hilary looked flustered. Finally she picked someone who mumbled his name so low that I didn't catch it. Hilary pressed the person to his right, then that person's partner and the next fellow. Then came the wizard. He bellowed, "I'm Corky and I'm an alcoholic." The group guffawed, all except Allison and Hilary. Finally it was my turn, and then a deep, lispy voice said, "Ah'm Beasley. Ah'm a grizzly and Ah'm addicted ta honey." Corky lost it, slapping his knees and chortling. A flutter of panic seemed to cross Hilary's face. She asked Ben to introduce himself.

The leaders neglected to introduce themselves and Hilary returned to prodding the group for a definition of wellness promotion. No response. Some stared at the floor or studied their cigarettes. One fiddled with a matchbook. A couple of men hunched in sullen belligerence. Ben sank behind Beasley's bulk. Hilary pounced on a few and got "I dunno", shrugs and blank looks. With a desperate tone, she turned to Corky.

He leapt to his feet standing at rigid attention. "Wellness promotion," he barked, "wellness promotion is when the boss wants to improve morale so he picks a worker who's had no sick time and perfect attendance for a year and promotes him to supervisor. And that's wellness promotion."

The room erupted in howls and cat calls. Hilary reddened. "Come on you guys. Be serious." But it took a whole minute to regain a semblance of control.

A half-hour passed. Allison and Hilary took turns lecturing about the virtues of nutrition. I wondered casually if either of them had ever tried it. A couple of the residents appeared to have fallen asleep. Ben meditated on an ashtray on the coffee table where smoke curled from a butt not quite extinguished. I looked at the time on my watch and I whispered to him, "Is it always this bad?"

"You think it's bad?"

"It's a therapeutic wasteland."

He looked relieved. "Thank God you think so. I was starting to be ashamed of my girlfriend for being a social worker."

Allison pontificated. "The only lasting solution to the problems created by alcohol are to *replace* it in your life. That's the idea behind wellness promotion. How many agree with that statement?"

A young man looked up with an earnest expression. "Don't we have to deal with the problems that led us to drink too much in the first place?"

"Yeah," somebody else said. I noted a couple of others show a spark of interest.

"You also have to get rid of alcohol," Allison remonstrated. "Look what it's done to *your* life, Dylan." I didn't know what alcohol had done to Dylan's life but I saw how his face fell and heard a sigh escape him.

"Who agrees with the statement Allison made?" Hilary bulldozed on. Men sank back into their seats. Ben jiggled Beasley up and down. I felt despair. *Ben and all these other guys need help. Some of them at least, are open to it. But there's no skill here.*

"Shelley? What do you think?" I jerked up my head at my name. *You don't want to know what I think.* Hilary waited expectantly.

"You seem to be saying that the way—the *only* way to overcome problems associated with alcohol abuse is total abstinence." Allison and Hilary nodded in unison. "I guess I don't agree. The literature shows that there is no one approach that helps everyone. I think Dylan has a point. If a person is using alcohol to medicate their pain, they need to address the issues in their life that led to this choice. Not everyone who drinks to excess follows the same pattern. A person may be hanging out with a crowd that rewards heavy drinking. If they haven't developed the physical disease of alcoholism they may be successful at eliminating problem drinking by changing their attitude to drinking and may need to develop a different set of friends."

I knew I shouldn't have done it. The two group leaders sat mummified in their chairs. Neither responded. Then Hilary's eyes shifted to a different part of the room. "Yes, um. Who else wants to comment on the idea of abstinence."

The talk drifted on. I checked my watch again and shifted uncomfortably. My foot had fallen asleep. Ben yawned. I nudged him. "Hey, if I have to stay awake, so do you."

He leaned toward me. "I think they're ignoring us," he whispered. "Have you noticed that they haven't asked us any questions in ages? They won't even look in our direction."

"Of course they're ignoring us; they're out of their depth. They're up against a bear, a clown and an expert." Ben snorted audibly, burying his face in Beasley's back. I snickered. Beasley shook. *No, this is a mad tea party. Nothing vital is going to happen for Ben here.*

On a low table, I deposited a stack of novels I'd culled from the shelves for Ben. From the rack on the wall, I selected half a dozen current issue magazines. It had been ages since I afforded myself the luxury of browsing through non-scholarly reading at the public library. I chose one of the low slung chairs arranged in a square around the table and sank into the leather. Sighing with pleasure, I picked a magazine from the top of the pile and thumbed through it till I came to an article that piqued my interest.

So completely did I shut out my surroundings that I wasn't sure what caused me to lift my eyes above the magazine. When I did, I found myself staring straight into the penetrating gaze of Brad Sparks.

He slouched in the chair opposite me but the bunching of his shoulders and muscles in his jaw betrayed a tension, like a cat about to spring. His eyes were too bright, as if with fever. He had not shaved in several days. His pants were rumpled and he wore a checkered lumberman shirt with the sleeves pushed up to the elbow. It was unbuttoned and untucked and worn over a black T-shirt.

Slightly unnerved, it took me a second or two to find my voice. "Hello Brad. You look like you just came off an undercover assignment." I meant it to sound light. He hitched a shoulder but his eyes never wavered.

"In point of fact," he said, his tone brittle, "I haven't been at work in a while. It was suggested that I take a leave. A *va-ca-tion*."

"Sounds like good advice."

He laughed without humour. "It was that or a reprimand. I don't think they liked me poking around in old records."

I looked away and took a deep breath before eyeballing him again. "Old records from twelve years ago?" His only response was a piercing stare. "Why Brad?"

"I have to know what happened to that kid who died in the car crash."

"And supposing you find out, what then?"

"If there was foul play something has to be done."

"Is this about Terri, or is it about you?"

"It's about justice. I became a police officer because I believe in justice," he declared, his voice rising in the quiet of the library. "How can I go about my job everyday wondering if people in high places in my organization engineered that boy's death? If they did, I want them brought to justice."

I let the magazine fall to my lap. "I admire your moral stance. But morality is more than an ethic of justice—allegiance to a written code. Real life is way too complex to allow for every eventuality to be codified." He glared, his face flushed.

"Morality," I continued, "is also an ethic of care. What's right and wrong between human beings depends on the context. You learned about Billy's death not as a police officer, but as a lover. Terri risked her newfound trust to share her experience with you. If you act in spite of her wishes, you betray that trust. How moral is that?"

The muscles in his face twitched. "I assume you know I haven't seen her since that day in your office. I wanted to call her but I didn't dare. I guess I thought she'd eventually call me." He paused but when I didn't respond to this disclosure, he asked, "Do I still have a chance with her?"

"Brad, I can't be having this conversation with you."

He looked away, gripping the arms of the chair with whitened knuckles. "Right. Confidentiality."

I wished I could think of a graceful way to end the encounter. "Listen," I offered, "your idealism is no small thing. I meant it when I said I admire your moral stance."

"Maybe I should change careers." He muttered with bitterness. "Policing doesn't seem like such moral work to be in after all."

"Every line of work has its share of corrupt individuals," I said. "Police, I know quite a few. Lots of them are great. Some," I hesitated, "aren't. Just because there are some bad apples doesn't mean the whole barrel is rotten. You've got to go on believing in what you do and what you stand for."

He hoisted himself out of the chair. "I believe in people getting what they deserve." He turned and made his way toward the reference section.

Tax Preparation While-U-Wait, Cash for Refunds, the storefront window advertised. I leaned on the glass door and stepped into a Spartan waiting area bounded by a counter. Behind it, a half dozen desks in two rows filled the office. A woman seated at one of the desks bent over a writing pad.

In the back corner, a customer sat opposite Ben, watching him pencil in information on a sheaf of papers. Ben glanced up and nodded to me. I'd half expected one of his goofy looks and a wave. But he went right back to his work.

I barely sat down when his customer rose and hurried out the door with his package. Ben pulled on his overcoat. "That's it for me, Glenda."

The other tax preparer lifted her head. "Night, Ben. See ya Monday."

At the house, while removing his coat, he asked, "Have you had dinner?"

"I grabbed a hamburger at a drive-through."

"Come downstairs while I make myself something. Dinner here is at five. I missed it." I followed him as he clumped down the steep dark flight to the basement. He moved about the tight little corridor of the kitchen with stiff tension, opening cupboards and the fridge, collecting the makings of a sandwich.

"What's wrong Ben?"

"Nothing's wrong."

I leaned back against the counter folding my arms. "Really? You've hardly said two sentences to me since I met you at your office."

"I'm hungry," he mumbled. "I need to get some food inside me." I retreated to the dingy dining room lit by a single tired lamp. I squeezed sideways into a chair at the corner of the table. Ben came in with plate and cup in hand and straddled a chair wedged between the end of the table and the wall. Silence stretched between us as he gulped down his sandwich and tea. I looked up when he finished.

"Wait here," he said abruptly, getting up. I heard his footsteps heavy on the stairs. After a brief interval, he returned. He plunked a cardboard box on the table.

"I had a visit last night…" I peered into the box, "from Parker. He returned the stuff he seized in the searches." Several cardboard accordion folders contained an assortment of papers and notebooks. Recognizing my journals, I drew one out. Little squares of yellow post-it note papers stuck out from the sides. I flipped open the book to one of these. On that page, I had recorded the conflict between Ben and I when he had told me he wanted an open relationship, freedom to be sexually involved with other women. I marvelled how Parker failed to grasp that cheating men aren't open and honest with their partners, don't negotiate agreements.

I turned to another sticker. Spilled across this page were my hurt and frustration over a night of sex that had gone sour. I felt heat rising in my face. These entries had never been meant for another person's eyes. Sick, I thrust the journal back in the box. I pulled out an envelope. Something fell out of it onto the floor. I reached for it. A semi-nude picture of myself stared back.

"Oh God," I groaned. The envelope contained several more.

"Kind of obvious what he was doing, eh," Ben growled.

I looked up, dazed. "What do you mean?"

"Parker. You can see what he was up to."

"Sure. Getting his jollies looking at these pictures you took. I never wanted you to take these. Now do you see why?"

He didn't seem to notice my recriminations. He pulled a couple of other envelopes and an address book from the box and flung them down in front of me. "Look, these have tags only by the names of women. Some are good friends, some I still talk to once in a while; some I haven't seen in years. Remember that poison pen letter I got after the second search, the woman who threatened me with a restraining order if I ever talked to her again?" I nodded.

"He pulled that stunt over and over. That bastard, Parker had a weak case against me. He probably thought he'd hit pay dirt in that first search. When he didn't he used every other chicken shit thing he could. The joint in the freezer, the crap in the garbage bag, your journals, all my friends, male *and* female, anything he could come up with to make a stink around me. He talked to practically everyone I've ever been friends with for the past twenty years. He made me out to be the worst piece of perverted garbage that walks the earth. He insinuated that I used the access I had to women's income tax files to blackmail them into giving me sex."

His voice had mounted to a hot pitch. "I could have lost a lot more friends than that one woman," he said bitterly. "And it cost me Sara."

"Come on, Ben. Parker didn't kill Sara."

"He didn't help either. Who knows how much the stress contributed to her dying? Why can't the police give more attention to criminals who really hurt people? That guy we saw in court who beat his wife. He walked. I just took money. Not even an individual's money, government money. Parker probably *spent* as much public money trying to catch me as I stole. Well, he'll regret that he tangled with me." Ben's mouth twisted in a snarl. Hate filled his black and burning eyes.

"Forget about him. It's behind you."

"Forget! You think I can forget all those days and nights locked up after Sara died? A person has to think about something when he's caged like an animal. I thought about Parker—about what he deserves. I learned a thing or two in jail about how to take care of a problem like that little Napoleon. It's not difficult to wire a bomb underneath someone's car."

"Cut it out, Ben. That's not funny."

"You think I'm kidding?" It was his hoarse whisper as much as his words that punched me in the stomach. A roar like an approaching tornado filled my ears. Shaking, I held up my palm to him.

"Stop it. I don't want to hear this." He twisted away from me, his breath exploding through flaring nostrils, his mouth set in resolute fury. "God damn it, Ben, I've stood by you through fire and flood. It's cost me too. Big time! But your doctrine of 'I don't get mad, I get even' is the rock on which you'll self-destruct. And I won't be in that boat with you," I shouted. "Not this time!" I lunged past him and bolted up the stairs.

"Shelley?"

I didn't answer.

"Shelley, don't go."

I was pulling away from the curb, when I saw him at the window in the porch, just standing there, watching me leave.

The evening expressway traffic swept the truck and my mind into its torrent. Thoughts bobbed, splintered, submerged and resurfaced. *It's murder he's talking! He* has *no morality. I've been a fool to think I could change him. Oh God! I stayed, wasted these years... like a dumb, loyal martyr in a two-bit romance. Leave him! Leave before he destroys your whole life.*

I didn't know whose voice sounded in my head. With my mind torn and battered, I steered through the night while headlights stabbed at me. Oblivious to how I got there, I began to register the dips and hollows in the road as familiar. A mile from the house I pulled over, reluctant to go there. I leaned my face against the back of my hands on the steering wheel. *Is this where it all ends?* I wept...for the loss of innocence, for the loss of time, for Shannon, for Sara, for myself.

At 9:01, my intercom buzzed. Tired and irritable from a night of troubled dreams, I'd hoped to hibernate through the morning behind paperwork and a closed door. "What is it Agnes?"

"Brad Sparks is asking to see you."

I took a deep breath before stepping into the waiting room but he cut me off before I could make my speech.

"I know, I know," he said. "You're not supposed to see me. But please, it's really important and it affects Terri."

I bit the inside of my cheek, indecisive. "Why don't you talk to her then?"

"I don't know what to do. Please, if you'll just listen I know you'll know what I should do, what's best for Terri."

Reluctantly I nodded. "Alright. Come in."

He sat on the edge of the chair in my office, taut and nervous. "I found something at the library after I saw you," he said.

I maintained a studied neutrality.

"I've spent the last two days trying to get a grip on myself. What you asked me—is this about Terri or is it about me? I realized, finally, that it really is about me. I pushed her to confront her father in spite of her fear that it could be catastrophic."

He clenched his fists, not looking at me and not saying anything more. I waited him out.

"When I was ten years old, a drunk driver killed my mother in a car accident. My whole world changed after that. My parents had been very close and her death devastated my father. He withdrew into himself, shut himself up in his room for hours leaving me alone. It was as if I lost my mother and father both.

"The driver was a prominent man in the community, a politician and a wealthy business man. He should have gone to jail for killing my mother, but he got off. I was incensed. That's when I decided to become a police officer. I would avenge my mother, be a white knight bringing scum like that to justice."

"It infuriated me when Terri's husband got a slap on the wrist for what he did to her. But when I thought that her father, another prominent citizen, might have arranged that boy's death and got away with it, it made me crazy! It was bitter irony that the very establishment I joined to fight crime and evil may have been an accomplice. It was enough to make me to lose faith in everything I'd built my world on since my mother's death."

He looked up directly into my eyes. His sober expression underscored his next words. "Terri's father didn't arrange Billy's death."

I felt myself jerk. "How do you know?"

"I went through the archives at the library looking through the newspapers around the time of his death. The accident appeared in the paper printed the day after New Year's. Billy hit a patch of ice. The paper went on to say that there had been a record number of accidents on New Year's Eve because of bad weather. I doubt if Terri ever saw the newspapers. She said her parents put her in the hospital and she was medicated. I'm almost certain that she never knew there'd been an autopsy. Her mother told the truth; the kid was drunk when he wrapped his car around a tree."

Brad dropped his eyes again. "You lectured me the other day about believing in what I do, what I stand for. I was ready to throw it all away, my career, everything, to get revenge. I let myself get totally caught up in the chase and lost sight of the possibility that Billy really did die accidentally. I feel like a fool, ashamed. I don't deserve to wear a badge." He fell silent.

At that moment a fragility in his pose made him look too young to be a police officer. I took the cue. "What would your mother tell you?"

He tried to laugh but failed. "She'd probably say she's still..." Something caught in his throat and the rest came out in a rasp, "proud of me. Jesus." He quit trying to fight back the tears that had already wet his lashes.

"You *are* a good police officer Brad. After all, you wanted to be a *white* knight. Still, your desire for revenge hurt the person you most care about. Unexpressed grief can do that; keep you stuck. You got stuck in the anger. The idea of a powerful public figure getting away with murder forced open the place where you shut up your grief. So welcome the feelings. They can't sneak up on you when they're out in the open."

Like a jolt of electricity, I heard my own counsel. *That's it! Ben isn't inherently perverse. But what chance has he had to express his grief in a safe, supportive place? Anger is a phase of grieving. Only unexpressed and unaccepted does it fester, become dangerous. I should have* listened *instead of shutting him down.*

Brad's release seemed to have produced a calm.

"Are you planning to tell Terri?" I asked.

"I don't know what to do. That's why I came to you."

"She has a right to know. After all, she's lived all these years in fear, believing that her father is capable of murder."

"I'm afraid she'll misconstrue my motives. I leaned so heavily on her to confront him. Maybe she'll think I'm just trying to remove an objection to doing so. I love her. It doesn't matter to me if she *ever* confronts him."

"Why don't you tell her what you've told me...about what was really going on inside you?"

"What if she won't listen to me?"

"Maybe she won't. I can't give you any guarantees. But it's time you took responsibility for your own feelings. I've got an idea she just might hear that."

I fought my way into the city through the evening rush hour. As if by the Devil's design, tonight traffic was a hellish snarl. I thrummed my fingers on the wheel. *Come on!* I muttered. The image of Ben watching from the window coalesced before me. I was awash in guilt; I'd let Florence Gallagher's self-righteous voice goad me. What had I said to Brad in the library? *Real life is way too complex to allow for every eventuality to be codified.*

It was nearly seven thirty when I rang the bell. Through the front window I could see figures huddled around the pool table, cues and cigarettes in hand, but no one answered. I leaned on the bell again, twice for emphasis. A moment later, Ben himself stepped into the porch. Seeing me, he stopped short. A pane of glass and chasm of twelve feet separated us. His expression was inscrutable.

My heart beat erratically. He approached and drew open the door. Wordlessly, he grasped my arm and pulled me into him, holding on as if he would never let go. "I thought I might have lost you for good this time," he choked. He cocooned me against his chest and I burrowed in more deeply.

"I'm sorry. I'm sorry I scared you, running off like that."

Chapter Twelve

Ben turned the key in Margaret's front door and opened it. I followed him inside, stooping to greet the ecstatic mutt wriggling and whining at my feet. Ben read the note on the fridge and handed it to me.

Thanks for agreeing to keep Jasper while we're away. Food for him is in the closet. Leash by the back door. M

Margaret had taken Ari to England to visit her mother, taking off for the first time since Ben had come home. By prior arrangement, Ari had left his key with us during his last visitation so we could pick up his dog.

"Come on, Pooch," Ben opened the back door, "outside." Jasper bolted on his short legs to the fenced freedom of the yard, racing in mad circles. "I'm going up to Sara's room," Ben said. "Want to come?"

The casualness of his question belied the expectancy that I knew he must feel. I had not been in her room since that day. The last time Ben had been there, Sara had been alive and still carrying on her cold war with him. I nodded.

He paused on the threshold, just as I had done six months earlier. Was he seeing in his mind's eye what I had seen then? Nothing had changed in the room except that the unicorn quilt had been smoothed over the bed.

"Everything is here," he murmured. "Everything of her. She left nothing with us." He moved over to the dresser, causing a rainbow mobile to pirouette by the window. I thought he touched something on the dresser but then he moved away and opened the closet. He fingered the fabric of each piece of clothing, before sliding the next hanger aside. He rooted through the boxes on the shelf above and the clutter on the closet floor. When he moved away, I noticed a poster pinned to the inside of the closet door, a yolk-coloured happy-face with the caption *Have a Nice Day*. Horns had been crayoned on the face and eyebrows that gave the grin a wicked twist. The first two words were crossed out. I smiled sadly, recognizing Sara's handwriting in two added words. *Nice day, isn't it.*

The thoroughness of Ben's inspection made me wonder if he were searching for something in particular but I pursued my own need to fondle everything with my eyes. An open cosmetic bag spilled its contents on the dresser, a compact, mascara, lip-gloss. Tangled in a hairbrush, the sight of blond hair sent a shiver through me.

"The inhalers are gone," I noted hollowly. He didn't respond. Then I saw the nail polish—pearl pink. An involuntary cry broke from me. I covered my eyes, retreating blindly. He caught me in his arms, spun me around and crushed me to him. "The nail polish..." I cried, "I can see her hands, her fingers. I *see* them!"

He sat on the bed, pulled me into his lap and held me. When my outburst subsided to a sniffle, he said quietly, "I wish I could do that."

"I wish you could too," I said earnestly, accepting the tissue he offered. "What were you looking for just now?"

"A couple of things." He reached into his coat pocket and pulled out a black velvet cube-shaped box.

"The pearl studs," I whispered. I took the box and opened it. "What do you want them for?" He shrugged but offered no explanation.

"What else were you looking for?"

"Her diary. The one you gave her."

"Her diary! Of course."

I tried the dresser drawers, rumpling through the clothes, while he did a more thorough search of the bookcase. "It would surely be in her room somewhere."

"Unless," Ben straightened up, "Margaret already found it."

"You could ask her."

"Hah! She wouldn't give it to me. Besides, if I ask her and she didn't know it existed, she will hunt for it and find it first."

"Come on, Ben. Don't make it something new for you two to fight over."

"Well, look," he swept his arm in an arc around the room, "she's got everything."

Quietly I answered, "She doesn't have Sara."

"Neither do I," he spat, building up a head of steam. "And what's more, she has Ari. You didn't notice the real estate books downstairs, did you? I'm afraid of her moving away taking Ari with her, maybe to England. She might be making arrangements at this very moment. I can't lose both of my children."

"Take it easy," I soothed, "you don't know that she's planning to move *away*. Maybe she just wants out of this house. That's understandable isn't it?"

I handed him the black jewel case I still held. He took it and pocketed it.

As soon as the truck rounded the corner, Jasper began whining and dancing in my lap. "Nearly home, fella?" I laughed. Ben eased the truck in behind Margaret's maroon Nissan. As soon as Ben cut the engine, I released the exuberant canine. Ari emerged from the house and Jasper met him like a breaker meets the shore.

In the cavernous living room with its high ceiling and deep windows, each of us occupied our own separate space like recent foes gathered for diplomatic talks. It was not a comfortable space... or topic but we had to agree, for these words would quite literally be written in stone. Ben explained the Hebrew symbols that normally appear on the headstones of Jews. "I thought it would be nice to have poppies carved on it." Margaret sounded hesitant as if having to ask permission to contribute. "They're symbolic for peaceful sleep." No one needed an explanation of her reasoning and Ben nodded his approval.

"What about you, Ari?" he asked. "Do you have ideas about something to go on Sara's stone." Burrowed in a recliner as if seeking shelter, he stole a sidelong look at his father, then his mother. "What about a harp?"

"That's a lovely idea, Ari," Margaret enthused.

I smiled. *Sara, our apprentice angel.*

"Yes," Ben agreed. "It's perfect. Now, what about the wording?"

We settled back into an uneasy silence. Ari picked up an elastic band, stretching and releasing it. Margaret fussed over Jasper.

Ben said, "I'd like the words, 'Sadly missed'."

"Oh no," Margaret protested. "That sounds so, so..." Her brow furrowed.

"Then what would you like," Ben shot back, tight-lipped.

"Oh, I don't know."

"Make a suggestion."

Tension flickered around the room like far off lightning.

"I can't think of anything."

"Just like always," he retorted. "Good at criticizing but you never have a positive suggestion."

"I'm not criticizing you."

"So what's wrong with 'Sadly missed,'"

"It sounds, I don't know, depressing."

His teeth clenched. "Well, I *do* miss her. I'd miss my son too if he weren't around anymore." Bewilderment crinkled her eyes as she stared at him. "Are you planning to take him from me too, Margaret?"

Jasper slumped unceremoniously to the floor as Margaret pushed him off her lap. She slipped soundlessly from the room, the dog trotting after her. The back door opened and closed. Ari sat pale and frozen. Without looking at either of us he suddenly clambered up and left the room in the opposite direction. His footsteps gained momentum as they climbed the stairs.

I sighed and gave Ben a baleful look. He met my gaze with a sour expression. "Go ahead. Say it. I shouldn't have lost my temper."

I shook my head, disgusted. "I'm not going to lecture. I'm tired of feeling responsible for keeping you in line."

"I'm sorry for doing it in front of Ari."

"But not for doing it?"

"No."

I turned away momentarily, then back again. "You figure out how to make amends with your son. I'm going to talk to Margaret."

She sat with her back to the house on a swing that hung from an aged oak in the yard. Jasper lapped tears from her face. I leaned against the tree trunk. Lacing my voice with irony, I said, "Nice day, isn't it." Sara's trademark expression had the desired effect; Margaret laughed through her tears.

"I seem to rattle his cage," she admitted.

"He does have quite a growl sometimes."

"I never could express my opinion with him very well. His temper scares me and then I get all tied up in knots and don't know what to say."

"Neither of you seem to communicate simple, clear messages to each other."

"Like him asking if I'm going to take Ari away from him?"

"Yeah, like that."

"Does he blame me for Sara?"

I studied the ground, scratching the dirt around the base of the swing with my toe. "No," I answered finally. "He's scared. He really *doesn't* want to lose Ari." I looked up pointedly.

"I *was* thinking of moving, maybe up north. I thought the change would be good. Besides this house is too big for just the two of us. I left those real estate catalogues out on purpose because I was too scared to tell Ben directly what I was thinking. I guess I wanted to run away from all the pain—as if I could leave it behind. But then while we were on vacation, I thought about what it would mean to Ari. He's lost his sister and he's gone into quite a shell since his father was charged and went to jail. I decided he doesn't need any more big changes just now. I regret upsetting Ben. I don't want to fight. I'm too shattered."

"I know," I nodded sympathetically. "Ben's shattered too. I'm relieved to hear you say that you've decided to stay. I worried, for Ari as well as for Ben, if you were to move away. I agree, Ari does need to be able to hang on to what is familiar, his friends, his school—and his father."

Margaret slid Jasper to the ground. Looping her elbows around the ropes, she toed the swing in a gentle arc. "I guess we couldn't come to an agreement about what to put on Sara's stone when there was that between us." I nodded.

"But," she went on, "I really meant it when I said I don't want anything depressing to be inscribed. I don't want to have something that enshrines the lowest point in my life. I just don't have any idea of what I do want. I'm not very good at this sort of thing."

"I have an idea, if you're open to suggestion."

"Oh please, anything to get us out of this impasse."

When I told her, Margaret's face lit up. "Oh yes," she murmured. "It's perfect."

Was I making a mistake staying with Ben, hoping life would get better? Misery and apathy clung to him. His efforts to find a new way to make a living lacked vision or focus. He'd gone back to the school bus job, getting sacked when someone in the company recognized his name from the newspaper. He lost a bookkeeping job when the business went bankrupt. He floundered from one dead end to another. Depressed and irritable, he was often depressing and irritating to be around. Often now, the yearning that came over me for the mountains and forests was compelling.

I shifted in bed to lay my head on his shoulder and broached the subject we'd both been avoiding. "That time you talked about harming Parker, you really scared me, you know."

"I didn't do it to upset you."

"But it did upset me. You're a loose cannon."

"What do you want me to say?" He sounded irritable again.

"This isn't about Parker, Ben; it's about Sara."

"No it isn't."

"Yes it is! Your rage is sadness turned inside out."

"Don't psycho-analyze me," he snapped peevishly.

I sat up, exasperated, turning my back on him.

"Come here," he muttered, sounding repentant. I ignored him. "Okay, okay, I won't kill Parker. I'll just hurt him a little."

"This isn't a joke."

I waited an eternity before he spoke again. "I don't know what I'm supposed to do. Don't you think I feel the pain? It's unbearable. I just don't know what to do."

I turned to him and touched the outer corner of his eye, slowly tracing a line down his cheek. "You're supposed to cry, Ben. Grief is what crying is for."

"Come inside with me," Ben said when he shut off the engine. "Ari may need help with his tie." A hound-like howl resounded when Ben rang the bell. Jasper rocketed up to the waist-high window in the door. On the rebound, he was joined by Ari. The two of them executed a perfectly choreographed bounce, appearing, disappearing, appearing. We laughed till Ari tired and let us in.

His white shirt and grey flannels matched his father's, his tie draped loose around his neck. Ben knotted it for him and we walked to the car, Ari poking his arms into the sleeves of his blazer.

Across town, we picked up Caitlyn. She had grown an inch and a half in the eight months since I'd last seen her. When Ben held open the car door for her, she stepped into the back seat like a debutante. Within minutes however, she regressed to a playful power struggle with Ari over the Rubik's cube he fiddled with.

Taking Caitlyn to dinner had been Ben's idea. It would be a relaxed atmosphere, he felt, in which to ask her if she wanted to attend next week's ceremony, the unveiling of Sara's headstone. The occasion would mark Sara's birthday, the first ever that the girls would not be celebrating together. From the back seat I heard Ari's entreaty, "Let me, Caitlyn. I know how to do it." Caitlyn had commandeered the cube. He attempted to show her the next move but she twisted away.

"No way. I can do it."

"Wrong," he heckled. "Wrong again."

She giggled. "Wait a sec, wait a sec." With a dramatic sigh she capitulated and handed it over. Deftly he twisted it this way and that, then held it out in his palm. "Ari," she deflected, "your hair's mussed up. I'll brush it."

She pulled a brush from her purse and swiped at his head. "Get away," he protested.

I interrupted their wrestling match "Okay you guys, we're here." As Caitlyn emerged from the car, her A-line skirt swished and resurrected a refined young lady.

With dessert cleared away, Ben slid cutlery and cups aside and leaned toward Caitlyn across the table. He held something flat between his palms. He spoke directly to her. "You spent last Hanukkah with us, Caitlyn. It was the second to last time I ever saw Sara. I remember it vividly, for it was the happiest I'd seen her in a very long time."

Beside me, I could not see her expression, but in her lap the knuckles of Caitlyn's hands whitened. Opposite me, Ari's face reflected the sadness that felt palpable beside me; sadness greater than children this young should know.

Ben handed her what he'd been holding. "Do you remember this?"

A sorrowful sound escaped her lips. Sara's twinkling eyes peered up from a photo now shaking in Caitlyn's hands. Sara was curled up on the couch in our living room holding a small object. "I forgot how pretty she is—was. She'd just opened the pearl stud earrings you gave her. She never got to wear..." Caitlyn choked and didn't finish.

"That's right, Caitlyn," Ben said softly. "She never got to wear them." From his pocket, he withdrew a small black velvet box and set it in front of her. "I want you to have them. To remember her."

"Oh Mr. Volski," she whispered. She opened the box and wept.

"Ben," I whispered, nodding toward Ari. He too was crying. Ben encircled him in his arm and I pressed my lips together but could not stem the flow of my own tears. Only Ben's eyes were dry.

Passing through the iron gates, Ben, Caitlyn and I were the first to arrive. The gates set apart this circumscribed world with its weeping willows and silent stone sentinels from the secular one a few dozen yards away. We proceeded along a path toward the only other moving thing in the cemetery, a white shroud billowing in the breeze.

Margaret's car with Ari inside followed ours and immediately behind it, the rabbi's. Moments later, Martin's silver Skylark appeared. The rabbi took his place at the foot of the grave. Caitlyn huddled against me, tense and somber.

The rabbi spoke in an intimate voice to us few, explaining the unveiling ceremony as a modern practice in the Jewish faith to allow mourners an opportunity to honour the memory of a loved one. He slipped into Hebrew; prayer has a comforting cadence that knows no language barrier. When he finished, he stepped up to the shrouded stone loosened the cords on it and pulled it free.

Etched in rose-colored granite, poppies framed a harp that played silent tribute to Sara's stilled fingers. Hebrew lettering bound her to her tribe and dedicated her to our memory. The final words were those I offered Margaret that day in her garden. Caitlyn mouthed them in a whisper then slumped against me with a cry. '*She found the end of the rainbow.*'

Shortly, the others headed toward the cars but Caitlyn held me rooted there, gripping my arm. "I turned fifteen three weeks ago," she said brokenly. "I'm going to keep getting older but Sara will always be fourteen." I pulled her into my arms and she wept against my shoulder.

The Sea-to-Sky Highway from North Vancouver to Pemberton delivers what its name promises. The road clings to the Coastal Mountains that rise almost vertically from the azure waters of Howe Sound. Many miles farther up, a mountain stream rips through a spectacular gorge and plunges over Nairn Falls.

Several hundred yards below the falls, a huge, flat boulder sits mid-stream. Steeling myself against the icy water, I picked my way toward it, notebook in one hand, sneakers and socks in the other. My perch offered a smorgasbord to the senses, sun-warmed rock, pungent pine needles, clattering treble of water over the stony river bottom, thundering base from the falls upstream. Dark-green spikes of fir, pine and hemlock feathered high above my head, reaching into an incredibly blue sky. Beyond the corridor of the river, the brooding eternal giants themselves kept watch.

Ben raised no objection when I told him I needed a vacation. Still on probation, he was forbidden from leaving the province. I departed right after the unveiling. I had pinned my hopes on the ceremony unleashing Ben's grief at last and was discouraged when it failed to do so.

I observed the river surging around my rock. *I could have it all again,* I thought. *The mountains, the forests… even a puppy.* I picked up my coil notebook and pulled a pencil from the spine. These notes would not make it back to Ontario. Never again would I fully trust that privacy was sacred, but at least here I felt safe to pour out my soul with only the mountains to look over my shoulder.

I miss Ben, the old Ben, funny, strong, dependable. It's him that I loved. Not this shadow, dark, angry and brooding.

I wonder if a drop of water slipping over the brink of the falls chooses to pass on a particular side of this rock? How long can it wait to change course after it has fallen? If I don't soon decide what course the remainder of my life will take, the flow of time will decide for me.

CHAPTER THIRTEEN

April 20, 1990
Dear Daphne
As I write, here on the deck, spring is awash all around me.
I can see Ben moving about in the orchard at work with his
pruning shears.

In your letter you sounded content, you and Eddie, happy
with each other. I can scarcely believe that Robin is a young
woman of seventeen and your little ones, no longer little.

Though Sara's absence pervades our daily thoughts, life
marches on. I defended my thesis last month and will receive
my degree in June. Just as I am finishing school, Ben will begin.
His application to the Faculty of Education was accepted. He
is to be a teacher, after all!

My sister-in-law, Melanie gave Jamie a daughter. They call
her Lily. Isn't that a metaphor for spring and regeneration!
When I hold my precious niece in my arms, I feel a wound
inside cauterize.

Healing takes time though. Many days I still feel heavy and
grey. And I wonder still, if I will ever again see in Ben the zany
show-off that so attracted me to him.

With all these reminders of new beginnings, we decided
the time has come to refurbish the room that belonged to
Sara. When I finish this letter, I'm off to scrub the walls in
preparation for the painting we will do this afternoon.

The sound of a car pausing at the end of the driveway made me look up.
It was the mail carrier. Dumping my pen and pad, I ventured down the
lane.

Movement caught my eye as I passed under the Purple Martin house
on its fifteen-foot mast. A lone scout hovered, then settled on the perch.
"Hi, there. Welcome back." He squawked a reply. His presence signalled
that the colony would be back in a week's time, their nest-building
operations in full swing.

I flipped through the wad of bills and junk mail. Among them was a small square envelope in gold lettering. It was addressed, *Ms. Shelley Gallagher and Companion.* I slit it open with my pinky and withdrew a folded card.

Mr. Bradley Sparks and Ms. Teresa Stone

invite you to

join them in celebrating

the joyous occasion

of their union in matrimony

on the twenty third day of June 1990

at two thirty in the afternoon.

A few weeks earlier in a lingerie shop, I stepped out of a change room, my selection in hand and collided with another customer.

"Shelley?"

"Terri!"

We regarded one another for an awkward moment, then she laughed an easy laugh. "I never expected to bump into *you* in this sort of place."

"Social workers are people too," I shrugged, only slightly self-conscious.

"Of course you are," she answered, teeth gleaming in a broad smile. "After all, it's you who helped me finally get comfortable with my own sexuality. You... and Brad."

"I'm happy for you Terri. Things sound good with you two."

A faint clatter of something falling to the tiled floor distracted me. Terri stooped for it. She came up with outstretched hand, a large black button pressed in her palm. "Yours?" she asked.

My eyes dropped to my front. I poked my finger through a button hole in my coat. Striking a Napoleonic pose, I looked sharply at her from under creased brows, feigning a thin-lipped indictment. For a split second she looked bewildered, then sputtered and laughed out loud. "It wasn't me!" she declared.

I smiled now at the memory of how happy she seemed and tucked the wedding invitation back in the envelope.

———

I lugged the bucket of dirty water to the kitchen and dumped it down the sink. Returning to the room, I stood in the doorway, hands on my hips, surveying. There was just the bed left to remove. Ben told me to wait till he came in to help, but I wanted to get on with it.

I grabbed the bare mattress and hauled it toward me. It tilted to the floor while I wrestled it into an upright position. Something slapped onto the floor out of my sight behind it. I put my shoulder to one end and propelled the awkward freight into the hallway, leaning it against the wall. Returning, I sat on the floor with the socket wrench to undo the bolts.

A splash of pink and blue on the floor caught my eye. I reached and picked up a soft-covered book and caught my breath. Sara's diary!

How had it been left here? The meticulous Sara who never forgot anything. The last time she was here had been Hanukkah. Yes! With Caitlyn. In the excitement of having her friend here, and it being hidden out of sight, she must have forgotten it.

I turned back the cover carefully as if the pages were ancient parchment. I read of infatuations with boys whose names I'd never heard. The names changed every week or so as different ones caught Sara's attention and others fell into disfavour. I read of giggling sessions with Caitlyn as they braved the phone to call up the latest crush, slamming down the receiver in panic as soon as the boy came on the line. I read of lonely days when asthma kept her home from school. As the previous fall turned toward winter, she wrote:

I'm thirteen but I feel thirty. I'm so tired. It's hard being the oldest when your parents are divorced. When Daddy left, Mommy had to work more. I had to look after Ari. He thinks things are normal. He doesn't have to worry about anything. Like if he gets locked out cause he forgot his key, he knows I'll have mine.

He has no idea about the tension between Mommy and Daddy. I don't tell him about the fights. He couldn't handle it. I have to protect him from the facts of divorced life.

I have to protect Mommy too. She's scared of Daddy. He doesn't scare me, though. I'm not afraid to fight him. I feel like Daddy divorced me too. He hates Mommy and he hates me. Ari is his golden haired boy. He never yells at Ari, but he ignores me and gets mad if I kick up a fuss to get him to notice me.

Because Ari's the youngest, they don't ask him to deliver messages when they aren't talking to each other. Only me. It's not fair that I have all this responsibility and asthma too. It makes me feel so old and worn out. So tired.

I leaned into my hands, a new grief washing over me. *Oh Sara, we did love you. If only you could have let us in; if only you could have talked to us.* I didn't hear Ben come in.

"Shelley? What is it?"

I couldn't find my voice. Instead, I held the diary out to him. He took it. For a moment he just stood, staring at the cover. Then he turned and walked out. I heard the back door close. Like a fluttering silent-movie reel, memories played through my mind.

I knew from my cramped, numbed body that I had not moved in some time. Unwinding myself, I waited for the pins and needles to stop, then went outside to look for Ben. I checked the orchard and the barn. The pond? Perhaps the steps.

His back was to me and he didn't turn though he must have heard my footsteps. I descended to where he sat on the bottom step. I could see the open diary on his knee but he wasn't looking at it. I knelt down.

His eyes were bloodshot and staring. I noticed now, the quiver that rippled through his body and the wetness on his cheeks. A deep and alien sound rose from his throat. I touched his sleeve. He fumbled for my hand and held it. "What have I done?" he groaned. "My stupid, stubborn pride. Look what I've done?"

I searched his face for an explanation but none came. My eyes dropped to the open diary. Easing it from his lap, I read the final entry.

I hate my asthma. I hate my skin...all broken out. No one wants to be your friend if you're different. I hate being the kid of divorced parents. I hate my Dad. Why did he do what he did? Nobody would ever want to be my friend if they knew. Sometimes I wish I had never been born. Sometimes I think it would be easier to be dead.

"She paid the price for my creed," he cried. She had so much pain and didn't know how to share it. *I* taught her that. I taught her to stuff it inside and put on a tough 'You can't hurt me' face to the world. And I can't get her back to tell her I was wrong."

He bowed his head and let me cradle him. The hurt and grief drained out into my arms. I looked down at the surface of the pond. Shining there, images of willow and oak and maple mirrored the April sky reminding me of all I had left behind. No mountains or graceful spruce reflected back. Gone were the alpine meadows and the ocean, the glacial lakes and tumbling rivers. In sweet surrender, I let it go. What I held in my arms was better.

Acknowledgements

I so appreciate my sister for galvanizing me to finally turn my dusty manuscript into a published work, by leading the way and publishing a book of her own. A special thanks goes to Ward Edwards, without whose knowledge, guidance and work on the technical logistics of getting published, this book would remain that dusty manuscript. He led and assisted me through a world about which I knew nothing.

I am deeply grateful for my Girl Gang, that extraordinary web of women friends who made it safe for me to reveal myself and who continue to accept and include me in the 'gang'. Last and most of all, thanks to my husband, who, when I said I wanted to write this story encouraged me to 'go for it',

About the Author

Donna Gannon is a retired social worker. Her rewarding career included counselling survivors of sexual assault and childhood abuse and couples caught up in domestic violence. Her passion for writing began in childhood. In her role as a social worker, her delight in the power of the written word took the form of creating promotional material, curriculum, manuals and dialogue for video presentations and writing policy and protocols for government and non-government organizations.

She lives with her husband in British Columbia in her beloved mountains, where they enjoy their two beautiful granddaughters.

Front cover design by Gayll Morrison — www.gayllery.biz